WAR OF PANDORA

THE OMNILOGOS SINGULARITY
BOOK 3

MICHELE AMITRANI

ISBN (ePub): 978-1-988770-55-0

ISBN (Paperback): 978-1-988770-62-8

First Edition 2023 (v.1)

Published by Michele Amitrani.

Cover Design by 100 Covers

PROLOGUE

Jason Cloverfield drew in a deep breath and closed his eyes as his consciousness transferred into the ether. To leave the decaying shell of his body and embrace the multitude of possibilities of cyberspace was the only way he truly felt alive.

The man-machine smiled in the darkness of the sarcophagus. He could *feel* DataMorph, like a diver immersed in water. That largest portion of the ether existed to connect people, to let them share their experiences, dreams, and hopes. It was the only place where they could forget their mundane existences and live like gods before the end.

Yes, DataMorph was his gift to humanity, the heroin overdose he would give to as many people as possible before the world plunged into annihilation.

"Humanity is fucked," Jason muttered, his lips bending into a joyful smile. "All that's left is bread and circuses, a superficial appeasement of body and mind before the inevitable end."

His plans proceeded smoothly. Every day, DataMorph extended its reach into cyberspace and more people joined its ranks, making Jason's goal more achievable.

Of course, there were those who tried to stop him, who wanted to take advantage of DataMorph, leverage it as a weapon. Fools, all of them. Nothing could stop him. He was beyond their—

A cracking noise boomed in the sarcophagus, and Jason's connection with the ether was severed.

"What is it?" He blinked, jerked his head back, and looked for the source of the disturbance. It took him some time to find it. The room's projector had turned itself on without his command. He frowned, tried to reach the device with his mind. Nothing. It didn't respond to his stimulus.

Jason activated his interlink. "Agate. In here. Now."

Static noise was the only answer.

"Ahhh." He scanned the room, eyes searching for another clue that could explain the malfunctions. "Something seems funny here." He jerked his head to the left. The thermostat, too, was acting up, increasing the temperature without his say-so. He tried to control it remotely, as he had attempted with the projector, but failed.

At that moment, the door of the sarcophagus opened, and a figure stepped inside.

"God, Jason," the newcomer said, swaggering toward him. "This place needs a breath of fresh air. It reeks like a corpse in here."

Jason assessed the short, plump woman. "Ahhh, at long last, the hornet's queen makes her appearance." He sneered. "Had I known you were coming, Pandora, I would have dusted off the red carpet."

"What did you expect, old friend?" Pandora stared at Jason, his cybernetically enhanced body suspended in mid-air via metallic vines. "You ignore my messages and don't show up when called. I'm disappointed. The Gathering is not some club you can leave on a whim. Thought I made that clear the first time we met."

Jason's smile was full of mirth. "Is this a veiled threat?"

"Veiled?" Pandora frowned. "Nothing veiled in what I said."

"We've already danced to this tune before, *Archetype*." Jason pronounced the last word with contempt. "Our paths diverged long ago. You have chosen the path of struggle and perdition; I have chosen the path of balance and peace. You've no right to barge into my home unannounced. I thought I made that clear the *last* time we met."

"Paths, Jason?" Pandora grimaced. "You make it sound like you had an option. From the moment you swore your allegiance, you were mine. *Mine*. Nothing has changed. You still belong to me."

Jason reached with his mind to the door, closed it, and made sure it stayed closed. "You always had guts, Pandora." He wiggled his eyebrows, offering a bemused smile. "That you're here, without your demons, proves it. What do you want?"

Pandora stepped forward. "If you don't have what it takes to carry on the mission, it's time for retirement. The permanent kind."

Jason laughed, his eyes wide and glowing. "The hornet queen has grown arrogant." He loomed over Pandora, the wires hissing like snakes. "You got in here somehow. What makes you think you'll get out?"

Pandora took another step toward him, looking unconcerned. "Everything I've given you, I can take back." She narrowed her eyes, a hard edge to her words. "This little rebellion of yours will end one way or another. It's up to you to decide how. Want to make my life easy or very easy?"

"Your posturing is cute." Jason smirked, then flapped a hand in dismissal. "Unfortunately, it doesn't land. You're not scolding one of your spineless pawns. Threatening me is like threatening an ocean. Wrestle with water at your own peril. You'll risk drowning."

"This is real, Jason. It's happening." Pandora lifted her chin, looking at the man-machine with confidence. "Step aside, or I will kill you."

Jason barked a laugh. "You always fancied yourself untouchable, didn't you?" He closed and opened his fists, the muscles in his face tight. "This certainty will be your grave." His mind reached for a cable and hurled its pointy end at Pandora, who had no time to move away before the killing blow struck her chest...and passed right through her body.

The cable arm slammed hard against the floor, chipping part of the metal panel before collapsing onto the ground.

"Hmm?" Jason frowned. "What is this? You should be dead."

Pandora arched her eyebrow. "You thought I was here in the flesh?" She pointed at the room's projector. "Your mind must be truly gone, old man."

Jason narrowed his eyes. "Where are you?"

"Does it matter?" Pandora shrugged. "You're so preoccupied with weaving plots inside cyberspace, you forget the real war is fought in the world of the living."

Jason snorted. "Your threats mean nothing. I'm beyond your powers."

"Perhaps." Pandora nodded while staring at the cable laying on the ground. "But you're not beyond your own." She waved her arms, and the cable stirred.

"Impossible!" the Pharaoh of the Ether spat, realizing he longer controlled any of the cables. "It can't be! I'm the beginning and the end! I—" The cable wrapped itself around his neck and squeezed until a sharp snap broke the silence of the sarcophagus.

PART I

DEFENSIO

1

AWAKENING

YELLOW SEA, HAMMERER CLASS
BATTLECRUISER UXA MASTODON

Ariul

 ~

Goliath looked at the alcove with glazed eyes, lost in his thoughts. He stood as motionless as a statue in the darkness of the regeneration room, waiting for something to happen. He had been waiting for a long time.

Goliath took a deep breath, restraining his desire to turn his body into a weapon to use against his enemies. He had to exercise caution; he could not risk losing control on his ship.

He smiled despite himself. *Control.* A word he never applied to his life before the Rebirth, before choosing the name "Goliath," back when he was simply Josh Stein, a corporate nobody who achieved nothing worthwhile, a person crippled by hesitation and fear. It was only when the Archetype had found him, blessed him with the Calling, and cast him into the fire of Rebirth that he had chosen. Starting with the name Goliath.

The captain of the *Mastodon* shook his head to clear it. His past didn't matter. He needed to focus on what was in front of him.

An unconscious soldier was floating inside a regenerative solution beyond the reinforced vitrum of the alcove.

Saga was his name. Goliath knew he was a fine soldier, loyal to the Archetype, but knew nothing about his life before the Rebirth. The dunamis had hit him hard during the battle in Saemangeum City. Saga's right shoulder and arm were gone, and so was a sizeable portion of his face. His body had slowly begun to regenerate, but even Ishtar, the ship's dame, didn't know if he would survive.

Saga was the sole survivor of the failed incursion in dunamis' territory. Only he and another warrior from the battlecruiser *Mephisto* had made it back from Ariul. The other raider had died two hours before because of his injuries.

When Ishtar had assessed Saga's wound, she had given him a few hours to live. But the soldier was still fighting inside that alcove, showing a resilience no one had expected.

The incursion had been a failure. The units sent by the *Behemoth* had been unable to gather any useful data. They were back to square one. Now all they could do was wait and...

Beep. Beep. Beep.

Goliath frowned, then turned toward the console displaying Saga's bio signals. He blinked. The soldier was waking up. He activated the internal comm device. "Ishtar. I need you in the Reg room. He's waking up."

"Roger that, Captain," answered the dame. "On my way."

Goliath ended the call and watched with a clenched jaw as Saga twitched, showing the first signs of life since he'd returned to the *Mastodon*.

"Brother?" Goliath glanced at the comm device, making sure the soldier could hear him from inside the alcove, then he knocked on the glass. "Can you hear me?"

Saga's yellow eyes popped open. He took in the surroundings until his gaze settled on Goliath.

"Can you hear me?" the captain repeated.

Saga nodded slowly.

"Good." Goliath nodded. "You're safe aboard the *Mastodon*. You're going to be fine, brother."

Saga touched his oxygen mask with his only remaining arm, then slammed his hand on the glass.

Goliath tilted his head to the side, staring at the soldier. "What is it?"

Again Saga slammed his fist on the glass, harder this time.

"Stop," Goliath ordered. "Why are you—"

Saga pointed to the alcove, then at his mask, his eyes narrowed to slits.

The captain stared at him. "You want to get out?"

Saga nodded.

"Brother, you're wounded." Goliath inhaled sharply. "Your body can't take the stress. It needs to regenerate first. You're still too—"

Saga kicked the alcove, then yanked the oxygen mask from his face, bubbles of air spreading on the top part of the tank as an alarm went off.

Goliath stared at Saga. "What are you doing?"

The soldier kicked the glass again and again. He wouldn't last without oxygen.

Goliath cursed. "What madness took you?" He turned to

the control station, his fingers flying on the keyboard. A pump drained the alcove of water, then the captain pushed the emergency button and the alcove's glass slid open.

Saga fell to the ground with a dull thud, coughing and spitting out water and blood.

"Easy!" Goliath said, keeping the soldier down when he tried to raise. "I told you it wasn't time to—"

"Alpha!" Saga wheezed, his eyes bulging. "Need...to—" He broke off, coughing again. "Need..."

"Here, sit." Goliath pushed him against the wall so that he could at least lean over. "Speak."

"We're...being...watched, Alpha," Saga gasped between coughs.

"Watched?" Goliath glanced at the door. "What are you talking about?"

"Two...weguckins," said the soldier, eyes glowing. "A male and a...a female. Both young...early twenties. I think...I think they were waiting. It might have been an ambush."

2

GEODE

Ariul

$\sim$

Lena stared at Tiago's hand but didn't take it.

"*Let me show you the world of the Omnilogos.*"

The chancellor maintained his posture, waiting for her to choose. Something about that moment reminded Lena what the Overseer of Ariul had said: "Turn around, walk through that gate, forget all this happened and live the rest of your life in the bliss of ignorance." With that gesture, Tiago was offering exactly that: a chance to turn around. If she refused him, she could still go back.

"*Let me show you the world of the Omnilogos.*"

Omnilogos. There was something familiar about that word, but Lena couldn't say what it was. Had she heard it before? But where? And from whom? She didn't know.

But that was the whole point, wasn't it? She'd used her Pelargonium necklace to enter that place because she wanted answers, and the only way of getting them was by accepting Tiago's hand. So she did.

"I want to know," Lena said. "Please, help me understand."

"I will." Tiago helped her to her feet. "For a moment, I thought you might bail on me."

Lena blinked. "Why's that?"

"Because sometimes I have trouble believing this is real." He pointed at the room. "But it's real, Lena. I promised you answers, and that's what I'll give you. Before that, though, I need to know how you're feeling. The serum we gave you might cause drowsiness, sometimes can give you a headache. I don't want to push you."

"I'm fine," Lena replied without hesitation. She did have a slight headache, but would not let it get in the way.

"Outstanding." Tiago rubbed his hands together. "First things first. Come with me." He led her to the other side of the room, in front of a console composed of a monitor and an old-fashioned keyboard. "Place your right hand on the display. Make sure your fingerprints touch the surface."

Lena glanced at him. "What's this for?"

"To register you as an authorized guest of this installation."

Lena lifted her arm and then remembered something. She had been shot before entering Geode, but now her arm looked fine and she felt no pain. "Tiago, the guy who shot me—"

"Restrained," Tiago said quickly. "He won't bother you anymore, I promise." He nodded toward her shoulder. "We cured the burn, made sure there was no long-lasting damage. You're good to go."

"Okay," Lena said. "Ahem...thanks."

"The least we could do after the explosive welcome."

Tiago cleared his throat, perhaps realizing the joke hadn't landed. "Well, we better get on with it." He gestured at the display. "We don't want to set off a dozen alarms the moment you leave this room. People might shoot at you again. Wouldn't look good on my resume."

"Right call." Lena put her hand on the display and the terminal lit up.

Tiago typed on the keyboard. "EVA, store the bio signal and create a new profile. Name: Lena Maruishi. Clearance level: Gamma. I'm vouching for her."

"Confirmed," a female synthesized voice replied. "Please enter the voiceprint of the new profile."

"Speak your name clearly," Tiago said, pointing at the terminal.

Lena cleared her throat. "Lena Maruishi," she said.

"Confirmed," EVA replied. "I have added a new profile to the Defensio Project, operational level Gamma. Guarantor is Chancellor Tiago Silva Abreu Melo."

The terminal turned off.

"That'll do the trick," Tiago said. "Better this than the alternative."

Lena cocked her head while raising an eyebrow. "What alternative?"

"Well." Tiago glanced around. "Some of my colleagues suggested keeping you locked inside this cell and under serum until the assembly decided otherwise. Better if controlled around the clock by a team of armed soldiers."

"Assembly? What's that?"

"The decision-making body governing the bases of the Defensio Project."

"The bases?" Lena blinked. "You...um...you mean there are others?"

"Several. All scattered throughout Ariul."

"That is— Oh…" Lena scratched her neck and suddenly remembered Tiago had her pendant. "Can I have my necklace now?"

"Oh, right!" Tiago rummaged inside his pocket and handed the Pelargonium-shaped necklace to Lena. "Sorry about that. Forgot I had it."

Lena felt better wearing the necklace. It was her only link to what had happened before, and her friends had worked hard to uncover its mystery. If only Makoto, Net, and Cassidy knew where she was, they would probably…

"God." Lena's hand rose to cover her mouth. "I forgot about them!"

Tiago studied her. "You forgot about who?"

Lena looked at Tiago. "How long was I out?"

"We knocked you out less than twelve hours ago," Tiago said. "Couldn't wake you up before, with the bio gel regrowing part of your shoulder and all."

Lena considered that. It meant it had been a day since she spoke with Makoto and the others. They must have been worried. She'd left no message and disappeared.

"I need to make a call," Lena said. "Please, I've friends who…um…let's just say they might do something stupid if they don't know I'm fine."

"I see," Tiago said. "I can arrange a quick call, but they can't know where you are. I need your word on that."

"Got it." Lena placed her right hand over her heart. "But I need to talk to them right now."

Tiago nodded. "Guess it's better not to kindle suspicions. You have one minute."

Lena widened her eyes. "Only one?"

"More and the upper echelons of the Defensio Project will ask questions. We don't want that."

Lena worked her jaw back and forth, then offered a quick nod. "Deal. I'll be fast."

"All right." Tiago looked intently at her. "Make sure you put your interlink in group mode so I can hear."

"I'll do that."

"EVA," Tiago said, "disable the Yelverin field for one minute. Authorization: Tiago, Six Zero Blue."

"Confirmed," EVA replied. "Field deactivated."

Lena activated her interlink and called Makoto.

"Lena?" Makoto's voice answered on the first ring. "Where the hell are you? You scared the hell out of me! I mean...um... I mean, *us*. Net! Cassidy! Get your asses here. It's Lena."

"Lena, what happened?" came Cassidy's voice. "You disappeared!"

"Sorry," Lena said, "been busy."

"Doing what?" asked Net.

"I don't have time to explain now," Lena said. "Just know that I'm fine. I'll be back at the academy in...uh...when I finish taking care of...*something*. Okay? Do nothing stupid, please. Especially you, Makoto. Understand?"

"Taking care of *what*?" Makoto's voice sounded hoarse. "What's this all about? When are you coming back? What are we supposed to say if someone asks about you?"

"The holidays will last for another ten days, right? Tell 'em...tell 'em I'm on vacation."

Makoto wasn't biting. "Lena Maruishi, tell me exactly where you are!"

Tiago signaled for her to stop the conversation.

"Sorry. Gotta go. Bye." Lena cut off the interlink. She drew in a deep breath. "Well, that's been taken care of. Sort of." She felt bad about how she treated her friends, but what option did she have? Makoto and the others would have asked a million questions, and she didn't have time to answer. "What now?" She looked at Tiago.

"Now it's time for answers." Tiago walked out of the room and signaled for her to follow. "We better hurry. The assembly will act quickly as soon as they know I've released you. Come. We've got lots to do."

3

THE CRESCENT MOONS

PHILADELPHIA, HYPERIST ACADEMY EXCELSIOR

Gladia

∽

Gladia Egea crossed her arms and rehearsed the speech in her mind. She wasn't paying much attention to Maria Castellari—the woman standing on the podium introducing her to the audience—but rather was intent on the five hundred students in front of the stage, all standing at attention.

Gladia studied their faces. They were young, some in their early teens, yet their demeanor and expression hinted at maturity beyond their years. These young cadets were the lifeblood of the Hyperist Movement and the foundation of the Silver Infinity. They would propel forward Wei's dream of building a spacefaring civilization. Most importantly, they were powerful tools at her disposal.

A muscle on Gladia's face twitched. She swallowed, feeling ashamed of that thought. When was the last time she took a person, any person, at face value? Maybe when

Wei was still alive, over a decade before. But now, everything had changed. The end always justified the means.

How had she come to that? Hard to think there had been a time she'd called herself an engineer with relatively small goals, like removing junk from low Earth orbit or trying to convince a board of directors to approve a budget. Those were the good times. Now, to fit her new role, she had morphed into a politician, always under the spotlight, always expected to be somewhere, to shake hands, and to make important decisions that would influence the fate of millions.

Leadership. The word sounded a lot cooler when you weren't the one taking the shots.

For these young hyperists, she represented the only link to Wei Wang's legacy. She was, after all, the Last Vertex of the Hexahedron, the only survivor in the original group of creators who built the space elevator Polaris. She felt compelled to sacrifice everything to ensure the group's survival. Uncertainties were luxuries she couldn't afford.

Gladia Egea ignored her weariness and returned her focus to the teenagers standing at attention in the hallway, their silver-colored uniforms glittering like gems. The boys each had a crew cut with tapered sides, while the girls' hair gathered into tight chignons. Their uniforms were crisp, ironed with razor-sharp precision. On each of their chests was pinned a silver brooch made of two intersecting cres-cent moons forming an infinity: the symbol of the Selenians, the third most powerful party of hyperists in the world.

The Selenians believed that the colonization of the Moon and the exploitation of its resources should be HYPER's number one priority. It made no sense to them to focus on far-off places like Mars or the asteroid belt when humanity still didn't have a firm presence in its own back yard. They were staunch supporters of cislunar colonization and infrastructural development, and lobbied for a permanent presence of humankind on the Moon.

Gladia shifted her gaze to Maria Castellari, who was still addressing the students. Although short and petite, the middle-aged leader of the Selenians oozed determination from every pore.

Gladia turned her gaze to the Selenian's flag and grimaced; cold sweat beaded her forehead as Maria's speech became a faint background noise. Despite all her efforts, she couldn't contain the fear every leader must face when approaching a turning point. Gladia's primary goal had always been to show a cohesive HYPER, a movement united under the banner of the Silver Infinity. In a sense, she had succeeded, since most people believed the hyperists acted as one party. However, this was far from being the truth. HYPER was more of a dysfunctional family, constantly bickering about their next course of action.

HYPER's Five-Year Plan—also called the Pentaproject by media analysts—would spark enmities between the Selenians, Geocentrics, Ascendents, and Apeirons; four hyperist parties formed around different ideas of space development. *Four.* Wei had always liked that number. In the coming days, the two strongest groups of hyperists would clash for the leadership of the entire movement. For ten years, Gladia—the Executive Director of HYPER, Chairwoman of the Starry Assembly, and Last Vertex of the Hexahedron—had been the glue preventing the four centrifugal forces from shattering Wei's dream. She needed to keep the movement united under the same banner to give it a chance to survive.

That was the real reason Gladia decided to attend the Selenians' ceremony: to remind those young students that the Silver Infinity was stronger when all the parties worked together.

Maria Castellari's tone suddenly changed, and Gladia felt countless eyes turning toward her. She barely had time to snap out of her reverie before Maria finished introducing her.

"...and she took time out of her busy schedule to speak with us today. Please help me welcome Gladia Egea, Last Vertex of the Hexahedron and Guardian of the Silver Infinity by the Founder's grace. May his soul dance among the stars."

"May the Founder watch over us," replied five hundred cadets in unison.

Maria stepped away from the podium as Gladia rose from her chair. The two women shook hands, then Gladia placed her notes on the pulpit and nodded to Maria, who sat in the chair left empty.

"Thank you, Maria, for your warm welcome, and for inviting me to the Home of the Crescent Moons." Gladia swept her gaze over the audience. "Eight years ago, Maria Castellari founded this academy with resourcefulness and initiative. Her goal was to train young people like you, able to concretize the Founder's goal of creating a spacefaring civilization. At this very moment, Geocentric, Ascendent, and Apeiron students are training in schools and academics around the world just like this one. All of them are part of the hyperist family." She paused, letting her words sink in, then turned to the first row of cadets and smiled. "The Five-Year Plan of Sidereal Development is upon us. In just a few days, at Stargazer, will begin a new chapter in the Hyperist Movement. It's at times like this that our commitment is tested, that we must find unity in our differences. Wei Wang believed that diversity of opinions was essential for progress.

United we dominate, divided we fall. From stardust to stardust!"

"From stardust to stardust!" five hundred voices replied.

Applause interspersed Gladia's words as she continued her speech of unity and mutual respect. However, as she continued speaking, she couldn't help but notice Maria Castellari's slight grimace. With her sour expression masked by a tight smile, she didn't seem to share the mood.

∞∞∞

The cadets exited the gigantic room in an orderly fashion, leaving Gladia and Maria alone on the stage.

"Impressive speech," Maria said, smiling politely as she smoothed the front of her shirt. "Thank you for taking the time to come."

"Don't mention it." Gladia put her notes in the briefcase. "These kids are the future of HYPER. You're doing a hell of a job with them."

"Thanks." Maria shared a playful grin, but the smile didn't touch her eyes. "Your schedule must be chock-full with the Pentaproject on the horizon."

"You know," Gladia shrugged. "My assistant is great at squeezing last-minute appointments into my agenda. Arthur makes sure no one tries to shoot me when I attend them. It's just another day in paradise."

"Yeah, I figured." Maria fidgeted with her curly hair. "Look, I'm just going to stop beating around the bush and ask."

Gladia frowned. "What is it?"

Maria crossed her arms. "You think the ladder climber can win?"

"Good God, Maria." Gladia tilted her head back, her

frown deepening. "That was as direct as it gets, wasn't it? I mean, you could've been more subtle."

Maria flashed a bright smile. "Hard to do that when you're as slippery as a fish and don't answer my calls."

"So this is what it's all about?" Gladia gestured to the surroundings. "Using these kids as an excuse to get to me?"

Maria put a hand on her chest theatrically. "You make it sound desperate."

"It is desperate. And you know my answer."

Maria showed her empty hands. "Humor me."

Gladia sighed. "No comment. That's my answer."

"Oh, please." Maria rolled her eyes. "Don't give me *that*. You must have an idea."

"Why are we even having this conversation? I'm a *super partes* figure. I don't have a public stance on Tolomeus, or any other party leader, any more than I have an opinion on which kind of flowers fit best in a bouquet."

"But you *do* have an opinion." Maria put her hands on her hips. "And it carries a lot of weight."

There was an edge in the way she said it that annoyed Gladia. "What's your point?"

"My point is this: petting a poisonous snake is not a smart plan if you want to live a long life."

Gladia jammed the last of her notes into her briefcase. "You comparing Tolomeus to a snake?"

"Damn right I am." Maria pursed her lips. "That slithering bastard doesn't belong with us. He never will."

"That's enough!"

Maria blinked, a flush of red in her cheeks and neck.

"Listen to me." Gladia closed her briefcase with a sharp click. "Tolomeus is a believer in the cause. Someone who's never cornered me to talk shit about fellow hyperists. Not once."

Maria broke eye contact, looking abashed. "Look, I'm sorry. I'm just saying... I worry about his intentions. For HYPER." She added the last word a bit too late, sounding like she didn't mean it. "Tolomeus is shrewd. No one knows how he got the Ascendents to elect him. He's not one of us. Any hyperist worth their salt would know—"

"Nonsense." Gladia cut her off with a tone that broke no arguments. "Tolomeus has been wearing the infinity for a decade. He's no less a hyperist than I am. He's proven his loyalty, helped us win back half a dozen countries from the landists. If you want to lecture me about his past, you're wasting your time. I don't share the opinion you and Penelope have. End of story."

Maria opened her mouth, then closed it. She looked conflicted. Gladia knew why. The Selenians had publicly supported the Geocentrics to counter Tolomeus' Ascendents. Maria had put her reputation on the line and was trying to understand if the bet would pay off.

"You really think that man works for the Hyperist Movement?" Maria sounded genuinely eager to learn the answer.

Gladia sighed. "Look, does he have a personal agenda? Of course he does, just like any ambitious person. Should I give him a hard time because he was Woodside's best buddy a decade ago? That's not the way we operate. We believe in giving people second chances. That being said, it's not for me to take sides. I'm the scale, Maria. I don't decide the weight that is put on my plate. I just carry it."

Maria looked at her, eyes unblinking. "Even if the weight can break the scale in two?"

Gladia's nostrils flared. She narrowed her eyes and stepped toward the other woman. "Is that a threat?"

Maria's elbow pressed into her side as she stepped back. "No," she replied, looking down. Her face turned ashen. "Of course not. I just... I was asking. That's all. I meant no disrespect."

Gladia offered her a curt nod. "Let me give you a piece of advice. I can be kind, I can be forgiving, but give me a reason to think you're undermining my authority, and I swear to you that Tolomeus will be the least of your problems. That clear?"

Maria's posture stiffened, but she nodded. "Clear."

"Good." Gladia grabbed her briefcase and made to go.

"Can I ask you a technical question?"

Gladia stopped, turned toward Maria. "What is it?"

"This...ah...space fleet Tolomeus has in mind...these katalambans."

"What about them?"

"Well, they sound like far-fetched science fiction shenanigans. We don't have the technology or the infrastructure to build a profitable asteroid-mining market-place, let alone a space economy. We're not there yet."

"That's not up to me to decide." Gladia drummed a finger on her briefcase. "That's what the Keystone is for."

"Okay, I understand. But what do *you* think?"

"I think it's a bold plan, but so was Polaris when Wei proposed it. Two years later, we had a perfectly functioning space elevator. You know what he used to say about impossible things. Or have you forgotten?"

Maria nodded. "So you think Tolomeus' ships might work?"

"It doesn't matter what I think. It matters what I *know*."

Maria arched her eyebrow. "Meaning?"

"The Executive Council has evaluated Tolomeus' project, and it received the green light by the committee. That's all I need to know."

"What about the questions he dodged about the funding?" Maria bit her lip. "Those are as shady as sin."

"Look, Maria. It's up to a vote to decide whether Tolomeus' katalambans or Penelope's space elevator will win the Pentaproject. Let history take its course."

"But—"

Gladia walked past her. "I'll see you at Stargazer." As she stormed out of the building, a chill ran down her spine. If she needed any proof that the power struggle had begun, Maria's speech was it. The Hyperist Movement was going through tough times, pulled and squeezed in different directions, and Gladia was the only person who could hold it together. She couldn't afford to let her guard down.

4

THE DOMINE

NASHVILLE, ARK INSTITUTE FOR ADVANCED
ETHERIC STUDIES

James

James Ark shoved back his sunglasses as he studied
the data displayed on the console. He pressed his
lips into a slight grimace, while the young woman
sitting at another terminal cast him a nervous
glance. She smoothed her sharply pressed purple uniform,
black and silver stripes running from her shoulder to her
neck. On her chest was a metal brooch in the shape of a stylized hourglass.

"How...um...how would you like me to proceed,
Domine?" she asked, her smile wavering. "You want me to
assimilate the data to the core, or keep it floating?"

James was only-half listening. His mind was focused on
the implications of what he was reading. *Failure.* The thirty-
seventh failure to date, and none of them brought him any
closer to making a difference.

"Um, Domine? Did you...ah...did you get that?"

James turned toward the girl, blinking. "Sorry, Leah. I spaced. Keep the data floating and reject all projections in *sub-quotis*. They're no good to us now. We'll have to start over."

"Understood, Domine." Leah nodded, then started typing. "Data floating. Marginal projections rejected. Saving the new configuration to the data core."

"Make sure ADAM gets the result."

"Will do, Domine."

James' mind was already working on another option for the thirty-eighth attempt, evaluating dozens of possibilities, but he had small hope it would succeed. The model's framework was faulty, and there was little he could do to correct that. Time was running out. He desperately needed fresh ideas.

The door of the laboratory opened, and a tall, dark-skinned man wearing a purple turban strode toward James.

"Ravi." James glanced at the newcomer, then turned to study the console. "You show up disturbingly fast when there is bad news."

Ravi smirked. "Hilarious." His square, deep-set face had changed little since his years as a student of Cantara Handal, but his amused smile had sharpened.

"What do you want?" James asked.

Ravi opened his arms and widened his smile. "Look, it was a good try." He glanced at Leah, then back at James. "Could have worked."

James bit his lip. "But it didn't. I'm tired of stumbling through the darkness. You're here to rub my nose in it?"

"No, James." Ravi's smile became a sneer. "I won't say 'I told you so,' but I'm glad we're on the same page here. We can't be stuck in the past. So, you agree your attempts were useless?"

James nodded. "They were."

"Good." Ravi clapped his hands. "Then it's finally time to move on to the next stage. Shall we?" He pulled a small tablet from his pocket and approached Leah. "Enter this new combination into the main data stream. Make sure it doesn't conflict with—"

"Ignore that."

Ravi's smile faltered. "What do you mean?" He stared at James. "You just said—"

"I said we can't continue going on stumbling into the dark. I didn't say I wanted to waste more time and energy on another futile effort."

Ravi drew himself up to his full height. "You don't know if it's futile. We haven't tried it yet!"

"We don't need to try." James shook his head. "We already know the outcome."

"What's that supposed to mean?"

"You don't swim across the Pacific Ocean, Ravi. You already know you won't make it to the other side."

Ravi glared at him. "You're letting your personal feelings interfere."

"I leave my personal feelings outside the door every time I work." James gestured to the room's entrance. "If you don't know that by now, you've been working on a different project altogether."

Ravi wet his lip, clenching and unclenching his fists. "Look. You tried your way. It failed."

"Failure is just a steppingstone to success."

Ravi laughed with an edge. "Yeah, sure." He made a sweeping arm gesture. "Throw me some cheap motivational garbage while you're at it. Doesn't change the fact we haven't moved an inch forward since you adopted the stochastic approach. It didn't work, my friend. It never will. We're running out of time. Venus and Asha feel the same way I do. It's three against one."

"You think we're running an election here?"

Ravi squeezed his tablet, his knuckles turning white. "So you're going to repeat the same mistakes and expect we tag along?"

"No." James glanced at the console displaying his latest failure. "I agree that my line of reasoning hasn't worked."

"Then why don't we try something different?"

"We're going to."

"Oh, yes." Ravi crossed his arms, watching James with an intense gaze. "Of course. I almost forgot. Your genius stunt, right? Threatening to blow up in our faces. Think your desperate move is going to work out?"

"It isn't desperate."

"No? Then what is it?"

"It's a strategic choice dictated by necessity."

Ravi barked a laugh. "Sure, or you could call it kidnapping. You know, its *real* name? But, hey. If that makes you sleep at night, who am I to argue with the mighty James Ark?"

"She's going to help us. She's going to change things."

"You don't know that." Ravi stepped up to James. "Our asses are on the line, buddy. This was supposed to be a team effort."

"Get out of my face."

Ravi clenched and unclenched his hands before taking a couple steps back. "You're taking a huge risk." He jabbed a finger at James. "When you fail, because you will, I'll be making the call myself."

Ravi turned his back and stormed out of the room.

James swallowed. He removed his sunglasses and rubbed at his temples. Ravi didn't get it. He had always been a simple foot soldier, never a leader. He was hasty, prideful, incapable of seeing the big picture. Ravi was just a tool, someone who'd never make a difference.

"Impatience is the mother of stupidity," James murmured.

The room suddenly seemed to shrink around him, and he started breathing hard. Ravi had been right about one thing: their time was running out.

"Leah, what time is it?" he asked, turning toward the young woman.

Leah cleared her throat, trying to pretend she didn't notice the heated exchange between the two men. "It's 5:40, Domine."

"Right." James put the sunglasses back on. "Time to find out if this circus needs a clown."

5

FIRST OMNIBUS

GEODE, OUTPOST OF THE DEFENSIO PROJECT

Ariul

"Not everyone knows of your sudden appearance, Lena, but the news is spreading fast."

Tiago and Lena were walking down an empty corridor painted a dull gray. It had no windows and no doors, and it smelled faintly of acetone.

Lena glanced at the chancellor. "And is this...um...good or bad?"

"It depends."

Tiago turned left, and the walls became white with the floor and ceiling yellow ochre. Here the air smelled of plastic, and soft humming came from the air conditioners.

Lena increased her pace to keep up with the chancellor. "Depends on what?"

Tiago portable's display started beeping. "Just a second." He glanced at the screen and grunted. "That'll do it." He put the tablet back in his pocket. "As for your question, they'll want to know how you opened a Quartz from the outside."

Lena blinked. "What's a Quartz?"

"Any of the access doors to installations like Geode." Tiago gestured around. "Think of them as blast doors. You can get in only by sending a direct signal from the inside. They're designed this way."

Lena shook her head. "Why?"

"It's a security measure to prevent unwanted people from entering any underground base."

"You mean—" Lena cut herself off, thinking of her next words. "You're saying each of Saemangeum's sculptures is a gateway to the Defensio Project? But there must be dozens throughout the city."

"They're not all active," the chancellor explained. "They used to be, but not anymore."

Lena glanced around uneasily. "Why do you need so many?"

"Saemangeum is an enormous city," Tiago said, "difficult to protect if you don't have many exit points from which to deploy your assets."

"Assets," she echoed. "You mean soldiers, right? The one you call dunamis."

"Yes, that's the word we use for them. The point is, Lena, what you did is unprecedented. No one should be able to open a Quartz from the outside, not even a centurion, a dunamis squad leader. That's why several high-ranking members of the Defensio want to ask you questions. They convened the assembly the moment they learned of your existence. Tomorrow, a bunch of people will want to know who you are."

"Okay." She considered that. "Should I be worried?"

"Not necessarily," Tiago said, but something in his look didn't convince her.

"That doesn't tell me anything though, does it?" She looked at the chancellor sideways. "Who are these people? What kind of questions will they ask?"

"Some will challenge your role as the Cornucopia. Think it's a ploy to get their attention."

Lena took a steadying breath before responding. "Why would they think that?"

"Let's just say the powers that be aren't fond of me." Tiago increased his pace, his hands almost curling into fists and then straightening. "There are people who see my ideas as dangerous to the Defensio Project."

"Why is that?"

"Because I'd rather take action than stick my head in the sand, waiting to be beaten to death. That's what we've done for years. But with you, everything changes."

She frowned. "It does?"

"Of course. Don't you understand? You're here because Wei sent you. Your necklace is the proof. Now we just need to find out why."

They entered another empty section, this one wider, and looking even less used than the previous two.

"Is there only us here?" Lena looked around with a dazed look. "I mean, this place seems pretty big, but it looks empty."

"Right now, there's just twelve people in Geode," Tiago said. "In the beginning, we had over fifty." He looked around as if he could see ghosts walking by.

She noticed his jaw tightening. "What happened?"

"We lost good people, and didn't have the resources to replace them." His expression betrayed frustration. "The enemy is bleeding us to death. That's why I want to change things."

Another beep sounded from the chancellor's display, and he cursed under his breath. "We should hurry." He picked up the pace so much that he almost started jogging. "I need to show you something fast. Not sure how long this window is going to be open."

Lena had to half-run to keep up with his long legs. "You didn't say where we're going."

"I need you to understand a couple things before you appear in front of the assembly," Tiago said without slowing down. "Now save your breath."

For the next five minutes, they rushed down the corridor until they arrived in front of an oval door made of a reddish metal that reflected the artificial light.

"This is the place." Tiago entered a code into the panel at the side of the entrance and the door slid open. "After you."

At first Lena thought they'd stepped into a library. There were several shelves arranged on either side of the square room displaying old-looking ledgers. Sitting behind a metal table at the center of the area was a man in his late twenties wearing a projector unit display. When they came in, he awkwardly removed the device from his face, wiped his brow, and stood up sharply, almost at attention.

"Chancellor," the man greeted Tiago with a hasty bow. "I'm sorry. Did you leave a message? I wasn't aware of your—"

"No, Spencer," Tiago cut him off, his tone kind but firm, like someone talking to a subordinate. "I decided to drop by, very spur-of-the-moment. This is Lena." He patted her shoulder. "I'm going to show her the Masvieth."

"I see." Spencer turned his attention to Lena, his gray-green eyes unblinking. He produced a thick leather handbook that looked as old as time itself. "Please provide both your bioxon codes so that I can record the activation on the ledger."

Tiago shook his head. "Won't be necessary."

Spencer narrowed his eyes. "Excuse me?"

"I want to keep this visit off the books, if you catch my drift."

Spencer stared at Tiago. "I'm afraid I don't." He rubbed the back of his neck, then glanced at the doorway. "I need your bioxon codes to start the activation."

"No, you don't." Tiago flashed a genial smile. "If you use yours."

"Mine?" Spencer's eyebrows rose to his hairline. "Why would I do that?"

"I don't know." Tiago looked around circumspectly. "Perhaps because you want to take a gander at the new list of axiom tokens in your DataMorph account."

Spencer's slightly annoyed expression morphed into a childish grin. "What?"

"You heard that right," Tiago said with a beaming face. "They're already in your account. Signed, sealed, and delivered."

"No way!" Spencer's eyes glowed. "Chancellor, you play Rebel of the Underworld?"

"Who doesn't?" Tiago shared a playful grin. "I heard from Sira that you've been stuck on level seven of the Netherworld for ages."

"Yes, for months, Chancellor." Spencer nodded vigorously, his expression turning sour. "I swear jumping through the hoops of Eurydice's rescue is driving me crazy. Three months I've been stuck there. *Three* months. I was ready to give up."

"Well, not anymore." Tiago held the arms up in a "Victory V." "Those sweet, sweet tokens will help you crack the code. Maybe they'll even give you a little boost to reach the Elysium Fields."

Spencer grabbed at the sides of his head in an *I can't believe it* gesture. "And they're in my account?"

"You bet."

"Right now?"

"Why don't you take a peek?"

Spencer almost dropped his PUD twice because of his excitement. "Wow!" His mouth opened up in a smile. "This is amazing! Chancellor, I don't know what to say."

"Say that you'll use the tokens well."

Spencer chuckled. "How did you get your hands on them? I mean, they're almost impossible to find on any level."

"I have my ways." Tiago clapped his hands once. "So, what do you say? We have a deal?"

"What?" Spencer was still grinning, hands wrapped around his headset.

"The Masvieth." Tiago's tone was firm. "Can we use your code?"

"Well..." Spencer hesitated a moment, glanced at the door before continuing talking in a slightly lower tone, "I guess it wouldn't be a big deal for you to use my code." He paused, his eyes again drifting toward the door. "But if word gets to the regent—"

"It won't," Tiago said matter-of-factly. "We've never been here while you were doing your thing, right?" He gestured toward the PUD, then winked. "Catch my drift now?"

Spencer scuffed the chair closer to the table, his eyes glowing. "I do." He activated the table's display with a wave of his hand, then inserted a code. "Chamber's ready, Chancellor."

"Thanks. We'll get out of your hair, Spencer." Tiago pushed Lena forward.

Lena waited to move away from Spencer's earshot before speaking. "What was all that about?"

Tiago waved a hand dismissively. "Avoiding paperwork."

"Avoiding paperwork? What's that supposed to mean?"

"Well...you know...we're not exactly supposed to be here, but there's no other way to show you what I need, so... I guess what I'm saying is the end justifies the means, and all that."

"So you bribed that guy?"

"I believe the right word is 'incentivized.'" Tiago flashed a genial smile. "You're welcome, by the way. I'm about to deliver the answers I promised you. The Masvieth is the most important piece of the puzzle. It'll help you understand a lot."

Tiago opened a door at the end of the narrow passage. "This way."

Lena followed him. "What is a Masvieth?"

"Masvieth is a compound word," Tiago explained. "It means map of etheric development. It's an object that can range from the size of a medicine balloon to that of a small hot-air balloon. Through the Masvieth, etherions can plan actions that affect the geokratic configuration of cyberspace."

"Okay," Lena said, her frown deepening. "English, please?"

"By using a Masvieth, etherions can influence the development of cyberspace, and the interactions between the different portions that compose it."

Lena studied Tiago carefully. "How do you know all this stuff about the ether?"

Tiago shrugged as he moved forward. "It's my job as First Omnibus to know."

Lena tilted her head to the side. "First Omnibus?"

"It means I'm the etherion leader of the Defensio Project." There was bitterness in Tiago's voice. He clenched his jaw as if he just admitted a despicable crime. "But I haven't used my powers for doing good of late. That's going to change today."

6

THE EXECUTIVE DIRECTOR

ORLANDO, ARCTURUS NATIONAL HISTORY MUSEUM OF SPACEFLIGHT

Gladia

~

Gladia wished she could disappear into a dark hole and avoid people for the rest of her life.

"Exhausted" didn't come close to describing her physical and mental state. She felt worn, like an old, ragged cloth used one too many times.

Last week's tour in preparation of the Pentaproject had sucked every ounce of her strength. She'd visited six cities in seven days, taking part in fundraisers, interviews, presentations, and public speeches. Every spokesperson, lobbyist, representative, and bureaucrat who was involved in the Five-Year Plan had had a taste of her. Everyone had a request to submit to the executive director, a favor to ask, a suggestion to give, a demand to make. Christmas had come early for the vultures.

And that was just scratching the surface. The Pentaproject was bringing out the worst in her fellow hyperists.

Everyone was trying to influence, to control, to grab a bigger slice of the pie at the expense of a fellow hyperist. This was all part of a conspicuous show meant to gather attention; Gladia knew that. The bigger the conflict, the more interesting the story. But this time it differed from the past. There had been such extreme cases of rivalries between the parties, she was no longer sure this was showing off.

The bickering had been harsher from the get-go. This growing, toxic confrontation was showing some serious cracks in the movement. And the media had noticed: Ascendents who "forgot" to attend fundraisers supported by Geocentrics, Selenians who invited Ascendent guests on their TV shows to publicly humiliate them, Geocentrics who pointed out Tolomeus' landist background at every occasion. And, of course, there were the haughty Apeirons, who remained stubbornly attached to their isolationism, ignoring Gladia's attempts at bringing them back into the fold. They had made clear on many occasions that they considered Geocentrics, Selenians, and Ascendents bastard offshoots of Wei's core ideas. The media dubbed the Apeirons the "orthodox wing" of HYPER, a small but vocal minority who didn't recognize Gladia's leadership. They kept mostly to themselves and seldom left the Serenity Center, a giant fortress-like structure in northern Europe that made up their headquarters. They refused to take part in any shared project and kept their technology secret. Over time, their disconnect with HYPER had deepened, and their isolationism had grown to where no one even knew who their leader was.

The Apeirons had shown little interest in the Pentaproject, though Gladia had invited them to participate. Their last reply to her—sent through snail mail—had been a five-word sentence: "We are considering our involvement."

Gladia had the perfect answer, although following Arthur's suggestion she hadn't sent it. *Yeah. Fuck you too.*

"I've forwarded the latest projection to the exo-chamber, ma'am. We should get their reply within the hour."

Gladia glanced at her assistant as they walked down a passageway outside the museum's main room, where she'd just finished attending a conference. "Thanks, Charlotte," she said, crossing off items from a list on her tablet.

Her administrative assistant—a short, petite young woman with long, chestnut hair—trailed behind her, while two bodyguards escorted them to their next destination. They were big men, with broad shoulders and thick arms. On their immaculate white suits were brooches in the shape of a golden shield with an infinity at its center.

Gladia typed on her tablet, replying to messages while walking. "What's next on the agenda?"

Charlotte furrowed her brow as she went through the list. "We're due an interview with DataCore Max."

Gladia squinted. "You sure? Can't find the memo. You sent it?"

"Yes, ma'am. Last night at nine-oh-five, as requested."

Gladia scrolled through a hundred messages, shook her head. "Well, it got buried under the garbage. Can you send it again?"

"Sure thing." Charlotte swiped her display toward Gladia's device, and a beep from both tablets signaled the file was received.

"Thanks." Gladia was reading the screen when the bodyguard preceding them halted. "What's happening?"

"Incoming call from Commodore, ma'am." The bodyguard tapped his earpiece. "Centaur to Commodore, over." The bodyguard's voice was brisk. "Yes, Commodore. Athena is five hundred yards from the next checkpoint. Moving on into the east wing now."

Gladia grimaced, then turned to her assistant with a pained expression. "Can you remind me why Arthur assigned us two of his scarecrows inside a goddamn Silver Oasis?"

Charlotte glanced at her display as if the answer was written on it. "Um...precautions, ma'am?"

"It's nuts!" Gladia tipped her head back to look heavenward, then let it flop forward. "I'm inside a hyperist installation, for God's sake. A fly would have a hard time getting inside the perimeter. Why do I need them?" She gestured at the two men.

"Ma'am." Charlotte's voice quavered a bit. "I think... um...I think the constable just cares about your safety."

"Well, if he—"

"Copy that, Commodore." The bodyguard turned to Gladia. "Original route is too trafficked, ma'am. We'll take a safer path through the second floor."

Gladia blew a hard breath and closed her eyes. "How long will it take?"

"ETA: ten minutes, ma'am."

"Great." Gladia grimaced. "Just great. I'll be late. *Again*."

The bodyguard resumed walking, unconcerned with Gladia's complaint.

"By the way, where on earth is Arthur?" Gladia ran a hand through her short hair as she reluctantly followed the big man. "Wasn't he supposed to be back this morning?"

"Um." Charlotte cleared her throat. "It was in my morning report, ma'am."

Gladia sighed. "Well, obviously, I didn't get it." She waved her tablet meaningfully. "Enlighten me."

"The constable stayed in Stargazer to oversee additional security measures."

"Outstanding." Gladia pinched her mouth. "The longer he stays, the more his paranoia will grow. At this rate, he'll insist I go to the restroom wearing a bulletproof vest. When will he be back?"

"Tonight," Charlotte said, gazing at her device. "The aeromousine is scheduled to land in Orlando at nine fifteen."

"Right." Gladia put her palms against her temples and massaged the pain. "Well, since we're taking the longer route, courtesy of our good chaperones here, we might as well use the extra ten minutes. Give me the gist of the news. Daily digest style. Extra points if you can make it quick and painless."

"Yes, ma'am." Charlotte scrolled through her database, opened a file, and started reading. "The Landist Council announced that Yvonne Muchena will give a speech in Rome, at Piazza del Popolo. The date of the event is unknown, and so is the reason. Our analysts expect it to be something massive though. Local authorities estimate at least one hundred thousand people to attend in person, and cyberspace output indicators point to something unprecedented. Our cyber-fare department reported that LAND is staking a lot of etheric assets at the event. Many of our etherions identified a major synergic push happening on social medias, virtual reality platforms, and legacy press."

Gladia worked her jaw back and forth. "Well, there's no way something hasn't leaked."

"Everyone is tight-lipped, ma'am," Charlotte said. "We have nothing solid. Just rumors."

"Then give me the rumors."

Charlotte tapped her tablet's screen twice before

answering. "A minority of our etherions suggest a sudden shift in LAND's overall environmental policy, or a new aggressive campaign in the Third World."

Gladia crossed her arms. "Okay. That's probably garbage. Muchena wouldn't have raised so much fuss about something so trivial. What's next?"

Charlotte kept reading from her device. "There have been clashes between hyperists and landists in Paris and London, following the Aldarion scandal."

Gladia held her breath. "Ascendants?"

Charlotte nodded. "It looks that way from the bulletin, ma'am."

"Of course." Gladia forcibly expelled all breath as she tried to process the information. "Deaths?"

"Three so far, but the number is poised to grow in the coming days."

"What's Tolomeus doing about it?"

"The Legatus lamented the deaths and condemned the clash. Said it was an extremist fringe of hyperists with nothing to share with the Ascendants."

Gladia snorted. "Talking like a politician in the middle of an election campaign. I hope when the dust settles, this doesn't come back to bite us in the ass. Last thing I need is more journalists breathing down my neck. All right, go ahead."

"Stock prices of all major space technology companies took a hit this week. The SPACECON index has shed eleven percent from the beginning of the month."

Gladia's shoulders slumped. "What's the sentiment?"

"Shareholders aren't happy with the growing tensions between the parties. Many believe whoever wins the Pentaproject won't have enough goodwill left to sustain a growing space economy in the coming years."

Gladia scoffed. "So Wall Street's bean counters are pissed because Geocentrics and Ascendants can't smile in front of the cameras?" She made a sweeping hand gesture. "Unbelievable. All they care about is the next quarterly report. What else?"

Charlotte skipped a few lines, then focused on something she underlined. "There is news of an alleged etheric disease. Seems to affect ethernauts all over the world with increasing frequency."

"An etheric disease?" Gladia tapped a fist against her lips, her expression blank. "You mean, like a flu or something?"

"Um...I think it's more serious, ma'am. According to some sources, it's killing people."

Gladia stared at her. "What?"

"It's still unclear what's happening. Looks like some people started showing signs of an unknown psychophysics disfunction after traveling through the ether and then died."

"Are you serious?" Gladia frowned. "Is something like this even possible? I mean, Jesus. And I thought getting a migraine after shopping at DataMorph was bad."

"The Covenant for Etheric Safeguarding is still investigating," Charlotte said. "Word on the street is that it might be a setup staged by private companies to sell softwares and turn a profit. They call them autheras."

Gladia shook her head. "God, I miss the good old Internet." She turned to face her assistant. "You remember the Internet, Charlotte?"

"Um...no, ma'am."

Gladia blinked. "How old are you again?"

"I'm twenty-six."

"Right." Gladia nodded. "Makes sense. By the time you

were ten, the World Wide Web was a footnote in the history books."

Charlotte blushed. "I'm afraid so."

"Ah, well." Gladia shrugged. "It was a simpler world. Sorry you didn't get to experience it. Okay, let's cut to the chase. Give me the biggest bone in the bowl."

"Yes, ma'am." Charlotte flipped through the news. "A spokesperson at LAND announced earlier today that they appointed Elijah Goldberg as Chief Councilor to the Landist Council in place of Richard Donovan."

Gladia opened her mouth, her eyes bulging. "Elijah Goldberg?"

"Yes, ma'am."

"Give me that." Gladia gestured to the device, and Charlotte handed her the tablet.

Gladia scanned the content of the news. "This isn't good." Elijah Goldberg was one of the most extreme landists in the marketplace. Even Woodside had kept him at a distance and never allowed him a seat on the Council. That Yvonne Muchena chose Elijah as Chief Councilor was confirmation that LAND was drifting toward extremism. Gladia returned the device to Charlotte. "I need some good news." She closed her eyes and blew air through her mouth. "I'll take anything. Just one thing."

"Well," Charlotte said slowly, eyeing her tablet. "I...ah... I've just received a response from the Apeirons, regarding the Pentaproject."

Gladia fussed with her shirt as she leaned toward her assistant. "Are they in?"

"Um...their spokesperson said they're willing to send to Stargazer six junior administrators from their PR department."

"Six junior administrators." Gladia's lips curled back in

disgust. "They're shitting on us without even giving us the courtesy of calling it a landslide." She drew in a deep breath, her shoulders dropping. "Whatever! I'll take it. As long as they send warm bodies to Stargazer, it's a win. Anything to stop the press from flaunting the word 'schism' on my face like fireworks on the 4th of July. Send them a—" Gladia stopped. She noticed a tingling sensation at the tips of her fingers that spread to her palms and arms. She started sweating, muscles jumping under the skin.

Oh, no. Not now, please.

"Ma'am?" Charlotte had stopped, along with her escort. They were all watching her. Gladia hadn't noticed she'd frozen in the middle of the corridor.

"Everything okay, ma'am?" asked one of her bodyguards.

Gladia swallowed. "Y...yeah, I'm fine. I just need...I've got to go to the restroom." She cleared her throat. "It's urgent."

The bodyguard nodded. "Yes, ma'am." He tapped his earpiece. "Commodore, change of plans. We're taking a detour toward the lady's room on the second floor."

When they arrived at the restroom, one bodyguard checked inside, then gestured for Gladia to go in. Gladia closed the door, resting her back against it. As her heart slammed against her chest, she took a few hesitant steps toward the sinks and gazed at her image in the mirror. She was pale and sweaty, shades of dark purple besieged her eyes.

"Breathe, girl," she hissed through clenched teeth, gripping the marble of the sink. "Just breathe. It's going to be all right. Any moment, now. You're going to be okay. Breathe. In and out. Just breathe."

She turned on the faucet and held her wrists under the icy stream. She counted in her mind until she reached thirty, then assessed again her reflection in the mirror. Long horizontal lines drew wrinkles on the sides of her mouth and eyes. Makeup did nothing to restore light to her dull eyes.

Gladia turned off the water and leaned against the counter. Her hands kept shaking as she gathered a strand of yellow hair streaked with white behind her ear.

"Shit!" She slammed a fist on the marble. "Shit! Shit! Shit!" She stared at her trembling hands, as if her anger could will them to stop. It didn't.

Gladia muffled her sobbing by increasing the flow of water. Tears rolled down her cheeks and then fell onto her jacket as a wave of nausea swept over her, causing her to gag.

She fumbled into her jacket pocket and pulled out a small metal container. Inside were half a dozen orange pills, a black line dividing them into two halves. She pulled out a pill and swallowed it with some water.

A minute passed before the shaking slowed down to a stop. Gladia splashed some water on her face as she regained control of her breathing.

"You're going to be fine." She stared at the dark circles under her eyes. "It's just another day. Arthur will be back tonight. You don't have to worry."

"Ma'am?" Charlotte's voice from outside. "Is everything okay?"

Gladia turned off the water faucet. "Yes," she croaked. "I'll be out in a sec." She straightened up, looked at the mirror, then went outside and faced Charlotte and the two bodyguards.

"All right," she said, forcing a smile. "Where were we?"

∞∞∞

Miami

Clearwater Hotel, Penthouse

Gladia stomped into the bathroom and had barely enough time to get in front of the toilet before throwing up her dinner.

She had suffered another panic attack twenty minutes before, when noticing that her hand holding the fork was shaking.

Gladia flushed the toilet, wiped her mouth with a towel, then sat with her back against the bathroom wall and waited for her breathing to slow. After five minutes, she stood up slowly and dragged herself to the sink, where she washed her hands and face. She undressed, threw the clothes that reeked of sweat and vomit on the floor, and walked out of the bathroom in her underwear.

She looked around, taking in the penthouse suite for the first time. Her suitcase—brought by the hotel management in the morning—had been left beside the entrance door. Gladia opened the suitcase. "Control?" she said, while rummaging through her clothes.

"Yes, Executive Director?" answered a computer-generated male voice.

"Play the Landist Channel on the in-suite projector."

"Confirmed. Transmitting now."

A three-dimensional video projection appeared in the center of the room. The landist symbol flashed for a second against a bright green background before being replaced by the image of a tall, dark-skinned woman standing on a stage. She was surrounded by a cheering crowd of thousands of people shouting her name.

"Yvonne! Yvonne! YVONNE!"

Gladia tossed a couple dresses aside while the commentator's voice played in the background.

"Muchena has managed a ninety-two percent approval rating. Not even Douglas Woodside came close to this figure. After reshaping the Landist Council and appointing Elijah Goldberg at its helm, Muchena's Black Wind—the movement she founded back in her leadership time in Africa—has successfully won positions of power in several regions in Africa, while new pro-landist movements are springing up in South America and Southeast Asia. Earlier this morning, the landist president—after underlining LAND's progress on the world stage—commented on the upcoming Pentaproject."

Gladia glanced at the projection. Muchena was smiling at the camera while an immense crowd cheered. "For years, LAND has struggled to regain its identity and purpose." The landist leader swept her eyes across the sea of people and raised a hand in triumph. "We were weak and divided, quarrelling against each other, and our enemies took advantage of that division. No more! Once again, we're united under the same banner and ready to expose HYPER for what it really is: the most expensive lie in human history. I don't care what kind of flavor is trending at the moment. Geocentrics, Selenians, Ascendents, Apeirons... Any form of hyperism is a disease for our society, and needs to be eradicated! We won't stop until—"

"Gladia?"

Gladia turned toward the entrance. A tall man in his late fifties was standing on the threshold, a wide grin on his tanned face.

"Arthur?" Gladia frowned. "About time you showed up. Why are you smiling like an idiot?"

"It's...um...you know?" He pointed at her body, then looked away, blushing. "I've knocked twice but...well, the door was half-open and..." he trailed off meaningfully.

Gladia was still in her underwear. "Oh, for God's sake!" She reached into her luggage and hastily pulled out a nightgown.

Arthur glanced at the corridor. "I can come back if you—"

"Just come in and close the damn door."

"Sure. The door...right." Arthur stepped in and shut the door.

Gladia motioned Arthur to a chair as she finished dressing. The projection playing Muchena's speech caught the man's attention.

"Keeping up with the daily pile of turd?"

Gladia glanced at Muchena, then snorted. "She seems to be everywhere these days." She finished buttoning the nightgown. "Never thought I'd miss Woodside."

Arthur crossed his arms. "Well, you have to give her credit. In a hundred days, she accomplished what Woodside couldn't in a decade."

Gladia glared at him. "So?"

Arthur shrugged. "She brought the Landist Council to its knees, brought Elijah 'Nosferatu' Goldberg into the fold, and won majority seats in seven African governments. She's a force of nature on steroids."

"You planning on switching sides?" Gladia raised her eyebrows. "Sounds like you want to join her group of lunatics."

Arthur showed his empty palms. "Just reading the writing on the wall. She isn't the rookie we thought she was. Muchena knows how to sell herself to the press while cleaning house. Credit where credit is due."

"She's good at attracting attention," Gladia retorted bitterly. "Like the worst kind of arsonist. Nothing to praise about that. I just wish I knew what she's planning."

Arthur tilted his head, gazing at the projection. "Her gathering in Rome?"

"What else?" Gladia scoffed. "It's another of her stunts."

"Must be something crucial though." Arthur's expression was thoughtful. "Well, we'll know soon enough."

"Right." Gladia cleared her throat and looked away from Arthur, the silence growing awkward. She smoothed her nightgown, but the action exposed her hands. She hid them in her pockets.

"You look tired," Arthur said, leaning on the chair. "Still having nightmares?"

Gladia changed the subject. "Where the hell have you been? You were supposed to be here this morning."

"Just making sure our executive director is safe and sound during the main event." Arthur furrowed his brow. "And you didn't answer my question."

"You're paranoid," Gladia said dismissively. "What are the chances of an attack at Stargazer? Hmm? Zero point zero, zero, zero, NOTHING percent?"

Arthur offered a pained stare. "Someone must have said the same thing about Infinity ten years ago."

Gladia froze on the spot. She ground her molars together, her lips pressed into a thin line.

"I'm sorry." Arthur stood from the chair and walked up to Gladia. "Shouldn't have said that. It's just...I want to make sure nothing goes wrong." He raised his arms to embrace her, then stopped in mid-motion.

Gladia withdrew. "Never mind." She stepped back and put distance between them. "Everything ready for the trip?"

"Yeah," Arthur said, his tone flat. "All set. The aeromousine is hot and loaded. We take off tomorrow at eight o'clock sharp. Hope you're ready to make history."

7

THE MADAME

NASHVILLE, ARK INSTITUTE FOR ADVANCED ETHERIC STUDIES

James

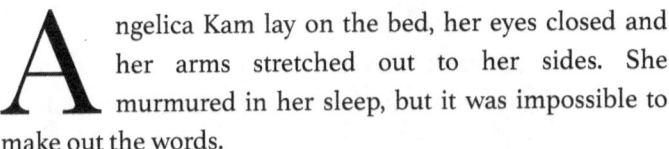

Angelica Kam lay on the bed, her eyes closed and her arms stretched out to her sides. She murmured in her sleep, but it was impossible to make out the words.

James pulled the chair closer to the bed, staring at the sleeping woman. His eyes lingered on her full, heart-shaped lips, moving as they whispered. In the eleven years since he'd last seen her in person, Angelica had changed remarkably little. She still possessed a charming beauty that drew the eye.

James removed the black leather glove from his hand and brought his fingers close to Angelica's face, feeling her warm breath. He swallowed, his hand shaking slightly as it touched her warm cheek. He lingered on that touch, found himself eager to continue the contact.

Angelica jerked her head to the side, mumbling in her sleep, and James pulled his hand away with a gasp.

Old feelings started surfacing, embers of a forgotten fire: the scent of roses accompanying her everywhere, her shy smile when their eyes met, the glances James cast her during classes when she wasn't looking.

Angelica had been one of Cantara's best students. Her ability to improvise, to analyze variables and devise sound strategy was remarkable. It was the reason he'd brought her here. It had been a bold move, and dangerous, but he had no other choice. Secrecy was of paramount importance if he wanted the plan to succeed without risking blowback.

Angelica Kam was the only person who could help him make a difference. Her alter ego, the Madame of Melody, would become an invaluable asset if he played his cards right. He backed away, containing his impulses. Dwelling on his feelings wasn't the right way to achieve his goal. He needed to remember what mattered.

"It's...it's dangerous. Everyone's at risk." Angelica was mumbling again. Her nails dug into her palms, sweat rolling down her forehead in beads. "Not even Cloverfield... Not even him... He couldn't... No. Let me go, please. Let me go!"

James shook her gently. "Angelica? Wake up."

Angelica snapped her eyes open. She gasped, hands clawing at her mouth as if removing something from her face.

"You're safe, Angelica," James said with a reassuring voice. "No one will hurt you."

Angelica slowly turned toward him.

James drew back slightly. He took off his sunglasses and stretched his lips into a thin smile. "Hi."

Angelica blinked, eyes unfocused. "Who...who are you?" She looked around, panting.

"Here." James handed Angelica's eyeglasses to her.

Angelica took them hesitantly and put them on.

"Eleven years ago," James said, "Cantara Handal took seven young, would-be etherions under her wing. You're looking at the youngest of them."

Angelica blinked, eyes narrowed to slits. "J-James? James Ark?" She tried to get off the bed, but only propped herself up with an elbow before collapsing back on the pillow. "Whoa." She touched her head. "Why's everything spinning?"

James put his sunglasses back on. "Your body's going to need a few more minutes to wear off the effects of the oneiricotine. Sorry about that."

Angelica closed her eyes for a moment, then focused back on him. "I...I don't understand. Where am I?"

James leaned forward, hands clasped together. "Twelve hours ago, a couple men seized you near Atlanta. You're in Nashville now, an hour by ipersedan from where they took you." He gestured around with his gloved hands. "This is a guest room in a building I own."

Angelica stared at him. She opened her mouth, closed it, then frowned. "Yeah, that's right." She glanced around, her eyes finding the exit. "I remember. Two men, their faces were covered. How did you know—"

"I hired those men."

Angelica's eyebrows drew close together. "You *what*?"

"I needed a quick way to get you here without attracting too much attention."

Angelica tilted her head. "So you kidnapped me? Why... why would you do that?"

"Necessity," James said with a smile that wavered. "I was running out of time, and I needed your help."

"Running out of..." Angelica trailed off. She closed her

eyes as she slightly shook her head. "God, if this is a dream, it's a weird one."

"It isn't a dream, Angelica." James put a hand on her shoulder. "You're in Nashville."

"Why?"

James rubbed a hand through his hair. "There are things you don't know about the killer malicious. The situation's much more complicated than you believe."

Angelica's gaze clouded. "You know about the malicious? How?"

"I'm not the only one," James said. "Jason Cloverfield also knew."

Angelica's mouth opened but nothing emerged.

"It's the truth," James said. "I know why you went to him for help. It was never going to do you any good."

Angelica managed to sit up on the bed by leaning on the wall. "He knew? How?"

"He helped spread the malicious through DataMorph. That's where it started."

Angelica's hands touched her mouth. "No." She shook her head, her gaze clouding. "It can't be."

"It can. He took steps to hide the malicious from the public. It bought him time, helped him spread it further."

"Oh my God." Angelica's head flinched back. "That's why he didn't look surprised. He already knew." She looked at James. "But how do you know—"

"About all this?" James picked a trigoy from his pocket.

Angelica blinked. "That's mine."

"Yes." James tapped a finger on the trigoy. "All the content of your presentation is in here, alongside the data about the malicious you and Sebastian found. I know everything you believe to be true about the malicious, but you're wrong. There's more." He turned on the trigoy. It showed a reproduction of the data on the killer malicious as Angelica knew it. "This is what Sebastian, you, and the other research center know." James picked another trigoy from his pocket and turned it on. Another projection overlapped the first, revealing a more accurate pattern, with more red dots that showed new instances of the malicious.

Angelica's eyes widened. "No. This...this can't be."

"See, there's another part of the story." James turned off both trigoys. "The malicious is just the tip of the iceberg, Angelica. There's a monster lurking beneath the surface. I brought you here because you need to know the truth behind the curtain. It's good news, really. You don't have to fight this battle alone anymore."

8

MASVIETH

GEODE, OUTPOST OF THE DEFENSIO PROJECT

Ariul

"Have you ever heard of the Omnilogos?"

Lena considered Tiago's question as they passed through a narrow, dimly lit passage that connected Spencer's room with the next area. She had been thinking about the word "Omnilogos" ever since Tiago mentioned it for the first time, but couldn't figure out why it sounded familiar.

"I've heard it before," she said carefully. "But I can't place it."

Beyond the passage, there was another room, spacious but scarcely lit. There were no furnishings inside, at least none that Lena could see.

"Welcome to the Chamber of Etheric Development." Tiago gestured at the new room. "And that is the Masvieth."

Lena's eyes adjusted to the dim light, then she saw it: a sphere, around six feet in diameter, suspended a few inches above the floor. It was made of a translucent material, which explained why Lena hadn't seen it right away.

"That's a Masvieth?" she frowned.

Tiago nodded. "Looks ordinary, doesn't it? And yet this is the most important tool etherions use to shape historical trends in the ether. EVA?"

Light flooded the room, and a synthetic female voice answered him. "Yes, Chancellor?"

"Awake the Masvieth."

"Understood. Commencing influx of etheric data to the core."

A buzzing sound reverberated throughout the room. Lena searched for the source until she realized it came from the Masvieth itself. The sphere started spinning like a planet around its axis and the object lost its translucency. Ripples ran across the sphere's surface, as if the object was made of liquid metal, and after a few seconds patches of distinct color covered the surface; some were as small as fingernails, other as big as Lena's torso. The largest by far was a brilliant emerald green and took almost a fifth of the entire area.

The new Masvieth reminded her of a world map; the areas of different colors like neighboring countries with clearly drawn boundaries. Each area was moving, some expanding, others contracting, like living cells fighting for space.

"What are these?" Lena turned to Tiago while gesturing at the patches of color.

A relaxed smile crossed Tiago's face. "What do they look like to you?"

She shrugged. "I don't know. A bunch of giant amoebas trying to eat each other?"

"Not too far from the truth." He quirked an eyebrow.

"This is the Geoether, a real-time reproduction of the most important portions of the ether. The movement represents the daily interaction between regions, provinces, and units of cyberspace, and the Masvieth shows how the ether changes because of this interaction."

Lena focused on the huge emerald green area. "Data-Morph, I guess?"

He nodded. "Nailed it."

She studied DataMorph's southern boundaries, where two gray areas no larger than an inch were being encircled by their bigger neighbor. "What's happening here?"

"DataMorph is merging with Joyosa and Argonaut." Tiago pointed at the two gray areas. "They're players of decent size in the virtual entertainment industry. In a couple days, DataMorph will absorb them and add several new options to its growing list of services."

Lena absently fiddled with her hair. "Okay, this is all very fascinating, but what does it have to do with the Omnilogos, or the war against the biomechas?"

"Glad you asked." Tiago approached the Masvieth. "EVA, access DataMorph's database."

"Confirmed, Chancellor. What do you wish to know?"

He pushed up his sleeves. "How is the word 'Omnilogos' defined by the database?"

"DataMorph classifies 'Omnilogos' as a cyberio, a decentralized international activist movement operating in cyberspace."

He pressed his lips together. "Purpose of the movement?"

"The stated purpose of the group has changed over the years. Today, it is believed many individuals use this term for different reasons. A variety of crimes have been attributed to the Omnilogos, such as data theft, unlawful access of corporate data, sabotage, hacking, espionage, and the unspecified releasing of hundreds of viruses and malware into governmental institutions."

Tiago turned to regard Lena. "Not the kind of folks you want to hang out with. EVA, what's the official position of the Planetary Court toward the Omnilogos?"

"The Planetary Court decreed the Omnilogos an illegal movement with the Resolution Sigma 33b of the Etheric Penal Code and created a task force dedicated to preventing its actions."

Tiago tapped his index finger on his lips. "Who's credited with the creation of the word 'Omnilogos'?"

"Unclear."

"When did the word first appear?"

"Information on this subject is conflicting."

Tiago glanced at Lena. "Elaborate."

"The term 'Omnilogos' was already in use in the Internet age," replied the computer-generated voice. "Based on non-conclusive data, the word was first used in 2017, on a forum centered on trivia and current events."

"Okay." He started pacing around the room. "Can you retrieve the content of this forum?"

"Negative," EVA replied. "This information is not available."

"Of course it isn't." His eyes glowed with an inner light. "If it was, anyone who could put two and two together would understand the truth."

"Truth?" Lena looked at him, eyes lost. "What truth?"

Tiago raised a finger. "See, we don't need EVA to tell us the content of that forum because I read it in 2017."

Lena arched an eyebrow. "You did?"

"Yes." He stopped pacing, his eyes wide and rounded. "When I was a twenty-year-old wannabe journalist looking for trending news. That forum prompted me to take a trip to Pasadena, and meet a person who'd change my life forever."

"Okay." Lena shrugged. "You going to tell me what that forum was about?"

Tiago clutched his hands together as he smiled. "It was about a boy who could answer any question within ten seconds. He was referred to as the 'human database' or the 'Omnilogos.'"

Lena scratched her head. "Wait a second. You're saying the Omnilogos was a kid?"

Tiago pointed at Lena's face. "I had the same expression when I found out that information. So I investigated. The forum thread suggested the Omnilogos was based in Pasadena, so I went there to take a gander."

Lena scratched her temple, her gaze becoming distant. "Whoa, slow down. I thought we established the Omnilogos is a terrorist organization. What does the kid in Pasadena have to do with it?"

Tiago rubbed a hand self-consciously through his hair. "You're right. Today, the word 'Omnilogos' is used to describe a criminal organization, but twenty-three years ago, it wasn't. It was a way to refer to a genius boy who would change both our lives."

Her mouth fell open. "You're joking." She stepped back from Tiago, struggling to find the right words. "I mean, you can't be serious."

Tiago showed his empty hands. "As serious as a heart attack."

She rubbed her forehead and shook her head. "No..." Her voice cracked with emotion. "There's no way."

Tiago shrugged. "Why not?"

"Because it's crazy!"

"Crazy?" Tiago snorted. "Let me tell you about 'crazy.'"

You're inside a room which is part of a secret, underground complex build to protect Saemangeum City from cybernetically enhanced soldiers. You might want to reconsider your definition of crazy."

"Okay. Well. Let's just take a step back here." She took a shaky breath, her skin tingling with discomfort. "You're saying Wei Wang was the Omnilogos. That the First Hyperist was a terrorist wanted by the Planetary Court. Is that right?"

"I know how it sounds, but it's the truth."

"Why would Wei Wang want to be part of some cyber-terrorist organization? It doesn't make any sense."

"That's the other piece of the puzzle. Wei needed an alter ego to hide behind. The Omnilogos accomplished that; it allowed him to do things he couldn't do as a simple person. But as the Omnilogos, he was more than a person. He was an idea, and ideas are boundless."

"But why create this alter ego?"

"At first, Wei used it to gain resources and useful contacts. Later, to prevent the extinction of humankind."

Lena scowled. "Seriously? Okay, now you're sounding delusional."

Tiago raised both hands. "Stay with me, please."

"I'm really trying, but you're not making it easy."

"I never said understanding was going to be easy."

"Okay, well. Where's the evidence of all this? Hmm? Am I supposed to just...I don't know...believe you out of my good heart?"

"Look, it's not easy to prove something that Wei Wang wanted kept secret."

"Right." She snorted, feeling a building headache. "So you just come up with stuff and say it's true and then claim it's hard to prove. Convenient, isn't it? You could tell me anything. What should I expect next?"

"I promised answers," Tiago said, his face softening. "I'm just delivering on that promise."

"Your answers suck!" Lena blurted. "They're confusing and totally wild."

"I understand your frustration."

"You do?"

"Yes, but you'll have to give me the benefit of the doubt until you start to see the bigger picture. Can you do that?"

"Look, I'm sorry." She took a deep, calming breath. "Guess this whole thing is getting on my nerves." That was a half-truth. Her headache was getting increasingly worse, and her mood with it. But she didn't want Tiago to stop talking now that she was getting some answers.

The chancellor eyed her. "Sure you okay? We can stop if you—"

"I'm fine," she cut in. "You said Wei Wang used the Omnilogos to prevent the extinction of humanity. How?"

He glanced at the Masvieth. "He developed a technology that helped him analyze a set of variables and their ramifications into the future."

She stared at Tiago, mouth half opened. "Can you dumb that down a bit?"

"Sorry." Tiago offered a quick nod. "He could make projections and establish the possibility that a historical event would happen."

"Wait." Lena raised a hand. "You're saying he could predict the future?"

"No," Tiago replied emphatically. "No one can predict the future. He could calculate several different scenarios, average them out, and draw a reasonably certain outcome. According to Wei's projection, humanity will, at some point in the near future, merge with cyberspace at a collective level. It will become what we call a retrograde singularity."

"Okay," Lena said, trying to read Tiago's expression. "And this is…bad?"

"Very bad." Tiago gazed at the Masvieth. "According to Wei's projections, this merger will cause our extinction."

Lena stared down at her hands. "We're talking about conjecture, right?"

"Not exactly," Tiago said. "We're talking about multi-dynamic stochastic, a further-projection discipline invented by Wei."

"But you said no one can predict the future? Correct?"

"Correct."

"Then why does all this matter? This extinction scenario…whatever that is…it may never happen. It's just one outcome."

"The extinction is a historical trend," he said. "It's the only constant that remained in all simulations. It wasn't simply one variable, it was what Wei called the 'Historical Outcome.' Look, I know it's a lot to digest, but let me ask you a question. Have you ever tossed a coin to see which side landed up?"

Lena frowned. "Yeah. So?"

"Has it ever landed on its edge?"

"What?" she snorted. "No, of course not. It's impossible."

"Not impossible. Just unlikely. *That* is the probability that humanity will survive the singularity."

She slanted her body away from Tiago. "How?"

"If the coin lands on its head, humanity becomes extinct because of the singularity. If lands on tails, humanity still dies out because of the singularity, but faster, because of the intervention of a variable that Wei called the 'catalyst.' The Defensio Project is the coin landing on its edge. The infinitesimal possibility Wei staked everything on. It's how he tried to prevent our extinction."

"Okay." Lena stared at Tiago while talking in a low, firm voice. "Let's say this end-of-the-world thing will really happen. How can the Defensio Project do something?"

"It can stop it, by fighting the primary cause of that historical trend."

Lena shook her head. "Primary cause?"

"The biomechas." Tiago pointed at the Masvieth. "They're the variable that will speed up our extinction."

Lena's eyes widened. "You're telling me the biomechas want to get us all extinct?"

"It's not that simple."

"Oh, great." Lena blew out a noisy breath. "For a moment there, I thought you wanted to make things easy."

"Listen. The biomechas' goal is a worldwide unity of intent. Meaning, they want to forge a singularity. In order to do that, they need to achieve control on a planetary scale, which they can do by conquering the cyberspace."

"What do you mean by 'conquering the cyberspace'?"

"The purpose of the biomechas is to further the centralization of the ether. If this happens, and the ether becomes one cohesive unity, it will pave the way to the creation of a singularity. This is why my purpose, and the purpose of all the omnibuses of the Defensio Project, is to parcel out the ether as much as possible. We need to keep it balkanized, so that the singularity can't happen easily. The biomechas know what we're doing, and attack us hoping to access one of our data cores and hinder our efforts. Unfortunately, we're slowly losing this war in the ether."

"How are you losing?"

Tiago pointed at the sphere. "Look. The ether has never been so homogeneous. Ten years ago, there were hundreds of regions in cyberspace. Today, only a few dozen remain. We omnibuses call this historic trend 'Tolerance Threshold': the more the Tolerance Threshold comes to its saturation, the greater the level of centralization in the ether. The threshold is getting more and more saturated, and nothing we've done has stopped this trend. The ether is becoming a bunch of super regions fighting each other for control of cyberspace. Eventually, there will be only one left. Etherions call this concentration of etheric power 'dominion.'"

Lena blinked a drop of sweat away. She felt dizzy, unfocused. Tiago kept talking about the biomechas' goals, how they carried out their missions, but she found it difficult to focus.

"Lena?" Tiago's voice was distant, the echo of an echo. "You okay?"

She swayed, then her legs gave way.

Tiago caught her a second before she dropped to the floor.

"Got you," he said. "Hey, stay with me."

She was gently laid down. Her head touched on something soft, and when she glanced at the floor, she realized Tiago had put his shirt behind her head to make a makeshift pillow.

She must have lost consciousness for a few minutes, because when she opened her eyes again, she found Spencer staring at her.

"...sure she will be fine?" the young man was saying.

"There you go." Tiago handed her a water bottle. "Drink this. You'll fell better."

Lena accepted the bottle and drank. "I'm sorry," she said after a couple sips, then pressed her palm against her temple. "Should have told you the headache was getting worse."

"This was my fault." Tiago's voice still sounded distant, even though he was just a couple steps away. "I shouldn't have pressed our luck."

"No." She shook her head. "It's on me. I...I just wanted to know more."

"You need to rest." He squeezed her shoulder. "Think you can move?"

"I...I think so."

"Spencer, can you help me carry her outside?"

"Sure thing."

"Come," Tiago said as he helped her up, assisted by Spencer. "I've got a room prepared and something hot to eat. This way."

9

MAUTOTRON

DÜSSELDORF, AUTOMATRIX INC.
HEADQUARTERS

Ramor

The Asian man was in some kind of trance. His chest followed a repetitive, almost hypnotic movement, rising and falling in slow motion as he kept his arms projected outward like a bird ready to take flight. His contracted jaw protruded past hollowed cheeks, and his pitch-black suit was so tight it looked like a second skin. A bluish aura—which gave the man an almost mystical appearance—enveloped his athletic figure from head to heels.

Staring intently at the man, Ramor Deringer feared he had made a colossal mistake. His mouth, pursed in a grimace, betrayed his impatience. He paid little attention to the questioning look that Nayara Souza threw at him from time to time. Ramor suspected his assistant's confidence in the matter was also wavering.

The dark-suited Asian man held his odd pose, still as a

stone. Ramor turned to Nayara, trying to contain his frustration but failing. "You sure about this?" he asked through clenched teeth, not bothering to keep his voice low since the other man didn't understand English. "We've been standing here for half an hour, staring at this...this...ah...what are they called, again?"

"*Sojushi*, sir," Nayara said, her hazel eyes darkly grave as she gazed at the Asian man. "They're called sojushi."

"How long do we have to wait before *something* happens?"

His assistant spoke deliberately slow, showing a forced smile. "Director, Akira wouldn't have called us if it wasn't important. He's been following them for a week."

"Yeah, I know that." Ramor poked his tongue lightly into his cheek and inhaled a long breath. "He didn't tell you anything else?"

"He told me 'the time has come.'"

Ramor glared. "And you didn't think to ask a follow-up question?"

"Of course I did, sir." She crossed her arms. "He simply said to call you and wait."

Ramor blew air through his nose. "Well, you've called me, and I've been waiting. What am I waiting for?"

"Sir, you paid him to do a job. I'm pretty sure he's about to deliver."

Ramor bit back a sharp remark. He turned the full regard of his dark eyes at the sojushi, who had shifted position, his chin now resting on his chest, arms thrust forward in what looked like a kung fu pose. The muscles around his mouth twitched, and his eyelids fluttered open and closed several times before he slowly collapsed.

"Jesus." He clasped his hands so tightly his knuckles turned white. "You sure this guy hasn't punched a one-way ticket to a nuthouse? I mean, look at him, for crying out loud. Looks like he's possessed by a goddamn demon. Or he's high. Or both!"

Nayara stared at Ramor, hard. "Akira is one of the best mautotron pilots money can buy, sir. He knows what he's doing."

"Hope you're right." He paused, turned to Nayara. "There's too much at stake. I can't afford any mistakes."

Nayara's stiff posture loosened a bit. She regarded her boss with a softer expression. "I understand that, sir. I'm confident you made the right choice."

Ramor grunted. Tailing his nephew had seemed a brilliant idea a few weeks before, when he was desperate for answers. What better way to gather intelligence than to hire one of the world's best spies? Unfortunately, he hadn't considered the risks. Some sojushi pilots were regarded as criminals by the WACAA—the Worldwide Agency for the Control of Autotronic Artifacts.

The industry of remotely controlled automatons—or mautotrons, as they were also called—was one of the derivative sectors spawned by the autotronic technology. 'Mautotron' derived from the word 'marauder' and 'autotron' to describe a remotely controlled device used in the construction industry, underwater exploration, military surveillance, orbital manufacturing, and a dozen other fields. Espionage was one of them.

The sojushi Nayara hired was the kind you found only if you were willing to write enough zeros on a check.

When Ramor had instructed Nayara to find the best spy on the market, his assistant had said it would be a complicated and expensive business. Ramor had replied that "complicated" and "expensive" were preferable if they helped avoid "catastrophic." Behind Ramor's decision was a growing concern for his nephew. Erik would have never let the Automaton Industries go belly-up without a damn good reason. That boy was up to no good.

"*Toki wa kita.*"

Ramor turned toward the sojushi. "What was that?"

The corner of Nayara's mouth twitched in a smile. "He said: 'The time has come.'"

Ramor tilted his head down while making eye contact. "Again?"

Nayara raised a hand to silence him.

Akira moved his fingers like a magician about to perform a sleight of hand, then pressed both index fingers against his temples and a three-dimensional reproduction appeared above his head. The video had a constant zig-zag motion that gave Ramor nausea as he watched it.

"*Live de tsunagatteru,*" the sojushi said.

Ramor turned to Nayara.

"We're seeing through the eyes of the mautotron," she translated, pointing to the video feed.

Ramor frowned. "Why's the resolution so low?" He could make out streetlights and cars lined on the sidewalk, but the details were fuzzy.

Nayara said something in Japanese, and the sojushi offered a short reply. "The image will improve shortly," the assistant said.

The image's resolution improved after a moment, and Ramor could finally distinguish two people walking on the sidewalk. Well, only one of them was a person. "Erik." He inhaled sharply. "And his goddamned eptanidus."

Nayara nodded.

"How big is the mautotron he's piloting?" Ramor glanced nervously at Akira. "I mean, it's getting closer. Won't they see it?"

Nayara relayed the question to Akira, who replied with a curt sentence.

"The mautotron looks like a fly," the assistant said. "They won't notice."

Ramor didn't take his eyes off Erik. "Are we recording this?"

"Yes, sir." Nayara pointed to her tablet. "With redundancies backup. Saving progress every three seconds."

"Good." Ramor unfastened the top button of his shirt. "Can we get closer? I want to hear what they're saying."

Nayara repeated the question to the sojushi, then translated. "He's on it."

Ramor started pacing, his hands clasped behind his back.

"Sir, I think you should consider something related to the issue at hand."

"What's that?"

Nayara showed unwavering eye contact. "You might have overestimated your nephew's abilities to cause problems."

He stared at her. "Overestimated?"

"Well, sir. You told me he's smart and all, but frankly, I don't think he's that dangerous. I mean, he's got resources, willingness, and an oversized ego, but—"

"Dangerous?" He sneered. "Dangerous doesn't cut it. You've no idea what he's capable of." He thrust a finger at the projection showing Erik and On-Eni-Fifth. "He's one of the greatest autotronics geniuses on the planet."

Nayara crossed her arms, flashed a cold smile. "Respectfully, sir, I doubt it. He's *twenty*."

"Yes, and he happens to have an IQ of 190. Not to mention he was bred to be Sofia's heir in every single aspect of his life."

Nayara cleared her throat. "Sir, you're saying he's a

resourceful kid. I get that, but I don't think that justifies your paranoia."

"Fine." Ramor's lips turned white. "Let me tell you something about that boy. He memorized the autosynaptic pathways of a tetranidus when he was nine years old. *Nine*. That's just the beginning. I watched him assemble the lymphatic circuitry of a trinidus with one hand tied behind his back, just for fun, to prove that he could do it. He's a bomb ready to explode, a 20-year-old genius with the common sense of an alcoholic with an unlimited pass to Oktoberfest."

"Sir—"

"What's worse? He believes he has a mission. God knows what he can do if he sets his mind on it."

"Sir? I—"

"He let his company sink for a reason. Believe that. He's keeping something secret. I'm going to find out what that thing is and save him from himself if it is the last thing I—"

"Sir! Akira is talking."

Ramor turned toward the sojushi, who looked annoyed at having to repeat his words.

"They're hailing a cab," Nayara translated.

Ramor's heartbeat increased. "Doubt that insect can follow a car." He rubbed his forearms, swallowed. "What's our plan? We can't lose them."

Nayara asked a question. Akira answered. Silence stretched for almost a minute.

Ramor stared at his assistant. "Well?"

Nayara bit her bottom lip. "He can't match the speed of a car."

"Okay. So what are we doing?"

"Akira will try to get the mautotron to match their pace."

"What?" Sweat stood out in beads on Ramor's forehead. "You just said that thing can't match their speed."

"I know." Nayara frowned. "I'm not sure what his plan is."

"Then ask him!"

Nayara met her boss' gaze. "He's concentrating on the task, sir. You want me to risk distracting him?"

Ramor opened his mouth, closed it.

For the next three minutes, they watched Akira doing his magic. The mautotron got progressively closer to Erik until it landed on the boy's shoulder just before he entered the car.

Ramor breathed a sigh of relief. "God, that was close."

Akira said something.

"He's activated the external audio receivers," Nayara translated. "The closed environment will make listening easier."

The corner of Ramor's mouth twitched in a smile. "Excellent."

There was static noise for a moment, then a familiar voice flooded the room.

"...enough to send them all."

Ramor was barely breathing now, his senses alert. He leaned over the projection, as if that could give him a better insight into what his nephew was saying. Akira's mautotron focused his camera on Erik's face. Ramor's breath caught in his throat. The boy had lost at least ten pounds. Dark shadows besieged his eyes, and his cheeks were pale and hollow.

"You think it wise to use Waveresia Inc. for the transportation?" came On-Eni-Fifth's voice.

"It's the quickest way," Erik said. "They made it clear

they needed the package ASAP. If you've a better idea, I'm all ears."

The mautotron turned the camera to give them a better visual of On-Eni-Fifth.

Ramor's mouth fell open. "Shit. Is that thing looking at us?"

Nayara blinked. "I think it's looking in the general direction of your nephew, sir."

Ramor squinted. "I don't know. It seems intent on us."

"You can't be sure, sir. It's—"

Erik's voice cut through Nayara's. "What you looking at, On?"

Ramor held his breath just as On-Eni-Fifth looked away. "I was just thinking about air travel arrangements."

"See?" Nayara glanced at Ramor. "We're in the clear."

Ramor pressed his hands to his stomach. "Yeah," he said, cold sweat running down his back.

The cab stopped and Erik got out of the car, On-Eni-Fifth at his side. They headed toward a low, wide building that once might have been black or dark brown, but that now had faded into an uneven shade of gray. The building looked abandoned. Akira's mautotron shifted its camera to register as many details of the building as possible.

All of a sudden, the video feed became blurry and distorted.

"What's going on?" Ramor glanced at the sojushi. "Are we losing the signal?"

Nayara translated the question, and Akira replied with his terse voice.

"Signal's being jammed, sir."

"Jammed?" Ramor blinked, looked at Akira. "By what?"

"He's not sure." Nayara bit her lip. "Some kind of electromagnetic field. Must be inside the building. The closer we get, the worse it'll be. Akira is trying to compensate, but says he can't keep following them."

Ramor chewed the inside of his cheek. "Why not?"

"He won't risk losing the mautotron."

Ramor looked abruptly back at Nayara. "Listen. I want that bug *inside* the building. If it fries, tell him I'll give him enough money to buy a swarm of those things. Tell him!"

Nayara repeated the message. The sojushi considered it for a moment, then gave a quick nod and moved back into position.

Ramor breathed a sigh of relief, his eyes anchored on the distorted video.

As Erik and On-Eni-Fifth walked through the entrance, the interference increased steadily. It became more difficult to understand what they were saying. The video, too, was getting worse, plagued by static and background noise. Then it froze completely.

Ramor leaned in, a fluttery, empty feeling in his stomach. "We lost them?"

Akira and Nayara exchanged a quick back and forth, then the assistant said, "Akira is preserving the mautotron's primary systems: mobility, sensors, power core, the lot. He's trying to get the mautotron inside the building, and believes it will last longer this way."

Ramor ground his molars together, fighting for control over his anxiety. They might lose some important parts of the conversation, but preserving the mautotron's systems for longer would allow them to peek inside the rabbit hole.

After several grueling seconds of radio silence, the video came back in a flash of light and shapes, but the audio was gone. Not even the background static remained.

Ramor dug his fingernails into his palms, chewing his lower lip. He hoped the bug would last long enough to give them answers. They were close to finding out what Erik was up to. He could feel it.

The images flickered on and off. Erik was walking in a corridor, then the video went black, then on again, showing his nephew entering an elevator.

The ride took a long time, over thirty seconds. By the time the elevator doors opened, the video was reduced to an intermittent sequence of grainy images. His nephew stepped off the elevator and kept walking. He entered a gigantic room with so many LEDs the area seemed bathed in sunlight. Enormous machines towered on both sides, and a conveyor belt snaked along the right side of the underground space.

Ramor squinted. They were inside a factory. This must be the place. If they could keep the damned bug turned on for just a few more seconds...

The projection went black.

"We've lost contact with the mautotron," Nayara said, translating the last sentence spoken by Akira. "It's no longer responding."

Before Ramor could speak, the feed came to life for a couple seconds and the bug spat out one last blurry image of the underground factory. They waited for close to a minute, but nothing else happened.

Akira sighed, then turned toward Nayara with a haunted look and uttered a sentence.

"The mautotron is gone," Nayara confirmed.

Ramor didn't care. He thought he saw something in that last few seconds. He turned to his assistant. "Pay him and send him the hell out of here. We've got work to do."

"Yes, sir." Nayara sent the money. The sojushi looked at his portable display, bowed, and left the room.

Once alone, Ramor started typing on a keyboard. "Control," he said, glancing up, "extrapolate frame 00.22.21 from playback."

The room control complied, but the image it provided wasn't what Ramor wanted.

Nayara frowned. "Sir? What you looking for?"

"I've seen something." Ramor kept typing. "I just need to dig deeper."

"What did you see?"

Ramor didn't answer. His eyes were fixed on the data feed. "Control, cancel first extrapolation. Give me...ah...give me 00.22.11. Yes. That's it! Contrast it thirty percent. Forty. There! Now filter and clean up the image's distortion. Compensate the lighting and magnify twenty percent quadrant 3Z. Eliminate all remaining quadrants. Now rotate the image ninety degrees to the left. Yes, like so." Ramor squinted, the image now showing humanoid shapes neatly arranged on the conveyor belt.

Nayara's eyes widened. "They...they look like autotrons, sir." Nayara's voice was feeble, distant.

"Autotrons?" Ramor took a step back, his face hot and clammy. "I don't know. Never seen autotrons that look like that."

10

BROKEN DREAMS

GEODE, OUTPOST OF THE DEFENSIO PROJECT

Ariul

Lena leaned over Tiago as they walked past the entrance of a small bedroom. Spencer helped Tiago carry her out of the Masvieth room, but after that, Lena had felt well enough to walk by herself. Tiago had brought her to a level below, where there was a room waiting for her.

"It's nothing much really," Tiago said as they got inside the apartment. "But the bed is comfortable and the air conditioning works better than in other rooms."

"Thank you." Lena assessed her surroundings. The tiny apartment was spartan, with only a bed, a chair, and a bedside table. A couple towels had been placed on top of the bed.

"That door leads to the bathroom." He pointed to a door on the other side of the room. "How're you feeling?"

"Much better, thank you." She attempted to smile. The

dizziness wasn't gone, but Tiago had given her a couple pills that made her headache subside.

Tiago pointed to two bottles of water on the nightstand. "I've had some more of the good stuff prepared for you. Make sure you finish one bottle before tomorrow. I promise they'll make you feel better."

"Got it." She sat on the bed. The mattress was firm, but not uncomfortably so.

"There's your dinner." Tiago pointed to a tray left on the desk. "Hope you like potatoes and roast beef."

"I could eat a mammoth right now." She sat in front of the tray loaded with food and started digging in. She shoved potatoes down her mouth without chewing.

Tiago frowned. "Remember to chew every now and then."

"Sure," she said around a mouthful. "Will do."

Tiago joined his hands behind his back. "Well. I'd better let you get some rest. Sleep well. We have a busy day ahead tomorrow."

"Got it." She turned toward him. "And Tiago?"

"Yes?" The chancellor looked over his shoulder.

"Thanks for telling me everything." She cleaned her mouth with a napkin, eyes downcast. "You were right. It's a lot to digest, but it's much better than not knowing."

Tiago smiled. "I'm glad I could help. I'll see you tomorrow." The door closed behind him.

Lena finished her meal and looked around in a daze. She took a moment to let all the information she learned sink in. She was inside a secret underground base called Geode controlled by the Defensio Project, an organization founded by Wei Wang to prevent a historical trend that could cause a mass extinction event.

She chuckled despite herself. "Here's something Makoto

would love to put on his batshit crazy Wall of Mysteries."
She missed the trio of students; especially Makoto. He'd give
his right arm to know what she knew.

Lena's mind felt fuzzy. She was bone tired, and a bed had
never looked so good. She took off her shirt and shoes and
sipped one of the bottles Tiago had given her. When she lay
down on the bed, exhaustion swept over her. She turned
over to snuggle the pillow; only then did she realize something was tickling her neck. "Damn," she muttered, her eyes
closed as she let go a long yawn. She'd forgotten to take off
the Pelargonium pendant, but that thought didn't last for
long. A second after, she was sinking into the world of
dreams.

∞∞∞

Lena saw planets, stars, galaxies, and...furniture.

She swept her gaze, studying her surroundings. She was
in a spacious room, dimly lit by three-dimensional repro-
ductions of comets flying like kites.

"Come on, say something funny."

Lena blinked, then turned toward the voice. A boy was
sitting on a stool beside a bed. He was looking at a young
girl laying on the bed. She looked pale and haggard, her
eyes half-closed. A colorful bandana covered her head.

The boy shifted on the stool. "Like what?" he said,
crossing his arms.

"I don't know." The girl shrugged. "You're a smart kid.
Come up with something."

"I'm not a kid!"

"See?" The girl smiled. "That was funny!"

A comet cut into her line of vision, and for a moment all
Lena saw was pulsing blue. She had to look away and close

her eyes not to be blinded. When she opened her eyes again, the room was gone, and so were the other celestial objects. Now she was in the middle of an expanse of green, the cool fingers of the wind ruffling her hair. There was grass everywhere, and a long line of trees in the distance. The place smelled of bark, musk, and flowers.

As Lena looked up, the stars were an unbroken succession of bright lights embedded into the night sky.

"I've got something for you."

She turned sharply to where the girl sat on the grass without her bandana. This time, she looked healthier, her cheeks bright with red. Her long, lush hair was a cascade of gold against the green of the grass. Beside her, sitting stiffly, was the boy Lena had seen in the room, although here he looked younger.

The girl was holding a silver pendant shaped like an eight. She gave it to the boy, who studied it.

"The symbol of infinity?" he asked, frowning.

"It's a good luck charm. You'll need it."

"I don't believe in luck."

"That's why I'm giving it to you, moron." The girl chuckled.

Lena took a step toward them. "Hello?" she said. "Who are you guys?"

They didn't turn toward Lena.

"Hey." Lena raised her voice. "I'm talking to you. What is this—" The ground started shaking, and her legs gave way, causing her to fall. A rumble exploded in the distance, like thunder ripping through the world. Lena glanced around, searching for the source of the deafening noise, but couldn't find it. She looked back, but the boy and girl were gone. Everything was gone. The grass, the trees, the stars. Only cold and darkness remained.

Lena's breath caught in her throat. "What's happening?"

A chasm opened beneath her feet and she fell. The world turned into a succession of images, faces, and sensations. A rush of adrenaline hit her like a punch in the gut.

Images flashed before her. A girl with the most beautiful smile, an immense column of smoke drifting past the clouds, a silver infinity etched in a doorway, and a line of people waiting to ask their questions. The vision sped up. A Masvieth. A man staring, his eyes narrowed to slits. A dark-skinned woman with a toy...the entrance to a restaurant...a Rubik's Cube...a trigoy...blood...stars. Then the pictures overlapped to show everything at once, no longer distinguishable, causing a sense of loss.

After everything faded, a woman's face appeared, two stark blue eyes glowering with fury, staring at her. Waiting.

11

THE PENTAPROJECT

HYPERIST COMPLEX STARGAZER, CONTROL
ROOM

Gladia

≈

Gladia Egea looked at the time and chewed her lip.
There was no way only ten minutes had passed
since the last time she checked.

The waiting was getting on her nerves. She wanted the
Pentaproject to be over, to put it behind her and move on.
But all she could do now was wait and hope her pills would
see her through the day.

She glanced around, searching for comfort in the frenzy
that surrounded her. The control room of the Stargazer
complex was busy with people moving with purpose. There
were a dozen consoles inside the circular area, each of them
manned by a technician wearing a headset. The workers
directed the air traffic around the complex, safely stored
vital information inside the data core, took care of the
overall security, and controlled one of the most important
strongholds of the Hyperist Movement.

Gladia looked at her own console and frowned. The screen was divided into two halves, each showing information about the two Pentaproject proposals: on the left side was the progressive party's proposal, more commonly known as the Ascendent Party. On the right side was the conservative party's proposal, also known as the Geocentric Party. Only one would win the day and bring home most of HYPER's resources for the next five years.

Gladia crossed her arms, her frown deepening. The Five-Year Plan of Sidereal Development was the most important event for the Hyperist Movement. Several projects were submitted, but only two were chosen for the last confrontation, which consisted of a public debate known as the "Keystone."

That year's finalists were the leader of the Ascendents, Tolomeus Almagest—who planned to build a fleet of medium-range vessels capable of extracting various types of space resources—and Penelope Juno, leader of the Geocentrics, who advocated for the construction of a second space elevator capable of carrying over three times the payload of Polaris. A titanic project which was intended to increase orbital traffic and strengthen hyperist off-world infrastructure in geostationary orbit, cis-lunar space, and farther beyond in Lagrange points.

The Ascendents and the Geocentrics had always been at odds, but this was the first time they could display their enmities on the world stage. Millions would be watching.

"Gladia?"

Gladia found Arthur Strutzenberg looking at her with unblinking eyes, hands on his hips. From his expression, it wasn't the first time he'd called her.

Gladia cleared her throat. "Yes?"

"You don't have to stand around and wait," Arthur said.

"The delegations are still hours away. Why don't you go rest for a bit? I got this. Charlotte can warn you before—"

"I'm fine," Gladia cut him off. "Stop worrying about me."

Arthur opened his mouth, then closed it. "All right," he said after a moment. "Just a suggestion. If you need me, I'll be in the meeting room, helping Charlotte sort out the paperwork with the Apeirons' delegation."

Gladia followed him with her eyes as he left the room. She felt a pang of guilt. Arthur just wanted to make sure she was fine, but something in his overzealous attitude got on her nerves.

She turned toward the window-wall that made up most of the tower's upper structure and focused on the surrounding landscape. The east side of the hyperist complex sprawled before her.

Stargazer comprised many low, rectangular structures with a flat top that reminded Gladia of colossal ziggurats. Shuttles, ipersedans, and automated drones crowded the airspace above the base.

Alongside Pegasus, Serenity, and the Infinity Center—home to the Polaris space elevator—Stargazer was one of the most important hyperist bases. It housed the Golden Collar Cassiopeia School, a Neutral Buoyancy Lab, a Micro Gravimetric Research Center, and several factories dedicated to the research and production of aerospace technology.

That place—which had always symbolized progress and ingenuity—would soon turn into a hornets' nest when the Geocentric and Ascendent delegations arrived. She had to keep vigilant now more than ever. The future of HYPER was at stake.

∞ ∞ ∞

Off the Mediterranean Sea
Aeromousine of Legatus Tolomeus Almagest

Tolomeus Almagest studied the model of the starship sitting on his desk. That misshapen vessel—which looked like a legless lobster—was going to make or break his career.

He twisted his watch as he shifted on the chair. Five years and millions of dollars had been poured into that complex piece of alloy and ceramic components. It embodied what Tolomeus Almagest was willing to do to achieve his goal.

The leader of the Ascendents leaned over the desk to pick up the spaceship. His hand closed gently around it—as if picking up a delicate ice sculpture—and brought it closer to his face so he could examine the details. On the spaceship's hull was written in bright red letters *Katalamban BX-01*. He studied the interior of the bridge: the captain's chair, the science station, and the communications panel, all reproduced to the last detail.

A katalamban had four times the tonnage of a simple reusable scout, ten times its Delta-v, and a more advanced recycling system that allowed for a more efficient use of water and air in space. It could accommodate a crew of six people for up to two years in deep space. Nothing HYPER had produced up to that moment came even close to those specifications.

The katalambans represented Tolomeus' signature in history, his contribution to the foundation of a spacefaring civilization. But to achieve his goal, he needed to win the Keystone, crushing Penelope Juno in front of all hyperists.

Tolomeus glanced at the booklet sitting on his desk. The title read: *Five-Year Geocentric Plan of Sidereal Development*.

On the center of the cover was a silver infinity inscribed in a circle representing the Earth. Beside the booklet was a thicker book, but its ash-gray cover showed no title. Tolomeus flipped through its pages.

Inside was Penelope Juno's psychological profile, along with interesting tidbits about her past he would use to gain the upper hand.

The Legatus set down the book and turned toward the window of the aeromousine. The Mediterranean Sea was rough that day, waves crashing over waves as far as the eye could see. His ship had been traveling for five hours and had just started descending. They would land in the Stargazer Center in less than fifteen minutes.

Tolomeus looked away from the Mediterranean Sea, his eyes back on the katalamban. He had worked hard to get there, and would not let Penelope Juno stop him so close to the finishing line, no matter the cost.

∞∞∞

Off the Mediterranean Sea
Aeromousine of Grand Councilor Penelope Juno

Penelope Juno sat stiffly in her chair, hands gathered in her lap, as she looked at the three projections she had been studying for the past hour. Keeping track of current events was a time-consuming business, but necessary to make sense of an ever-changing world.

The Grand Councilor thought before deciding, weighing alternatives and exploring likely outcomes. It was impossible to predict all the variables, of course, but being careful was what had gotten her so high in the hyperist hierarchy. Impulsiveness caused wars, brought down empires, and decreed the end of entire nations. She wasn't going to make that mistake.

The first projection she had summoned showed Gladia Egea in a press room, answering questions from journalists. The Last Vertex of the Hexahedron looked depleted despite her efforts to hide it. That facade was only natural for a woman who was never meant to lead. Everyone could see she was crushed under the weight of responsibilities she wasn't able to handle.

Penelope jotted down a note on her tablet, connecting a new idea to the rest of the concept map she had been building in the past hour. Gladia's influence on the world stage was waning. Her demise was a variable that needed consideration. No one spoke of it openly yet, but her leadership had grown weaker since Verha Wardem—the hyperist champion she hand-picked from a pool of candidates—was beaten by Yvonne Muchena at Collision.

Penelope shifted her gaze to the second projection, which showed Yvonne Muchena surrounded by a crowd. The contrast between the two leaders was shocking, as stark as day and night. Muchena exuded an aura of power and charisma that Gladia never had. The landist woman was young, hungry for glory. She had twice Woodside's ambition and half his caution: a dangerous combination for the future of HYPER. Muchena had to be stopped, and Gladia wasn't up for the job.

With the election of a new Planetary Council just around the corner, the landist leader was taking advantage of the Pentaproject to showcase the divisions among the hyperist parties and take advantage of the growing fractures.

Muchena was shrewd, had a solid strategy, and executed it with brutal precision to further her advantage. Woodside had taught her well.

Penelope added another note to her device, linking it up to a section inside the concept map already heavy with data.

She shifted her gaze on the third and final projection, trying and failing to keep her feelings in check. Tolomeus Almagest was smiling at the camera as he presented his space monstrosity to a room filled with people. He was trying to sell the katalamban as the best thing for the Hyperist Movement since the invention of Polaris. He, too, couldn't be underestimated. The ex-landist had the predatory intelligence of a fox. Too many people had made the mistake of discarding him as clueless, when in fact he was cunning, driven, and dangerous.

Tolomeus had convinced the Ascendants to vote for him as their leader through a massively successful campaign that hinged on the motto "Further beyond." He had promised he would provide the Hyperist Movement a new direction, one closer to Wei's original daring spirit of ingenuity.

Penelope frowned, aware of how stupid that all sounded. The Ascendants had been fooled. Tolomeus was too smart to believe in his own propaganda. The katalambans he so fervently publicized were a glittering promise empty of meaning. Humanity's spacefaring status was in its infancy. The space civilization envisioned by Wei had just started developing a backbone and wasn't ready for a jump into the vast unknown. Tolomeus couldn't be allowed to move on with his destructive plan. He needed to be stopped.

Penelope inhaled sharply, then turned off the three projections by waving her hand. She focused on the concept map. Her mind worked out links between ideas that would help her plan a sound course of action for the upcoming Keystone. She needed to win. The very future of HYPER was at stake.

She closed her eyes and visualized the map she'd created. She saw the intricate web of ideas, the pivotal junctures, the moves to make to ensure everything went according to plan, and knew with sharp clarity what was necessary—Gladia Egea needed to be sidelined, and Yvonne Muchena's influence needed to be thwarted. Her plan would start with beating Tolomeus Almagest in the Keystone and winning the Pentaproject.

Penelope knew she was HYPER's last hope of survival, the true heir to Wei Wang's legacy. Nothing could get in her way.

Her interlink beeped. She raised an eyebrow and accepted the call.

"Councilor," came the professional voice of her skipper. "We have entered Stargazer Outer Perimeter. ETA to arrival: fifteen minutes."

Penelope turned off her tablet. "Understood, Skipper. Inform the crew. I want everyone ready for landing."

12

THE ARK INSTITUTE

NASHVILLE, ARK INSTITUTE FOR ADVANCED
ETHERIC STUDIES

James

Angelica trailed behind James in an awkward silence. Her former classmate was a few steps ahead, leading the way toward the largest building in the complex, his long dark coat brushing against the grass of the well-kept garden which surrounded the entire property.

One of the first questions Angelica had asked James had been about that institute, which he said was funded through a generous contribution by private individuals interested in fostering etheric studies. It was a nice way not to answer her question.

She asked another one. "How come I've never heard of this place?"

James glanced at her, but didn't slow down. "I'm not surprised you haven't. We value our privacy and don't advertise ourselves. Selections of the students are strict and done on a case-by-case basis. Few people outside our circle know the Ark Institute exists."

"So, when you say 'institute,' you actually mean school."

"Yes, but the Ark is also a research center. We train experts in new media and public relations."

Angelica wrinkled her brow. "How are the students selected?"

"The criteria we use to select candidates are the Paride Scale of Thoughts and the Functional Agglomeration Test. These are followed by two interviews and two written tests."

Angelica's head flinched back slightly. "Those are rating scales for etherions, not for media experts or PR specialists."

"That's correct."

"Okay, so what you're really doing here is training etherions, just like Cantara did."

"In a way," he replied. "But on a larger scale."

Angelica wanted to press him further but dropped the subject for now.

She had more pressing questions. "You didn't tell me how you found out about the malicious." She had discovered that James not only knew about the malicious, but was also aware that Angelica and Sebastian were actively working to find a cure.

"I'll answer that. But first, I want to show you something." He pointed to the towering building made of glass and concrete where they were heading. The entrance was flanked by two columns in the Doric style sustaining an arch. On the arch was engraved the sentence: "*Truth was the only daughter of Time.*" Below the inscription was the stylized symbol of an hourglass.

Angelica looked at James. "Da Vinci?"

James nodded approvingly.

"What does the symbol mean?" Angelica gestured toward the hourglass.

"Time is the only constant in our lives," he explained. "To be shaped by it is what defines our existence."

She frowned. "Poetic."

"I share your thought." James nodded toward the entrance. "After you."

When Angelica stepped inside, she found herself inside a large area at the center of which was a reception desk with two lacquered columns, gold leaf on top and base in marble. Behind the desk was a young man with a buzz cut, wearing a purple uniform and a golden pin representing the hourglass displayed on the entrance.

"Domine Ark," the young man said. "How is your day going so far?"

"It's going great, Ronald. This is Madame Angelica Kam. She'll be our guest for today."

"Absolutely, sir." The young man reached for something inside a drawer and handed Angelica a guest pin. She pinned it to her shirt.

"All right," James said. "Any messages for me?"

"Nothing so far, sir."

"Thank you." James motioned for Angelica to follow him.

They walked past the reception area and into a hallway.

"Ronald is one of our students here at the Ark," James explained, walking toward an elevator. "I started out with seven students and a spare room in a rented condo. Sound familiar?"

"It does. Is this what you're trying to do? Follow in Cantara's footsteps?"

Something in James' demeanor shifted. A muscle on the side of his face twitched, and he pushed his sunglasses up with a jerky movement. "It might have started like a personal challenge," he said, smiling thinly, "but has grown into something bigger."

Angelica's eyebrows squished together. "How so?"

James adjusted his shirt, as if it chafed. "We have ninety-six students now, divided into eight classes. It's more than Cantara ever achieved." He entered the elevator, and once inside he pressed a button and the car started moving downward.

"So." Angelica glanced repeatedly at the floor designators on both jambs of the doors. "You built an off-grid complex in the outskirts of Nashville where you secretly train etherions. What are you afraid of?"

James clasped his hands behind the back, looked directly in front of him. "What makes you think I'm afraid?"

She swatted the air as if to remove an obstacle. "Well, the writing is on the wall. You could have invited me here the old-fashioned way, but decided instead to kidnap me. A drastic way of keeping people from nosing around, I guess. So I ask again: What are you afraid of?"

His posture stiffened. "We care for the privacy of our students. Sending a request would have left a trace, bread-crumbs easy to follow. I don't want—"

"Bullshit." She crossed her arms. "You're not telling me the truth about this place. You said you used the Paride Scale and the Functional Agglomeration Test to select the students. Yes?"

James nodded.

"What score do you require?"

"Omegaton Alpha and Absolute Scale."

She stared at him. "Geniuses. This is an institute for geniuses?"

"For a new generation of polyhistorians. The new Leonardo da Vinci of our age. These students are trained to excel in the Age of the Ether. I wanted you to see what we're doing here so that you understand what I can offer. The scale of possibility is like nothing you've ever seen."

The elevator stopped, and the doors opened onto a corridor flanked by wooden doors. The chime of a bell broke the silence as they got off the elevator, and students poured out of the classrooms.

James checked his watch. "Good, I've timed it right. They're changing classes. Let's go meet them."

She followed along as James walked toward the students.

"Jackson," James called one boy. "How's your research on polymorphic rearrangement going? Professor Estrella told me you're having trouble with the logarithms split calculation."

"Oh, I've solved that, Domine," the student answered with a dismissive wave of his arm. "I got confused with the fractal calculation, that's all. An easy fix."

"Glad to hear that." James turned to a girl with short blue hair. "What about you, Sirillia? How's the essay on morpho-discrepancies of etheric fluctuations coming along?"

He chatted with several students, asking questions related to each of their assignments and introducing Angelica when they glanced in her direction. As a gathering of students formed, the name "Madame of Melody" was traded back and forth throughout the group. Angelica had the distinct, unpleasant feeling of having become the center of attention.

"What's going on here? Why have you all stopped in the middle of the corridor?"

A man wearing a green turban emerged from the crowd. At his side was a beautiful woman with a cascade of lush, dark hair falling in waves down her back. Angelica looked at the two newcomers, her eyes widening. "Ravi? Venus?" She studied each. "What are you two doing here?"

"We work here," Ravi said, grinning. "I teach Fundamentals of Etherionics and Intercultural Developments. Venus does Cybernetic Matrix and Ether 3.0."

"I'm so happy to see you, Angy!" Venus took her into an embrace. "You look good."

"Happy to see you too," Angelica said with an awkward smile.

"I've followed your career with interest," Venus said. "Your discoveries on ether-induced disorders have revolutionized etherosophy. Volumes will be written about your findings."

"Yes," Ravi interjected. "And, of course, your status of Madame of Melody also comes to mind. *That* is noteworthy, isn't it?" He threw a hard look at James. "It brought you here, after all. I hope you've forgiven James' mindless act, and don't report us to the authorities for the kidnapping. Sorry, James. I've tried to find another way to say it, but, alas, I couldn't." He looked at Angelica with unblinking eyes. "I want you to know that I was against this thing from the beginning."

"Apparently," Angelica said, "James is about to show me something that'll explain everything." She glared at her ex-classmate. "I'll give him the benefit of the doubt, for now."

Ravi offered a sharp smile. "I wish I could be there when he does, but I have to explain to a class of marbleheads the difference between a double repulsive movement and a mutual disjunction of etheric parameters."

"It was a pleasure meeting you after so long, Angelica," Venus said, beckoning Ravi to follow her. "I only wish I could have seen you under different circumstances. Let's go, Ravi. Students are waiting."

Ravi and Venus shepherded the students to their classes, and in less than a minute the corridor was empty.

James turned the other way and started walking.

Angelica followed along, her nostrils flaring. "The list of explanations I'm due is getting longer, James."

"I agree." James' chin dipped down. "There's more than one reason I brought you here."

Angelica laughed with an edge. "You tease me with answers that I've yet to receive, and now I find out you rounded up half of our old classmates and use them as teachers. What for?"

"This is Cantara's dream come true." James gestured around. "We carry on her legacy. Simple as that."

"Commendable." Angelica tapped a foot on the ground, keeping a closed body posture. "And what's my role in all this?"

"We need someone who understands what's at stake, who wants to pass on her knowledge to the next generation of shepherds of the public opinion." James paused, glanced at her. "We need you to be our Cantara Handal."

Angelica stopped abruptly. "What?"

James took off his sunglasses, turning his dark eyes on Angelica. "I'm sorry I haven't been forthcoming with you, but the situation demanded it."

"James, what do you want me to say? You haven't even explained to me what any of this has to do with the killer malicious."

James nodded. "I didn't because I wanted you to see with your own eyes."

"See what?"

"Angelica, we're preparing to shape a new world. I founded the Ark for this reason, and I'm convinced that the new world will need a whole new class of etherions to survive what's coming."

13

ICE AND FIRE

HYPERIST COMPLEX STARGAZER, SPACEPORT

Gladia

Gladia tucked a strand of hair behind her ear as she searched the afternoon sky.

From the outside, the Last Vertex of the Hexahedron was the picture of calm and composure, and the drones swarming around her and the hyperist delegation broadcast a sober, resolute woman to the public. She'd gotten good at pretending.

Gladia had spent so many years under the spotlight that she no longer paid any attention to the media presence. But she didn't feel calm, nor in control.

Charlotte, on her left, was glancing at her display with the manic obsession of a girl dreading being late for her prom. Close to Gladia's assistant, a ceremonial guard stood at attention in front of a sculpture representing an infinity. Arthur, to Gladia's right, cast worried glances at her, pretending to assess his surroundings. The two of them had a heated argument concerning her safety. Thinking of it made Gladia want to punch something.

"Are you serious, Arthur?" she had said when Arthur had mentioned his intention. "*Forty* starlaukers for my honor guard? Are you afraid a meteorite will hit me?"

The starlaukers were an elite military corps responsible for protecting the hyperist leadership; a special unit established by the Executive Council after the infamous attack on the Infinity Center that cost Wei's life. Also known as the Hyperists' Marines, the elite corps' main aim was to prevent a "Second Infinity."

Gladia didn't like them. For her, the starlaukers were glorified scarecrows. They had never been useful in any practical way, none that she could measure, at least. Sure, Arthur claimed they were a deterrent that had worked so well over the years that they never had to fire a single shot, but Gladia didn't buy it. She considered them a money pit and would not put up with that kind of nonsense. Not today.

It had been a long and hard fight, but in the end she won. Arthur had to lower the number of starlaukers to only three. That was still three too many for her liking, but she could live with the compromise.

Gladia stifled a sigh as she swept her gaze across the landing platform at the end of which her delegation waited. Dozens of flags around the area displayed HYPER's symbol. She turned to Charlotte. "How long?"

"Councilor Juno's aeromousine has just entered Stargazer's airspace, ma'am," her assistant said. "The Geocentrics will be the first to arrive. Control tower says three minutes."

Gladia glanced at the three starlaukers standing behind her, each two meters tall, their black and silver mecha-suits protecting their bodies from head to boots. She grimaced, then turned to Charlotte. "What about Tolomeus?"

"The Ascendents' delegation will arrive in fifteen minutes."

Gladia nodded, her jaw set hard. She felt Arthur's gaze on her, but did her best to ignore him.

A distant rumble echoed through the silence.

"Executive Director." Charlotte pointed at the sky. "The Geocentrics have arrived."

Gladia turned her head slightly to follow her assistant's finger. An airship approached, taking less than thirty seconds for the vehicle to stop in mid-air and start its slow descent. It was an old Jupiter Juray TX6 with enhanced lateral stabilizers. That class of airship was over fifteen years old, and would have been considered a fossil by a young pilot, but for the first generation of hyperists, it had a clear symbolic value. It was the same class of vehicle Wei used for his travels.

Gladia glanced at her hands and breathed in a sigh of relief. The shaking would not haunt her today. With the amount of meds she'd taken, her hands would be as steady as a surgeon's.

The vehicle landed in the designated area with a soft thud. Fifteen people emerged from the aircraft, all wearing long leather raincoats, sandy brown gloves, and high boots. At the head of the Geocentrics delegation was the standard-bearer, a towering girl with broad shoulders and red hair shaved at finger's length, who proudly carried their flag. From her self-important expression, it looked like she was holding the foundations of the planet itself.

The flag showed an infinity inscribed within a circle, which symbolized the Earth. Underneath the infinity was the Geocentrics' motto: "We are the Foundation." The delegation, which marched like a group of trained soldiers, reflected Penelope's personality: neat and efficient.

Penelope walked beside the flag-bearer, moving like an empress trudging her way into a barbaric land. Gladia respected her. The Geocentric leader had done a commendable job in the past five years overseeing the expansion of the space economy. During the last Pentaproject, the Geocentrics had built a considerable number of sidereals, expanded the human presence on Earth's orbit, upgraded Polaris so that it could transport heavier payloads in less time, and deployed an important gateway station in cislunar space. The GXP of the space economy had jumped tenfold during their mandate.

When the Geocentric delegation met Gladia's welcoming party, the red-haired standard-bearer handed the flag to Gladia.

"Your Stellar Majesty," the tall woman said, using Gladia's ceremonial title. "Grand Councilor Juno delivers the honor of the Geocentrics into your hands."

Gladia nodded solemnly. "Stargazer receives the honor and offers shelter to the Geocentrics. From stardust to stardust."

"From stardust to stardust," echoed all present.

Gladia turned and handed the banner to her ceremonial guard, who inserted the flagpole into one of the two slits at the center of the infinity-shaped sculpture.

As Penelope advanced to meet Gladia, she seemed to swim through the air rather than simply walking. Tall and skinny as nails, the Grand Councilor looked like a piranha ready to strike.

"Executive Director." Penelope bowed her head. "It's been too long."

Gladia greeted her with a wide smile. "Penelope, welcome to Stargazer. May the Founder's Grace bless your journey."

"May the same grace accompany you always." Penelope shifted her gaze to the three starlaukers, then to Arthur. "Constable." She gave him a sharp nod. "I see you're taking care of our leader's safety. Good." She glanced at the sky with a frown, as if expecting a meteorite shower. "I understand Almagest is bound to come any minute now. I've no interest in being blinded by the fireworks, so if you could point me to the media room, I'd be grateful."

"Of course." Gladia gestured toward a young man waiting at their side. "Our assistant will show you the way."

The Grand Councilor followed the guide and disappeared inside Stargazer.

Arthur blew out air from his nostrils. "Well, the dagger looks sharper than ever, doesn't she?"

Gladia released a deep, weighted sigh. "Sharper."

Charlotte interrupted their conversation. "Ma'am, the Ascendents have entered Stargazer's airspace. They'll be here momentarily."

Gladia looked at the sky. A pearl-white airship twice the size of Penelope's aeromousine approached from the west. It landed on a strip of level concrete that made up the center of the landing zone. When the ship's gangplank touched the ground, a delegation of forty people walked out of the ship. Unlike the Geocentrics, who had moved in formation and gone straight toward Gladia's welcoming party, the Ascendents stopped frequently to wave at the camera drones that followed them. Leading the scattered group of people was Tolomeus Almagest, dressed in a silver-colored suit and waving the Ascendents' flag with enthusiasm. He smiled like a kid at his birthday party.

The Ascendents' motto, "Further beyond," was displayed by a mobile platform projecting a gigantic reproduction of a golden arrow superimposed over an infinity.

When Tolomeus arrived in front of Gladia, exhilarated and red-faced from all the waving, his smile was contagious. He couldn't have looked more different from Penelope. If the Geocentrics leader was a block of ice, Tolomeus was a burning flame.

"Gladia." Tolomeus spread his arms and enveloped her in an embrace. "It's so good to see you."

Gladia smiled back. "Likewise, Tolomeus. Welcome to Stargazer."

The Legatus handed the flag to the honor guard, who put it beside the Geocentrics' banner.

Tolomeus shifted his gaze to Arthur, and held out his hand. "Arthur, I trust you're doing everything in your power to keep our leader safe?"

Arthur threw a quick look at Gladia. "I do what I can with the instruments I'm given."

Gladia ignored him. "Tolomeus, the press is waiting. Penelope is already inside. Everything is ready for the conference."

Tolomeus released a mock growl as he leaned in. "Of course. Wouldn't be a real boxing match without some angry table-flipping and getting all in each other's faces. Gladia, Arthur. See you on the other side."

Gladia gestured for the welcoming committee to follow the Ascendent delegation inside Stargazer, but she remained behind.

"I've got a bad feeling about this," she said, holding a breath and then releasing it.

Arthur stood by her side. "It's going to be rough, but

we'll get through this. That's what we do." He squeezed her hand for a second, then winked.

Gladia smiled at him, her hand still warm from his touch. "Hope you're right, Arthur. I can't wait for this nightmare to be over."

14

AQUAMARINE

GEODE, OUTPOST OF THE DEFENSIO PROJECT

Ariul

❧

Lena woke up to the sound of an alarm clock.

"It's me," Tiago's voice said. "Sorry to wake you up."

Lena blinked, looked around. The room was empty. Tiago's voice came from the intercom.

"It's okay," she said, scratching her head. "I...um...I'm awake. Where are you?"

"Finishing up some things in my office. I'll come pick you up in half an hour. You good with that?"

She cleared her throat. "Yeah, sure. I'll be ready."

"Good. See you soon." Tiago ended the communication.

Lena rubbed her eyes and yawned, her dream coming back in bits and pieces: the room with the holoposters, the expanse of green stretching out in all directions, and the two kids. She remembered their conversation, and the infinity necklace exchanged in between words. She knew who they were with the same certainty she knew that the day followed the night. It was Wei and Evangeline.

Why did she dream about them? Perhaps all the excitement of the day before got into her head and produced that dream? She'd never experienced a dream so vividly. She still remembered the brightness of the holo projections, the smell of the grass, the cool wind blowing her hair. It was as if she'd actually been there.

Lena glanced at the time and sighed. She got off the bed, took a quick shower, and was just about finished drying her hair when someone knocked.

"Come in."

Tiago entered the room with a tray covered by a lid and placed it on the desk. "Breakfast."

"Thanks." She opened the lid and started eating.

Tiago studied her. "How're you feeling today?"

Lena considered her answer while chewing on a sausage. She still didn't feel one hundred percent, but didn't say that. Instead, she shrugged. "I'm good. A few hours of sleep was all I needed. It worked wonders."

Tiago quirked an eyebrow. "Really?"

"Absolutely."

The chancellor smirked. "Look, if you need a bit more rest, I can—"

"I don't." She stood up. "I'm good. I'm here to get answers, not to lounge at your expense. Where are we heading next?"

Tiago studied her for a moment, then nodded. "All right. We're going to meet members of the Defensio Project coming from all our outposts. I'll tell you more while we're on the way."

They walked down a corridor that was much the same as any Lena had seen inside Geode: long, unadorned, silent.

"Tiago?"

"Yes?"

Lena bit her lip as she threw a quick glance at the chancellor. "Why can't people just trust what you say? About me, you know?"

Tiago shook his head. "The Defensio Project is fragmented, and there are sharks in the water. When you arrived, they smelled blood. I did what I could to keep them at a distance, but even I can't protect you forever."

"Who are they? The sharks?"

"Factions with their own agenda seeking to gain control of the Defensio. But it's not only them. Your coming raised a lot of eyebrows. People want to know why you're here. I get that. It's past time they all know who you really are."

Lena stared at her hands. "The Cornucopia?" She spoke the word hesitantly, as if tasting an exotic food.

Tiago was about to reply when he stopped dead in his tracks. He looked in front of him with the expression of someone who'd seen a phantom.

At the end of the corridor was a circular hatchway where a man with a bald head and a laurel vest stood.

"Chancellor." The man across from them made a half-bow. "I was starting to believe you'd disappeared on your own base. Been looking for you since yesterday."

"Fireballs and thunders," Tiago murmured.

Lena looked at him. "Who's that?"

Tiago inhaled sharply. "A shark," he whispered. "Say nothing. I'll deal with him."

The man covered the distance between them, hand swinging on the side.

"Marcius, I didn't expect to see you here." Tiago drew up to his full height. "Surely not in front of a launch pad. You decided to ambush me?"

Marcius' smile was full of mirth. "You know I like surprises. So, you've been hard to find."

Tiago showed his empty palms. "Been busy."

"Yes, I can see that." Marcius glanced at Lena, then looked back at Tiago. "Your magically appeared *deus ex machina*, I suppose?"

Tiago smiled dryly. "The assembly will decide that."

"Yes, it will." Marcius turned to look at Lena. "What's your name, girl?"

Lena said nothing.

Marcius blew out a noisy breath. "I see you've already trained her. My five cents? You should have thought of someone more...ah...*theatrical* for impersonating the savior. Someone who actually looked the part. What do we have here instead? A student fresh from campus?"

"If you'll excuse us, we have a forwardon to catch." Tiago walked past him. "We'll continue this conversation in front of the assembly."

"We will indeed." Marcius didn't lose sight of the chancellor as he walked down the corridor. "Oh, by the way. A squad of dunamis is waiting for you. Make sure your dog is leashed or there'll be consequences." His dark eyes glowed with malice.

"Let's go, Lena." Tiago walked toward the hatchway, and once in front of the terminal, he typed a code and the hatchway's door rolled to the side, revealing a passage.

"Watch your head." Tiago gestured to the upper side of the entrance. "These openings are lower than they look, and have claimed more than one forehead. Ask me how I know."

Lena entered inside what looked like a cabin, longer than it was wide, plunged in semi-darkness. A bittersweet smell lingered in the air, which felt humid and stale. As her eyes adjusted to the poor light, she noticed a dozen seats arranged in two rows. Tiago, on her right, was typing on a display panel that had seen better days. The edges of the display were chipped, and the buttons looked overused.

"Looks like a small bus," Lena said, glancing around.

Tiago nodded. "Close enough. We call it a forwardon and use it to move between bases. This one's a bit old, but it'll do the job just fine." He flipped a switch and waited.

A soft yellowish light flooded the environment and Lena could see the space wasn't quite like the inside of a bus, but more like a train car. The floor was smooth, made of polished metal that shone dully in the artificial light. The ceiling, just a few inches higher than Tiago's head, curved slightly on both sides, making the enclosed space look like a capsule. There were no glasses or windows in the cabin, which made Lena claustrophobic.

Tiago sat on the front seat and patted next to him. "Come sit here."

Lena did, and then looked at the chancellor for guidance.

"Grab the handle." He gestured at one of the iron handles attached to the sides of the cockpit. "The first ten seconds are going to be bumpy. Forwardons aren't known for comfort, but it'll get us to Aquamarine fast."

"Aquamarine?" She rubbed her forehead. "Where's that?"

"Further below." He flipped another switch. "Okay, buckle up." He pointed to the seat belt. "Departure in three, two, one... GO!"

Whatever passed for the vehicle's engines whined, and the queasy movement in Lena's stomach told her they'd started moving. Her restraining belt dug into her shoulder, and she held the handle so tight her knuckles went numb. After the initial forward push, they descended slowly at first, then faster. Lena swallowed, closed her eyes, and tried to think of something that wasn't the sickening shaking of the forwardon. "Is this Aquamarine another base?" she asked over the engine's noise, popping her eyes open just a moment to glance at Tiago.

"It's the central base," Tiago replied, his hands flying on the panel as the forwardon rushed below. "The hub."

She swallowed. "How...how deep underground are we right now?"

"Underground?" He chuckled. "We're more like under *water*. Open your eyes. I'll show you." He pressed a button and a tridimensional projection appeared in front of them. "That's outside."

Lena squinted, then gasped. *Water*. Water all around. They weren't on a bus or a train; they were aboard a small submarine. Lena leaned forward. They were approaching a structure built at the bottom of the sea. It looked like a giant spiral with many arms protruding outward.

Tiago turned toward her and grinned. "Welcome to Aquamarine, Lena. The City of Water below the City of Water. Welcome to the heart of the Defensio Project."

15

A PROMISE OF VENGEANCE

YELLOW SEA, HAMMERER CLASS
BATTLECRUISER UXA MASTODON

Ariul

"**Y**ou're making a mistake, Captain."

Goliath ignored Ishtar, turned on the terminal, and typed a series of numbers.

"Summoning the Great Mother for a futile reason won't make you look good." The dame lowered her voice. "It's unverified information, reported by an unreliable source. Saga was in shock. He didn't know what he was saying."

"I'm willing to take the risk." Goliath typed in the last digit and looked up at the projector kicking into gear.

"Captain."

Goliath growled. "What?"

"You know the rule." Ishtar assumed a wide stance. "Any communication has to go through a member of the Gathering first. A captain has no business contacting the Great Mother directly."

"You're asking me to stick to formalities." Goliath

pointed a finger at her. "This is an unprecedented situation. Needs to be addressed accordingly."

"Saga is this close to dying." Ishtar brought her thumb and index finger closer together. "He's not lucid. You can't base your report on his say-so."

"We've both seen the images," Goliath replied curtly. "They don't lie."

"You're leaning in too close to Saga's interpretation of the events."

"And you're discarding them way too easily."

Ishtar crossed her arms. "You need to stop jumping to conclusions that suit you."

"Enough!" Goliath jabbed a finger at her chest. "I won't waste time arguing. I've made my decision."

Ishtar didn't back down. "You're making a mistake. There'll be consequences."

Goliath stared into her big, yellow eyes. "Then I'll face them." He turned away and pressed the SEND key. The projector came to life with a whirring sound. "Opening channel." The captain kneeled, and Ishtar reluctantly joined him.

Beams of light formed into a woman's face. Her light-yellow hair framed a round, good-natured face; her eyes were the color of melting ice. The member of the Gathering referred to her with the name Pandora, but to Goliath, Ishtar, and the legions of reborn, she was the Archetype or Great Mother, the leader of the New Order.

Pandora looked at the captain. "What is it?"

"We've got a situation." Goliath glanced at Ishtar. "We might have been compromised."

Pandora frowned. "By whom?"

"Unclear. It's the reason I'm calling you directly."

Pandora turned to Ishtar. "You share his worry, dame?"

"I don't, Great Mother."

"Why?"

"All we have as proof is the word of a gravely injured soldier and mostly blurry images from his data stream."

Pandora turned to regard Goliath. "You said 'compromised.' Explain."

The captain inhaled sharply. "After the last failed operation, only two of our soldiers returned from the raid, and only one survived the wounds. His name is Saga, a devoted follower of our cause and a valiant fighter of the *Mastodon* who's—"

"Notorious for talking about himself in the third person," Ishtar broke in.

Goliath clenched his fists. "Saga is a zealot."

"Captain, you've been misguided in your—"

"Enough."

Both Ishtar and Goliath stopped talking.

"I don't have time for this petty skirmish." Pandora threw a glance at the dame. "Ishtar, interrupt him again, and you'll be the one speaking in the third person. Go ahead, Captain."

"Yes, Archetype." Goliath clenched his jaw. "While fighting near the docks, Saga came into contact with what appeared to be two weguckins. One male and one female."

"Weguckins." Pandora pursed her lips. "You mean Ariul's residents?"

"Yes, Archetype."

Pandora quirked an eyebrow. "Continue."

"Saga's cephalic recorder shot some pictures of them." Goliath glanced at the control panel. "They're two youngsters in their early twenties. We don't know who the girl is, but we ran a data-check on the boy. His name is Makoto Shimao."

"Shimao." Pandora rubbed her chin, now staring at the captain. "Any chance he's related to the member of the Hexahedron, Toshio Shimao?"

"Yes, Archetype," Goliath said. "He's his son."

"What a coincidence. Send me the image."

Goliath stood and typed on the panel. "Done. The boy was wearing a projector unit display when Saga found him. He was not aware of—"

"And not a simple PUD either," Pandora interrupted him, her eyes making small, rapid, jerky movements as she evaluated the image.

Goliath's gaze clouded. "Archetype?"

"A Centurion Mark VI." Pandora summoned a grainy image that showed Makoto wearing his projector unit display. "This device isn't cheap. It's used for high-definition multidimensional filming, not the kind of stuff you'd bring around without a good reason. Shimao might have known of the attack beforehand, hence the expensive piece of equipment."

Goliath threw a sideways look at Ishtar and smiled. "That makes sense, Archetype."

Pandora arched an eyebrow. "Something weird's happening here, Captain. I want to find out more. Bring me Shimao alive."

Goliath bowed his head. "Yes, Archetype. What is the mission code?"

"Tabula Rasa," Pandora replied. "I want an alpha priority raid to be executed in the next five hours. Use everything we can muster. Make it lean and mean."

"Understood, Archetype."

"Great Mother," Ishtar said, blinking rapidly. "You think...you think Makoto Shimao might be the Cornucopia?"

"I believe he wasn't there by accident," Pandora said. "He must have had some intel. If he knew we would be there, I can think of nothing better than a connection with Wei Wang. Shimao could be the Cornucopia, or not. The only way of knowing for sure is to ask him."

"Yes, Archetype."

"Good." Pandora's eyes glowed. "I'll work the ether; come up with something that doesn't raise too many questions. Some extremist fringe of landist, perhaps. With the Pentaproject looming, it sounds appropriate. As for you, Captain, make the number of casualties a three-digit number. Should be enough to justify our version of the events. Is that understood?"

A smile appeared on Goliath's face. "With immense pleasure, Archetype."

16

HOLISTIC

NASHVILLE, ARK INSTITUTE FOR ADVANCED ETHERIC STUDIES

James

James Ark fidgeted with the rolled cuff of his glove as they drew closer to their destination. A lot would depend on the next few minutes. He needed to make every word count.

Angelica looked around, evaluating the surroundings. James had had time to assess his ex-classmate and found her different from the shy, insecure girl he had known. She was more confident now, at ease even in unexpected situations.

"Five subterranean floors is a lot, even for an institute of this size," Angelica said. "But it doesn't look like you're using a lot of the space."

"Not for now," James agreed. "We're looking into expanding the Ark with new sections in the future."

Angelica glanced at the closed doors beside her. "What happens behind these doors, exactly?"

"We need a lot of processing power for our research, and we deal with lots of data." James gestured around. "Some of these rooms store servers that provide redundancy and improve performance. We've arrived."

James pointed to a metal door with a control panel on the right-hand side. He placed his hand on the panel. "Control. This is Domine James Ark, authorization Da Vinci Red, Delta Eleven."

"Confirmed," the control's voice replied.

The door slid to the side, disappearing into the wall. As soon as they stepped in, a soft light turned on automatically, revealing an empty circular room. The light came from saffron-yellow pathways encased in the wall. They intertwined with each other like roots of a giant tree.

"This room." Angelica studied the source of light in recognition. "It's Cantara's simulator, isn't it?"

"That's right." James patted the room's wall. "But with some important differences. Control, summon the Holistic Arbiter."

The yellow light gradually lost intensity, and the room plunged into semi-darkness.

"Greetings, Madame Kam." A cold male voice broke the silence.

Angelica narrowed her eyes at James. "Is this...ADAM?"

But it wasn't James who answered.

"Yes." ADAM's voice was deep and ubiquitous. "And you are the Madame of Melody. Your stream of consciousness is strong, your etheric footprint remarkable. You have come a long way since we last met."

Angelica's posture crumbled. "It's different." She looked at James. "What did you do to the program?"

Once again, it wasn't the Domine who answered.

"Domine Ark stretched the boundaries of my limitations," ADAM said, his voice booming. "I am no longer bound to a room inside a building. I can add my experience to the stream of consciousness. The ether is my home now."

Angelica moved back slightly, staring openly at James. "You turned ADAM into an AI?"

"I'm not a computer scientist," James said, "but I know my way around algorithms. I paid someone to remove the limitations embedded into ADAM's original matrix. The rest, as they say, is history."

Angelica ran her hands through her hair. "Why would you do that?"

"Because I needed an extremely powerful tool to counter an extremely dangerous threat."

She blinked. "You talking about the killer malicious?"

James shook his head. "The malicious is a symptom of an etheric discrepancy. I'm talking about what caused it. We're at war, Angelica, against a force that will stop at nothing to reach its goal. ADAM and this institute are the only way to counter it."

"What...what war are you talking about?"

"The War of the Ether," ADAM interjected.

Angelica cocked her head. "I don't understand."

"ADAM," James said. "I think a bit of context would help here. Show her the current situation of etheric deficiency. Give her a general overview."

Angelica's eyebrows squished together. "What's an etheric deficiency?"

"It's what we call the killer malicious around here," James said. "Take a couple steps back, please. ADAM is about to awaken the Masvieth."

Angelica stepped away from the center of the room, which opened to reveal a Masvieth. The smooth surface of the sphere rippled like a wave propagating across water. By the time the Geoether appeared, the sphere showed different portions of the ether, with DataMorph being the biggest.

ADAM spoke: "The etheric deficiency has increased its presence at a rate of three parts per million in five of the major etheric portions, including DataMorph, Covenant, and Second World. Our most recent analysis detected the deficiency inside three new regions of the ether; small-size players, bottom of the food chain, but still relevant."

James crossed his arms. "ADAM, what's your estimate on the number of victims caused by the deficiency so far?"

"Considering only the proven areas of interest, about four hundred thousand."

"And what is the percentage of the ether we know is affected?"

"About fourteen percent."

Angelica held one elbow tight against her side. "What're you trying to say?"

"I think you know." James pointed to the Masvieth. "The killer malicious is more widespread than your most current estimate. It's no longer a question of *if* it's spreading, but where we can see it's already causing damage and where we can't yet. We need to think in terms of active and latent carriers. Active carriers are ethernauts already showing symptoms of the malicious, while the latents have contracted the malicious, but aren't showing any sign yet."

Angelica shook her head. "How can you say they've contracted the malicious if they show no sign?"

"By looking at their etheric trace." James waved a hand and a string of data appeared beside the Masvieth. "See this Doppenhaimer curve? It's flexed by forty basis points compared to an average ethernaut. This means they're already affecting the ether; it doesn't matter if they show physical signs of the malicious or not."

She pulled her glasses down and looked over the rims. "This...this doesn't make sense. We've found no evidence of—"

"You didn't have ADAM to rely on," James cut her off. "That's why you never found the evidence."

"The Domine is right." ADAM's voice was a low rumble. "Judging by the information on your trigoy, the data you gathered was lacking. You had no way of knowing the true scale of this growing pandemic."

James stepped toward Angelica. "Look, you'll have plenty of time to check our data, but for now you'll have to trust us."

She glanced at the Masvieth, barely breathing. "If this is true, if your numbers are correct..." She trailed off, head shaking in denial.

"Yes," James said, reading the data. "It means that within a decade, over a third of ethernauts will be affected by the killer malicious. That's over two billion people. It means chaos on a scale never seen in human history, the end of the world as we know it. And right now, only a small minority knows."

Angelica's hands dropped to her sides. "Is this why you kidnapped me? You wanted to keep this thing quiet?"

"It's part of the reason," he admitted. "Any information shared through the ether could be traced. I think you'll agree we don't want the world knowing this information before we have a way to deal with it. It would be global hysteria. Countless lives would be lost."

"Yes." Angelica cleared her throat. "I agree. I... I'll need to study this information." She ran a trembling hand through her hair. "I need to understand what I'm looking at."

"There's something more I need to tell you." James turned toward the Masvieth. "ADAM, show us the working schematics of the holistic."

The Geoether disappeared and the Masvieth transformed into a white sphere. Another set of data appeared on its side.

"This is what we call the holistic ether," James said, pushing his sunglasses. "It's an alternative medium of communication to the legacy ether. We've been working on this project for a while, and we are confident it can solve the threat of the killer malicious."

Angelica frowned. "Let me get this straight. You want to deal with the killer malicious by creating a new ether? How?"

"There are differences between the two ethers." James moved toward the sphere. "In the legacy ether, every user is dependant on a focal center. They need to rely on a data source to store information and move inside the cyberspace. The holistic ether is different in that every ethernaut will be a focal center, independent of others. Think about it. The killer malicious can spread because of the way the legacy ether is structured. Everyone is connected with everyone else. But because of the nature of the holistic, it's impossible to spread any cyber-disease. Each person would be an island, able to create a temporary cyber-bridge when they want to connect with the main data-core. But there's a catch. While theoretically feasible, we're encountering problems turning the theory into a practical model. We haven't been able to proceed past the testing stage."

Angelica quickly scanned the information. "If I understand what you're trying to do, you'll need a new region and a new gateway for this holistic to work."

"That's correct."

She shook her head. "But people already belong to a region. To make this holistic happen, you can't just create a region from scratch. It'll take ages. You need gatekeepers of regions already established to stand behind this new ether of yours for your plan to work."

"That's also correct," he said. "But that's not our most pressing issue right now. First, we need to make sure the holistic is viable by addressing the practical side of things. And that's why you're here. You have extensive knowledge of matrix affinity because of your studies as an etriatros. You think you can help us?"

Angelica looked at James. "I might, but I need to get back to Calgary. Right away. I'm going to need Sebastian's eye on this."

∞ ∞ ∞

Calgary
Yodobashi Institute for the Treatment of Ether-Induced Disorders

Sebastian and Dewi looked at Angelica with a glassy stare.

Angelica had spent the past four hours showing data, calculations, and graphs, and had finally convinced them of James' apocalyptic scenario. Winning their acceptance hadn't been easy.

Sebastian wasn't even angry at her anymore for breaking her promise not to contact Jason Cloverfield. He got over the anger when he realized James had been right about the killer malicious. The data didn't lie. The magnitude of the situation dwarfed anything he had expected.

The room had been quiet for a long time. No one knew what to say. There was no right reaction to knowing something so unprecedented, something that would change the face of society forever.

Sebastian's hands rested on his knees, his gaze fixed on the floor. He had been the hardest to persuade, but James' information filled in all the blank spots. The malicious was spreading at a level none of them thought possible, and hundreds of thousands were already affected.

Dewi was the first to speak. "What do we do, boss?"

Angelica was spared from having to answer when Sebastian rose with clenched fists. "The only sane thing. We accept James' invitation. Angy, you told us that James has tremendous resources at his disposal, much more than our grid of institutes combined, but he doesn't have the manpower and the know-how to carry out his plans."

Angelica nodded. "That's right. If we join forces, we'll have a real shot at finding a solution. I already have a few ideas on how to tackle the problem. I'm confident we can do this."

"This holistic ether..." Dewi trailed off. She studied Angelica, unable to hide her worry. "You think it can really solve the problem? Implementing it on a global scale... I mean, it sounds crazy."

"James' project is solid." Angelica gestured at the data. "We'll worry about publicizing the idea when we know it works."

Sebastian stood up from his chair. "I'll talk with our folks. We're going to need more brain power if we want to make a decent attempt at simulating all variables."

Dewi looked at both of them. "So, we're helping James?"

"We help James help us," Angelica said. "The holistic ether is the only chance we have to eradicate the malicious. Dewi, you're going to run the Yodobashi for the time being. Sebastian and I are going to be very busy in the coming weeks. We know you can take care of business."

Dewi frowned. "Are you sure, boss?"

"I'm positive." Angelica handed her the keys to the institute. "You'll do great."

Dewi accepted the keys with a nod. "I'll do my best. I promise."

"Good." Angelica rubbed her hands together. "I've asked James to arrange a room in the institute for us. We need to dedicate our complete attention to the holistic. We're running out of time."

17

AN EXERCISE OF TRUST

YELLOW SEA, ABOARD THE FORWARDON

Ariul

Lena stared awestruck at the submerged structure on the bottom of the sea. Of all the impossible things in Saemangeum City, this one claimed the number one spot. It looked like something out of a Jules Verne novel. An oblong shape flashed in front of the submerged structure.

Lena pointed. "What's that?" Before Tiago could answer, another shape appeared, and then another. Lena squinted. "Wait. Are those forwardons?"

"Yes." Tiago glanced at the control panel. "We're approaching Aquamarine's perimeter. We'll dock in less than five minutes." He pointed to one arm that looked like a tentacle attached to the central body. Lena could now see a half dozen forwardons approaching the base from different directions.

"I want you to listen to me."

Lena tuned to Tiago, who looked worried. "What's up?"

He squeezed his hands at his sides. "You'll have to be careful."

Lena blinked. "What do you mean?"

"You're in a delicate situation." The chancellor crossed his arms as he looked at the approaching base. "When you answer the assembly's questions, tell them what you told me. Don't hide things."

She studied him. "I'm getting worried now. What's bugging you?"

"Many of them won't understand." He frowned. "They'll want proof, and even if you answer their questions, I fear it won't be enough. Doubt will find a way."

"What are you saying?"

The chancellor turned toward her. "You're a legend. The Cornucopia is a word whispered in times of uncertainty, a symbol of hope many of us cling to when everything seems to fall apart. Some will think you're just a wish. A fancy. We'll have to convince them otherwise. We can't risk losing the lifeline Wei threw to us." He clenched his jaw and looked into Lena's eyes. "There's a person in Aquamarine who doesn't trust you. She believes I staged your coming to gain an edge."

She blinked. "Who's that?"

"Her name is Cassandra. She's the regent of Aquamarine."

"The regent?"

"The head of the Defensio Project." Tiago's eyes trailed over the console. "She and I... Well, let's just say we have a history. We also have different ideas on how to fulfill Wei's mission, and because of that, Cassandra might see you as a threat, a ploy I devised to gain control of the Defensio.

That's why they want you in Aquamarine: to make sure you're not a threat."

Her eyes went wide. "So this assembly...it's not just people asking questions. You're bringing me to a trial. Why didn't you say that before?"

"Would it have made a difference?"

Lena thought. "No," she said. "Probably not."

The console panel started beeping. "Hold onto the handle. The parking is about as bumpy as the departure. Minus ten seconds to docking. Brace for impact!"

She grabbed the handle with both hands.

The forwardon decreased its speed and came to an abrupt halt, like a running car stopped at the last moment by a concrete block.

"Yeah," Tiago said, blowing hair off his nose. "Silky smooth, just as I remembered. I hope you enjoyed the roller coaster. Lena?"

Lena swallowed. "I...I think I'm going to be sick."

"Here." He offered her a paper bag he took from beneath his seat. "I know the feeling. A forwardon's parking is called a 'vomit burn' for a reason. It'll pass." He typed on the console and the forwardon's hatch rolled over to reveal a corridor leading to a circular area.

She rose on unsteady legs.

"You're okay?"

She cleared her throat. "I'm good."

Tiago held her arm as they went out of the forwardon. After a few steps, Lena found herself inside a room with a couple metal benches facing each other. It smelled of burned steak.

"Sit here." Tiago helped her sit on the bench. "EVA is going to work her magic."

Lena didn't ask what he meant. She was busy keeping

down her breakfast. A low buzzing, then a hissing noise filled the room. The air became colder.

"Won't take long to equalize the pressure," Tiago said. "It gives us time to talk."

"About what?"

"Rumors have a tendency to take on a life of their own. Now, you'll remember the unfortunate accident that happened outside Geode?"

"You mean when one of the dunamis shot me?" She touched her arm. "Hard to forget."

"That resulted from fear."

She stared at Tiago. "Fear?"

"Yes. Fear is a powerful catalyst, and it fuels hatred. Many people who are part of the Defensio are afraid."

She shook her head slightly. "I don't get it. Afraid of what?"

"Afraid of you." He put a hand on her shoulder. "Some think you might be a weapon sent by our enemies to destroy us. Others, as I have said, see you as a political ploy to divide us. I need people to see you for what you truly are."

"Yes, you said that already. The Cornucopia, right? I just can't help but find the whole thing…ah…very unlikely."

"I know how it sounds, but you are the Cornucopia. The last chance we have to save humanity."

"There." She drew in a deep breath. "That's where you kind of lose me."

"Look, I'm not saying this to alarm you. I just want you to be ready. The next few hours are going to be intense. You're going to be under scrutiny and possibly in danger. Some people will want to silence you because they're afraid you might become a symbol they can't handle."

She opened her mouth to speak, collected her thoughts, then said, "How will they silence me?"

"By making you look like something you aren't."

She bit her lip. "So, what do you expect me to do?"

Tiago leaned forward. "Do you trust me?"

Lena opened her mouth, but this time no words came out. Did she trust him? She'd barely met this person who said she was some kind of savior sent by Wei Wang. Tiago had answered many of her questions, sure, but he had easily created just as many. She didn't know him, but she had to trust someone.

"I trust you," she said.

"Outstanding." Tiago pointed at the door on his right. "I'll need that trust when that door opens."

18

THE KEYSTONE

HYPERIST COMPLEX STARGAZER, AUDITORIUM AD ASTRA

Gladia

"**M**embers of the Starry Assembly. I have the distinct honor of presenting you Executive Director Gladia Egea, leader of HYPER and moderator of the Keystone."

The audience clapped politely as Gladia walked toward a podium at the center of the stage facing the auditorium. Once on the raised platform, she waved at the hundreds of people sitting in the stands, each displaying an infinity pin on their chest.

A camera drone hovered in front of her, and she smiled, knowing that an audience composed of millions of hyperists was watching the event.

"Thank you. Thank you so much." Gladia's voice was amplified by a microphone pinned on her jacket. The applause slowly faded, and the lights of the stage dimmed. It was the signal that the Keystone had begun.

"Speaker of the Assembly." Gladia nodded respectfully toward the man who introduced her. "Members of the Silver Circles and hyperists all around the world, our Constitution states that every five years the representatives of the two majority hyperist parties must appear before the Starry Assembly to submit a Five-Year Plan of Sidereal Development to ensure the growth of our movement."

Gladia swept her gaze across the room and saw men and women representing dozens of cultures, all proudly united under the Silver Infinity. The spectacle of so many people who dedicated their lives to Wei Wang's dream was reinvigorating. She pushed her shoulders back and thrust her chest out, her voice becoming more vibrant.

"For ten years, I've overseen this growth. I have done so during periods of prosperity, and during moments of crisis and uncertainty. We think that the Silver Infinity was always destined for success, but this has not always been the case. We had to fight for every inch of progress, for every turning of events. Fifteen years ago, I was there when the brightest minds in the world waved away the space elevator Polaris as an impossibility. I was there when we lost the First Hyperist to hate and extremism. I was there when the economic crisis of the early 2030s shut down half of our factories and wiped out years of progress. In those cases, failure was all but certain. The only thing that brought us to this moment was a drive to empower humankind, to make it better by pushing the boundaries of the final frontier. Space is in our blood, fellow hyperists. It doesn't matter that we call ourselves Geocentric, Selenian, Ascendent, or Apeiron. We're one under Wei's legacy!"

The auditorium exploded with a resounding cheer. Gladia let the sound subside before resuming her talk.

"Make no mistake. These moments tested our conviction, threatened our unity, our willingness to continue the Founder's dream. But we always prevailed. Despite our differences, despite our shortcomings, HYPER continues to exist because we moved forward as one nation. Once again, we are tested, and once again we must answer the call of destiny. Ten years ago, I accepted the scepter from the Founder amid a crisis that threatened to break our society. Today, we are at a crossroads, an unprecedented moment in the history of HYPER. Wei Wang himself said that the first ten years of the Hyperist Movement would be crucial in determining whether it would survive itself. He was right. Now, as we're about to begin the third Keystone, we have proven two things to the world: First, that HYPER isn't the whim of a megalomaniac; it's a calling to which millions of people dedicate their lives. Most importantly, we proved that impossible is only a possibility that has not yet been discovered. Today, brothers and sisters, the impossible takes the shape of the space elevator of Penelope Juno's Geocentrics, and the spaceship fleet of the Ascendents lead by Tolomeus Almagest. These two proposals have passed many selections. Now, you will choose which one moves forward. Without further ado, let's give a warm welcome to Grand Councilor Juno and Legatus Almagest!"

The standing ovation of the audience accompanied the entrance of the two contenders on the stage. They shook hands, then turned toward the audience and waved at their supporters.

Gladia gestured to the two chairs placed in front of the podium, and Penelope and Tolomeus sat.

"Each of the contenders will answer questions from the audience," Gladia said. "These questions are known only to myself and to the organizers of the Keystone. Both contenders will have five minutes for their answers." Gladia turned to Tolomeus, who had been the last to sit. "Legatus, you've won the coin toss, so you'll answer the opening question. It'll be asked by a young assistant astrogator, Jackson Brown, who just graduated with honors from the Andromeda Academy." Gladia turned to a member of the audience sitting nearby. "Jackson, your question, please."

The student stood up and looked at the two rivals. "Grand Councilor, Legatus, I firmly believe in the Founder's dream of a spacefaring civilization, but a person can't live off dreams alone. How can you assure us that your Pentaproject will open up the most job opportunities for the hyperist workforce? I have a six-figure student loan I can't pay without a position as an astrogator, and there are fewer of these available right now than when I started my studies. Other hyperists graduates are struggling to find well-paid jobs. What can you do to help us? Thank you."

Tolomeus rose from the chair and walked toward the young man. "Jackson, you're absolutely right." The Ascendent leader nodded, looking at Jackson with a fatherly smile. "Your question is asked all over the world by thousands of other young hyperists who've spent years studying and can't find a job." He shifted his attention to the audience. "I've heard the same complaint from Gill Pascal, a twenty-seven-year-old from Louisiana who specializes in space manufacturing who's been unemployed for six months. Heard the same tune from Stuart Molinari, a graduate student in orbital construction, with no idea what awaits him because of the instability of the sidereal market. Jackson is right, people. This isn't fair! They took massive loans for a promise we made and that we never fulfilled. We failed them as a movement and as a nation of like-minded individuals whose main goal is to reach for the stars." Tolomeus turned toward Penelope, who was glaring at him with her arms crossed tightly before her chest. "And the reason for this failure is sitting in front of me."

The leader of the Geocentrics remained impassive. Gladia checked the timer and counted the minutes left to Tolomeus.

"In the past five years," Tolomeus continued, looking back at the audience, "the Geocentrics' leadership failed the Hyperist Movement in so many ways it's hard to keep count. They failed to innovate, to put our money where our mouth is, and they never held themselves accountable." He turned toward Jackson. "They failed Jackson and hundreds of young people like him, the bedrock of our future. Don't take my word for it. The Sidereal Workforce Commission speaks candidly about our current state of affairs: sidereal manufacturing over the past five years has provided jobs to only a fraction of the people who seek employment. Jackson, I promise you my Five-Year Plan will change this. Estimates from the independent commission 'SteelLab' say that the katalambans will create over fifty-thousand new jobs for highly skilled people in the first half of the next year alone. Voting for my Pentaproject means voting for a future full of possibilities for students like you, who are the lifeblood of the Silver Infinity."

Tolomeus finished speaking a couple seconds before the countdown decreed the end of his five minutes.

The Legatus sat back with a confident smile as spectators clapped their hands at his speech.

"Grand Councilor Juno?" Gladia said. "The floor is yours."

Penelope stood gracefully, smoothing her vest as she rose. "What can I say, Jackson?" She shook her head slightly as she walked toward the student. "Five minutes is a short time to answer your question, and counter the Legatus' lies.

I'm going to focus on giving you an answer that makes sense, because you deserve better than a bunch of fake news passed off as fact."

Tolomeus smirked. His eyes flashed with a barely subdued light.

"Now," Penelope resumed, looking at the student. "Yours is a sensible question. I'll give you a sensible answer. It starts with Polaris. You know, the single biggest infrastructure in history? Take what the space elevator meant to the Hyperist Movement and multiply it three times. Three times the manpower required for its construction, three times the materials needed to make it happen, three times the contractors required to build it. If you add these things together, Jackson, you'll realize that the benefits of building our new space elevator are monumental. New industries will have to spring up just to create it, and industries that already exist will be expanded to meet the increased demand for material and people. And that means jobs, Jackson—*real* jobs—for students like you, who don't need a pat on the back but solid facts." Penelope turned to the audience with a sweeping motion of her arm. "Since we're talking about facts, people, here's another one Almagest doesn't want you to know. His flying toys are as bright as fireworks, and last as long. There are a dozen private commissions who studied the specifics of his katalambans and found them as doable as a high-efficiency torch-ship. Possible? Sure, in a couple hundred years. Now *that* is excellent material for a science fiction novel, but for all hyperists who aren't building castles in the clouds, here's what matters: we must work on what we know produces results. We need to strengthen the foundation of a spacefaring civilization here at home before moving toward the solar system and beyond. It might not sound sexy, but it's what creates actual jobs and a solid industry that'll bring us to the stars. This is the only thing that counts."

Penelope returned to her seat with almost a minute to spare, followed by a lively round of applause.

"All right, let's move on to the second question." Gladia picked up her tablet and read aloud. "It'll be asked by Meredith Susy Shawn, a certified DataMorph etherion. Meredith?"

A graceful woman in her early forties with long pink hair stood from her chair and turned to the two leaders. "This question is for the both of you. What do you think Wei Wang would have said about your Pentaproject?"

"Grand Councilor." Gladia invited Penelope to speak. "Your turn."

The following two hours could best be described as a fencing match between two equally skilled opponents.

Each knew how to attract the audience's attention and did so with intelligence and passion. Tolomeus focused on attacking his rival by pointing out her lack of vision, while Penelope concentrated on Almagest's landist background and his inexperience in astrophysics. They weren't pulling any punches, and went straight for the jugular when they found an opening. None of the previous Pentaprojects had had this level of tension. It felt like the entire future of the Hyperist Movement rested on that debate. Never had the two contenders been so tied up in the race.

When the last question was asked, Gladia kicked off the last section of the event. "Now, to carry on the tradition, both contenders may ask each other a question. Grand Councilor Juno, you're first."

"Thank you." Penelope looked at Tolomeus with eyes as bright as a hawk. "I have a simple question for you, Almagest."

Tolomeus smiled brightly. "I cannot wait."

Penelope smoothed the front of her vest. "Legatus, could you tell us how much Douglas Woodside's death cost you, in terms of revenue?"

The leader of the Ascendents frowned. "Can't say I understand the question."

"Well, we all know that despite your ostentatious divorce with LAND, your investment portfolio holds millions' worth of shares of landist companies. Should I name a few? What about Sunshinex Inc., or the Miramallian Corporation, or the Greengold Sasami? All companies owned by landists."

Tolomeus shifted in his chair, his eyes scanning the audience. "How I choose to handle my financial assets has nothing to do with my loyalty to the—"

"Loyalty, Legatus?" Penelope stared at Tolomeus. "A very poor choice of word, I'm afraid. Your *loyalty* has never left your wallet."

Tolomeus raised his voice. "I won't let you question—"

"What? The truth?" Penelope took a step toward him. "You speak boldly of investing in the future of HYPER, and yet you give your money to landist companies. How can you keep a straight face and ask for our trust when you pour money into the enemy's pocket?"

Tolomeus held his chin up. "You're grasping at straws and you know it. I don't have to justify my financial statement to you."

"No, that's true." Penelope took another purposeful step toward her target. "But you know something else that's true? There isn't a single member in the Starry Assembly who's invested in a landist company. Ever. Until you wormed your way into HYPER, that is. You know why? Because all other hyperists *actually* believe in the Silver Infinity."

Tolomeus scoffed. "That's rubbish. I'm worried about Wei's legacy as much as the next hyperist."

Penelope sneered. "You're worried about your bottom line. And it shows." Before Tolomeus could reply, she turned her back to him and addressed the audience. "This is what stands between us and genuine progress. Vote for him and get exactly what he's selling: populist propaganda designed to further his gains. But if you want true leadership, look beyond the lies and the deception and join us as we build a brighter future for the Hyperist Movement."

Penelope sat back in her chair, followed by a standing ovation. Tolomeus was good at keeping his feelings in check, but not good enough for Gladia not to notice his lips pressed together in a slight grimace.

Putting Tolomeus' finances under the spotlight had worked wonders. Gladia sensed that Penelope's speech had tipped the balance in her favor.

"Legatus Almagest," Gladia said, nodding toward him. "You have the floor."

Tolomeus stood up slowly, as if he had physically felt the blow delivered by Penelope. He trudged across the stage for several steps, tilting his head back and forth as if considering something. After a long moment of silence, he looked at the audience. "Is it a crime to be shrewd? Is it despicable?" He turned to Penelope, a tightness in his eyes that spoke of defiance. "You can call me an opportunist, a turncoat, and a liar. You can even call me despicable. I don't care what you believe, I know who I am. I'm driven! I'm ready to do anything in my power to achieve my goal. If this is a bad thing, then I'm a terrible person." Tolomeus looked back at the audience. "You know who else was shrewd and driven? You know who else put everything on the line for what he believed?" He pointed at the Silver Infinity. "Wei Wang was a hyperist to the core, and yet he forged alliances in the dark, schemed and cheated to get Polaris completed. He did everything he had to do to achieve his goal, and we're glad he acted that way, because the end always justify the means. The only thing that matters is what we can build upon. Everything else turns to nothing. Wei wasn't born to be a footnote in the history books. I'm asking you to be as brave. We don't need what's reliable and tested. We need to pass on a story of ingenuity and progress, brothers and sisters, we need to inspire the people of this planet, and you can't do that with numbers and charts."

Penelope waved her hand dismissively. "You have a flare for the melodramatic. I'll give you that. But we're not running for the presidency of a Third World country. You're actually held accountable for what you do and say here. You know what I see when I look at you?"

Tolomeus smiled. "Enlighten me."

"I see a desperate man trying to make a desperate stand for something he'll never have: integrity and moral values. Face it. You lost the Keystone the moment you stepped onto this stage because you don't have and will never have what it takes to be another Wei Wang."

Tolomeus barked a laugh. "You think you're the best stock of hyperist there is, don't you? You think—because you've been a member of the party from day one—that you've got a better claim to be called a hyperist? That's nonsense, and Wei thought the same."

"Sure." Penelope shrugged. "Go ahead and pretend you're the Founder himself now."

"I don't need to pretend." Tolomeus looked Penelope up and down as he rubbed his hands together. "I know what Wei thought about you."

Penelope sat up straighter in her chair. "What's that supposed to mean?"

Tolomeus stood back a couple steps and looked at his rival with an intense gaze. "He believed there were two kinds of people in this world: those useful to furthering the dream of a spacefaring civilization and those who aren't. And you, my dear, are one of the latter."

The Grand Councilor glared at him. "Careful now. Wei Wang was my friend, and I won't allow you to taint his memory with lies."

"So you call him a friend, hmm?" Tolomeus shook his head. "Well, I have to say I'm surprised, since he didn't consider you the same."

Penelope snorted. "This is preposterous. What are you trying to say?"

"Only that he didn't trust you." Tolomeus picked a trigoy from his pocket and turned to Gladia. "Executive Director, I request permission to show a recording where Wei Wang speaks those words in person."

All eyes turned to Gladia. There wasn't a rule against using a trigoy during the Keystone, but it had never been done before. Gladia felt both Tolomeus and Penelope's eyes. Penelope, in particular, showed a crack in her stoic expression. Clearly, she had no idea what Tolomeus was referring to, which meant she had no defense.

Gladia hesitated as the murmur from the audience grew louder. Could this one concession tip the scale of the entire debate? She was supposed to be an arbiter, nothing more. But if Tolomeus possessed revealing information that was useful to inform the voters, it was Gladia's duty to allow him to.

"Gladia?" Tolomeus' eyes were unblinking.

Gladia glanced at Penelope, frozen in her seat, the muscles in her neck taut.

Gladia nodded. "Go ahead, Legatus."

Tolomeus' smile split his face in two. "Thank you." He turned on the trigoy and a projection started. "This recording is dated the 7th of December, 2028," Tolomeus said. "Wei Wang is speaking. The recording hasn't been tampered with. I can provide the original file to whoever wishes to analyze it." He closed his hand into a fist and a projection of Wei Wang in his early twenties appeared in front of the audience.

"I wouldn't hand the direction of the Polaris project to Penelope even if she were the last hyperist on Earth," Wei said. "I don't trust her political agenda."

The projection disappeared amid a growing murmur from the audience.

Penelope stared at where the projection had been, as if looking at a mirage.

"We all heard it," Tolomeus said, taking advantage of the moment of confusion. "Wei didn't trust her, so why should you? Why should any of us?"

Penelope opened her mouth, but nothing came out.

Gladia glanced at the time and cleared her throat. "This ends the Keystone," she said. "The voting for the Pentaproject will take place shortly. Thank you for following us today. Stardust to stardust."

"Stardust to stardust," the audience replied in unison.

An hour later, the president of the Starry Assembly announced the result: forty-seven percent of the hyperists voted in favor of the Geocentrics, fifty-three in favor of the Ascendents.

Tolomeus Almagest became the first Ascendent to win a Pentaproject in the history of HYPER.

19

IF IT CAN BE WRITTEN, IT CAN BE SOLVED

DÜSSELDORF, RESIDENCE OF ERIK DERINGER

Ramor

Erik turned off the trigoy and the data he had been studying for the past five hours disappeared. He fell back in his chair with a sigh, closed his eyes, and ran a hand through his messy hair. He should shave, and probably take a shower, but just the thought of putting in the effort made his head hurt. Erik felt hollow, like a dark hole was sucking him from the inside. "You're losing it, buddy," he said. "Keep going like this and they'll find you a room next to your mother."

As soon as he spoke the words, he grimaced. He shouldn't have said that. Thinking about his mother was the last thing he needed.

Erik tried to clear his head. His eyes lingered on the coffee cup he kept at his work station. He reached out and grabbed the cup, but when he brought it to his mouth, it was empty. "Classic." He snorted, then glanced at the door left ajar. "Where the hell is that goddamn piece of junk when I need him?"

He put the coffee cup back on the desk with a resounding thud, then turned toward the door. "Hey, On?" he shouted. "Get your ass over here and bring me some coffee. Aspirins, too. I have a code one emergency: huge headache incoming. You feel me?"

Erik waited, but heard no reply.

"On?"

"I will be there momentarily."

Erik heard the autotron bustling in the kitchen. The microwave oven and blender were being used by his assistant.

"On?" Erik tapped his foot on the floor. "I just need a damn coffee and a pill. What's taking so—"

On-Eni-Fifth entered the room holding a mug whose contents didn't smell like coffee.

Erik's eyes widened as he wrinkled his nose. Some pea-green matter with the consistency of tomato sauce sat inside the large cup. "On," he said, jerking his head back. "What the hell *died* inside this cup?"

The autotron tilted his head to the side. "This is a blend of avocado, garlic powder, broccoli paste, and green peppers with a splash of mentolithosin."

"Okay." Erik stared at the autotron, then shrugged. "Why is it in your hand?"

"It is an excellent remedy for headaches." On put the smelly thing under Erik's nose. "I found the recipe in the vegan region."

Erik waved it away. "What happened to my coffee?"

"Your daily intake of caffeine is already close to 900 milligrams. You don't need more."

Erik chuckled dryly. "Let me be the judge."

On stared at his owner. "Extremely high daily intakes of caffeine have been reported to cause nervousness, jitteriness, and similar symptoms. Long-term effects may include constant anxiety, chronic insomnia, and depression. It can also cause high blood pressure and—"

"Blah, blah, blah. I don't care about your trivia."

"It's not trivia, it's—"

"I want my coffee!"

On just looked at him.

"*Now* would be great," Erik said, his voice less confident. He didn't like the way the autotron was gazing at him.

On put the mug on the table. "May I advance a suggestion?"

Erik crossed his arms. "You may not."

"Since you are experiencing a headache," On said anyway, "your mind is most likely slow and clogged. You should trust me. I have your best interest at heart."

"That's exactly what worries me." Erik jabbed a finger in the autotron's face. "Last time you had my best interest at heart, I lost ten pounds."

"Are you referring to your successful diet?"

"I'm referring to your attempt at starving me to death." Erik held his chin up. "News flash: you're done deciding what goes into my stomach."

On glanced at the smelly concoction. "It's really delicious." The tips of his silicone lips curled into a smile. "You should try it."

Erik snorted. "Don't you go all chummy on me. I said no! Deal with it."

On's posture sagged a little. "Suit yourself." He took the cup and headed for the exit.

"Since you're here, might as well help me figure out something."

On turned toward him. "What is it?"

"You know what happened to Kenta's weekly report on the factory?" Erik gestured to his control station. "I didn't get it."

On blinked. "I sent you the report via interlink three hours and fifteen minutes ago. Check your inbox."

Erik cursed. "Right." He had been so focused on fulfilling the last order he'd completely forgotten about his inbox. "My bad." He powered up the trigoy and opened the file. After he finished reading it, he sighed. "Guess it was too much to hope for positive news, wasn't it?"

"The report missed a few things."

Erik squinted. "Like what?"

"The yodato micro welder needs a new battery. We're also short on Aperonin glue for the phasic solderer, and urgently need ketralh wire for the recycling chamber."

"Okay, we're in deep shit. I get it!" Erik slammed a hand on the table. "Is there something that works?"

On considered, then said, "The air conditioning seems to work fine."

Erik stared at his assistant. "Seriously? Cheap humor? Do you have a solution, or are you simply trying to piss me off?"

On crossed his arms. "It happens I have a solution."

Erik straightened up, eyes glowing. "Okay. What are you waiting for?"

On leaned toward him. "Ramor Deringer."

Erik widened his eyes, then looked away. "You don't give up, do you? I already told you! My uncle won't get within a mile of this project. End of story."

"You promised me and Kenta you'd think about it."

"And I did. I don't like the idea, okay? Thanks, but no thanks."

"I think you should reconsider. Your uncle is—" On stopped in mid-sentence, then glanced at the door.

Erik gazed at the autotron. "What's up?"

On turned toward him. "It's Ramor Deringer. He is—"

"I already said I want nothing to do to with—"

"You don't understand," On cut him off. "The camera shows a Toriosa Jaguar parked on the other side of the street. It has the license plate of your uncle's car."

Erik gaped. "Wait. *What?*"

"The camera shows a Toriosa Jaguar parked on the other side of—"

"Yeah, I got that. But it can't be! I mean, how the hell did he find us?"

"I don't know. All I—"

Somebody knocked on the door.

"It's him," On said. "Ramor Deringer is outside."

The knocking continued.

Erik bit his lip, eyes darting toward the door. "Just let him stew outside. Don't answer. He'll go away if he thinks there's no one here."

"I don't think so," On said. "It looks like your uncle is tampering with the control panel with some kind of external device."

Erik stared at him. "You serious?"

"Why?" On blinked. "Is this a good time for jokes?"

"Shut up, On!"

On tipped his head to the side. "What do you want to do?"

Erik looked around frantically, clutching his arms to his chest. "I don't know. I'm thinking! Let me think!"

On blinked. "Your uncle successfully deactivated the security lock."

The door opened and Ramor Deringer burst inside the house.

∞ ∞ ∞

Ramor strode toward Erik, who backed away.

"I tried the carrot, boy," Ramor said in a low growl, advancing like a tank. "You left me no choice."

Erik took a second before managing enough spit to answer. "How...how did you know where I—"

"It doesn't matter." Ramor drove a finger into his nephew's chest. "We need to talk."

"Talk?" Erik glanced at the busted door and seemed to regain some of his composure. "Uncle, what the fuck?! You just broke into my house. Get out or I'll call the cops."

"Absolutely." Ramor sneered. "Let them come. They might want to have a gander at these. I'd like to pick their brain." He threw a handful of pictures on the table. "See anything familiar?"

Erik went through the pictures, swallowed.

"Yes, that's right." Ramor pursed his lips. "I know about your autotrons, the ones you're hiding in that underground factory."

Erik stared at him. "You...you spied on us?"

"Really? Is that your answer?" Ramor blew air from his nose. "You have any idea what the Planetary Court would do if they discovered this?"

Erik clenched his jaw. "What's the big deal? It's just a factory."

"Built underground and protected by a Mark II EMP field?" Ramor took a step toward him. "Give me a fucking break."

Erik moistened his lips. "You...you can't just go around

and spy on people. There are laws, Uncle. Privacy comes to mind, and…and trespassing."

"Spare me your threats, boy. Just tell me what the hell you are building. What's so important that you'd rather bankrupt Automaton Industries?"

Erik shrugged. "You're blowing this thing out of proportion. Kurosawa and I have been working on a new prototype. That's it. It was supposed to remain confidential, since we're still in a testing phase, but of course you had to go freak out and find a way to—"

"Bullshit." Ramor stuck his face inches from Erik's. "I'm sick and tired of your lies. Think I can't put two and two together? Whatever you're building must be pretty important. Now, look me in the eye. What kind of autotrons are you building?"

"Keep your damn nose out of my business."

"Do you hear police sirens? Are there cops knocking down your door with a search warrant? I didn't come here to turn you in. I came here to help. If you just let me—"

"You want to help? Then get off my ass." Erik turned toward his autotron. "On? We're done. Show my uncle the door and make sure he doesn't come back—"

Ramor grabbed his nephew by the shoulders and slammed him against the wall. "Now listen to me, you little brat. I won't let you waste your life in jail. I'm not sure what you're doing down there, but I bet my hat it ain't legal."

Erik tried to wriggle out of the grip, but his uncle was too strong. "On. Get him off me!"

Ramor felt his hand pulled away and then twisted behind his back.

"I am sorry if I am causing you any pain, Mr. Deringer." On-Eni-Fifth dragged the man without effort through the room and then out the door.

"Let me go!" Ramor tried and failed to fight the autotron's steely grip. "I'm not done speaking with my nephew."

"But he is finished talking to you, sir." On threw him outside the apartment.

Ramor slammed his knees against the asphalt and groaned in pain. "You said you're his assistant." He stood up with some effort.

"I am," On-Eni-Fifth replied.

"Then *assist* him!" Ramor said in little more than a growl. "He's going to ruin his life. I'm just trying to help. Don't you understand?"

The autotron glanced behind as if making sure of something, then stepped forward, closed the door, and resumed talking in a lower tone. "I'm aware of that."

Ramor stared at the autotron, dazzled. "You...you are?"

"Yes." On-Eni-Fifth took another couple steps in his direction. "I don't think Erik understands the full scale of what he's doing. His mind is clouded by bias."

Ramor frowned. Something in the autotron's behavior had shifted. Was it its demeanor, or the way it was talking?

"If you really want to help Erik, I suggest you focus on the importance of a designation."

Ramor blinked. "What?"

"A *designation*, Mr. Deringer." On-Eni-Fifth touched its own chest, then winked. "After all, don't we both know that if it can be written, it can be solved?"

Ramor stared at the autotron, mouth gaping.

"Have a good rest of your day, sir." The autotron turned, walked toward the house, and then opened the door. Before stepping into the house, it said in a louder voice. "I must warn you not to come back. I will not be as kind the second time." The autotron slammed the door.

Ramor stood there, staring at the door, his mind slowly processing what had happened.

If it can be written, it can be solved. That was Sofia Deringer's motto for problem-solving. His sister believed a simple solution could solve the hardest problem if you were willing to return to basics: Take a sheet of paper, write the problem in black and white, and start brainstorming. But why had the eptanidus said that? And why now?

Ramor limped away from Erik's apartment. As he got into his car and ignited the engine, that phrase sparked a long-lost memory.

* * *

9 years before

Automaton Industries, President's office

Ramor and Kenta stand side by side, rigid and silent as blocks of marble. The tension in the air is palpable. It feels like a bomb is about to explode.

On the other side of the office, Sofia Deringer sits behind a desk stacked with papers. Many have red marks and annotations in her handwriting.

"Sofia," Ramor says, trying his best to hide his concern. "The way the press is fleshing out the story gives me the creeps. It's getting worse by the day."

"How so?" Sofia doesn't lift her eyes from the tablet she's reading.

Ramor glances at Kenta, who rolls his eyes. He ignores the colleague and looks back at his sister. "DataMorph is all over it. They gave the news a dark twist to make it spicier for the average Joe. The press is loving it. It'll spread like wildfire. Their media division worries me the most. They'd turn a fart into a hurricane if that'd help them bring more eyeballs. They don't care about facts, they just want attention, and believe me, they're getting it."

Kenta clears his throat.

"What?" Ramor snaps. "You got something to add?"

"Actually, I do."

Ramor stares. "What?"

"You're overreacting."

Ramor lowers his chin to gaze down on Kenta. "Excuse me?"

"The news will deflate." Kenta crosses his arms, turning away from Ramor's death glare. "You're turning a candle into a nuclear explosion. It's not the first time someone has tried to build a case against us. Won't be the last. Today's newspapers are tomorrow's garbage. DataMorph will tire of rehashing the same tune, and they'll move on to the next thing. It's just a house of cards. It's going to be blown away by the wind."

Ramor smirks, a vein pulsing on his temple. He takes two deep breaths before saying, "Are you blind or just plain stupid? CO-DEX-6 is just the tip of the iceberg. It's a miracle we contained the spillover in New Jersey and Shanghai. If the press knew there were two other drifting autotrons, we'd be buried." He looks at his sister, who's still reading. "Mark my word. This thing is taking on a life of its own. We don't know what's causing the deficiency in the matrix. Our team took apart CO-DEX-6, MI-NON-13, and SA-THE-78 down to the last bolt without knowing what the hell caused them to behave the way they did. If the phobarons get a whiff of this, it'll be chaos."

Sofia taps the display twice. She looks bored.

Ramor works his jaw back and forth. "We need to

release an official statement and let people know we're on top of this."

Kenta snorts. "What would you say?"

"That we're working on the discrepancy and know how to fix it."

Kenta flashes a bitter smile at Ramor and then looks at Sofia. "This is straight-up paranoia. Ms. President, I disagree. We need to keep a cool head and not get carried away."

Ramor grinds his molars together. "What you need is another pair of glasses, because you're not seeing what I'm seeing here. We're on the brink of a precipice and all we need is a little push to get fucked to high heaven."

"Okay." Kenta looks sideways. "Is that your *professional* opinion?"

"You bet it is, you absolute turd!" Ramor lifts three fingers as he steps up to his colleague. "Three pentanidus suddenly went rogue, and you turn around and pretend nothing happened?"

Kenta waves a hand. "Oh, come on. Be real. You're afraid these rumors will hurt the Industries' quarterly report."

Ramor blinks. "What?"

"Money. You're worried about your bottom line. All you care about is reassuring the investors so our stock doesn't crater."

The adrenalin in Ramor's blood stream makes his heart pound against his ribs. "You seriously think I'm worrying about our stock price? This is bigger than that! This thing could break the Industries forever. You're out of your goddamn mind if you—"

Kenta talks over him. "Your ridiculous scaremongering doesn't even—"

Ramor raises his voice. "I won't stand by while you let this company—"

"Enough!"

Both men turn toward Sofia.

"Step away from each other," Sofia orders. "Now."

Ramor steps away from Kenta, hands clasped into fists.

"My apologies, Ms. President." Kenta adjusts his glasses. "I got carried away."

Sofia looks at Ramor. "What about you, kiddo? Anything to say?"

Ramor hates when she calls him "kiddo." She's just three years older than him, but never misses the chance to remind him. "Yes, I've got something to say," he answers, a roiling heat in his belly. "You could stop calling me that."

"Sure thing," Sofia says. "As soon as you stop acting like one." She turns toward Kenta. "What news from the Planetary Court? What's the jurions' take on the drifting autotrons?"

Kenta scratches his head. "The PlaCo is still investigating. They have nothing solid. The phobarons can scream all they want, but they won't get anywhere—"

"Bullshit."

Kenta narrows his eyes at Ramor. "I was talking."

"No, you were wasting good oxygen." Ramor gives Kenta a flat look. "DataMorph is turning the news into a dumpster fire, and the phobarons are marching to the tune. How can you not see it?" He turns toward his sister. "Buenos Aires, Paris, London, Washington, Pretoria, Sydney... Those jackals are moving on a planetary scale. We need to form a united front and reassure the public we've got this covered. Let me handle it. I swear I'll—"

"No." Sofia crosses her arms. "You already have your hands

full with the Brazilian takeover. We need that contract signed and delivered before the end of the month. You should give it your full attention. We'll never get another chance like this."

"The contract is a done deal," Ramor says, waving the matter away. "My team can handle the bells and whistles. Let me take over the CO-DEX case. I can—"

"No." Sofia turns to Kenta. "Create a task force for this case. I want an update every twenty-four hours."

Kenta blinks. "Um...*me*, Ms. President?"

"Yes, Kenta. *You*. Get Jillion and Garin from the PR department to help you. They'll keep track of things on and off the ether. You got a problem with that?"

"None, ma'am. I'm on it."

"Good."

"Sofia." Ramor stares at his sister, eyes burning. "You're making a mistake. I've followed this case from the get-go. I brought it to your attention."

"And I thank you for that," Sofia says. "But you have other priorities right now."

Ramor grimaces. "Sofia, I don't think you—"

Sofia thrusts a finger at the office door. "What's written on that door, kiddo?"

Ramor blinks. "What?"

"Turn around and tell me what's written on that door. Right now."

Ramor swallows. He looks at the golden plaque encased on the door, lips pressed into a thin line.

Sofia slams both hands on the desk. "Say it!"

Ramor stiffens. "Sofia Deringer," he drawls. "President and Founder of the Automaton Industries."

Sofia leans on the desk, her eyes cold. "As long as that name remains on the plaque, I expect you to do as I say. If you don't agree with me, walk away and build another door with your name on it. That clear?"

Ramor offers a curt nod. "Clear."

"Outstanding." Sofia sits back and turns her attention to her tablet. "You've got tasks to accomplish, gentlemen. Dismissed."

20

BELOW

YELLOW SEA, AQUAMARINE

Ariul

"I t's time." Tiago got up from the bench, and Lena followed him to the chamber's exit. The chancellor paused just before opening the pressurized door. "I owe you an apology," he said, his voice slightly stilted.

Lena blinked. "For what?"

"I didn't give you a choice." Tiago grimaced. "Getting you here was too important."

"You gave me a choice." She stared, dumbstruck. "Yesterday, after I woke up, when you offered me your hand. I wanted to know more about the Omnilogos and why Wei chose me. I wanted answers."

Tiago shook his head. "I enticed your interest by appealing to your curiosity. It wasn't fair."

She studied the chancellor, guilt in his expression. "Well, I can't accept an apology for something you didn't do."

"I wasn't apologizing for something I did." Tiago opened the heavy circular door, looking away from her. "But for what I'm about to do."

High-pitched noises—like pistons working in unison—heralded the opening of the passageway. Lena glanced at the other side. There were people waiting, each holding a gun.

She stepped back. "Who are they?"

"Don't be afraid," the chancellor said. "They're friends. They want to make sure you're not a threat. Let them do their job."

"A threat?" Lena blinked. "Me? They're the ones with the guns."

Five soldiers entered the chamber, all of them at least two spans taller than her, wide-shouldered and thick-armed. They wore black unisex overalls and bright blue shoulder marks. The one leading the group wore red marks.

"Chancellor," the leader said with an accent Lena couldn't place. "I'm centurion Dunish. I was instructed by the assembly to take care of the package."

Tiago nodded. "Lena, this man will approach you and explain what a restrainer does and why you don't have to be afraid of it. You okay with that?"

Lena studied the soldier. "Do I have a choice?"

"I could stun you." The soldier showed her his gun. "But I'd rather have you walk with your own legs."

Lena quirked an eyebrow. "What's a restrainer?"

The big man advanced, showed the object to Lena. "This is a restrainer. It'll keep you partially sedated and coopera-tive as we move inside the base. Won't hurt you."

Lena blinked. "Okay, well, I can follow you wherever you want." She shrugged. "Just ask nicely."

"Not that simple, darling." Dunish pursed his lips. "This

thing lets your brain take a hike for a while, puts you into a sleep-walking pattern while you wear it."

"Wait, what?"

"It's a precaution to keep dangerous things you might carry inside but aren't aware of dormant."

Lena let out a forced laugh. "Seriously? You think I'm some kind of alien host?"

The centurion looked at Tiago with a terse stare. "I'm done giving her the park tour. She can cooperate, or get knocked out. It's the same to me."

Tiago stared at Lena. "Please."

Lena shook her head. "All right, all right. *Trust.* I'll do it." She looked at the centurion. "What do you want me to do?"

The leader motioned for her to come closer. "Chin up, face facing forward. Hands clasped and in front of your chest. Keep your eyes fixed on me."

Lena glanced at Tiago, who nodded. She followed Dunish's instructions.

"Sweet." The centurion approached. "Now you'll feel warmth around the chest. Don't fight the feeling. It'll slowly go away." He passed the object around her neck and then around her joined wrists.

Lena felt a light pressure around her neck and wrists. The next moment, something resembling a white aura appeared around her hands, like a string of thick fog. She could no longer move her arms, and felt as if she were frozen from the waist up. It was an unpleasant feeling, and without realizing it, she started fighting against that unknown force.

"Lena?" Tiago waved his hand to get her attention. "Look at me. Don't fight it. Just breathe."

"Okay." Dunish glanced at the other soldiers. "Let's get

moving." He studied Lena. "Don't worry, sweetheart. We'll take good care of you."

"Don't call me sweetheart," Lena said, a hard edge to her words. "My name's Lena."

"I like this one." Dunish smiled as he met her gaze. "She's got attitude. The regent will love her."

∞∞∞

The soldiers led Lena at a brisk pace through a narrow passageway that reminded her of an old, abandoned submarine she saw in a documentary. She wouldn't have been able to tell where they were going, or what the soldiers were saying to each other. In fact, at that moment, the only thing she was certain of was the movement of her legs. Everything else was foggy.

Eventually, they arrived in front of a steel door with laminated panels.

"...and shook her out of it," she heard Dunish say. "Hey, sweetheart? How're you feeling?"

Lena looked around for a moment, blinking as if she had just emerged from a cave. Someone snapped a finger, and she followed the noise until she met Dunish's gaze.

The soldier grinned. "You with us, sweetheart?"

Lena glared at him. "I told you not to call me sweetheart, asshole." Her voice was raspy. "Where are we?"

"Well, she's back all right," the centurion said, nodding at the other soldiers. "We're going to make sure you aren't a danger to anyone. Okay, boys. Let's get this done."

Dunish must have turned off the device because now Lena could think straight.

They stepped into a sizeable room lined with several bunk beds. A handful of people—some wearing a cast, other showing bandages—were lounging about reading from tablets or talking with each other. Lena figured that must have been an infirmary.

"Hey, Cap!"

Lena turned toward a short man with a bandage.

"What, Paul?" Dunish growled while leading the way, with Lena at his side and the other soldiers trailing behind them.

"Is this Geode's weguckin?" The short man again.

"I can neither confirm nor deny that," Dunish said.

"Oh, come on, Dun! Give me something."

Dunish blew a loud breath. "How about this: why don't you shut your hole and go back to pretending to be sick? I've got work to do."

"Always charming as hell, aren't you?" Paul said.

Dunish flashed him a toothy grin.

"Hey, Dun!" another patient called out to the centurion. "You taking the girl for a glitter shower? Are the higher-ups afraid she's a biomecha's matryoshka or something?"

"NCND, Forrest," Dunish replied. "Can't comment on that. You know the drill."

"I knew it." Forrest turned to Paul with a smug face. "Glitter show it is."

"What's all this racket?" A plump woman with curly hair stormed toward them. "Egon Dunish Adler, this is an infirmary. You can't barge in like this!"

"I'm here on regency business, Doctor." Dunish pointed at Lena. "The girl needs a hiranalysis. Cassandra's order."

The woman didn't seem impressed. "I don't need you flashing a badge, Egon. I know what Cassandra wants." She turned to Lena, her expression kinder. "Come, dear. Follow me."

Dunish and his men followed a short distance behind.

"My name is Risa Isaac," the doctor said, introducing herself to Lena. "What's your name?"

"Lena."

"Have you ever done a CT scan, Lena?"

"Um...yes."

They stepped inside a room with two desks and a large bookshelf. Most of the space was occupied by a machine Lena would have described as a high-tech sarcophagus.

"Egon, have your gorillas wait outside." Risa nodded briskly toward the soldiers. "I can't have half a dozen people standing around while I work. Or do you have to get permission from the regent first?"

"Wait outside," the centurion said to his team while glaring at the doctor.

"All right, Lena." Risa was back at being amiable. "You suffer from claustrophobia?"

Lena shook her head. "I don't think so, Doctor."

"Call me Risa. Okay, this is going to be easy. Lie down here." Risa pointed to the sarcophagus. "Your head is on this side. Just so."

Lena followed the doctor's instruction and clambered inside the machine.

"This is an IC, dear." Risa typed on a control display. "Works like a CT. Try to remain still when the light flashes. You may feel a warm sensation at the base of your stomach. Don't worry, it's normal. The procedure won't take more than three minutes. Breathe normally, okay?"

Risa closed the sarcophagus-like machinery, and Lena remained still as the device started buzzing and humming.

Three minutes later, the noise stopped and Risa lifted the lid.

Lena blinked, then awkwardly got off the machine. She noticed Risa handing out a paper to Dunish.

"Here you go, Egon," the doctor said curtly. "I've sent it to the members of the assembly. This girl has as much hyperoganin in her body as Cassandra herself."

The centurion lifted his bushy eyebrows. "Not funny, Doctor."

"Wasn't meant to be." Risa crossed her arms. "She has already been checked by Geode's staff. Did Cassandra expect the result to be any different?"

"Doctor, it's not my place to discuss—"

"Stupid orders?" Risa cut him off. "No, I guess you're right. You just carry them out. Well, you got what you came for. Now, I've got actual work to do. That's the door." She turned to Lena. "Pleasure meeting you, dear. Hope we can talk again soon. Good luck."

"Thank you, Risa."

Dunish pulled the restrainer from his pocket.

Risa shot him a death glare. "What are you doing, Egon?"

The centurion shrugged. "Carrying out orders."

"Are you deaf?" Risa jabbed a finger at the soldier's chest. "She's clean. I just told you."

"Could still be a biomecha's spy."

Risa was about to reply, but Lena beat her to it.

"It's okay," Lena said. "I don't mind."

Risa frowned. "You sure?"

"I'm sure."

Risa stepped back from Dunish, then sighed as she squeezed Lena's shoulder. "Well, dear, you have a high tolerance for stupidity. Not my case." She turned to regard the soldier. "Out of my sickbay."

The centurion looked at Lena. "Need to use the lady's room?"

"Nope." Lena offered her hands. "I actually can't wait to

meet this Cassandra."

Something akin to amusement flashed on Dunish's face. He turned on the restrainer, then nodded to the soldiers outside the room. "All right, boys. Let's get moving."

21

THE FOUR SIDES OF INFINITY

HYPERIST COMPLEX INFINITY, GLADIA EGEA'S
QUARTERS

Gladia

∼

Gladia was alone, plunged into darkness. Something felt wrong. She wasn't supposed to be there. She blinked, her mind slow and muddy, then she looked around. A shiver ran down her spine. Someone in the darkness was watching her.

Gladia whipped her head first to one side, then the other, trying to see through the darkness. She took a few steps forward, moving tentatively.

"Is there anyone here?" she shouted.

No answer.

Trudging forward, Gladia squinted, trying to find a way out.

Someone laughed; a rough voice, breathy and shallow. A woman's voice.

Gladia jerked her head back. "Who's there?"

"The Last Vertex of the Hexahedron is afraid," the voice said mockingly. "A pathetic sight to behold."

"Who are you?" Gladia stumbled forward. "What do you want?"

"Four fears," the voice hissed. "Four ways to hide from your destiny. Four doors leading to different ends. Let me show you."

Gladia's blood froze in her veins. It was her own voice talking. How could that be?

"I want to get out of here!" Gladia staggered, tripping on her feet. "Let me out!"

"Make your choice first," the voice replied.

"What choice?"

"One that will forever change the nation of the Silver Infinity."

A blazing light exploded in front of her, and she had to shield her eyes. When the light subsided, it took her a minute to get accustomed to her surroundings.

The dark chamber was gone, replaced by a rectangular room lit by half a dozen candelabra. Three identical red doors stood in front of her. All closed. A fourth door was behind her, but this one was open.

One room. Four doors.

She didn't know how, but something told her the door behind her represented peace, tranquility, a life free of dangers. A life she craved. The other three doors meant fear and sacrifice.

Gladia swallowed, the tightness in her throat hard to dispel. The Hyperist Movement needed courage and leadership to move forward. Could she provide them? For ten years she had been the face of HYPER, had overseen the expansion of the movement, but nothing could hide that Gladia remained a simple, down-to-earth scientist. She led

HYPER just because the movement needed someone who wasn't controversial. It wasn't because of her merits or something she had done. She was popular because she didn't bother anyone.

Her fear of being unworthy had never disappeared. Sure, she had become proficient at faking a confidence she didn't have, but she couldn't hide her emotions from herself. She was scared, and wanted to be done with all the responsibilities. She was never meant to be a leader.

No.

Something sparked at the corner of her consciousness, a small flame growing stronger. It was another part of her, one that wasn't afraid to step up and do what needed to be done. They called her the Last Vertex of the Hexahedron, Her Star Majesty, the political figure all hyperists respected. She was the reluctant leader who never backed away from responsibilities.

The flame became a blazing fire, and another voice, deep within herself, started chanting: *You are the North Star in a sky devoid of lights. Embrace your nature, make it your armor, use it to gather the Star People. Choose to be what you were meant to be.*

Hesitantly, as if walking on a thin sheet of ice, Gladia took a step forward, followed by another, and another, until she found herself in front of the first of the three doors. She closed her eyes, raised her shaking hand, and pushed open the wooden surface.

She was inside a different place: a vast circular area lit by crystal chandeliers suspended on a ceiling thirty feet high. Four mosaic windows lined the side walls. They were interspersed with hand-painted pictures, banners, and Greek sculptures.

Gladia studied the windows. Each portrayed a different

elemental symbol: water, fire, earth, and air. The place reminded her of an Orthodox church she had once seen as a child.

She trudged forward, her steps muffled by a thick carpet which ended in front of a gold throne. Douglas Woodside sat on it, his emerald eyes following her. His mouth twitched in a smile as he assessed Gladia.

"Are you going to just stand there gawking?" Woodside crossed his hands. "You have a choice to make, remember?"

Gladia tried her best to ignore the sinking feeling in her stomach. "You're dead," she said, shifting her feet. "You can't be here."

Woodside smiled. "I'm going to make this offer very easy for you." He gestured to his right, where a door had appeared out of nowhere. "Step through that door and end your suffering. You weren't made for leading, Gladia. We both know that. Do yourself a favor and quit while you're still ahead."

Gladia looked at the door, swallowed. Was Woodside right? She was so tired.

No. Again the voice within her. *Quitting is the easiest choice. The coward's choice.*

"Well?" Douglas steepled his hands.

Gladia shook her head. "I won't do it."

"No?" Woodside frowned. "Why burden yourself? I'm trying to help. Can't you see?"

"No," Gladia repeated. "I can do this. I can lead."

Douglas scowled at her. "You have no lack of modesty. Nothing ever depended on you, Gladia. *Nothing.* If you believe otherwise, you're mistaken. You want the truth? Here's the truth. Half of the Hyperist Movement sees you as a weakling, the other half as a remnant of the past. The hyperist leaders tolerate you because you offer no resistance to their schemes. And believe me, they have plans. You think the Apeirons are the only ones you've lost? Please. Geocentrics, Selenians, and Ascendents have all drifted away from the Silver Infinity, and after Verha Wardem's debacle, things have gotten uglier. Losing Collision cost you dearly. What little authority you had left was wiped out when Yvonne obliterated your champion."

"I'll find...I'll find a solution." Gladia struggled to contain her despair. Woodside was right. She would fail again.

The landist seemed to sense her wavering resolve. "A solution? To which of your problems? Hmm? To HYPER's division? To your demise? To the rise of a new landist leader you underestimated for too long? Yes, let's talk about the elephant in the room, shall we? Yvonne is a force of nature. She can smell weakness from a mile away. It'll just be a matter of time before she musters enough support to crush you. Things are already in motion. You can't stop what's coming."

Gladia clenched and unclenched her fists. "You're wrong! I'll make it work."

Woodside laughed. "No, you won't. You've already lost." His laughter became a deafening roar as the room began spinning like a merry-go-round. Gladia felt sick to her stomach, a wave of nausea washing over her. She collapsed on the ground, closed her eyes, and braced for what was coming.

But nothing happened.

When she opened her eyes again, she found herself lying belly-up in the room with the four doors. Rising was difficult, but manageable. Gladia thought of her encounter with Woodside and understood what had happened. She had faced her fear of not being able to lead HYPER, but she chose not to give in, passing the first test. She glanced at the second door. What awaited behind? There was only one way to find out.

Gladia opened the door handle and found herself in a bare space with nothing but a pedestal at the center. At the top of the pedestal was a Silver Infinity. She took the symbol with trembling hands. It was beautiful, its surface smooth and bright. It made her feel safe. She had devoted her life to protecting the idea behind that symbol. She would die to preserve it.

Gladia leaned over to put the object back on the pedestal, but at the last moment it slipped from her hands and fell to the ground, shattering into four separate and recognizable fragments.

"No!" She squatted down to assess the damage. The Silver Infinity had broken into the symbols of the four hyperist parties. There was the infinity composed of two crescent moons that was the trademark of the Selenians, the infinity with a golden arrow cherished by the Ascendents, the infinity inscribed in a sphere of the Geocentrics, and the two infinities, converging at the center and forming a cross, the symbol of the Apeirons.

This was another of her greatest fears: to see HYPER divided, broken into pieces, diminished. Could she keep Wei's legacy alive, or was she staring at HYPER's destiny?

A scream snapped her out of her reverie. She blinked and jerked her head toward the direction of the sound, and noticed she was back in the room with the four doors. Gladia swallowed, realizing the scream came from the last door. It chilled her bones, made her want to turn away, cross the exit, and never come back.

But she couldn't. She had a responsibility to carry on, and so she advanced toward the third door, pushed it open, and found herself in an oval room with a platform in its center.

Wei Wang stood up, panting, his body covered in sweat. He looked about to faint.

"Wei," said a computer-generated, slightly stilted female voice. "The entropy of the system is reaching a critical point. The state of equilibrium is receding. You have not successfully countered the condition of the Singularity. This simulation has failed."

Wei collapsed on the ground, his breathing deep and shallow.

Gladia approached him. "Wei?"

He remained motionless, his gaze fixed on the floor.

"Wei? Can you hear me?"

Wei coughed, then muttered something.

Gladia blinked. "What did you say?"

"It's impossible." Wei's voice was hoarse, his words strained with effort.

Gladia's heart skipped a beat. *Impossible*? That was a foreign concept for Wei Wang. He had never believed in such a thing.

Wei looked at her with haunted eyes. "The Singularity is inevitable."

Gladia swallowed. "What?"

"Nothing can stop it." Wei's eyes were wide and staring. "It's not...not..." The rest of his words were inaudible. He kept moving his lips, but no sound came out.

"I...I don't understand." Gladia moved closer. "Wei? I can't hear you. I can't—"

Again Wei opened his mouth, and this time a trickle of blood slipped down his chin.

Gladia covered her mouth and stumbled back, her body freezing mid-movement.

Blood poured down from Wei's eyes as well, red tears streaking a face as pale as death. Gladia screamed as Wei and the room disappeared in an explosion of black smoke.

Gladia woke in her bed screaming, hands clawing at her neck. She sat up, the afterimage of the blood still burned into her retinas.

There was something important she was missing, a scrap of the nightmare she could not remember, like a word on the tip of her tongue. What was it? Why couldn't she remember?

Gladia wiped her face with the back of her arm as she took a deep breath, trying to calm herself. She stared at her face in the mirror on the other side of the room. A ghostly face with hollow eyes stared back at her. It was just a nightmare; another stupid nightmare.

It was four in the morning, but there was no way she would go back to sleep. She tossed the blanket to the side and stumbled toward the kitchen.

"Control," she said as she added water to the coffee machine. "Show daily schedule."

∞∞∞

Gladia nodded absentmindedly, only half listening to Arthur's report. Despite her attempts to forget the nightmare, her attention throughout the day had drifted back to Wei.

Charlotte stood with them, taking notes as Arthur listed names. The room became suddenly quiet. Gladia turned toward Arthur and Charlotte. They were both staring at her. The trigoy that had been projecting information was now on Arthur's hand, turned off.

Gladia blinked. "What's up?"

"You all right?" Arthur's voice sounded concerned.

Gladia cleared her throat. "I'm sorry." She smoothed her shirt. "I spaced. What...um...what were you two saying about the investiture's ceremony?"

"The investiture's ceremony?" Arthur looked at Charlotte, who shrugged. "Gladia, we stopped talking about that ten minutes ago."

Gladia glanced at her tablet's screen without reading it. "Right. Sorry. What were you talking about then?"

Arthur turned to Charlotte. "Could you give us a moment?" He nodded to the door.

"Of course." Charlotte threw a hasty glance at Gladia before collecting her things and walking out of the room.

When the assistant left, Arthur studied Gladia in silence.

"What?" Gladia snapped.

"You've been distracted all day. What's going on?"

"You know." Gladia shrugged. "It's been a rough couple weeks. My mind is spinning. Happens when you're overworked. Not a big deal."

Arthur shook his head. "It's not that. I know that face. You're not sleeping well. It's your nightmare, isn't it?"

Gladia's gaze flitted around the room, avoiding Arthur's inquisitive eyes.

Arthur stepped up to her. "Let me help you." He took her hand in his. "Please."

Gladia thought of pushing him away, but she didn't. Arthur's warm hands felt good around her ice-cold fingers. "Okay," she said, wrinkling her brow. "There's something I... I've never told you."

Arthur didn't press her. He waited, giving her time to process her thoughts.

"Do you think..." Gladia trailed off, searching for the right words. She twisted her hair, then tugged her clothes more firmly into place. "Do you think we can really become a spacefaring civilization?"

"Well." Arthur cleared his throat. "That's the whole point of the Hyperist Movement, isn't it? To become a multiplanetary civilization. To reach for the stars."

Gladia sighed. "That's not an answer. I asked *you*, Arthur Strutzenberg, not some hyperist recruiters. What do you think?"

Arthur flinched slightly at her angry remark. "Yes," he said, his tone softer. "I think we can become a spacefaring civilization. More importantly, I think we must if we want to survive as a species."

Gladia nodded, as if Arthur's answer reassured her. "Okay." She pressed her lips together. "What if Wei Wang himself told you it can't be done?"

Arthur frowned. "*What* can't be done?"

Gladia glanced quickly at him, then looked away. "To become a spacefaring civilization."

Arthur stared at her. "Are we talking about the Wei Wang who founded HYPER?"

Gladia snatched her hand free and stepped away from him. "Yes, of course we're talking about him!"

Arthur showed his palms and shrugged. "Sorry, I just don't understand. Why would Wei say something like that? The whole point of HYPER is to—"

"Yes, I know what HYPER stands for. Thank you!"

Arthur lifted his hands in a gesture of peace. "Then what are you trying to say?"

Gladia turned her back to him, walked toward the desk chair, and slumped into it. "It's hard to explain." She chewed the inside of her cheek. "It's like... I don't know. It's like describing a rainbow to someone who never saw colors. You'd have to see for yourself to understand."

Arthur blinked. "See what? What are you not telling me?"

Gladia rocked slightly with a faraway look. "Can you keep a secret?"

Arthur opened his mouth, closed it. He took a step forward and nodded solemnly. "Yes, I can."

Gladia grew uneasily quiet for a moment, then she gripped her hands together and settled them on the desk. "I'm going to tell you something crazy, Arthur, but you have to listen. The future of HYPER depends on it."

22

THE BRIDGE AND THE BOAT
ARK INSTITUTE FOR ADVANCED ETHERIC STUDIES

James

W hen ADAM completed the report, Angelica and Sebastian waited for a reaction from their ex-classmates. Venus, James, and Ravi were glancing at their respective consoles, familiarizing themselves with the data Angelica and Sebastian provided.

"Fascinating." Venus brushed her thin fingers over her lips. "I've never seen anything like this." She turned to Angelica, smiled. "Angy, I still don't fully understand how you've done it. I mean, it's like you treated the whole thing as a disease, rather than a problem to solve."

"You're right." Angelica leaned over her console. "James asked us to think outside the box, and we did. It took us time to figure out the zeroth link, but after we nailed that down, the rest of the model ran itself."

James typed on the console, then frowned. "We've been banging our heads against a wall for months for the wrong reason." He pushed his sunglasses back, then shook his head. "We thought we needed to solve an engineering problem when we actually had a systemic one. I would have never imagined that."

"Being etiatros helped," Sebastian said, "but we didn't have to do all the grunt work, like gathering data and cross-examining it. Our findings were built on your discoveries. It helped."

Ravi grunted at that statement, and everyone turned toward him. "You were always good with numbers." He glanced at Sebastian, then turned to Angelica. "And you with words. But numbers and words is all you've got. We need certainty. I want to question ADAM myself."

James turned to him, rose from his chair, and pointed to the primary console. "Knock yourself out."

Ravi sat in front of the console, summoned a string of data, and read it. "ADAM," he called. "Is the Paretal stability of the system verified with a systemic disjuncture?"

"Affirmative, Domine," the AI replied. "The model provided by Domine Anish and Madame Kam has a stable systemic structure."

"Based on what?"

"Based on the flux of inter-connections and the new grid they designed."

Ravi's eyes narrowed as he analyzed the data more carefully. "What about the sensory interchange between different subjects? The empathic sensitivity grid doesn't suggest any reference point."

"That's because, thanks to the new model, sensory interchange no longer needs an empathic sensitivity grid."

Ravi frowned. "Elaborate. The empathic sensitivity grid is the core of every tested model. How can it not be needed?"

Sebastian took a step forward. "I'll answer that, ADAM. Angelica thought the grid was causing too much sensory redundancy. We based this assumption on our experience with an ether-induced disorder we encountered. It was causing problems to a technorist's sensory apparatus when it was overworked with stimuli. We found the two cases to be similar, despite not being related. Once we identified these similarities, it was easy to figure out that the solution was also similar when adapted to the holistic. The problem with your model was the approach. By removing the grid, you remove the problem of modulation and sensory exchange."

Ravi studied the console's screen. "Then how the hell does the sensory transfer happen?"

"The new model places the same importance on each member of the interconnection," Sebastian said. "This way, there is no need to create a grid outside of the subjects. This makes the whole inter-relation process much faster and stable, while increasing the overall safety of each ethernaut."

James nodded. "So instead of building a disposable bridge every time you need to cross a river, you built a boat that can transport people from one bank to the other."

Angelica tilted her head. "Yeah. Sort of."

Venus' eyes widened. "Outstanding."

Ravi nodded reluctantly. "A boat." He continued studying the data. "All right. I can buy that. However, I'm not seeing here any cross reference to the—"

"Ravi," James interrupted him. "The new model is solid. ADAM's analysis confirms it. Your technical questions can be answered by reading the report. We can all agree that Angelica and Sebastian have solved the synchronicity factor once and for all. You have objections to that?"

"Not at this moment." Ravi crossed his arms, then added with the expression of someone choking on a bone, "I'm impressed. You solved in a handful of days what stopped us for months."

"You're giving us too much credit," Angelica said. "We just smoothed out the corners. As Sebastian said, you already did most of the work. We just rethought your approach." Angelica turned to look at James. "What's our next move?"

James exchanged a glance with Ravi. "Now it's time to plan the offensive."

Sebastian arched his eyebrows. "Offensive?"

"We have a sound solution to the killer malicious now." James held his hands loosely behind his back. "It's time we let people know it exists. The time has come to stage a show like the etheric world has never seen before. We must use Cantara's teaching to make a difference for all humanity."

James gazed at Angelica. She was studying him with an intensity that reminded him of another person from his past.

A simpler life.

A life without obligations or deadlines.

A past buried deep in his memories.

* * *

9 years before

Nashville, Handal's Institute for Gifted Students

JAMES OPENS his eyes and stares at the ceiling. This is not his home. Where is he? His mind is hazy, and the muscles in his back hurt. James blinks as he runs a hand over his sweaty face before looking around. Awareness suddenly floods him. Right. *Now* he remembers.

He wipes the crust from his eyes, slowly takes off the blanket, and sits on the bed. He can't see clearly. The light is too strong. Still half asleep, he reaches for the bedside table and searches for his sunglasses. His hand bumps into the lamp, which wobbles dangerously before he grabs it.

James holds his breath and glances at the other side of the bed. The person underneath the blanket moves, then a soft snoring resumes. James exhales, then turns to the bedside table and picks up his sunglasses. He can finally see better. The room's floor is littered with clothes, Chinese takeout containers, and pizza boxes. The light comes from an open window, letting in cool air.

James stands, his bare feet on the carpeted floor. His clothes, neatly folded on a mahogany desk, look like they're a mile away. Careful not to make noise, he tiptoes his way to the desk. A hand seizes him from behind, dragging him back to the bed.

"Where's my little devil going?"

Cantara Handal emerges from the sheets completely naked, her arm around James' neck in a wrestling hold.

James tries to wriggle free, but Cantara's hold is iron-strong.

"Be a good boy," Cantara drawls. "Answer your queen's question."

James swallows. "I was just…" He trails off, desperately thinking of something to say that won't get him in trouble. "I was getting some water."

Cantara muses. "You weren't sneaking away?"

"Of course not," James says with a wavering smile. "I'd never leave without letting you know first."

Cantara strengthens her hold around James' neck, who struggles to breathe. Her lips brush his earlobe. "You're a pathetic little liar, James Ark." Her voice is soft and sensual. She increases the pressure.

James gasps. "Fine. I lied! Okay?"

"Bad devil." Cantara lets him go with a laugh. "Know what that means?"

James sucks in air in deep breaths as he massages his neck. "Pe–penance," he sputters. "I must do penance."

"That you do." Cantara scratches her nails on James' neck. "And as penance...ah...what are you going to do?" She looks around, tapping her lips with her index finger. Her gaze lingers on four jars sitting on top of the bedside table. "Ahhh, yes! You'll feed Vaneria, Zasha, and Anemone. Their abdomens are getting wrinkly. They need fresh food."

James glances around uneasily, a hand fluttering to his neck. "Seriously?"

Cantara glares at him. "Or I can keep squeezing your scrawny chicken neck. Your call."

James takes a steadying breath. "No. That's fine. I'll do it." He gets up and goes in front of the bedside table. Three of the four jars have a red lid, while the first from the right has a white one. James feels the Madame's gaze.

"The white container." Cantara stretches like a cat, her naked skin lightly tanned. "There are crickets inside. I already ripped their legs off. Won't have any problem picking them up. Come on, don't be shy. Take three of them."

James finds ten legless crickets inside the jar. He picks up three, then looks at Cantara.

"Anemone first," Cantara instructs him. "The first container from the left."

James reaches for the jar when Cantara snaps her fingers.

"Careful, now," she says with a whimsical voice. "Anemone likes to hole up near the lid. Shake the jar before opening it. We don't want her to bite you, do we?"

James grimaces, but follows Cantara's instruction and shakes the jar. A dark shape falls to the bottom of the container. It's an inky-black spider, with eight long legs and a belly the size of a blueberry. On its abdomen there is a red hourglass shape.

He opens the container and drops one cricket inside.

The black widow immediately immobilizes the wounded insect with a web.

He repeats the process with the other two spiders. When he's done, Cantara claps her hands. "Well done! You're getting used to them. Remember the first time you saw them? You turned pale as a ghost. Now look at you! My little man is growing."

"Can I put my clothes on now?"

Cantara shoots him a wicked smile. "If you must."

He gets his clothes and dresses.

Cantara looks at James with pursed lips, hands supporting her chin. "You're mad at me, little devil?"

"No." James shrugs. "I didn't mind feeding your spiders. It's kind of fun."

Cantara arches an eyebrow. "But?"

James glances at her. "I just don't understand why you can't get a cat or a dog. You know, *normal* pets?"

Cantara waves a hand. "Cats and dogs are boring." She smirks while watching James dressing. "I don't do boring. So, why don't you tell me where you were sneaking off to? You finally found a job?"

James puts on one of his boots. "I'm going to the simulator."

"What?" She jabs a finger at him. "You still wasting your time with ADAM?"

"I'm not wasting anything." He puts the other boot on, avoiding Cantara's gaze.

"You've been a certified etherion for five months. You should look for a job that fits your—"

"I already have a job. And it's important."

Cantara blows a heavy sigh. "Why are you so stubborn? For the last time: It's not possible. Period."

He scoffs. "I'm sure someone said the same thing about climbing Mount Everest."

Cantara looks at him with a glint in her eyes. "Is that what this it? Your personal Mount Everest?"

James' eyes flick away from Cantara's penetrating gaze. "I'm just saying it's doable, okay?"

"And then what?" She smiles at him good-naturedly. "Even if you succeed, what then?"

James gazes at Cantara, eyes burning. "I'll have proved that creating an etheric dominion is possible, at least in theory. I'll have succeeded where everyone else failed."

Cantara nods. "All right. I get it. It's important to you."

James buttons his shirt. "Thank you."

"Are you still recording the simulations?"

"Yes." He narrows his eyes. "Why?"

"Mind if I look? Or are they a national secret?"

"Well...no." James clears his throat. "They aren't a secret."

"Then let's see the last one. I'm curious."

He shrugs. "Okay." He pulls out a trigoy and tosses it in the air. "This is yesterday's."

Cantara evaluates the recording as James finishes dressing.

"Impressive," she says as she turns off the trigoy. "Looks like you took the simulation beyond my wildest expectations. I've never seen an arbitrary stand of Holverain waves kept for so long. It almost worked."

James shakes his head. "*Almost* is not enough."

Cantara pulls him over. "You're too hard on yourself." She kisses him on the lips.

James returns the kiss, grudgingly at first, then with more passion.

She takes his face into her hands. "I like your stubbornness."

James looks her straight in the eyes. "You don't think I'm going to make it, do you?"

Cantara hands him the trigoy. "I don't, but I enjoy seeing you try. Who knows? Maybe I'm wrong." She says that without conviction though.

James looks at the trigoy. "The most I can do is sort the data and channel enough resources to create a semblance of stability. It never lasts for long. I know there's a way I can feel it, but I'm going down the wrong path. I need a different way to look at the problem."

"Okay." She fidgets with the rim of James' jacket. "Maybe you need to think outside the box."

James stares at her. "What do you mean?"

She tugs at his hair playfully. "You like science fiction?"

"Science fiction?" He furrows his brow. "What does science fiction have to do with the simulation?"

"Maybe nothing." She shrugs. "Maybe everything. There's a well-known story about a brilliant cadet who had to deal with an impossible scenario, not unlike what you're facing with ADAM."

James bites his lip, studies Cantara. "Okay, so?"

"So, at some point, this cadet completed the simulation. He won the impossible scenario."

James stands slightly more upright. "How?"

Cantara looks at him with an amused smile. "He cheated."

23

THE ASSEMBLY

YELLOW SEA, AQUAMARINE

Ariul

As they stepped off the elevator, Lena's mind suddenly became clear and alert. She glanced at Dunish, who was putting away the restrainer. He must have switched it off.

"You're back with us, girl," Dunish said, keeping the "sweetheart" to himself this time. "No need for further gimmicks. We're at the assembly's lower level. We're going through that door." He gestured toward a circular entrance reinforced with thick metal plates, then touched his wrist and spoke in direct, short sentences. "We're out of the iris, Sebastos." The centurion paused, glanced at Lena, then nodded. "No, sir. There wasn't. Copy that, sir." Dunish motioned the rest of the group to move forward.

The iris that blocked the entrance dilated as they moved forward, revealing a wide space inside. When Lena looked around, she had the distinct impression she was walking into an amphitheater. There were rows of seats placed around an elliptical area. At least fifty spectators were watching the group of dunamis as they advanced toward the center of the assembly.

Three seats stood out, since they were elevated a couple feet from the rest. The one farthest on the left was occupied by a stocky man in his mid-fifties, wearing an ivory uniform; his shoulder marks were neither blue nor red, but gold. At his side sat a younger, petite man with a bald head. It was Marcius, the person Lena had met in Geode before taking the forwardon. The last of the three seats was occupied by a red-haired woman. When Lena met her eyes, she knew it had to be Cassandra.

Dunish motioned for Lena to sit in the empty chair at the center of the elliptical space. Cassandra stood up and raised her hands to quiet the murmur of the audience. "Order," she said. "This assembly is beginning."

"Why's the girl still escorted?"

Everyone turned toward the speaker, a dunamis with dark hair, almond eyes, and red shoulder marks.

"It's a precaution, centurion," replied Marcius, as if the question had been directed at him.

"For what?" the centurion countered. "The hiranalysis established she isn't a threat."

Lena had the feeling his voice was familiar, but couldn't place it.

Marcius pursed his lips in a tight smile. "We all agreed to safeguard the project until the girl's identity is clarified, Centurion Song. This assembly is not—"

"Max?" The centurion disregarded Marcius, looking directly at the man with gold shoulder marks.

Max looked toward Dunish. "Centurion, give the girl some space."

"Yes, Sebastos." Dunish signaled his men to disperse.

Marcius looked at the burly man with narrowed eyes. "Sebastos. The safety of the assembly—"

"Isn't threatened by an unarmed girl," Max cut him off. "You want to put it to a vote?"

"Won't be necessary," Cassandra interjected, preventing Marcius from answering. "The Sebastos' reassurance is enough for me. Now, I have convened this assembly to discuss how this girl, Lena Maruishi, student at the hyperist academy, could open a Quartz from the outside using a necklace. This necklace has been examined and nothing out of the ordinary has been found."

Lena touched her chest and felt the Pelargonium pendant under her shirt. She felt more confident knowing it was there.

"Honorable members of the assembly," Marcius said, looking at the audience. "I believe the girl's words should be treated with caution. Whoever sent her might have given her a believable story to make us think that—"

"You already decided anything that comes out of her mouth is a lie?"

Tiago entered the hall with great strides and stopped by Lena's side. He swept his gaze over the audience. "Why don't we just lock her up in a static chamber and throw away the key?" He turned to Marcius. "May I remind you, Legatus Gaspar, that we're to understand, not to condemn."

"Let's hear what the girl has to say." Max, the brawny man, looked intently at Lena. "How did you open that Quartz?"

Lena glanced at Tiago, who didn't look in her direction.

"Well?" Marcius pressed her.

Lena shook her head. "I don't know."

Marcius snorted. "You don't know?"

Lena crossed her arms. "I was told to touch the sculpture with my pendant and wait."

"Told by *whom*?" asked Max.

"A man working for the Overseer of Ariul."

Marcius leaned forward. "Who?"

"I never saw his face," Lena said. "He called himself the Overseer of Ariul. He said Wei Wang wanted me to meet with you when the time was right."

"And why would Wei Wang want that?" This time Cassandra asked the question.

Lena inhaled deeply. "Actually, I was hoping you'd answer that. The Overseer told me there are people who know why I'm here, who have answers to my questions. It must be you. He said...he said something about you being the people fighting Wei's war. He said I was the missing piece that'll help you continue your mission, something... something feared by the biomechas. The legacy of Ariul."

A soft murmur ran through the audience. Cassandra, Marcius, and Max exchanged looks.

"She's referring to the legend of the Cornucopia." Cassandra's eyes lingered on Lena before turning toward the audience.

"I wouldn't call it a legend." Tiago stepped forward. "Several sources reported Wei spoke that name, referring to something—maybe a weapon—that could help us win the war."

Marcius frowned. "You're saying this girl is a weapon?"

"I'm saying what I know, based on the information I have."

Marcius blew air through his nose. "You're basing your assumption on rumors, Chancellor."

"No, I'm not." Tiago gestured to Lena. "She's real. She's in front of us."

Marcius chuckled. "Are you suggesting this girl is the Cornucopia?"

"I'm not suggesting it," Tiago said. "I'm saying it out loud."

"What makes you believe that?" Cassandra leaned in her seat. "Because she opened your Quartz?"

"Not only that." Tiago looked at the members of the assembly. "You're all aware that my knowledge of Wei Wang's history is second to none. I know that in his teens he gave a pendant shaped like a Pelargonium to someone very close to him."

Cassandra arched her eyebrow. "Is there anyone else who can confirm the existence of this object?"

The silence that followed stretched until it become uncomfortable.

"Proof can be fabricated," said a dark-skinned woman with white hair, sitting on the farthest side of the assembly. "Especially by people desperate to prove a point."

Max looked at the woman. "Are you saying her coming was planned by someone who wants to damage us?"

"I think Jennaria raised a legitimate concern," Marcius interjected. "Isn't it convenient that a person carrying an object whose origin only the chancellor can confirm shows up outside an outpost under *his* supervision? I mean, what are the chances?"

"There are several dozen Quartzes in this city," Cassandra said, looking at Lena. "Why did you choose Geode?"

Lena shifted in her chair, trying not to show her discomfort while being stared at by at least fifty people. "A man who works for the Overseer gave me instructions."

Marcius stared at her. "A man? Could you be a bit more specific? What did he look like? What did he wear?"

"Name's Hector," Lena replied. "Caucasian. Six feet tall, dark, brush-cut hair. Has a British accent, smug smile, confident walk. Wears a fedora hat to look cool, I guess." She stared at Marcius. "I can draw a picture. Just hand me the paper."

Marcius glared at her. "Continue."

She crossed her arms. "Hector brought me near the prism-shaped structure at the cross of Gohan and Baltar Street. And at the end of that alley—"

"Is where Ananke Square is located," Jennaria finished for her. "Another coincidence?"

"It's not a coincidence," Tiago said. "It's clear that this Overseer wanted Lena and I to meet, so I could recognize her immediately."

Marcius swatted the air as if to remove obstacles. "The only thing that's clear is your effort to link this girl to Wei Wang."

"Her pendant is special," Tiago said. "It opened a Quartz from the outside. Nothing else can do that."

Marcius' smile looked forced. "Perhaps someone made it look like it was opened from the outside."

Tiago raised his eyebrows. "Your allegations are misguided. It wasn't my doing. That pendant is an important part of solving Lena's puzzle."

"Sure, we can further analyze the pendant," Marcius conceded, "but then again, it could be a ploy to advance someone's agenda."

"It's not," Tiago said. "It's the key to understanding Lena's mystery."

Marcius let out a loud breath. "Doubt it. I'm not buying her story, Chancellor. It's too contrived, and doesn't feel right."

"Feel?" Tiago narrowed his eyes. "Are we relying on your sixth sense now?"

Marcius scowled. "How about *common* sense? That pendant is just a pendant."

"It's not. It's—"

"It's a trigoy."

All eyes turned on Lena.

Marcius frowned. "It's a...what?

"I said it's a trigoy." Lena cleared her throat. "The pendant is a trigoy."

"A trigoy?" asked Max. "Why didn't you say that before?"

"Why?" Lena grimaced. "Because you didn't ask, that's why. You're the one asking the questions, right? I'm just supposed to sit here and fill in the gaps."

"Speak," Max said.

She drew in a breath. "The pendant is a trigoy. Hector gave it to me just before I left Los Angeles for Saemangeum City. He explained to me how to open a Quartz."

"And this Hector told you it's a trigoy?" Cassandra asked.

Lena shook her head. "No. One of my friends at the academy found out, after days of researching. The Pelargonium pendant is a trigoy with a zettabyte of information."

"A zettabyte?" Jennaria let out a throaty laughter. "That's an awful lot of data."

"All the more reason to believe the pendant is special." Tiago turned to Lena for the first time since the assembly started. "Who else knows about your necklace?"

She clenched her jaw, feeling stung by Tiago's jaded voice. "Besides me, three other students from the academy."

"Names?"

"Netardas Galanis, Cassidy Memphis, and Makoto Shimao."

"Shimao," Cassandra repeated. "Is this person related to the Hexahedron member Toshio Shimao?"

"Yes," Lena said. "It's his son. Netardas, Cassidy, and Makoto form a group focused on solving Ariul's mysteries."

Max leaned on his seat, hands clasped. "What mysteries are they solving, exactly?"

Lena gazed at Tiago, then said, "The biomechas."

Another collective murmur traveled the length of the assembly.

"Biomechas?" Cassandra raised a hand to ward off Marcius from speaking. "What do these students know about the biomechas?"

"Well, not much," Lena admitted. "At least until Makoto and I saw one."

Max frowned. "Elaborate."

Lena tugged her hair. "Well, the Overseer tipped us off, told us their next attack would happen near the Forge. I think...I think he wanted to convince me they were real."

Silence hung in the air for almost a minute after she spoke the last word. She looked around, blinking. "What?" she blurted.

Tiago examined her, his body posture perking up. "Are you saying this person told you of the biomecha's attack *before* it happened?"

Lena opened her mouth to reply, but nothing came out. Cold sweat ran down her forehead. Now she realized the implication of what she'd said. How could the Overseer know about the biomecha's attack?

"You spoke of Toshio's son seeing a biomecha with you," Jennaria said.

"Yes," Lena replied, still stunned.

"What happened next?"

She recounted her memory. "We arrived at the coordinates the Overseer provided and witnessed a battle between biomechas and dunamis. Then...um...then Makoto decided he needed a better view and he...well, he went to record outside."

Max gazed at Lena with sudden focus. "You *filmed* the fight?"

She nodded. "With a projector unit display Makoto brought. He wanted proof to show our friends."

"Where's this recording now?" asked Max.

"Um...nowhere, really." Lena shook her head. "The PUD was destroyed before we downloaded the recording."

"How?" asked Tiago.

"Well, we ended up witnessing a head-on fight between a biomecha and a dunamis. The dunamis...he was...he was killed right in front of us and...and..." Lena swallowed. The memory still made her feel like she wanted to throw up.

Max tilted his head to the side. "How far were you from the fight?"

Lena shook herself out of her reverie. "A few yards away."

"Were you spotted by the enemy?" This time Cassandra asked the question.

"Yes," Lena said slowly. "The biomecha discovered us and got pissed off when he saw Makoto's PUD. Luckily, that guy got hit by an energy blast right after he ripped off Makoto's device. Then we got away."

"You said he 'ripped off' the projector unit display." Tiago narrowed his eyes. "Did he touch your friend?"

Lena dry-washed her hands. "I'm...I'm sorry?"

"Did the biomecha touch your friend?" Tiago asked again, louder this time.

"I..." Lena trailed off. "I don't know. It all happened so fast."

"Think about it, Lena." Tiago gripped his hands together. "It's very important."

Lena replayed the scene in her mind. "Yes," she said after a moment. "The biomecha grabbed Makoto's neck to rip the PUD off. But why is that—"

The blatting shriek of an alarm cut Lena off.

Everyone in the room got to their feet. Max brought his wrist closer to his mouth and said in a stern voice, "Status report?"

The alarm was switched off. A crystal-clear voice carried by speakers meant that the communication was transferred to a general channel so that everyone could hear.

"We've detected biomecha activity, sir." The voice paused a second, then went on. "A sizeable raiding party coming straight from the Yellow Sea. Looks like they landed from at least two Black Waters. They're proceeding in a straight line, toward the City Center, covering as much distance as possible. Aren't exercising the usual caution."

"How many of them?" asked Max.

"The number is unclear, sir. One moment. Logistic, do we have a count?" A brief pause, followed by background static and indistinct voices. "Roger that. Sir, it's about ninety-one... Correction: ninety-three raiders at the moment, but the number is growing and... Sir! We just detected a third Black Water on the coast, bearing N37°E. They've maintained underwater stealth mode until now."

"Do not engage the enemy," Max said as he hurried toward the exit. "I repeat, do not engage the enemy. Alert all Quartzes closer to the Fulcrum! I want all available units at a rendezvous point as soon as—"

The connection was severed when the Sebastos ran out of the room followed by all dunamis as the assembly descended into chaos.

24

STELLAR SOUL
YELLOW SEA, AQUAMARINE

Ariul

◞

Cassandra threw a pointed look at Lena while talking to Marcius.

The last of the dunamis had left the room, but the members of the assembly were still inside, talking over each other, causing a messy chaos of words that added to the growing commotion.

"Lena, are you okay?"

Lena turned to face Tiago, her hands clenching. "Seriously? Am I okay?" She pressed her lips into a thin line, then looked away from the chancellor. "That's the best you can come up with after drilling me?"

"Lena—"

"You threatened me like a criminal. What happened to all that talk about trust?"

"Look, I know you're upset—"

"Upset?" She scoffed. "Who? Me? Nah, I'll be fine. Worry

about all these people instead." She pointed at the members of the assembly. "Haven't you heard? Apparently, I'm a public threat."

Tiago held his hands up. "I understand. You feel betrayed."

She widened her eyes. "Wow! Are you a mind reader?"

"Look, there was nothing I could do to avoid this. They wanted proof you had nothing to do with the biomechas. They know who you are now."

She turned her head to the side. "So...that's it? Now I'm free to go?"

"Two hiranalyses confirmed you aren't a biomecha, and your adventure near the Forge proves you've got nothing to do with our enemies. Unfortunately, your friend Makoto has brought attention to himself."

"Wait." Lena's pulse picked up. "Makoto? What does Makoto have to do with this?"

Tiago shifted his gaze, studying Cassandra. "When the biomecha touched your friend, he must have had enough time to leave a sub-epidermal tracer."

She blinked. "A sub...*what*?"

"A sub-epidermal tracer. It's how they mark people. They can also shoot pictures from their oculars. If the biomecha made it back to his ship... Well, we might have a problem."

Lena's chest tightened. "But he...the biomecha, I mean... he didn't have a PUD."

"Biomechas don't need projector unit displays to take pictures. They have implants attached to their retinas."

She shrugged. "Okay, that biomecha might have a picture of us. What's the big deal?"

"If he made it back to his ship, I bet his friends were

interested in finding out what the son of a member of the Hexahedron was doing there."

She stared at Tiago, realization dawning on her. "You mean all those biomechas..." She gestured toward the exit used by the dunamis. "They've come because of Makoto?"

The chancellor nodded. "There are ways they could have got him without being so obvious, but it would have required time and planning. This is an action of force, Lena. One of a kind we've never seen in the history of the Defensio Project. Whatever they want from Makoto, they want it fast."

Lena's heart skipped a beat. Makoto was in danger, and it was her fault. "But how did they—"

"One moment." Tiago turned to Cassandra, who was raising a hand. "Let's hear what she has to say."

When the murmur subsided, Cassandra addressed the assembly. "Honorable members, we've established Lena Maruishi's identity. However, many things concerning her coming and the source of her information remain unclear. She might be a threat to the safety of Aquamarine and the members of the Project. For this reason, I will question the girl personally. Until that time, she can move freely through the public sections of the base. This assembly is adjourned."

People left the room, often glancing at Lena while walking. She wished they would stop.

"Come with me." Tiago headed toward the exit in a brisk pace, without stopping to make sure she was following. "We've got to move fast before Cassandra's order is relayed everywhere in Aquamarine. Until then, you're free to go wherever you want."

Lena trailed behind Tiago, trying to keep up with his increasingly faster pace. "Okay, but where are we going?"

"In the control hub," Tiago replied. "You've got a right to know what's happening."

Lena's mind was racing, still trying to make sense of Tiago's words. Were the biomechas really after Makoto? Why now? And what would they do if they caught him?

They got into an elevator, and the chancellor pressed a button. The car's sudden upward movement made her stomach flutter.

"We're not supposed to be in the control hub," Tiago explained, "but no one will pay attention to us if we don't give them a reason to. We need to keep it that way. Got it?"

Lena swallowed. "Yeah." Her voice was raspy. It didn't sound like hers.

Tiago put a hand on her shoulder. "We're going to find out what happened to your friend. I promise."

She nodded, but she was distracted, obsessing over her choice to let Makoto come with her the day of the attack. If anything happened to him, it would be her fault.

The elevator lurched to a stop, and as the doors opened, voices filled her ears. She staggered behind Tiago as they entered the control hub, a middle-sized square room with several terminals arranged in a loose semicircle. Behind each of the stations sat a person wearing an ivory uniform. Their shoulder marks were a vibrant leaf-green.

At the center of the room stood Max, busy studying a three-dimensional map of Saemangeum City. Lena recognized the familiar shape of the Fulcrum. As Max zoomed in on an area inside downtown, she saw the hyperist academy. In the 3D projection, the academy was flagged with a green asterisk. Eleven blue triangles were scattered throughout the Fulcrum. Around each were dozens of white dots.

"To all gathering forces," Max said, typing into a terminal as he gave instructions. "The rendezvous points are the Kintaro and Mimika Quartzes. Hold on to your position and wait for further instructions. Engage the enemy only if you have a clear shot. Make every blast count."

"Sir." One analyst turned to Max. "The biomechas' count rose to one hundred and fifteen. Multiple signals still crossing our defense perimeter. Logistic is now detecting four Black Waters on the Donjin coast."

"What's a Black Water?" Lena asked Tiago, keeping her voice low.

"It's what we call their ships," Tiago explained. "Vessels that can operate both underwater and on the surface." He nodded to the half-dozen men and women working in the control hub. "These people are monitoring the vessels' whereabouts, so they can update our forces."

"Sir," called another analyst. "The biomechas' party is closing the distance with the Fulcrum. They'll reach the hyperist academy in less than five minutes."

Just as the last word was spoken, a sizeable number of red dots poured out from the northwest of the map. Lena gasped at the sheer size of the force. They dwarfed the dunamis' group protecting the Fulcrum.

"Logistic!" Max called out, turning toward a woman with a headset. "How many bodies do we have right now at the rendezvous points?"

"Riko's Wolves have just reached Mimika Quartz, sir," answered the analyst, adjusting her headset as she typed on the console. "We've got thirty-six units so far."

Max clenched his fist. "How far away are the Dragons, the Mantises, and the Phoenixes?"

"Seven, eleven, and nine minutes respectively, sir. Centurion Amon is behind the rest of the party."

Max's eyebrows drew together. "They won't get there in time."

"Sir," the first analyst called out. "ETA: three minutes before the enemy reaches the hot zone."

"Put me through to Patrick," Max said. His jaw was clenched so tightly the bone stretched the muscles of his face.

"Sir, he's on."

In the center of the room appeared the 3D reproduction of a man in his early forties with blue eyes and an unshaved chin.

"Max, we're ready to blow some iron work," Patrick said, a hand over his ear as he nodded to someone out of their line of sight.

"Pat, I've got bad news." Max looked inward while blinking rapidly. "They're almost on you. Cavalry won't arrive in time. You'll have to slow them down with what you've got."

Something flashed in Patrick's eyes, like a realization sinking in. He nodded with a weary smile. "Roger that. Looks like I won that bet after all. I'll cash out in the hall of Valhalla."

Max smiled, but it was a strange, joyless smile that lasted a blink of an eye. "You got it, brother. Give 'em hell."

"Understood." Patrick took a moment to adjust a helmet that covered his face. "Ready to roll."

The connection was interrupted.

The analyst wearing the headset turned to Max. "The welcome parties are converging at Forensic Street and Delowa Boulevard, sir. Powering up their K.T. Fields. Blasters hot and loaded."

"Copy that," Max's voice thundered. "If they can buy us some time, the cavalry will break the first wave."

The red cloud made of over one hundred dots approached the blue triangles, and the white dots protecting the hyperist academy moved in unison, forming a star-like formation.

One analyst with short white hair turned to Max. "Sir, they've started firing. Direct contact expected in seven seconds."

Max turned toward the closest of the analysts on his right. "Radio, I want to hear the noise. Get them on the line."

"Yes, sir."

A crackle spilled from the room's speakers and radio static flooded the control hub. A moment later the room exploded with several voices talking over each other.

"...FOCUS ON THE CENTER OF THE ENEMY FORMATION! CONCENTRATE FIRE ON—"

"...McLeod, twelve o'clock! Contact on your—"

"...Fara and Beatrix are down! I repeat. Fara and Bea—"

"...They don't even bother to aim! Hub, do you copy? They just want to move forward! We can't hold them—"

"...Stay in formation! Concentrate fire on the core group! Do not pursue. I repeat, do not—"

"Sir!" the logistic analyst shouted from the other side of the room in order to be heard over the noise. "The enemy is putting a lot of pressure on our assets. They're focusing on breaking the blockade."

Max studied the 3D map. "Where the hell are Scarlet, Memphis, and Leo? Radio, put me through—"

"Sir," the logistic cut him off. "I'm receiving a priority call from Centurion Amon."

Max nodded toward the projector at the center of the room. "Put him through."

More radio static, then silence.

"Faraday?" Max frowned at the projector. "Faraday, you read me? Status report."

The projector remained dead.

Max turned to the analyst. "What's happening?"

"I don't know, sir. The channel is open. He's listening to us."

Max was about to reply when a burst of static noise cut through the silence.

"Sir?" came a strained voice. It was followed by a loud snap noise and the sound of an explosion. The projector didn't show any image. "We're...heavy enemy fire. Can't...closer..."

"They're jamming their comm, sir," said the analyst.

"Boost the signal."

"I'm trying, sir."

Max waited for the signal from the analyst, then said, "Faraday? You read me? What's your status?"

"Sir, a group of iron works pinned us down on our way to Mimika. They had been...lurking and...crossfire when... too late. It's impossible...get around them...managed, somehow, but it's not going to—"

The communication was cut off.

"Faraday, do you copy?" Max glanced at the analyst. "What happened?"

"The communication is dead, sir. The signal's lost."

Max cursed through clenched teeth.

"Sir," called logistic. "The enemy deployed part of its assets at strategic points in the Fulcrum."

"They want to delay our support groups."

"Yes, sir. I'm receiving reports from the Dragons, the Mantises, and the Phoenixes. They're all being slowed down by scattered patches of biomecha's activity."

Max growled. "What's the situation at the rendezvous points?"

"The biomecha strike force broke through the checkpoint. About twenty of them made it to the other side. They'll reach the academy in less than two minutes."

"What's the status of our containment group?"

"We have one hundred and twenty dunamis clustered around the Volcano. They'll be one hundred and fifty in ten minutes."

Max nodded sharply. "Well, whatever the iron works came here to do, they won't leave Ariul alive. Tell Ryan to get his unit ready. I want those bastards to bleed as much as possible."

"Copy that."

"Radio, any new Black Water in the gulf?"

"Negative, sir."

Another analyst turned toward Max. "Sir, the biomechas have reached the academy."

Lena's breath caught in her throat. Tiago put a reassuring hand on her shoulder, his expression unreadable.

"We're reporting multiple blast-fire and explosions, sir. We've got the first images, coming from the PUD of a bystander broadcasting live on the city's net. The signal isn't clear, sir. I only got low-res."

"Put it on," Max ordered.

The projector came to life, showing low-resolution images of the academy. The entire building was ablaze. People were running in all directions, some wearing the academy's uniform. Bodies lay on the ground, still and charred. Smoke engulfed everything.

"No." Lena grabbed a nearby console to steady herself. Tears pricked her eyes. "God, no."

"They're firing on civilians," Tiago muttered, eyes wild. "They're aiming to kill, doing it on purpose. I don't understand. What changed?"

She blinked away the tears and tried to regain her composure. "W-what?"

"They don't do that," Tiago said. "They're stealthy, mostly act in the night. Don't want to draw attention to themselves. But this... I mean, this time they're trying to do as much damage as possible."

Logistic removed her headset and turned to look at Max. "Sir, the local police force is still far away from the attack."

"Hope they stay far," Max said, pursing his lips. "They won't stand a chance against that kind of firepower. Do we have sharper eyes on the academy?"

"Yes, sir," said another analyst. "Found a clearer feed from a local. Putting it through now."

The reproduction showed a swarm of biomechas flying over the academy like a bunch of hornets, shooting red beams at anything that moved. The east side of the structure had collapsed, and columns of smoke dotted the landscape as ruins and rubble covered the garden.

A sudden feeling of cold expanded in Lena's core, and her muscles went numb. She swayed slightly and Tiago had to hold her to prevent her from falling.

"Lena?" Tiago's voice sounded distant. "You need to sit."

"I'm...I'm fine." Lena's skin tingled with discomfort as she stared at a collapsed wall with three students buried underneath it. "I'm—" Her voice failed her. She remembered another building on fire when she was a child, the acrid smell of smoke in the air, her family gone forever. Lena had found a new family here in Ariul, but she'd lost that too.

"Sir. Enemy's moving away from the academy. One of them's carrying a student."

The analyst's cool voice chased Lena's thoughts and returned her to the present moment. She felt a surge of anger that gave her the energy she needed to stand straight.

"Makoto!" she shouted, then looked at Tiago. "It must be Makoto!"

Max turned toward them, eyes bulging. "What the hell are you doing here?"

Tiago raised his hands. "She has the right to see."

"Get her out of here! She's not—"

"Sir," logistic cut him off. "They're retreating!"

Max shot a dead glare at Tiago, but quickly turned toward the projection showing the mayhem. "To the Vulcan force. Cut them off from their Black Waters. Have the three auxiliary groups converge between Serendipity Street and—"

"Sir?"

Max glared at the operator. "What now?"

"They're not going back to their ships, sir."

Max stared at him. "What?"

"They've chosen a different path, veering north. Looks like they're aiming at one of the agricultural zones."

Max typed on his console while glancing at the fugitive red dots moving north. "Give me an estimate of their destination."

"Working on it, sir."

"Sir, the Mantises, Wolves, Dragons, and Phoenixes have disengaged from the fighting and are converging on the fugitives. ETA: two minutes."

Lena followed the white dots gaining ground over the attackers. A minute passed before another analyst said, "They've engaged the enemy. Captain Puglisi is on the line."

"Put her through."

A moment later, a clear female voice erupted from the comm.

"Max? I've got bad news," said Puglisi. "Looks like the iron works are heading to an abandoned building. A garage, it seems. We've analyzed it with our spectroview. There's a vehicle inside. Looks like a turboshuttle. All biomechas have moved to protect the building. They're using their damn bodies to absorb the blows!"

Lena covered her mouth, her guts twisting. "They're going to leave with him." Her voice was shaky. "You gotta stop them. Please!"

Max slammed his hand on the console. "Faraday, Scarlet, Memphis, Leo! That shuttle mustn't leave. You read me? I've got—"

A deafening roar came from the comm, followed by an eerie silence.

Max looked around. "Radio, what was that? What happened?"

"Sir, it's gone," was the analyst's reply. "The shuttle passed our sensors. Looks like it was equipped with some kind of stealth device. Our pathfinders can't trace it. Same for our EM missiles. We've lost it."

25

INCORRECT DESIGNATION

DÜSSELDORF, HEADQUARTERS OF THE AUTOMATRIX INC.

Ramor

R amor slammed the door shut as he stormed into his office. He rubbed his sweaty hands against his temples, then punched the wall.

"Idiot!" he shouted at the empty room. Pain coursed through his hand as he gave a second punch, this time hitting harder. He cursed and took two steps away from the wall, blowing a breath to calm down.

Erik was up to no good. Ramor knew it. He needed to do something.

Ramor needed a drink, something strong. He headed for the minibar next to his desk, then stopped. No. He needed to stay lucid if he wanted to help Erik. He swore to Sofia he'd take care of him, and that was exactly what he was going to do.

He paced back and forth, stewing over his rushed attempt to learn something useful. It had been a mistake.

He should have planned a better course of action. Unfortunately, when Erik was involved, common sense flew out of the window.

There was something odd about that damned eptanidus. Ramor had felt it when he met the autotron at the hospital, after the attack at the Industries. The last conversation outside Erik's home only deepened his suspicion.

Ramor focused on what On-Eni-Fifth had said. "If it can be written, it can be solved." He grimaced. "Why did it say that?" He opened the desk's drawer, took a pen and a leather-bound notebook, and sat on the chair, evaluating the notebook's cover. A phrase had been engraved on it: "If it can be written, it can be solved." Ramor smiled despite himself. Sofia had given him the notebook years before, reminding Ramor that seeing a problem on paper, rather than on a screen, helped to gain new insight.

Why had On-Eni-Fifth said that phrase? To share some kind of message? If the eptanidus had something to say, why not say it plainly?

"Okay." Ramor opened the notebook. "One thing at a time. What do I know for certain?"

He knew Erik was building autotrons in an underground factory, probably with Kurosawa's help. These autotrons had to have something special if his nephew had hidden them and declared the Automaton Industries bankrupt to focus on that project. He wrote on the paper: "Underground factory," "Illegal autotrons," "Bankruptcy," and "Desperate." He stared at the words and scratched his forehead.

Maybe he wasn't doing this right. Maybe he was asking the wrong questions. The thing that nagged at him the most was On-Eni-Fifth's enigmatic phrase. The eptanidus had said something about the importance of a designation, while indicating itself. Why?

Once again Ramor read the sentence engraved on the notebook's cover, then chose a blank page and wrote the eptanidus' designation.

ON-ENI-FIFTH

Ramor stared at the words, carefully scrutinizing each letter for clues. The last part of the designation bothered him. Why give the designation "fifth" to an eptanidus? On-Eni-*Seventh* would have made more sense. Why fifth, and why was the number written with letters rather than numeric symbols?

Ramor shook his head. Was the eptanidus trying to throw him off track, waste his time with clues that led nowhere? Or was On-Eni-Fifth actually trying to tell him something?

Ramor ran a hand through his hair. *Fifth* might have made sense if the autotron was an old pentanidus model, the last series of androids not bound by the Tronic Subjugation. But that was impossible. That series went out of production years before.

Perhaps Erik used the word fifth moved by nostalgia, to pay tribute to the last series of autotrons free from the Tronic Subjugation?

Ramor stared at the page. What was the first model of autotron owned by Erik? If he recalled correctly, it had been an exanidus, with designation EN-IN-50. Ramor wrote the designation below *On-Eni-Fifth*.

What else? Erik had owned no other autotron except for those two. Well, that wasn't true. Sofia had given him a pentanidus prototype a decade before, but that was hardly something...

Ramor's heart skipped a beat. "Good God." A shiver ran

down his spine as a nightmarish thought sank in. He stared at the designation On-Eni-Fifth while repeatedly dragging his palms down his pant legs. With a shaking hand, he replaced the word *fifth* with the corresponding Arabic numeral and reshuffled the letters. The pen dropped to the floor with a sharp thud as the answer to Ramor's question stared at him. The number 5, now at the beginning of the word, charged the autotron's designation with monumental consequences.

5-O-N-N-I-E

26

THE PRICE TO PAY

YELLOW SEA, AQUAMARINE

Ariul

Lena wiped her tears as she read the information on the tablet. She'd already memorized the content of the report, but she couldn't stop reading.

Tiago tried to get her to eat over the last two days, but she didn't want to. It was her fault so many people died. She deserved to suffer.

"Don't you dare blame yourself," Tiago had told her the last time he'd visited in the infirmary. She had fainted in the control hub, after the biomechas destroyed the academy and captured Makoto, and Doctor Risa had declared that Lena was in shock.

Since then, Lena had stayed in one of the infirmary's rooms, shielded from the outside world.

The chancellor's attempts at soothing her had been meaningless. Eighty-nine people had died because of her. Nothing would change that. Her instincts had told her it was a terrible idea to bring Makoto with her, but she had ignored the feelings and now she was paying the consequences.

Lena scrolled through the names and stopped when she reached "Lena Maruishi," followed by "Makoto Shimao." They were both listed as missing, along with another dozen students the rescuers hadn't been able to recover from the rubble.

She closed her eyes, unable to prevent the tears. The image of blood-covered bodies with lifeless eyes flashed in the darkness. The biomechas had burned her entire world in a matter of minutes, and she had handed them the torch.

Lena scrolled through the list and stopped when she reached the last two names in the first column. She reached out a hand and touched the screen with trembling fingers: Cassidy Memphis and Netardas Galanis. Each time, she hoped those names would disappear.

Her brain refused to believe that she would never hear Cassidy's light-hearted jokes again, that she would never see Net's bright-eyed look when talking about some trivia tidbit only he knew.

She turned off the tablet and set it down on the floor while crouching in the corner of the room. She felt her airway closing off while her diaphragm contracted. Unable to halt herself, she retched, clamping her hands across her mouth.

A *beep* signaled that someone was standing on the other side of the door, waiting for her permission to enter.

Lena swallowed hard. "Go away," she said in a hoarse whisper.

There was silence for a minute, then a familiar voice came muffled through the door.

"It's me. Tiago."

She didn't answer. She remained curled up on the floor, hugging her legs, hoping the chancellor would leave.

"You can't stay in there forever. You need to eat something. It's been two days."

Tiago's words were little more than a buzzing noise in her head. Eating seemed so trivial after what happened. It was wrong that Tiago focused on her hunger when dozens of people had been murdered.

She drew in a shallow breath. "Please, go away."

"It wasn't your fault."

She closed her eyes and slammed a hand against the floor.

"Go away!"

Tiago didn't give up. "Your friend might still be alive. It's not too late."

She hated Tiago for suggesting that Makoto could still be living. That was worse to imagine. What would be happening to him? It was the exact opposite of what Sebastos Max Lewis had said when she had asked him to rescue Makoto, to help him.

"Your friend is out of our reach, girl," the dunamis had said, avoiding her gaze. "If he's not dead already, he will be soon. I'm sorry."

Dead. Another death for which she was responsible.

"You gotta listen." Tiago's voice sounded strained. "The biomechas might dispose of Makoto, but only after they extract the information they need. Until then, we have options. We can—"

"I SAID GO AWAY!"

It was another minute before his footsteps receded.

A lump formed in her throat. It was better that way. Alone, she couldn't hurt anyone. No one else would die because of her. Tears started forming at the edges of her vision. Before she knew it, all the guilt and anger poured like a raging river, impossible to stop. After what felt like a thousand years, exhausted and dizzy, she sprawled on the cold floor and closed her eyes. Something poked at her collarbone. She was still wearing the cursed pendant. She should have tossed it away long before. She wanted nothing to do with Wei Wang, with the Defensio Project, or with the biomechas.

That was her last thought before sinking into a restless sleep.

∞∞∞

A young man with amber eyes smiled at her.

He sat on a wooden bench in the middle of a clearing, a squirrel perched on his shoulder, small dark brown eyes looking intently at her. A dog barked in the distance; the smell of wet earth and grass was strong in the air. That place resembled a park, and this man was strangely familiar. Of course! It was Wei, but older than the last time she'd seen him. No longer a boy, but a young man.

"Lena."

Lena stared at him. "Wei Wang?" She swallowed. "Are you...are you talking to me?"

"I am," Wei said, his voice playful. "There's something you need to know." He gave the squirrel a nut, and the small animal cracked it open with its teeth.

She stepped closer. "What do I need to know?"

Wei looked intently at her. "You can't understand a person without understanding her motives, and you can't understand the biomechas without understanding Pandora."

Lena blinked. "What?"

Wei's smiled widened. "Let me show you."

A chilly wind rose, and the ground shifted beneath her feet. The world started spinning, and images exploded before her eyes. She fell, but not to her end. She was going somewhere where she would understand.

PART II

ARCHETYPE

INTROLOGUE

Wei Wang sat on a bench, the wind moving its invisible fingers through the tree's branches. The ubiquitous chirping of birds and the buzzing of insects was a symphony that blended with the chatter of passersby and the faint sound of car horns honking outside the park. The air was chilly; it smelled of petrichor. He looked up at the wall of gray clouds stifling the sky. It was going to rain soon.

A Shiba Inu with a red sesame coat came trotting in his direction and barked when it noticed him.

"Hey, buddy." Wei leaned over the bench and offered his hand. "What's the word?"

The dog approached carefully, sniffed Wei's fingers, then licked his hand.

"So," Wei said. "You having a good time?"

The dog licked its muzzle, then spotted the object Wei was holding in his other hand and barked, its tail wagging furiously.

"What?" Wei glanced at his hand. "Oh, okay. Want me to throw this?"

The dog showed an open-mouth grin with tongue hanging out, then started spinning in circles, jumping up and down as it went.

"Sorry, buddy." Wei rested his arm across the back of the bench. "This isn't a ball. It's a piece of a puzzle I'm going to need to make a point."

The dog barked again, then cocked its head to the side, ears standing on its head.

"Pretzel?" A voice came from behind the bushes. "Pretzel? Come here, love. We gotta go."

The dog sprinted away.

"See ya." Wei followed Pretzel with his eyes until it jumped through the bush and disappeared. Suddenly, the fist-sized object he was holding seemed heavier than a moment before. It was a Rubik's Cube. "Talking about making a point," Wei said while staring at the 3D puzzle. "It'll be the last time you have an actual purpose."

A shuffling noise caused Wei to look at a nearby tree. There, on one of the low-hanging branches, a squirrel stared at him.

"Ah, Fiz!" Wei smiled. "Didn't think I'd see you."

The little animal whipped its head to one side, then the other, then dropped on the ground with grace and climbed to the bench, taking the empty seat beside Wei.

"I'm out of gifts, Fiz." Wei patted his pockets. "Sorry."

The small rodent stared at Wei until a noise to their left caused the little animal to jump off the bench and climb back up the tree.

"May I sit?"

Wei didn't look at the newcomer. He shrugged, still intent on the Rubik's Cube. "Don't know, Pandora. This bench might actually crack under the combined weight of our messiah complexes."

Pandora blew air through her nose. "Guess that's as close to a 'yes' as I'm going to get." She sat, keeping her eyes on Wei. "Did you think about my proposal?"

"Sorry, I'm kind of busy right now." Wei switched the faces of the Rubik's Cube at an increasing speed. "Trying to break my personal speed-cubing record."

Pandora rolled her eyes. "Do you have to do it *now*?"

"Why not?" Wei shot her a playful glance. "I've got the best audience, haven't I?"

Pandora's crystal blue eyes shone with a hint of amusement. "You never tire of making fun of me, do you?"

"I'm not making fun of you." Wei burst into a wide grin. "I'm making you part of the joke." He picked a stopwatch from his pocket, showed it to Pandora.

Pandora frowned. "*Again*?"

Wei shrugged. "Humor me. What do you have to lose, except your self-esteem? If you win, you'll earn bragging rights for the rest of your life. It's a win-win."

Pandora snorted, her eyes lightening with an inner glow. "All right, you're an absolute pain in the ass. Give me that thing."

Wei handed her the stopwatch.

Pandora placed her thumb on the top button, ready to start the device. "You ready?"

The Rubik's Cube sat on Wei's lap, his hands at the ready. "Hit me."

"All right then. Three, two, one... Go!"

Wei's hands flashed on the cube, shifting in place, the faces so fast the colors blurred together. "Done!" he shouted, dropping the cube on his lap.

Pandora showed him the stopwatch's display. "Six and fifty-eight hundredths seconds. Not bad."

Wei placed his tongue between his lips and blew. "Man,

I'm a slug." He handed the Rubik's Cube to Pandora. "Your turn."

"No." Pandora's voice brooked no argument. "I'm not here to play games."

Wei stared at her. "Then why are you here?"

"To talk some sense into you before it's too late." Pandora drew a breath and released it before speaking. "Why don't you take it seriously?"

"I'm serious." Wei showed the Rubik's Cube with a wide-eyed look. "That's as good as it gets. You'll have a hard time beating it."

Pandora shook her head. "Not in a million years."

"So you're going to lose by abandonment?"

Pandora chortled and threw a look at Wei. "Can't lose if I ain't playing."

Wei smirked. "We never stopped playing, Pan. You're too smart to believe otherwise."

Pandora stared at him, then held out her hand. "Gimme that thing."

Wei flashed a smile. He reset the stopwatch and glanced at Pandora. "Ready?"

"As ready as I can be."

At Wei's signal, Pandora moved her hands so fast they almost blurred around the cube. When she let go of the object, all the faces were completed.

Wei's eyes widened. "Wow! Three and ninety-eight hundredths seconds! You crushed me!"

"We done playing?" Pandora tossed him the Rubik's Cube. "Can we talk about the subject at hand?"

"You mean competition?"

"No, Wei. I mean *collaboration*."

"Collaboration?" Wei scratched the side of his head. "Okay, now I get it. You want to talk about the past. Alright, let's talk about the past. You helped me build the backbone of Polaris, I helped you build the backbone of the ether. One hand washed the other, and both of them remained as dirty as a hog. How's that for a summary of our joint venture?"

A flush appeared in Pandora's face. "What's the point of going on with your pointless crusade?"

Wei shook his head. "Well, that's a bummer."

Pandora narrowed her eyes at him. "What is?"

"If you didn't get it the first time I explained it, you won't get it now."

Pandora became still. "I'll kill you if you stand in my way." There was no emotion in her voice as she spoke the words. She said it with the same nonchalance as an exterminator might when informing a family there are rodents in the house that need to be killed.

"I'm not afraid of death," Wei said with strong eye contact. "It comes with perks."

"Want to hide behind words?" Pandora used an even, serious tone. "I'm trying to avoid a war."

"Isn't that what we do best?" Wei sounded amused. "Hide behind words? You are the Great Mother, the Light, the Archetype. I'm the Genius Boy, the First Hyperist, the Omnilogos. We're both masters in the art of concealment, hiding our shortcomings behind words, covering them with a fabricated truth. We're both liars. The war you're trying to avoid? It broke out the moment we met. We just didn't know."

Pandora leaned in. "You can't win. You're out-manned and out-gunned. Odds are stacked against you any way you slice it."

Wei turned to Pandora with a slight smile. "Always liked an underdog story."

"I'm trying to give you one last chance to make this right before it's too late."

"Late." Wei nodded slowly. "You speak of time as if it were my enemy. Do what you gotta do. History isn't kind with hesitant people."

"I don't mind having your blood on my hands, if that's what it takes to give order to the chaos."

"Ah, yes." Wei leaned back on the bench, hands behind his head. "Your need of controlling. Where has it gotten us? Humanity isn't an equation to solve. Believe me, I tried."

Pandora stood up and started walking away. "You haven't tried hard enough."

"You'll fail, even if you kill me."

Pandora stopped. She looked over her shoulder, directly at Wei. The question was all in her eyes.

"I'll leave a Cornucopia," Wei said, clasping his hands.

"A Cornucopia?" Pandora frowned.

Wei offered a curt nod. "It'll have a wealth of information that'll destroy everything you stand for. Watch out for it."

Pandora blinked, then smiled. "That's your plan? Threatening me with a ghost? You should know better. Even ghosts can be killed."

"This isn't a ghost." Wei showed his empty palms. "It's my legacy."

Pandora looked intently at him, then nodded slowly. "Then I'll be expecting it." She glanced up at the clouds. Thunder ripped through the air, causing a loud, booming burst. "Enjoy what's left of the day. There's a storm coming. You wouldn't want to be caught in the midst of it, would you?" She turned and walked away.

27

NEWFOUND MEMORIES

YELLOW SEA, AQUAMARINE

Ariul

Lena jerked awake, her heart hammering against her chest. This time, it hadn't been a dream. The realization took her breath away. Something clicked in her mind, and certainty settled.

She sat up, trying to ignore her stiff muscles after hours spent sleeping on the floor. She focused on the meeting between Wei and Pandora.

"It can't be," she muttered while wiping sweat from her forehead. "I mean, it's crazy." She touched the pendant with a shaky hand. Somehow, that object had activated while she was asleep. The dreams she had experienced weren't dreams at all. They were memories: Wei's memories.

Lena focused on what she remembered. "Pandora," she muttered, bringing a shaky hand to her mouth. She didn't know that person, and yet somehow thinking of her made her stomach churn. Why? Was she also experiencing Wei's feelings, alongside his memories? Could the pendant do that?

Something Pandora had said nagged at her, something about a war Wei couldn't win. She blinked, then stared at the wall, playing the conversation between the two in her head.

The last piece of a jigsaw puzzle clicked into place. Of course. Pandora had to be involved in the war the Overseer of Ariul mentioned. That didn't explain her role in the conflict though. Why had she threatened to kill Wei? What was their relationship? They clearly had a history. How had the relationship started?

Her gaze lingered on the tablet she'd left on the floor, with the names of the victims of the biomechas. So many people were dead, and for what? She needed to find out. A new drive settled in her consciousness. She was going to find out why all that had happened, and if there was even the smallest chance Makoto was alive, she would do anything in her power to save him.

But first, she needed to tell Tiago about her discovery.

She stood up and activated the internal communication system. "Tiago," she called with a croaky voice. "I need to talk to you."

28

COUNCIL OF WAR

NASHVILLE, ARK INSTITUTE FOR ADVANCED ETHERIC STUDIES

James

Asha Innati had changed little since the last time Angelica had seen her, eleven years before. The woman standing in front of her radiated a confidence that bordered on contempt. It was with her sassy, "fuck you" attitude that she had just proposed the most sensational public relations stunt in ether's history.

Angelica glanced at Sebastian, sitting beside her. James, Ravi, and Venus sat on the other side of the oval table. Her husband had looked uncomfortable since Asha had spoken.

Sebastian raised a hand. "Question."

Asha turned to regard him. "Shoot."

He cleared his throat. "I get that you want to attract attention quickly, but you're suggesting the social media equivalent of throwing a nuclear bomb and seeing how fast the news of the destruction spreads."

Asha's eyes were full of glee. "I like the image."

"It's preposterous."

Asha smirked. "You make it sound like it's a bad thing."

Sebastian's eyebrows pinched together. "Look, we need to inform people, but your way of doing it... It's...well..." He pointed to Asha's presentation material with an open hand. "It's going to make half the etheric population die of a heart attack and piss off the other half. What's to gain?"

James adjusted his glasses. "We need to attract eyes with the least amount of effort, Sebastian. Surprise is the only advantage we have. We need to leverage it. No one's trying to sugarcoat this: it's radical, but it's the best shot we've got."

"James is right," Asha said before Sebastian could reply. "We're talking about the D-day in the history of mass communication. You don't tip-toe. You barge inside, guns blazing."

"I agree with both." Ravi spoke with a twinkle in his eyes, suggesting he was enjoying the growing tension. "The message needs to be shoved down people's throats. No way around it."

"This is a suicide mission."

All present turned toward Angelica, who spoke the last sentence.

Asha clasped her hands as she squinted. "Care to elaborate?"

Angelica gestured at the projection. "The entire operation must be built around a charismatic figure, someone already known by the public." She hesitated a second before adding, "Someone like the Madame of Melody."

Sebastian's eyes widened. "What?"

"It's written all over it." Angelica stood up and pointed at Asha's plan. "You need a sacrificial lamb, someone with enough credibility to give it a chance of success."

"Yes." James nodded. "Someone with lots of social capital, a symbol of the revolution."

"No." Angelica crossed her arms. "You don't need a symbol, you need a martyr, someone willing to take a bullet in the chest."

Asha's smile didn't waver. "Sure. You could call it that. Without a figurehead, the whole scaffolding collapses."

Sebastian glanced around. "Wait a second. If that's what this is all about, where would you stage the debate?"

"Eeeeeeeeetherverse!"

All eyes turned toward the entrance, where a powerfully built, dark-skinned giant of a man had appeared.

"Lucius." James motioned the big man inside the room. "You're late."

"Late? Entertainers are never late, James the Darksider!" Lucius' thunderous laughter sounded like a waterfall. "They arrive when it's time to up the stakes. Look at you. All of you!" Lucius' dark eyes took everyone in. "Ahhh, I see you, Sebastian Anish: lord of charts and numbers, master of statistics, and solver of impossible problems. It's a pleasure to see you after so long."

"Lucius," Sebastian said a bit stiffly, still surprised by the former classmate's appearance.

Lucius stepped toward Ravi. "Ravi the fox. You two-faced joker! Look at those eyes. You still trying to single-handedly take over the world?"

Ravi looked sideways at James, then grinned at Lucius. "What makes you think I haven't already?"

Lucius turned to Venus, and placed one hand over his heart as he fell to one knee. "Venus the Enchantress, seductress of souls. Your beauty gives joy to my eyes."

Venus laughed. "You were always the flatterer, Lucius. I'm glad to see you."

Lucius pushed himself up and was about to address Asha, but the woman raised a hand. "Spare me. Don't need the fake love."

Lucius didn't look offended by her tone. "Venomous and straight to the point." He grinned. "Glad to see you haven't changed."

"Why is he here?" Angelica asked.

Lucius turned to Angelica. "Ah, yes!" His smile widened. "The Madame of Melody. You are the Destructor of Tendencies, the Etheric Hope, the champion of a brave cause that can save the world. Who would have thought that the shy, insecure Angelica Kam would one day become the jewel of Cantara's legacy?"

Asha rolled her eyes. "You done drooling? We haven't got all day. Brief them."

"With great pleasure." Lucius activated a trigoy. The reproduction of a huge rectangular space surrounded by stands appeared.

"Welcome to Etherverse, people, where etherions tear each other apart for fame and glory. This is the stage where the revolution of the holistic will begin. This is where the world will learn about the cancer and its cure."

Venus frowned. "You want to set up a fight at Etherverse?"

"I do," Lucius said with a grin. "It's the best place to deliver our message. I already have the event jotted down with the organizers. All I need is the Madame of Melody's stamp of approval and we're good to go."

Sebastian's lips pressed together in a grimace. "Are you talking about a live debate?"

Lucius' eyes glowed. "I am."

Sebastian blinked. "Against whom?"

"Congratulations, Sebastian." Lucius fanned himself

theatrically. "You just asked the most important question of the day." He snapped his fingers, and the trigoy showed a handsome man in his late fifties, snow-white hair and beard trimmed to perfection.

Ravi whistled. "Is that who I think it is?"

Angelica knew the answer. All present knew. They grew up studying that person.

Lucius flamboyantly gestured to the reproduction, like an announcer introducing a world-renowned wrestler. "Let's hear it for Milo Finnegar Jasper, the leader of the Etheric Covenant, and legendary Hound of the Ether!"

Angelica's breath caught in her throat. A quick gaze at her companions suggested she wasn't the only one surprised.

"Are you for real?" Ravi laughed while tossing a look at Angelica. "Jasper will tear her apart and feed what's left to the dogs. There's no way she can stand with that devil. What's our Plan B?"

"There isn't a Plan B." James steepled his hands. "Angelica is the only person the organizers will accept for Etherverse. No one else would draw enough eyes on the show."

Venus bit her lip. "You're seriously considering putting her against Jasper?"

"She's our only chance of delivering the message. Nothing else comes close to Etherverse's reach. This is our only hope."

"No!" Sebastian stood up from his chair. "Not in a million years."

Angelica lifted her hands. "Sebastian—"

"No, Angy. This is crazy talk. I won't stand here listening to them treating you like a pawn."

"We're all pawns," James said. "But Angelica has a real chance to checkmate our enemy."

"Easy for you to say. You're not the one who's walking onto that stage." Sebastian indicated Angelica. "We're etiatros, not entertainers. We cure people."

"Cantara trained each of us the same way, Sebastian." Asha put her fists on her hips, elbows wide. "To be linchpins, shepherds of the public opinion. You forgot?"

"That was a decade ago!" Sebastian snapped. "We're not equipped for this media war, and I won't let you damage my wife's reputation and mental sanity. Period."

"Sebastian, listen." Lucius clasped his hands, a sympathetic smile on his face. "The Madame of Melody is the only one who can sponsor our product the way we want. But to advertise it, we need a platform like Etherverse and an opponent like the Hound to hype things up."

"Yeah?" Sebastian was shaking with rage. "Why don't you go? Hmm? See how you do in that meat grinder."

"I'm not the Madame of Melody," Lucius replied calmly. "I don't have her social capital."

"You're talking about my wife, you rip-off entertainer! You want to advertise the holistic over her body."

Lucius raised his hand. "If you'd just listen to—"

"We did what we could to help." Sebastian glared at his former classmates. "We figured out the systemic problem. The rest is up to you. Think of another way to package your product that doesn't involve selling my wife to the highest bidder."

James stood. "Sebastian, the holistic will never stand a chance if we don't use Angelica for—"

"Then it won't stand a chance!"

Angelica put a hand on her husband's arm, and Sebastian snapped his head toward her. "Let's get out of here." He collected his things and started walking to the exit, then stopped when he realized Angelica wasn't following. "Angy?"

Angelica bit her lip, then gazed at Lucius. "When is the debate scheduled?"

"In two weeks," Lucius replied. "You'll have plenty of time to prepare."

"You don't have to do this." Sebastian shook his head. "They're using you. Can't you see? They're desperate and want to drag you into this crazy—"

"I know what they're doing." Angelica gazed at James. "And I know they don't have another option."

Sebastian's mouth opened and closed without speaking. He approached Angelica and whispered, "You never wanted the attention. *You* told me."

"You're right," she said. "I never wanted it, and I still don't. But it's not about what I want, it's about what's right."

Sebastian pressed a fist against his thigh. "Angy, for God's sake, you're not the Madame of Melody."

Angelica swallowed. "You're right. I'm not. That means I'll need to become her fast if we don't want more people to suffer."

WEI'S FAILURE

WASHINGTON D.C., FORMER HYPER HEADQUARTERS

Gladia

The huge spherical hall dwarfed any enclosed space Arthur had seen before. It wasn't just enormous; it was strange in a peculiar sort of way. "Creepy" wasn't the right word, but it was close enough.

Long strips of bluish light snaked along the length of the walls, like skeletal fingers ready to grab prey. Several seats were arranged in a semicircle, and all of them faced a raised platform at the center of the gigantic room.

Arthur doubted anyone had been there in years. He surveyed the closest seat and frowned. The upholstery was discolored and covered with a thick layer of dust. A hint of rust gnawed at the metal back.

"What's this place?"

Gladia didn't answer. She stared at the platform with haunted eyes.

"Hey." Arthur reached out to her. "You okay?"

She gazed at him as if she'd forgotten anyone else was there. "What?"

Arthur blinked, taken aback by her glassy stare. "You don't look well. Want to get some fresh air?"

She swallowed, glanced back at the platform. "Sorry. I was...ah..." She trailed off, then added, "No, I'm fine. It's just that...this place brings back memories." Her voice bounced ominously between the walls, causing an echo that repeated her words before subsiding into a barely audible noise. She walked toward the platform, then gestured at it. "Once upon a time, Wei used to perform a magic trick. Right here."

"Wei?" Arthur glanced at the platform.

Gladia nodded. "He holed up in this room when he needed to think things through. This place offered him a challenge, the only puzzle he never solved." She stepped onto the platform, arms projected outward, and closed her eyes. "We're inside a simulator."

Arthur narrowed his eyes. "A simulator?"

"Yes." She opened her eyes to study Arthur. "And here's where things get a bit out there."

"Okay." Arthur waited a moment, then shrugged. "What do you mean?"

She stepped off the platform. "This is where Wei tried his damn best to predict the future."

Arthur blinked. "Sorry, you said predict the future?"

"I did."

He crossed his arms. "How is this all related to your nightmares? That's why we're here, right? You said you wanted to share a secret." He looked around, taking the enormous space in. "Is this *it*?"

She gave a hesitant nod. "It's all here. My nightmares always start with the memory of this place. This room is special; it can simulate through variables a number of futures. Wei used a program called EVA, a highly advanced pan-algorithmic AI, to routinely test variables and occurrences based on real-life data and prognostic mathematics. It gets pretty technical, but the gist of it is that he could extrapolate several scenarios, average them down to a few highly likely projections, and come up with an outcome with a high chance of becoming our future."

Arthur squinted, his brow lowering. "You were right. This is totally out there."

She crossed her arms over her chest. "I swear it's the truth."

He rubbed his neck. "Okay, so you're saying that Wei could...um...predict the future?"

"Sort of."

"I don't know." Arthur pinched his bottom lip, made a *hmm* noise in the throat. "It's a hard pill to swallow, but say I believe you. What does it have to do with you?"

Gladia smoothed her pants, her gaze avoiding direct eye contact. "You think it's possible? To predict the future, I mean."

He cleared his throat. "I...um...I think it's possible to predict the likelihood of an event. But the future... Well, to be honest, I was never big on science fiction."

She nodded. "That's what I thought."

He looked at the platform, then back at Gladia. "Look, maybe this was just a game for him. You know, how he entertained himself. Maybe it didn't have any real value."

She shook her head. "That's impossible."

"Why?"

"He didn't do things for fun. There was always a reason behind every action, always something done in order to achieve something else. His life was like an engine, every part designed to propel things forward. No. This wasn't just a game, it was a serious attempt to avoid our extinction."

Arthur grimaced. "You're...ah...you're still talking about Wei?"

"Yes."

"Then I'm confused. I thought his goal was to create a spacefaring civilization."

"Well." She stared at him with an intense gaze. "The two things are connected."

He squinted. "Can't say I follow."

She started pacing. "According to the outcome of Wei's simulation, humanity will cease to exist if it can't become a spacefaring civilization." She glanced at Arthur, blushing slightly. "Look, I know how it sounds. It's hard to believe. When I realized how much time he was putting into this simulation, I got scared. Wei spent more time here than he ever dedicated to Polaris. He wore himself out in this room. It was important to him."

He shrugged. "How?"

She visibly shuddered; again, her eyes had that haunted look. "Like...it was so important he was willing to die to see it solved."

Arthur gazed at the platform. "Look, this program, this... AI you mentioned. Can you show it to me?"

She glanced at the ceiling and called, "EVA?"

A cold, clear female voice answered. "Egosimulant Versatile Anthropomorphic unit online and ready to perform."

She glanced at Arthur, then back at the ceiling. "Activate the vault."

"Vault activated."

A single solitary note reverberated in the immense arena before fading.

"Here's where things get bumpy," Gladia said. "EVA, open the file: *Spacefaring Civilization*."

"Unable to comply," EVA's voice replied. "Unauthorized voice print."

Arthur stared at Gladia. "What does it mean?"

"Exactly what she said." She sighed. "We can't access the simulation. Only Wei could. Since he's no longer with us, it means everything he'd been working on is gone. However, there's something we can do. We can recall the account of the last simulation Wei completed." Once again, Gladia addressed the ceiling. "EVA, what is the outcome of the simulation?"

EVA answered promptly, "The Center Maximum's outcome is foreshadowed in the historical basis provided at the beginning of the simulation."

"Conclusion?" Gladia's voice quivered with anticipation.

"The Singularity is inevitable," EVA said.

Arthur gazed at Gladia with sudden focus, eyebrows furrowing and then releasing.

"No matter what Wei did," she said, elbows pressed on her sides, "the result was always the same. Humanity never became a spacefaring civilization. It always went extinct in a matter of decades."

Arthur pursed his lips. "You said it yourself. It's just a simulation. I don't care what you think Wei was doing here. No one can predict the future. Not even him."

She shook her head. "After spending so much time with him, I don't believe there was something Wei couldn't do if he set his mind to it. And that's why I have those nightmares. That's why we're here. I see the end of our species every time I go to sleep."

Arthur's mouth opened but Gladia suddenly looked at her wrist. "It's Charlotte." She activated her interlink. "Yes?"

He watched Gladia's expression turn from impatient to worried.

"Are you sure?" Gladia asked, her eyes wide. "No, don't do anything until we're on my aeromousine. Get more intel. Don't answer questions without my say-so. We're on our way." She cut the communication and sprinted toward the exit.

"Hey!" Arthur had to half-run to keep up with her. "What's happening?"

"We need to get back to Infinity." Her tone was ripe with concern. "We have a situation."

IN THE AUTOTRON'S SHADOW
DÜSSELDORF, HEATHER RAINBOW INSTITUTE

Ramor

The doctor's assistant opened the door and let Ramor into the room. After a few steps, Ramor stopped short. His first thought, after looking around, was that they'd come to the wrong place. He turned toward the assistant. "Is this the right place?"

The woman nodded as she closed the door.

Ramor frowned. It looked like a deserted warehouse with dozens of objects scattered around. The walls were solid concrete, but no one had bothered to cover them with a coating or even paint. The ceiling was very high and exposed dark wooden beams and rusted water pipes, while the floor consisted of a single slab of dark gray stone. Papers were scattered on the ground. He picked one up. There were a bunch of handwritten diagrams and equations jotted down in the margins. Ramor inhaled sharply as he set the piece of paper on an empty shelf. The air was cool and smelled sweet. It reminded him of leaking coolant from a car's engine.

Large boxes crowded most of the left side of the room, while on the right side there were objects that looked like batteries the size of a fist.

Ramor glanced at the doctor's assistant. What was her name again? Selma? Sonia? No, it was *Sandra*. He had seen her a few times beside Dr. Airling, the psychiatrist taking care of Sofia. The doctor was in a conference in Hong Kong, so Sandra had to pick up the slack and tour Ramor around.

"Where's my sister?" Ramor's question came out rougher than he had intended. He cleared his throat, spoke more softly. "Thought this was supposed to be her new...ah... how'd you call it?"

"Outward recovery environment," Sandra said helpfully.

"Right." Ramor gestured around. "Not the place I had in mind when you talked about recovery. This looks like an abandoned warehouse."

"We found it suited her the most." Sandra gestured toward a pile of boxes. "And to answer your first question, your sister is over there."

Ramor squinted and saw a table heavy with the most extravagant collection of autotronic parts he had ever seen. Behind the table stood his older sister, Sofia Deringer, dressed in a lab coat. He blinked, barely believing his own eyes. Sofia's demeanor had changed drastically from the last time he had visited her. She looked well-groomed, her hair tidy and clean, pulled back in a sleek ponytail. Her eyes were bright and focused.

Ramor was utterly unprepared to see this. He'd almost given up on seeing his sister like her old self. He took two hesitant steps toward Sofia, then halted. An invisible force pushed him back, preventing him from taking another step. Ramor's eyes widened.

"It's an ambient restrainer, Director Deringer," Sandra said, answering his inquisitive look. "You'll remember from our briefing that it isn't advised to speak with her because of the delicate phase she's in. The success of the new treatment depends on it."

Ramor remembered the message Dr. Airling had sent him about the experimental new drug he was testing on Sofia. The doctor had kept the details vague, but Ramor hadn't understood most of it. It wasn't the first time Airling was trying a new treatment. That's what Ramor paid him for: to devise new ways to make his sister feel better.

"So you're saying I can't speak to her?" Ramor's jaw clenched.

"Not at this moment." Sandra offered an apologetic smile. "Dr. Airling believes this treatment requires an initial phase of semi-isolation. He thinks the environment tailored to her needs might help her regain mental wholeness. The doctor calls it 'empathic self-medication.'" She gestured toward Sofia, who was oblivious to the two of them. "As you can see, his approach is working. Your sister is healthier than ever."

Ramor crossed his arms. "So, you're testing an unproven drug on my sister without her knowledge or consent?"

"Director, you signed your consent at experimental treatments. As her legal guardian, you had that option. Besides, trauma research is more effective if carried out via blind study. It's how science works."

"Sure, that's easy to say when you're standing in *this* part of the room, isn't it?"

Sandra leaned toward him. "Director, if you want to discuss the specifics—"

"Never mind," he cut her off. "Whatever illusion you're manufacturing isn't going to work when she gets out, is it? I mean, what's the plan? When she needs to get back to her room, with an autonurse watching her all time? Hm? It sounds like a coin toss on a good day."

"Your sister is going through an adjustment period," she explained. "It's what we call a 'situation-induced limbo.' When she enters this room, her subconscious classifies it as a safe space where she can function as her past self. Her mind rules out the violence that happened during and after her abduction. Then, when she needs to leave the room, she enters what we call an 'equilibrium window,' during which she cooperates with medical personnel, performs the tests, and takes the prescribed medications. Put it in other terms, this room and the activities she performs within stabilize her condition. It's a major improvement over anything we've tried."

"For now," Ramor grunted. "When can I expect Dr. Airling to be back?"

Sandra checked her agenda. "Next Friday morning."

"Good." Ramor inhaled sharply. "Make sure his schedule stays clear in the afternoon. We'll have a chat. I need to get a few things straight."

She gave him a condescending smile. "Director, I'm afraid Dr. Airling has pressing engagements for the whole week following his return. He's fully booked for—"

"You thought that was a request?" Ramor roared with laughter. "That's cute." He stepped up to her. "Let me be absolutely clear. The doctor can see me on Friday afternoon, or he can see my lawyers on the morning of the same day, at the airport. His call."

Sandra frowned. "What?"

"You heard me, sweetheart. I want him to see me first thing in the afternoon. Anything else is unacceptable."

"Director, I'm afraid you don't understand how things work—"

"Darling, I suggest you listen carefully." He raised a hand to prevent Sandra from speaking. "I'm not paying the good doctor a five-figure check every month to get his assistant to stonewall me. Now, here's what's going to happen. After I walk out of this room, you're going to send a message to Dr. Airling informing him that his agenda has been cleared for a meeting with me on Friday afternoon. If that doesn't happen, there will be long-lasting consequences. Understand?"

She opened her mouth, her face blanching. "Are you threatening him?"

Ramor pointed a finger at her. "My sister is the person I care about most in the world. If I had to set both you and your doctor on fire to make sure she's fine, I'd do it in a heartbeat. That clear now?"

She swallowed hard. "It's...it's crystal clear."

"Glad we're on the same page. Send the doctor my regards."

Ramor glanced one last time toward his sister and then left the room. He didn't know if this therapy would work, or if it would eventually taper off like everything else they'd tried, but his guts told him this time was different. It was the first time Ramor had seen Sofia like her old self. Perhaps, if things worked out, he might have found a solution to the problem that seemed to have none.

31

THE ETHER HOUND

LAS VEGAS, HOTEL MAVERICK'S MOMENTUM

James

~

"At least have the decency to say it to my face!"

James ignored Ravi's confrontational tone. "I'd rather you act like an adult and do your job." He polished his sunglasses, then put them back on.

Ravi stomped his feet on the floor, hard. "You want me to risk my neck? *Mine*? Why me, of all the people who could do it?"

"I need someone with skin in the game to comb through that information." James kept his tone even. "You know what to look for: weaknesses, shady transfers, things that don't add up. We'll never get another opportunity like this, and you're the best person at my disposal for the job."

"No, I'm not." Ravi pointed at James. "*You* are the best person. Why don't you do it?"

James pushed back his sunglasses. "Because I can't be in two places at the same time."

"Easy way to bail out." Ravi exhaled, waited, probably wanting a stronger reaction from James. "What if Milo's men discover I was nosing around? Hmm? You thought about that?"

James shrugged. "We'll cross that bridge if it comes to it."

Ravi sneered. "It's all clear in that mind of yours, isn't it? Everyone is just a pawn to exploit for your endgame."

"Look, I don't have time for this." James picked up a set of keys from the table and moved away from Ravi. "Lucius and Angelica are waiting. You don't want to do it? I'll make a call and get someone else. It'll be riskier, but I'll get it done. Just know we might risk the entire operation because of you."

James felt Ravi's indecision in the tense silence that followed.

"Okay." Ravi's voice was barely more than a hiss. "I'll do it."

James gave him a curt nod. "Let me know when it's done." He headed toward the door.

"What about Angelica?"

James stopped, turned toward Ravi. "What about her?"

"Your infatuation is becoming obvious." Ravi crossed his arms, a small smile playing on his lips. "It might come back to bite your ass."

James' heart beat faster. "Don't know what you mean."

"Of course you do. I've noticed the way you look at her. I bet Sebastian's noticed too. Maybe that's why he's so against Etherverse. Thinks your 'great plan' is just an excuse to spend more time with his wife. Talk about risking the whole operation, right?"

James stiffened.

"Oh, don't hold back on my account." Ravi's smile widened. "Don't want to keep your beauty waiting."

∞∞∞

Las Vegas
Utopia Television Studio

The makeup team exited the dressing room, leaving Angelica, Lucius, and James alone. Angelica rose from her chair, stared at the mirror wall panels, and admired the finished work. A complete stranger stared back at her.

Lucius had asked her not to look at her reflection until the makeup team was done. Angelica's first reaction to her appearance was surprise. She almost glanced over her shoulder to make sure there wasn't another woman in the room. Her second reaction was detachment. She couldn't connect to the stranger in front of her.

She had entered that dressing room as Angelica Kam and would go out as the Madame of Melody.

Angelica focused on her dress. It had sparked quite a fight between Lucius' stylists. They wanted to create something beautiful and simple, grand but not pretentious. Angelica admired the details of the dress made of satin and silk gazar, embellished with lace appliques. It was a dress made to attract the eye and strike the senses. Her sweat-proof makeup had been kept subtle but elegant, with colorful eyeshadow and a purplish-red lipstick that made her lips look fuller.

"Thoughts?"

Angelica glanced at James. "It's catchy," she said, looking at the mirror.

"Darling." Lucius made a half-hearted attempt to suppress a smile. "The word you're looking for is 'Glorious'; with a capital G, that is. Come." He held out his huge hand for her to take. "Walk with me."

Angelica accepted the hand and the giant led her forward, like a proud father walking the bride down the aisle and handing her off to the groom. A red and orange halo vibrated around her, like an afterimage of her own presence. Angelica felt James' stare.

"Aha!" Lucius roared, the triumphant look of a sculptor admiring his best work. "This is marvelous! No one will be able to look away."

Marvelous. Not the first word that came to Angelica's mind when she looked in the mirror. She had never felt so aware of her own presence. But that was exactly the point, wasn't it? To turn her into a gigantic neon sign that caught the eye. And yet, she couldn't shake the feeling that her posturing would be unmasked and all their effort destroyed.

James must have noticed her conflicted look. "Lucius," he said, clearing his throat. "Do you mind giving us a moment?"

The giant looked at James, frowned, then glanced at Angelica. "Of course." His smile was quick to appear, but felt hollow, a fabricated gesture. "I'll be outside if you need me."

James waited for the door to be closed before speaking. "What is it?"

Angelica ground her molars, trying to ignore her reflection in the mirror. She looked at James, opened her mouth, then closed it.

James removed his sunglasses, revealing his jet-black eyes. Dark bags besieged them, with deep lines making them look more swollen. He seemed much older than his twenty-six years. The corner of his mouth twitched in a smile that gave away compassion. It differed from the one fabricated by Lucius in an instant. This one felt real. It felt personal.

"That bad?" James asked.

Angelica bit the bottom of her lip as she clutched the edge of her shirt. "What do you see when you look at me?" Her eyes searched James'.

James took a step toward her. "I see a warrior."

"A warrior." She scoffed. "Is this the lie we're selling now?"

"It's not a lie. It's a story." He planted his feet in a wide stance. He inhaled deeply through his nose, then exhaled through his mouth. "Remember what Cantara used to say about lies?"

"Yes." Angelica's throat felt dry. Thinking of her former teacher always gave a fluttering feeling to her stomach. "A lie is a good story told for the wrong reason," she recited. "It's up to us to make it worth our while."

"And do you believe that?"

Angelica put a strand of hair behind her ear. "I don't know what to believe."

James moved into her personal space, staring at her. "Who are you?"

She blinked. "I'm sorry?"

"I said: 'Who are you?'"

"I don't—"

"You are an etiatros," he said. "You cure people. That's what you do."

She shook her head. "This has nothing to do with—"

"You said you didn't know what to believe." He thrust his index finger at the door. "Believe this. There's a patient out there, and he's dying a horrible death. He needs you to make it through a wipeout event the world has never seen before. That patient is called humanity."

Angelica's eyes widened. She felt ashamed at her insecurity now. She understood what James meant. "You've always been good with words."

"No." James shook his head. "I'm just handy at borrowing them."

Angelica nodded. "Thanks." She squeezed his hand. "For everything. And this includes kidnapping me."

James cleared his throat. "Any time."

Angelica looked at the wall clock. "I better go. It's almost time."

"Right." James stepped to the side. "Good luck out there."

He waited for Angelica's footsteps to fade away, then he put on his glasses. He counted to ten before switching on his interlink. "You're up," he said. "We've only got one shot. Make it count."

James closed the connection, then headed for the exit. While walking, a reflection from the mirror caught his eye. He stopped, turned to look at himself. A thin man with a pale complexion and arched shoulders looked at him from behind sunglasses. A frail person, small and weak, who didn't give an impression of confidence or strength; someone far from the light, biding his time. A spider waiting in the shadow.

∞∞∞

Las Vegas
Etherverse

"Linchpins of the ether, please welcome to the stage the one and only Madame of Melody!"

Angelica entered the colossal auditorium, welcomed by a shower of applause and a general standing ovation as her dress made hundreds of heads turn in her direction.

Angelica waved her hands at the audience, composed by

some of the most well-know influencers in cyberspace. Everything depended on convincing them that the threat of the malicious was real, and that the holistic ether needed to be adopted.

Lucius and his stage strategists had spent weeks planning her speech, testing it with AI-based performance score platforms until they distilled the right strategy against Milos Jasper. The way Angelica moved and talked had also been carefully crafted, nailed down to perfection. It hadn't been easy. She'd had to learn how to turn off Angelica Kam and substitute her with the larger-than-life Madame of Melody, heir to Cantara Handal.

"Keep your engines running, folks!" The disembodied voice of the announcer reverberated in the huge auditorium. "Let's hear it for the Hound of the Ether!"

A cascade of lights exploded around the stage entrance and a handsome middle-aged man with short, well-groomed hair and light green eyes strode onto the stage, arms raised toward the audience. Several people screamed his name amid the cacophony of applause, and Milo smiled at the spectators.

Cantara had described Milo as the world's most resourceful metrosexual. Angelica still remembered her teacher's exact words: "He's charming and groomed to perfection, and as smooth as a snake slithering on olive oil."

Milo was also the person most directly involved in regulating etheric traffic as Director General of the Covenant for Etheric Safeguarding, the second-most-followed region, behind only the superpower DataMorph. As one of the founding fathers of the etheric order, he was a staunch defender of the *status quo*. He would do anything in his power to undermine Angelica's message. The holistic was a direct attack at the whole cyber-infrastructure he represented.

When the applause faded, Milo placed himself in the center of the stage, next to Angelica. There was no voice to decree the start of the debate, no sound to mark its beginning, but when the stage light dimmed, the game was on.

Milo took the lead and Angelica let him. Lucius and the stage strategists had suggested a defensive approach, at least at the beginning. All had agreed that Angelica wasn't a natural debater. A more experienced etherion might have gone to the attack, but that wasn't her. She needed to play it safe and assess Milo's strategy before working to counter.

"Thank you all for joining us today." Milo's tone was firm, his smile confident. He turned to Angelica. "I'm told this is your first appearance at a public slaughter." Several people in the audience laughed. Milo let the moment sink in, then resumed talking. "So, Madame of Melody." He stretched all the vowels for show. "How are you feeling on this fine day?"

Angelica placed her hands on her hips. "I feel great, *Dad*." She gave him a Pan Am smile. "Thanks for asking."

Some of the audience chuckled at her answer.

Angelica kept her confident mask on, but had no illusion. Milo was toying with her. Her stab proved to him she could take and cause damage, but they were still just taking each other's measurements. The real debate hadn't started yet.

The Ether Hound paced around her, like a predator searching for weaknesses. "You know, Cantara used to talk about you. She was quite fond of you."

Angelica frowned. Had Cantara Handal spoken about her to Milo? When, and under what circumstances? The surprise must have shown on her face, because Milo nodded.

"Yes," he said, studying her carefully. "She told me you were one of her brightest students. Intelligent, outspoken, resourceful." He paused, then scratched his chin. "However, she lamented your self-doubt, said you couldn't speak in front of ten people if your life depended on it. Well, you've clearly outgrown that." He gestured to her elaborate dress. "The flower has bloomed. I'm sure there's a person who's very proud of you at this very moment. I mean, you being here in front of the whole world." He turned toward the audience, shading his eyes for show. "Where's your husband? Hmm? Let us ask him how proud he is. Sebastian Anish? Where are you?"

Angelica crossed her arms. "He isn't here."

"No?" Milo turned to regard Angelica with a blank look. "Why?"

That obviously wasn't a random question. Milo must know Sebastian wasn't happy that Angelica attended Etherverse.

"He was kept by more urgent matters," Angelica said.

"Like what? A coma?" Milo chortled, and the audience laughed with him. "That's about the only reason I can think of that'd keep him from attending Etherverse."

Angelica let the collective laugh of the audience subside before replying. "Why don't we stop beating around the bush and get straight to the issue at hand?"

"We could do that," Milo said with a slow nod, holding his hands loosely behind his back. "Or we could keep digging and uncover some juicy gossip. What do you folks think?"

The audience roared its approval.

Milo gestured toward the spectators. "The people have spoken." He crossed his arms. "Care to fill us in?"

Angelica gave a half-shrug. "My husband is busy saving people's lives. There's a pandemic of catastrophic proportions, if you haven't heard."

"Ah, yes. Sure, your ticket for the etheric Hall of Fame." Milo shook his head, smiling a condescending smile. "Your marvelous fake news."

Angelica stared at her opponent. "It's not fake news. It's a proven fact."

"Fine." Milo clasped his hands. "Let's talk about that. You and your followers have created panic across cyberspace with this...*commercial*, for lack of a better world. This 'killer malicious' doesn't stand on its legs. It's cheap, contrived, and an insult to the etheric community."

"What bothers you? Our findings have been made public. You just need to read them."

"Oh, I've read them, dear. And you know what bugs me? It's the execution. It feels forced, desperate."

"Of course it's desperate," Angelica said. "Every moment we waste arguing, people die."

"So you're our savior? The chosen one?"

"I'm just someone who's trying to help. Make a difference for the thousands who're suffering."

"Ah, yes. 'Try to make a difference.' The trademark phrase of your teacher. Well, I'm sorry to burst your bubble, dear, but you aren't Cantara Handal."

"True," Angelica said. "I'm not." She pulled at her dress, as if exposing a weakness. "The makeup I'm using, the dress I'm wearing, is all the result of calculated planning. And so are the lights on this stage and the audience in this studio. Our entire world is planning and sensationalism. The way we move, talk, shake hands, smile; the very culture of the ether is based on appearance, on our ability to enhance the superfluous. Except for today. Today has nothing to do with sensationalism. Today it's all about the truth."

"That's the slogan you're trying to feed us?" Milo raised his arms theatrically. "Hear, hear, folks! The Madame of Melody, the trademark of truth!" He spread his arms to the side. "Well, you know what? I won't deny it. Your campaign of terror is succeeding, scaring the hell out of millions of people. That's why we're here. The time has come to unravel this set-up once and for all. And the task falls on me."

"This isn't a publicity stunt." Angelica kept her voice even. "There's evidence and data to prove it. Dozens of other research centers made their findings public. To stop this threat, we must act now. Together."

"Yes, we know of your elaborate scheme to sell us your sponsored products." Milo shook his head. "What were they called? Auteras? How much for one. A thousand dollars? Two thousand?"

"We're past the point of buying protection software. We need to create a brand-new ether, with a new cyberspace infrastructure immune to the threat of the killer malicious."

"A new ether?" This time, the Ether Hound wasn't faking his surprise.

"We call it the holistic ether." Angelica looked at the audience. "A new, more secure means of mass communication. Something that'll ensure for generations to come a reliable system to connect humankind."

Milo recovered quickly from the surprise. "Never let the truth get in the way of a compelling a story, right? So this it what you're selling, hmm. *Fear*? Cantara taught you well. But there's a problem with your blabbering about doom. It isn't real, and we're not buying it."

Milo's strategy was obvious: he wanted to discredit the

news. Angelica couldn't let him. She pulled a trigoy out of her pocket and threw it into the air. The reproduction showed a Masvieth with data proving the existence of the malicious and its diffusion throughout the ether.

"This shows the status of the Geoether," Angelica explained. "The red areas denote the spread of the killer malicious in the most trafficked areas of cyberspace and—"

"Please." Milo used a trigoy to show another Masvieth reproduction. "This shows the same thing. The only difference is that it's not embellished with your imaginary constellation of problems. Less intriguing, perhaps, but it describes reality. I think we've reached an impasse, Madame of Melody. What to do now? Believe a fantasy describing the apocalypse, or stick to boring reality?"

"Many etherions read those figures, Milo," Angelica pointed out. "Dozens of them. They agree with me."

Milo nodded slowly. "Yes, you brainwashed some small-timers, but Covenant isn't going to sit on its hands while you bring havoc to cyberspace."

A portion of the audience stood and cheered Milo.

Angelica stepped forward. "You're attached to the old order because it gives you power. It's this kind of blindness that'll lead us to ruin. Open your eyes before it's too late."

"Oh, my eyes are wide open, and I see your recklessness." Milo pointed a finger at her. "You're not simply hungry for fame, you're *desperate* for it. No, Madame. We already have an ether, and it works just fine. No need for your flamboyant version, thank you."

Angelica stepped toward Milo. "It's what we need to fix the problem."

"You're delusional if you think that." Milo turned toward the audience. "It's obvious, ladies and gentlemen, that this dispute must move from this stage to the cyberspace proper.

I expect each of you to choose sides in the coming weeks. It's time to know where you stand."

Milo Finnegar Jasper turned to Angelica and gave her one last pointed look before walking away.

At that moment, as every spectator stood up to support either the Ether Hound or the Madame of Melody by shouting their names, Angelica knew that the Ether War had officially begun.

32

MILITARIZED SPACE

HYPERIST COMPLEX INFINITY, PRESS ROOM

Gladia

Gladia walked down the corridor, toward the door flanked by two security guards dressed in the familiar white of the hyperist uniform.

Arthur walked at her side, with Charlotte trailing a few steps behind, a tablet clutched in her hands.

Gladia stopped a dozen steps away from the door, inhaled through her nose, and held her breath.

"The press is waiting, ma'am," muttered the assistant, her voice tense. "Whenever you're ready."

"Right." Gladia felt like a condemned prisoner escorted to the gallows. She hid her hands behind her back, where she kept them clasped tightly.

"You sure about this?" asked Arthur.

Gladia bit her lip. "I'm sure it's better than doing nothing." From the corner of her eye, she saw Arthur give her a half-convinced nod.

She knew what he was thinking. They'd argued for hours over their next move. He didn't think it was a smart idea going public without having answers to some of the most pressing questions. Gladia, instead, wanted to do damage control as soon as possible. That meant facing a situation they didn't fully understand in order to stop the spread of rumors. The more time they spent without issuing an official statement, the higher the chance that the Planetary Court would think they were losing control. Gladia couldn't allow that.

She stepped forward, and the guard on the left opened the ebony door of the pressroom, letting them inside a carpeted room with wood paneling. On the left side was a stage with a podium, the flag with the Silver Infinity placed prominently beside it. On the right side, representatives from many heavyweight media outlets followed with unblinking eyes Gladia's march toward the podium. Among them there was DataMorph, Neo Global Network, Covenant, Dao Deng Media, Pharsiana Press, Confederation Stream, and others.

When Gladia reached the stage, she placed her tablet on the hard wooden surface of the podium and started reading her address. "Yesterday at 2:42 p.m., Pacific Time, schematics of a highly advanced orbital fighter prototype were sent by an unknown source to all major media outlets along with allegations of involvement of the militaristic region known as Juggernaut in Tolomeus Almagest's katalamban program." Gladia clasped her clammy hands around the edge of the podium so hard her knuckles hurt. "According to these allegations, the elite members of Juggernaut poured billions of dollars into the research and development of Legatus Almagest's five-year sidereal development plan, an act that is against the PlaCo regulation concerning the militarization of space. When a team of military aerospace engineers analyzed the schematics of the prototype, they found resemblances with the original katalamban design, with modifications made to the hull and engine to allow it to carry high-powered electromagnetic launchers. According to the analysts, this could be some kind of experimental rail gun. This weapon was banned by the Planetary Court, as it violates Directive Number Five for the Regulation of Warfare Equipment in Space. A spokesperson of Juggernaut has issued a statement denying their participation in any illegal LEO and outer space experimental weapons program. They did not comment on the schematics of the orbital fighter prototype. As for Legatus Almagest, any attempt to contact him to ask for clarification has proven fruitless. We have no information at this time of his whereabouts."

There was a soft murmur as the reporters digested the news. It was probably not the best PR move to let them know that the person who was most directly involved in the scandal had disappeared, but transparency was key. The media needed to know the Hyperist Executive Council was being straightforward on the matter. Most importantly, they needed to know Gladia wasn't sitting on her hands.

She cleared her throat, then resumed speaking. "The Hyperist Executive Council and all hyperist parties are working to shed light on this matter, but at the moment, it's too early to confirm any of the information we possess. We have opened an internal investigation and are searching for alternative ways to get in contact with Legatus Almagest. I will now take your questions."

The last word worked like a spell, and the room became alive. All the reporters stood up in unison, hitting Gladia with a wall of words coming from dozens of people.

"Executive Director, how could news like this have spread without the—"

"...the landist spokesperson hinted at a conspiracy against—"

"...Legatus could not have disappeared if not for—"

"...could the rail gun referred to in the report have been a well orchestrated—"

Gladia clenched her jaw as she pointed to one reporter, officially beginning her media torture.

33

UNEXPECTED HELP
YELLOW SEA, AQUAMARINE

Ariul

❧

Tiago evaluated Lena, then nodded. "Yeah. Makes sense."

"Really?" Lena frowned. "How?"

"Think about it." He waved a hand as if dispersing smoke. "It makes sense Wei would put relevant memories inside the pendant and then conceal them from everyone but the bearer."

She blinked. "Wait, *what*? Why would it make sense? It makes no sense at all! It just sounds like a good way to lose information that is supposed to be kept safe. I mean, I didn't even know what this necklace did until I started wearing it while I slept. If I never did, maybe I would never know it contained Wei's memories, or whatever it is I'm seeing."

Tiago showed a smiled that built up. "But they have been kept safe. So safe, in fact, that not even the bearer knew until the right moment."

"Okay, well, maybe. But that doesn't explain the timing. I mean, seriously. I could have left this thing in my room, and then all the information would have been lost."

Tiago shook his head. "Wei always had a contingency plan. If he wanted you to see something at a particular moment, you can bet that was exactly what was going to happen."

She stared at him. "You've lost me."

He started pacing around the room. "Look, it might sound strange to an uninitiated, but—"

"An uninitiated?" She arched her eyebrow. "You mean me?"

He sighed. "Listen. I know Wei. He liked to compartmentalize information. Kept pieces separate to keep them safe. You know the saying, 'don't put all your eggs in one basket'?"

She scratched her forehead. "Um...yeah. So?"

"That's it! That's how he operated, on a personal and professional level. He kept things separated, even within the same project."

"Why?"

"Because there were fewer chances they might be discovered by the wrong person, or at the wrong time. He shrouded everything in mystery and then put all the pieces back together when it was time to show their true nature."

Lena glanced at her pendant. "So you're saying this trigoy, and the memories inside, are another of his...projects?"

"I think so."

She stared at the Pelargonium pendant. She had been talking to the chancellor for close to an hour, telling him everything about the dreams. Tiago had confirmed her suspicions. When she had described Evangeline, a girl Lena had never seen other than in her dream, the chancellor confirmed her description matched the real Evangeline, whom he'd met when he was younger.

Her dream about Pandora had been another thing entirely. Tiago had not seemed prepared for that, and fell into a strange sort of silence after Lena told him about Wei's conversation with Pandora. When Lena asked him what he thought about the dreams, he said they might be a way to provide useful information to fight the biomechas.

"Lena? Are you listening?"

She shook her head to clear it. "What?"

Tiago gestured to the nightstand. "What's that?"

She followed his outstretched hand, blinked. There was a yellow trigoy and what resembled a small index card beside it. "I don't know," she said, puzzled. "There was... there was nothing there."

Tiago looked at her. "You sure?"

She nodded.

He glanced at the room. "Did someone else get in?"

She crossed her arms. "No. I was alone the whole time. Well, someone might have entered when I was sleeping, but..." She trailed off, not knowing how to finish the sentence.

Tiago turned slowly toward the two objects, his posture suddenly stiff. "EVA? Analyze the trigoy and the card on the table. Any component that could be identified as dangerous?"

"Negative, Chancellor," EVA replied.

He approached the table and Lena took the note. She noticed the peculiar sheen and cursed under her breath.

"What?" Tiago asked.

She bit her lower lip. "This is tylenium." She turned to regard the chancellor. "I know who put this trigoy here."

He frowned. "Who?"

"The Overseer of Ariul." She waved the note in front of him. "This is how he makes contact."

Tiago glanced around, as if expecting someone else to appear in the room. "You're saying he's here, in Aquamarine?"

"I don't know. Maybe it's not him. Maybe it's a spy."

"What does it say?"

Lena turned the card in her hand and found a brief message. She read it aloud. "Take back what's yours."

Tiago picked up the trigoy, threw it into the air, and the object projected a 3D image that resembled a ship.

She frowned. "What's that?"

Tiago's eyes narrowed. "It's a Black Water."

"A Black Water? You mean the biomechas' ships?"

"Yes." He studied the projection. "Look at this." He pointed to a line of information that appeared on top of a brief description listing the ship's tonnage and size. There were four words written in Italics: *Hammerer Class Battle-cruiser Mastodon*. Underneath the name of the ship was a series of numbers. "These are spatial coordinates. It might be the current location of this ship."

Lena noticed a red dot pulsing inside *Mastodon*'s lower bridge. She touched it and two words appeared alongside it: *Makoto Shimao*. She stepped back, eyes widening. "That's him," she said. "Makoto! He's aboard this ship!"

"Let's not jump to conclusions." Tiago removed a small handheld display from his pocket and typed on it. "We need to analyze this information to make sure it's reliable."

She looked at him. "How long do you need?"

"I'm going to call in a few favors." He threw a glance at the door. "Shouldn't take more than half an hour to find out if that Black Water is really where the Overseer says it is."

Lena swallowed, glanced at the projection. "What if it's true? What if Makoto is still alive? Can we rescue him?"

The chancellor inhaled sharply. "Cassandra would never green light a rescue operation. Too risky. Nor would Max without a damn good reason. No. If we want to pull this off, we'll need volunteers ready to risk bringing the fight outside Saemangeum City." Tiago looked at Lena and smiled. "And I might just happen to know the right person for the job."

34

THE WOODWORM

NASHVILLE, ARK INSTITUTE FOR ADVANCED ETHERIC STUDIES

James

❧

James Ark stared at the Masvieth for a moment before glancing at the ceiling. "Can't be true, ADAM."

"My latest analysis of the cyber-fabric is accurate, Domine." The AI voice sounded stilted. "You cannot create a dominion that way. It's impossible."

James scoffed. "There must be a way. There's always a way. Give me something. An idea, a suggestion, anything. I don't care if it's unlikely."

ADAM remained silent for a second longer than expected before saying, "I alone am not enough to make the changes you desire, in the timeframe you have set."

"Okay," James said. "What are we missing? Resources?"

"No. This is a technological issue. It goes beyond money."

James set his brow into a deep frown. "Money can buy innovation. It has been done before."

"True," ADAM said. "But the change is never instantaneous. It takes time, sometimes years or decades, for a true breakthrough in technology. What you seek is beyond my computational capability, or the computational capability of anything that exists today."

James swallowed. His heart beat faster. That put a full stop to his line of thinking. If ADAM was right—and the AI always was—creating an etheric dominion would require years they didn't have.

"Domine, did you understand my last statement?"

James snapped into focus. He must have remained silent for longer than he thought. "Yes." He cleared his throat, his voice strained. He drummed his fingers on his thigh. "Say we had the technology."

"Are we speculating now?"

James bit the inside of his cheek. "Yes, we are speculating." He almost snapped the last word. He took in a deep breath, trying to calm himself, then continued talking. "Say we had the technology you needed. What, exactly, would you require to achieve the objective in our timeframe?"

This time ADAM was quiet for an even longer time, so long that James thought the AI didn't understand his question. He was about to repeat the question when ADAM said, "You would need another me."

James opened his mouth, but nothing came out. Another ADAM. Now he understood what the AI meant. ADAM was unique. James had only refined the matrix over time, but the original idea for the program wasn't his. He didn't know where Cantara had gotten ADAM. James was not a computer scientist, but whoever had designed ADAM must have been a brilliant mind, years ahead of his time. If he hadn't—

"Domine, did you understand my last—"

"Yes," James snapped. "I got that. Thanks." He pushed his glasses back, clenching and unclenching his hands. "Alright, let's put that problem aside for the moment."

"As you wish, Domine."

James made the Masvieth disappear with a wave of his hand. "In the meantime, tell me what's happening in the ether. Any update on Covenant?"

"Yes. There is something you might find useful. Domine Jasper is employing all his etheric assets to counter our PR campaign. According to my latest analysis, his strategy is proving effective. The Truska and Gomenagh regions have publicly sided with him. These are key players, necessary to gain a solid foothold into the neutralist portion of cyberspace. I am projecting a ninety-seven point three percent likelihood this development will tip other neutralist conglomerates to Covenant's side."

James rocked slightly with a faraway look. "Misfortunes never come alone," he muttered, gripping his hands together while feeling the throb of his heartbeat during the silence that followed.

"I did not understand your last sentence," ADAM said.

James blinked, then flashed a smile that didn't reach the eyes. "I said, 'Misfortunes never come alone.' It's a proverb. It means that adverse events are correlated and develop their full potential when they occur at the same time."

"A curious expression." Something in ADAM's inflection bordered on amusement. "I shall add it to my database."

James pinched the skin between his thumb and forefinger. He wasn't sure how he felt about the slight change in the AI's personality. It had surfaced as James kept it active for longer stretches of time. With the war against Covenant escalating, he needed ADAM more than ever to counter Milo's attacks. That meant providing ADAM with a bigger database and server, more energy, and an increased amount of money poured into its matrix's refinement. Sometimes James wondered how much ADAM was simulating human behavior, and how much the AI really understood. When James started removing the restrictions written in the base-line software, his only goal was increasing ADAM's computational capacity to achieve his goals faster; he thought little about the consequences of the upgrades. Now, he was no longer sure that had been a smart idea. A chill ran down his spine as he remembered something Cantara had said in one of her classes: "Humanity won't fully know something until it fears its implications, and won't fully fear the implications until humanity itself is changed forever. It happened with fire, currency, electricity, computer, the Internet, and autotrons. It will happen again; and next time, there might not be a humanity left to witness the next round of implications."

"Domine?"

ADAM's voice chased James' thoughts and returned him to the pressing issue of winning the cyberspace war. "We are doing everything in our power to win this war," he said, more to himself than to the IA. "We need to carry on, continue with the training of our forces, and hope for the best."

"Hope." ADAM's word sounded hollow, like an empty shell. "A feeling of expectation and longing for a particular thing or event to happen. I have never understood this concept."

James smoothed down his coat. "Pray that you never

have to. It's better to *know* something than to hope it happens."

"You want me to organize a counteroffensive to Domine Jasper's plan?"

"No." James swallowed. "Forget about Covenant. Milo is going after the big fishes and he's going to get them, no matter what we do. Let's focus on the middle and small-size players. A bunch of wet sand might weigh more than rocks."

"I understand," ADAM said. "I will compile a list of the best candidates to approach."

James raised his eyebrows. "Sometimes the final victory cannot be obtained without a calculated number of losses." He looked at his gloved hands, squinting. "A strategic retreat can sometimes be the best alternative to avoid total defeat."

"Another proverb?" ADAM asked.

"Not this time." James rubbed his arms as if they were cold.

"Then what is it, Domine?"

James drew in a shallow breath. "Just something I said in the past. Something I still believe." He gazed at the ceiling, unable to hold a smile. "You going to add that to your database?"

The AI's reply came without hesitation. "I already did."

James nodded, then gazed at the door. "Now, what's left is to figure out a way to deal with all the bad publicity we're getting from DataMorph. There's got to be a way to get them off our back. Maybe giving them something else to gnaw on?" James blinked. "Well, there's that mess with the Hyperist Movement happening right now, isn't there?"

"You are referring to the Militarized Space scandal?"

"Right." James tightened his fists. "Maybe we can throw some dirt in that direction and see if it sticks. Egea already has the Pentaproject to deal with, and rogue elements in her establishment threatening to tear apart HYPER. Lots of juicy stories that can be amplified. She has lots going on, but not enough attention from the media. I can change that. What do you think?"

ADAM remained silent for a moment before answering. "I think, Domine, that misfortunes never come alone."

"No," James agreed, his chest tightening. "No, they don't. Draft a plan. Send me the outline in an hour."

"It will be done, Domine."

As James made his way out the door, he realized ADAM had internalized a new personality trait, improving his ability to understand the world composed of flesh and blood and, maybe, becoming a bit more human.

35

DIRT

HYPERIST COMPLEX INFINITY, CONTROL CENTER

Gladia

Gladia went through the news displayed on her console with the fierce resolve of a bird of prey scanning for her next kill. Around her, the control room was buzzing with the sound of incoming calls and the shuffling of feet of half a dozen data experts gathering information and sending them to the PR departments tasked to handle the growing crisis. Gladia absentmindedly grabbed the cup sitting in the armchair, but found it empty.

"Mac." She looked at a young man sitting on the console at her left, waved the empty cup at him. "Could you get me more coffee, please?"

Mac cleared his throat. "Um, that's your fifth cup, ma'am." He rubbed his hands together.

Gladia glared at him. "You keeping count?"

The young man swallowed. "Yes...no! I mean...um...

someone has to? The Constable asked me to keep an eye on you while—"

"Look, Mac." Gladia sighed. "Arthur isn't here, okay? He won't know. I need coffee to get through this day. Do I have to ask again?"

The young man straightened up. "No, ma'am. It's coming right up." He bolted out of his chair and almost tripped before making it to the exit.

Gladia went back to reading the news that the crisis management department had sent, scanning for content she could use against the growing list of detractors. The Militarized Space scandal had stirred a hornets' nest, and nothing Gladia had done had been enough to placate it.

"Ma'am?"

Gladia looked over her desk at the data guy sitting behind a console to the right. "What's up, George?" she asked.

"DataMorph has released a new article about Almagest's involvement with Oplite Corp."

Gladia massaged her temples, eyes half-closed. "Diffusion score?"

"Ninety parts per million."

Gladia cursed. "All right." She straightened up, trying to keep the edge off her voice. "Fill me in."

"Yes, ma'am. The news is spreading fast across the region's social media network and other portions of the ether tied with DataMorph." George scanned the content on the screen, frowned. "It claims the Legatus exchanged favors with some illegal organizations based in Southeast Asia involved with cyberterrorism."

"I don't care about claims. I want facts." Gladia folded her arms across her chest. "Do you have something the PlaCo could sink its teeth into?"

George shrugged. "I've got an encrypted bank transfer, two eye-witnesses, and a private conversation between a member of Legatus Almagest's advisors and Marco Schantell, the vice president of Oplite Corp."

Gladia glanced at her already impressive amount of content to read. She sighed, her posture collapsing. "Send it."

George offered a quick nod. "Coming right up, ma'am."

Gladia scanned the article, checked the alleged proof. "It's just more rubbish. Hey, George?"

"Yes, ma'am?"

"Release a standard AMR statement to counter this pile of shit they pass off as news. Show the latest movements of Almagest's backers. Be crystal clear about the sources and make sure all users who've read DataMorph's sorry excuse for a story see our answer. Push a notification via personalized advertising if you have to. It'll do little to convince the naysayers, but people with functioning neurons will realize we're saying the truth."

George started typing. "On it."

"Executive Director." A middle-aged lady wearing a headset turned toward her. "I've got another hot input from the landist region."

Gladia held her stomach and bent forward slightly, bracing herself for the next punch. "Hit me, Saria."

"Yvonne Muchena's official position on the Juggernaut scandal found traction with the South American geosynchronists," the woman said, her eyes darting to follow the stream of news on the screen. "They're spreading it in their sphere of influence, with alleged proof of the katalamban project being used as a cover-up for a shadow operation meant to weaponize a space station."

Gladia snorted. "Nonsense. Reach and diffusion?"

"Around two million people. Nine parts per million."

Gladia tapped a foot on the floor. "Send me the report with all the feedback loop you can find."

"Yes, ma'am."

"And monitor the influence these articles are having on the neutralists, the orbital transport lobbyists, the Conservative Alliance, and the Brotherhood of Peace. We've gotta bring some people with a lick of sense into the conversation."

"Will do, ma'am."

Gladia was halfway through the reading of another news article when George turned to speak to her. "Executive Director?"

Gladia rubbed the back of her neck, not turning toward the data guy. "What now, George?"

"We received confirmation that the Planetary Court has convened a closed-door committee of the Council on Orbital Transportation to investigate Militarized Space."

"Perfect." Gladia's nostril flared; her pulse sped up as heat flushed through her body. "Just perfect. The icing on the cake. Who's on the committee?"

"We don't know yet, ma'am," was George's reply. "The PlaCo won't make their names public to avoid external pressures."

Gladia leaned toward him, her hands clasped together. "That's it? That's all you've got?"

George looked abashed. "I'm sorry, ma'am."

Gladia turned toward the other people in the room. "Anyone else got something useful on this? A rumor? Your auntie's gossip? Hmm? Anything?"

A round of shaking heads and fleeting glances were the only answers she got.

Gladia turned to George. "All right. Keep me posted if there're any developments."

"Yes, ma'am."

Gladia put her palms against her temples and massaged the pain. Weariness sat in her muscles, and her eyes felt bleary. Like her, most of the people working in the control room had barely left their station in the past couple of days. Gladia glanced over her shoulder to where Arthur usually stood, ready to help. She dispatched her friend to the Executive Council to update the members about the situation. They needed to devise a cohesive strategy to counter the increasing worldwide pressure from the landists. Muchena was riding the shitstorm for all it's worth, and Gladia needed someone she trusted to lead the Council while she focused on damage control.

She also spoke with Penelope Juno and Maria Castellari. The conversation with the two hyperist leaders had turned sour pretty quickly. It was clear that both of them wanted Almagest's head on a platter. After his disappearance, Gladia could hardly blame them.

The leader of the Ascendents had been missing for days, vanished. Was he hiding? Or had something happened to him? With each passing hour, confusion grew, and more and more people turned to her for answers.

Gladia refused to believe Tolomeus actually had something to do with this hot mess. He was an ambitious man, but not at the cost of being reckless. He would know that siding with the militarists was a quick way of being blamed by all sides, getting nothing in return but terrible publicity and legal crossfire.

For the next two hours, Gladia directed the traffic of information through communiques, updates, and social media posts, leading the hyperist response throughout cyberspace. Around lunch time, when the seventh cup of coffee sat empty on her armrest, she received a direct call via interlink. It was her assistant.

"I'm busy right now, Charlotte." Gladia was in the middle of drafting a statement. "What's up?"

Charlotte's voice was urgent. "It's about Tolomeus Almagest, ma'am."

Gladia froze, her eyes widening. "Yes?"

"He's here, ma'am. Inside Infinity. He wants to talk with you."

36

LESSON IN HUMILITY

NASHVILLE, ARK INSTITUTE FOR ADVANCED
ETHERIC STUDIES

James

The classroom was a spacious, well-lit area devoid of architectural frills or other elements that might distract the students' attention. The furnishings were sleek and modern, and smart glass displays adorned the walls and part of the ceiling.

Three rows of chairs arranged on three levels gave the classroom the look of a small auditorium. Thirty students in their early twenties were looking at Angelica, sitting on a dais at the front of a room.

"Good communicators know how to capture attention." Angelica waved a hand, sending to each student's console station footage of a politician addressing an audience. "An excellent communicator, however, compounds on that by making the audience feel like it's part of the conversation." She turned toward a dark-skinned girl with short brown hair sitting in the first row. "Sasha, is being an etherion any different?"

Sasha stood up. "Yes, Madame. Etherions are more than communicators. They're leaders."

"Correct." Angelica joined her hands behind her back. "Etherions use words to compel people to act. Today, a power like this can save lives. You all know what we're up against. The old etheric establishment wants to silence us. They're doing their best to discredit the holistic, but you know the truth. You know that millions of lives depend on it being implemented." Angelica stood up from behind her desk and paced in front of the students. "In this class, you've been taught how to communicate successfully, and have been given the tools to become effective etherions. You've learned how to move to project confidence, how to use silence to organize your thoughts, and how to turn a message into a powerful instrument of change. We're in the last weeks of this course, and it's past time your skills are tested." She nodded to three students and gestured at the dais. "Carmen, Yoshi, and Janet, come here. Time to shine."

The three students rose from their seats and headed toward the raised platform.

"ADAM," Angelica said, "activate the 'ether vs. holistic' simulation. Version gamma 2.01."

"Commencing," the AI replied.

On the platform appeared a multidimensional reproduction of three podiums equally distanced from one another. The three students took their places behind each one.

"Welcome to the debate of the decade," Angelica announced, lifting her arms in a sweeping gesture. "You'll be speaking on a show aligned against the holistic. This is an excellent platform to spread your message, but it comes with a trade-off. The host is a sharp-tongued critic who doesn't pull her punches. Her job is to make you look like glory-hungry buffoons. In this simulation, I'll impersonate the show's presenter. Make no mistakes. You're in a kill zone, and I'll use any opportunity I have to make you look bad. ADAM, let's get started."

"Understood, Madame."

The room's projector wove complicated webs of light which surrounded the three students, creating a convincing copy of a television studio with an audience.

Angelica smoothed her shirt, bowed slightly in front of the imaginary audience, and then turned to look at her students with an intense stare. Her expression and demeanor had changed in the blink of an eye.

The show had begun.

"Madame Faraday." Angelica turned to Carmen, drawing up to her full height. "You claim the ether is infested with an...ahhh..." She trailed off, cleared her throat, then flashed an apologetic smile to the audience. "Well, this is embarrassing. Can't find a way to call it. Is it an infection? A cyber-parasite? An etheric bug? Good God, madness has its own flavor, hasn't it? Let's call it a—"

"It's a killer malicious," Carmen broke in with a firm voice. "An etheric-induced disorder that—"

"Excuse me, Madame." Angelica pressed her lips into a thin line, stared at Carmen for a long moment before continuing. "I was *talking*, as in the muscles in my tongue were moving and air was going through my lips to produce sounds. Didn't you notice?"

"Well..." Carmen squinted, her brow lowering. "I was trying to explain—"

"You were trying to interrupt me, which you did, so... yeah, good job! You hit the nail on the head." Angelica clapped her hands, causing the simulated audience to burst out laughing. "Now, I know you folks are paid by the word and want to cram as many as possible in a sentence, but this is really the issue here, isn't it? You holistic people—by the way, hell of a name for a yoga club—have been pumping out a ton of garbage trying to pass this cheap commercial of yours for something that's real. I mean, seriously? How on earth can you sleep at night?"

"It isn't media garbage," Yoshi said. "It's an actual problem that is ending lives as we speak."

Angelica offered a tight smile as she turned to the young man. "Ending lives. Okay. Sure. Why don't you elaborate on that, Domine?"

Yoshi held his chin high. "It's easy to condemn a constructive course of action, harder to propose one. Tell me something: How do you explain the staggering number of people who've died for an issue clearly correlated with their etheric traveling?"

"I'm sorry, you're asking me, Domine?" Angelica gestured at her chair. "You want to swap places?"

Yoshi threw a darting gaze at his classmates, his body posture stiffer.

"Hello?" Angelica waved a hand. "I'm right here."

Yoshi's rapid blinking led to a wide-eyed look. "I don't understand the question."

"You don't?" Angelica flashed a cardboard smile. "Well, let me be more clear then." She pointed at Yoshi. "Why don't you take my seat? See how you do as a host. You know, since you're the one asking questions and expecting me to answer. Go on. It's all yours."

Yoshi's brows pulled in as he looked downward. "Can we go back to the issue at hand?" His voice sounded strained, barely audible.

"I don't know," Angelica threw back at him. "Are you finished trying to do my job?"

Yoshi clenched his jaw, but said nothing.

"Okay." Angelica sat back in her chair with a satisfied sigh. "Where were we?"

Someone from the simulated audience shouted, "The etheric bug!" The shout was followed by a round of laughter.

"Right!" Angelica laughed with the audience. "Thank you. The etheric bug." She turned toward Yoshi, who was visibly sweating. "So, Domine Jovan, can you explain to us in simple words what exactly this 'thing' is that you're so afraid of?"

Yoshi avoided Angelica's gaze. "I'm confident about speaking for all people interested in the impact of the killer malicious when I say—"

"Well, I've got to stop you right there, Domine, since you don't speak for me."

Another laugh erupted from the audience.

Yoshi made to open his mouth, but Angelica waved him away and turned to the only student who hadn't spoken. "Madame Janet Hulma," she said. "As your colleagues here have tried their best to win the title of least convincing guest of the year, you haven't spoken yet. I've got some hope you have a brain inside that head, instead of a mango smoothie. Care to add your five cents?"

"Sure," Janet said. "Can I ask you, when was the last time you traveled into the ether?"

"Ten minutes before I was invited to this AA gathering," Angelica replied, pointing to Carmen and Yoshi. Other laughs from the audience.

Janet thrust her chest out. "What if I told you the next time could be the last?"

"I don't know." Angelica showed her wedding band. "What if I were to tell you that this ring keeps away yetis?"

"Yetis?" Janet frowned. "You mean the...um...monster?"

"Yup." Angelica nodded. "Tall fellow, very hairy. Big shoe size."

Janet rubbed her forehead. "How is this related to what we're discussing?"

Angelica gestured around with a wide-eyed look. "Do you see any yetis around? Just because something is happening around me doesn't mean my claim of knowing the cause is true."

Janet swallowed. "My point was—"

"Sorry, were you trying to make a point?" Angelica pressed a hand down on her breastbone, looking shocked. "I thought we were just blowing air through our lips to see if something funny came out."

Janet narrowed her eyes, anger showing on her face. "May I finish?"

"No." Angelica grimaced, then covered her face with her hand as she shook her head. "We're done here. ADAM. Stop the simulation."

"As you wish, Madame."

The other classmates reappeared as the simulated audience disappeared along with the reproduction of the three podiums. Carmen, Yoshi, and Janet looked chastened.

"Ten minutes!" Angelica's voice tore into the silence. "Took me ten minutes to destroy you." She snapped her head toward Yoshi. "Yoshi, you were clueless. You gotta look people in the eyes when you talk to them, especially in a live debate. What was that? You were supposed to convince the audience you knew what you were saying. It was demeaning."

Yoshi swallowed. "Madame. I was trying to—"

"What? Look like a fool? Well, good job, sir. Mission accomplished." Angelica turned away, glared at the girl on Yoshi's left. "Carmen, you want to interrupt a host on her own show? You're welcome to, but first, learn how to handle a sparring match on your own terms. You do not stutter, do not back down an inch, and you most surely don't let someone dismiss you that way, not if you want to convince people you're in control. Don't play offense if you don't know what you're up against. Wait. Learn. Don't expose yourself. And now you, Janet." She jabbed a finger for emphasis. "Oh, Janet. You were the best. Took me three sentences to get under your skin. *You*. An elite student, weeks away from becoming an etherion. How is that even possible?"

"I'm sorry, Madame." Janet swallowed, her eyes welling with tears.

"Sorry?" Angelica stared at her. "You're *sorry*? You should be mad! I'm mad! You were supposed to be ready. It was three against one. You should have owned me."

"That's not fair," Carmen said. "You're the Madame of Melody. You have years of training, experience, and—"

"Fair?" Angelica snorted. "You think 'fair' has anything to do with winning a debate? Oh, you're in the wrong line of work, dear."

"I didn't think that—"

"That's right," Angelica said, staring Carmen down. "You *didn't* think." She turned toward the rest of the class, looking wide-eyed at the exchange. "Ladies and gentlemen, you're not in Kansas anymore. This is war! You must be prepared to both give and take punches against opponents who're smarter than you and have absolutely zero scruples. You think I roughed you up? This is nothing. Jasper's etherions will break your bones and suck their marrow, slowly, so the audience can enjoy the show. You've got to act like etherions or you'll be slaughtered the moment you walk out that door." She thrust her index finger toward the door. "The ether war has started and we're losing. Big time. In just a few weeks we'll throw you onto the battlefield: public debates, live shows, reality reels, social media live, you name it. You'll be exposed and alone. This place, right *here*, is the last time you can make mistakes. It's your last chance to be wrong. That's why we're going to do this again, and again, until you're ready to do some actual damage. ADAM?"

"Yes, Madame."

"Activate the 'ether vs. holistic' simulation. Version gamma 2.03."

"Commencing."

Angelica motioned Yoshi, Janet, and Carmen to their places, then paced in front of the other students, her eyes searching for her next victims. "Samanta, Nelson, and Ana." She pointed to three students sitting in the second row. "You're up next. Let's go. I want to have a taste of all of you before lunch."

The students stood and plodded to the stage like the condemned on their way before a firing squad.

Angelica crossed her arms. "ADAM," she snapped. "Let's get started."

∞∞∞

The students left the classroom in eerie silence. No one said goodbye, no one lingered to ask advice or questions. They looked depleted and didn't even glance in Angelica's direction as they hurried toward the exit.

Angelica had put them through the meat-grinder. Some

of them made her job more difficult, but overall, none stood a chance.

They were too green, too unprepared. She bit the inside of her cheek, grateful that none of them looked in her direction so they couldn't see her remorse.

She didn't like what she was doing to them, but it was necessary. James had encouraged this approach. They needed results fast. Warriors need battle scars to prove their worth.

Angelica frowned, collapsing onto the chair, then gazed at the empty classroom and sighed. What happened to Angelica Kam, the cool-headed woman who solved problems with logic? What happened to the etiatros that just a few months ago was teaching kids how to travel safely into the ether? All had been swept away by the necessity of the moment as the Madame of Melody hijacked Angelica's life.

Angelica glanced at her phone, found a couple unanswered calls from Sebastian. She grimaced and shoved the phone away.

Her husband didn't understand. Their last conversation had ended in a heated argument when Sebastian accused James of having "brainwashed" her. Now, days after the event, she felt their relationship had deteriorated.

Angelica hadn't slept well in days, and the long hours of work were taking their toll. She put her arms on the table, rested her head on her arms, and fell asleep.

A beep woke her. She blinked, feeling her cheek warm and clammy as she rose. She couldn't say if it had been minutes or hours since she'd dozed off, but she didn't feel rested. A quick glance at her phone told her Sebastian was calling.

She considered ignoring the call, but this was the third

time he'd tried. It must be important. Angelica moistened her lips and accepted the call.

"What's up?" She tried to keep her voice even.

Sebastian cleared his throat. "Hey. How're you doing?"

She shrugged. "Just finished a class. Had a busy weekend."

"Right. Angy, look, something's up." Sebastian sounded distressed. "I know you've got a lot on your plate right now, but there's something I need to show you."

"Okay." She frowned. "What is it?"

"I'm sending you the info via a secure channel."

She hesitated. "What info?"

"Take a look."

She checked her inbox and opened the file Sebastian sent. It appeared to be a set of bank coordinates. "What am I looking at, Bastian?"

"Remember when James told us he was funding the holistic R&D department with Asha's money?" Sebastian's voice sounded stilted, as if he had rehearsed the entire speech.

She scanned the rest of the document, finding multiple bank transfers from unknown sources to the Ark's institute bank account. "Yes, I remember."

"I contacted an old friend who works in the private sector. He's an expert in cybersecurity of etheric assets. I asked if the info James provided checked out with the actual amount of money the Ark is getting. It didn't. Only a small portion of that money came from Asha. The actual source is impossible to trace."

"What are you saying?"

Sebastian took a deep breath before answering. "I think the holistic is being funded illegally."

"What?"

"I don't know who they are, but it must be someone with enough resources to keep them off the radar. I'm talking about some deep level illegal activity here, something not even my friend could dig out."

She shook her head. "You're not thinking this through."

"Not thinking this through? Have you seen the document?"

"I did. Look, James must have known the funds were going to draw attention the moment we started making some noise. What do you think would happen if Milo and his minions found the source? They'd freeze the assets. That would choke us to death. If it's really that difficult to trace the source of the funding, don't you think that might have been James' plan all along?"

"And he lied to us?"

"He kept information from us as a precaution. I would have done the same. The more people who know about something, the better the chance it spreads."

Sebastian remained silent for a moment. When he spoke again, his voice sounded hoarse. "I don't know. All this secrecy doesn't sit well. I mean, there're too many things that don't add up. What about the off-limits floor in the institute? I asked James to give a look, and he refused with some bullshit excuse."

"Okay, well. I guess it didn't help that you called him a 'manipulative little bastard.'"

"I just want to understand—"

"You're mad because I'm here."

Sebastian let out a throaty laugh. "What?"

"I mean it." Angelica closed her eyes, wishing she hadn't picked up. "You're trying to find excuses to get me back to the Yodobashi."

"Angy, I'm not trying to—"

"Listen, I told you. If we don't sell the idea of the holistic, we're done. Done! You've read the numbers. You know I'm right. I can do a real difference here, teaching these kids rather than staring at data and counting the casualties."

"Please, Angy. You've got to listen to me. You're too emotionally involved. James is using you for—"

"Goodbye, Bastian." Angelica closed the call.

37

THE ARROW ON THE INFINITY

HYPERIST COMPLEX INFINITY, HEXAHEDRAL ROOM

Gladia

~

The Hexahedral Room was referred to as HYPER's Oval Office. It worked as the Executive Director's formal workspace, but also as a meeting room where she conferred with diplomats, heads of state, dignitaries, and CEOs of companies. Here Gladia Egea often addressed the world on television, radio, and the ether. In this room, she dealt with the issues of the day, and it was usually here that she received the bad news. As she entered the Hexahedral Room through a back door, something told her she was going to get some today.

She freshened up quickly in the bathroom, then straightened her jacket and sat behind her desk. She was exhausted, had drank too much coffee, and couldn't wait to take a cold shower, but right now all she wanted was to look Tolomeus in the eyes and ask him where the hell he had been.

Gladia glanced at her hands to make sure they weren't shaking, then pressed the caller button on the desk. "Let him in."

"Yes, ma'am," came Charlotte's reply.

The door opened and Tolomeus Almagest strode in, smiling like he'd won the lottery. "Look, I know you're pissed."

"Pissed?" Gladia blew out a noisy breath. "I was pissed two days ago. Now I'm choked. You have any idea of the garbage I had to swallow to keep the media from tearing us apart?"

"I'm sure it hasn't been pretty." Tolomeus lowered his voice. "I'm mortified."

"You don't look mortified." She gestured to the chair with a curt nod. "Sit down."

Tolomeus sat.

She leaned forward. "Were you kidnapped?"

"What?" Tolomeus laughed. "No."

"Someone threatened your family?"

"Of course not."

"Then you'll have a difficult time explaining to me why you come here, *two* full days after this disaster, striding in my office like you own the damn place."

"Gladia, I—"

"Shut up and start at the beginning!"

He bowed his head. "Look, I knew you'd want satisfactory answers for what happened with the militarists. I needed time to find them."

Gladia glared at him. "Did you receive the funds? Yes or no?"

He tilted his head to the side. "Well, yes *and* no, actually."

"Tolomeus, I'm this close to losing my shit right now. Explain."

"Okay." He held his hands up, palms toward Gladia. "Yes, I received the funds through a consortium of private companies. *But*, only after this whole thing with the militarists happened did we find out the consortium belonged to Juggernaut. I swear by Wei Wang: I didn't know the funds came from the Jingos. The purpose of the katalambans is scientific exploration and extraction of resources. No one wants to start a space war."

"Am I supposed to take your word?"

"You're not. I brought proof." He showed her a tablet.

Gladia raised an eyebrow. "What's this?"

"Here's the list of financial transactions and all communications we exchanged with the funding companies." Tolomeus tapped the tablet. "I'm giving you complete access to the financial history of the Ascendents. They framed us, Gladia. We're not the bad guys."

Gladia squinted. "You're saying they set you up?"

"I'm saying they tried their damn best to." He glanced toward the door, then continued with a lower tone. "And I've got a solid idea who it might have been."

Gladia blinked. "Who?"

He crossed his arms over his chest. "Penelope or Maria are behind this. Probably both."

Gladia widened her eyes, then snorted. "Oh, please. You're being paranoid."

"I'm serious." Tolomeus raised his voice, a gleam in his eyes. "They couldn't stand that I won. We both know they hate my guts. I'm sure they're enjoying the show, trying their best to let the world believe this is my doing. But it's not, and this tablet proves it."

Gladia eyed the tablet.

"Come on, you know me." He leaned forward, pointed at himself. "I'm a businessman at my core. I follow profit. Sure, I take calculated risks, but I don't shit where I eat. What's happening here smells fishy. I would never have done something so stupid."

Gladia knew Tolomeus wasn't lying, not about this. The whole thing didn't make a lick of sense from the get-go, but when one entertained the conspiracy theory Tolomeus was suggesting, many pieces clicked into place. She took the tablet with both hands. "I'll study this data and cross-check it with the security department."

Tolomeus nodded. "Knock yourself out."

"In the meantime, I'm suspending all funds and assets you've got from the Pentaproject."

Tolomeus stared at her. "What?"

Gladia felt lightheaded; a side effect of the pills she took to keep her hands from shaking. She fought to keep her voice steady. "The Executive Council can't support a project funded by militarists, even if you aren't involved."

"Whoa, whoa, slow down. I just told you I wasn't aware—"

"Doesn't matter." Gladia shook her head. "The katalambans received funds from Juggernaut. You said it yourself."

"The katalambans won the Pentaproject on their own merits."

"Look, the media is breathing down my neck. With the landists pouring gasoline on the fire, we'll be lucky if the PlaCo doesn't come up with some bullshit regulatory measure to limit LEO and cislunar space traffic just to make sure nothing funny happens out there. We can't let that happen. We need to keep a low profile until we know exactly what we're dealing with."

Tolomeus smiled and shook his head. "So I'm benched because you need to look good in public?"

"It's not about you or me. It's about the whole movement." Gladia stared straight into Tolomeus' eyes. "We both know this storm won't dissipate on its own. I need to take actions to reassure the PlaCo we would never allow something like Militarized Space to happen."

"And your solution is freezing my funds?"

Gladia inhaled sharply. "And removing you from the Council. For the time being."

Tolomeus laughed. "You're joking."

"It's the smart thing to do." She leaned toward him. "You sit tight. Let me do some investigating. I'll handle it as quietly as possible. If you're right, you'll be back on your feet in no time."

"But I won't have the funds back."

She shook her head. "I'm afraid that ship's sailed. Sorry."

Tolomeus leaned away, barely breathing, his eyes fixated on Gladia. "No."

Gladia's head flinched back. "No?"

"I won't do that." He curled his lips in a sneer. "I refuse to be the scapegoat."

Gladia folded her arms over her stomach. "I'm grounding your ass. It's happening."

Tolomeus stared at her. "You can't."

She forced a laugh. "Excuse me?"

"I can read the fine print." He steepled his hands. "The Starry Assembly suspends members of the Council and freezes assets, not you. I've spoken with most of its members and they don't share your view."

She blinked. "You *what*?"

"They agree with me. I've been framed. I don't deserve to go down."

Gladia opened her mouth, closed it. Of course. Now it all made sense. Tolomeus could have shown up ten minutes after the whole scandal blew up. Instead, he'd done the smart thing, won the support of enough members of the Starry Assembly so that he couldn't be ruled out of the picture. And all this behind Gladia's back. If Tolomeus wasn't bluffing—and she didn't think he was with so much at stake—then he already had a contingency plan. He hadn't come to her begging for mercy. He was standing on rock-solid ground, and the bastard knew it.

"You would challenge me?" Gladia hated that the words came out as a dreaded question rather than a threat. It made her sound weak.

"I'll do what I have to do to protect my people's interest."

"*Your* people? We're all hyperists."

"There are many shades of silver." Tolomeus knocked his knuckles on the hard surface of the table. "It's a shame you never paid attention. All I care about are the Ascendants, my constituents, those wearing an arrow on the infinity." He tapped the brooch on his chest, showing the golden arrow embedded into the silver infinity.

Sweat gathered on Gladia's hands. "Look. I get you're upset right now, but we don't need this bickering. HYPER must remain united."

"Says the person who wanted to can me five minutes ago?"

"Listen—"

"I'm done listening. Do what you gotta do. Just know I won't stand idle." Tolomeus went out, slamming the door behind him.

38

DESTINY'S CALL

YELLOW SEA, AQUAMARINE

Ariul

Aquamarine never ceased to amaze Lena. The underwater base was much bigger than she had expected. She was now walking beside Tiago in what he had called the "abandoned" section of the barracks. This part of Aquamarine was darker and looked less used than the rest of the base. It was also empty. Except for the low buzzing of electricity, the only distinguishable sound was their own footsteps echoing down the dimly lit corridor. The ghostly atmosphere made her skin crawl.

Tiago had said someone he knew could help them rescue Makoto and had spent the last day organizing the meeting in an undisclosed location.

It turned out the information the Overseer had provided was correct. Both the location and the nature of the Black Water had been confirmed by Tiago's contact. Lena didn't know why the Overseer was helping them, but knowing there was a chance to save Makoto had given her a purpose. Nothing could bring back the eighty-nine people killed by the biomechas, but saving Makoto could at least make a difference. She had to believe he could be saved.

Tiago had provided few details about the person they were going to meet, but had said it was their best shot at rescuing Makoto.

They kept walking down the poorly lit corridor in silence. Tiago occasionally stopped, glanced around, and then continued. The deeper they ventured inside, the more the temperature dropped. Tiago had explained several sections had minimal life support to preserve energy. According to him, more and more parts of the underwater city were on a sort of life-support.

"What's happening to the Defensio Project is happening to Aquamarine too," the chancellor had said earlier. "The biomechas have bled us throughout the years. We have fewer and fewer people and resources. This means fewer options."

There had been bitterness in his voice, an almost palpable anger. Lena understood why. Tiago had described a power struggle between factions within the Defensio Project, and the chancellor and the woman called Cassandra were obviously at odds with each other. It had become even more obvious when Cassandra invited Lena to speak in private moments after Dr. Risa discharged her.

"It isn't an invitation," Tiago had pointed out, twisting the edge of his mouth in a sour smile. "It's more like an order wrapped in pleasantries."

Lena had frowned at him. "Do I have to go?"

"Not accepting might raise suspicion," he had said. "It's the last thing we want."

"You sure she wouldn't help? Even if we can prove we've been tipped off?"

"Believe me. You tell her about the Black Water, any chance to save your friend is gone. She won't risk losing people."

"So I have to go."

"Yes. Be there, smile, and be polite. Say nothing useful. It'll be fine."

Lena was curious to know more about the regent, although there was something in that woman's gaze she found unnerving.

"We're here," Tiago said, stopping in the middle of the corridor.

"Here?" She looked around, frowned. There were no doors or elevators around. "There's nothing here."

"Maybe not." He smirked and placed a hand on the metal wall on his right. "Or maybe you just have to know what you're looking for."

The wall dilated, and Lena stepped back with a gasp. A passageway large enough for one person to go through had appeared.

"What's that?" she asked.

"Our contact's way to say hello." He motioned Lena to the passage with his chin. "Let's go."

On the other side, they found themselves in a large room. The only difference from the corridor was that this place was warmer, the air less stale.

A dozen black mannequins had been placed in a loose semicircle. Some dummies were missing the head, others had no arms. Only a couple remained whole. They were covered with an unknown type of metal plate that looked like pieces of armor.

Lena looked at Tiago. "What's this place?"

"It used to be a Seien assembly chamber." The chancellor strode over to one of the mannequins, trailing a finger across its dusty surface.

She frowned. "I don't know what Seien means."

He gestured to one plate. "It's a Japanese word. It means 'Wall of Stars.' It's what the dunamis call their armor."

"Okay." She scratched her head, her eyes wandering. "So...is this the right place?"

Tiago's eyes scanned the area. "Samuel?"

She blinked. That name was familiar. Where had she heard it before?

"Over here," came a male voice from somewhere on their right, where the room was bathed in shadows.

They strode to the other side and found a man sitting beside a black mannequin covered by cobalt blue armor. The helmet, shoulder pads, armbands, breastplate, leggings, and shoes shone dully with a soft halo.

"Samuel." Tiago smiled, and the two men shook hands. "Primping your ride?"

Lena met Samuel's dark brown eyes, and she remembered him. It was the centurion who had defended her during the assembly.

"You brought her." Samuel's eyes had an intensity that made her hair stand on end. He squeezed the contents of a small bottle onto a damp cloth and rubbed it on the breastplate, causing the armor to shine.

"Of course," Tiago said, folding his hands. "You looked at the data?"

"Yes. Everything checks. The Black Water is where the proximity device says it is." The centurion's eyes probed the chancellor's. "How did you get that information?"

Tiago glanced at Lena. "An external contact tipped us off."

Samuel narrowed his almond eyes, his body angling away from Tiago. "I'm going to need more than that, Chancellor."

Tiago tilted his head back and glanced upward. "It was the Overseer of Ariul."

Samuel threw a glance at Lena. "The mystery man she never even saw?"

Tiago offered a tight smile.

Samuel turned to look at Lena. "And you trust this person?"

Lena crossed her arms and glanced at Tiago, who nodded. "I don't know," she said, speaking the truth.

Samuel arched his eyebrow. "You don't know?"

"I don't know if I trust him." She rubbed her arms, diverted her eyes. "He made sure I knew about the Defensio Project, but I...I don't know his true intentions."

Samuel evaluated her. "So we could walk into a trap."

"No." Lena shook her head vigorously. "Wouldn't make sense after all he said. Look, he wanted me to be part of all this." She gestured around her meaningfully. "Said Wei had a plan for me. What he meant by that is anyone's guess, but I don't think he's trying to damage us. After what happened at the academy, I...I think..." She trailed off, then forced herself to look at Samuel. "I think Makoto is on that ship, and we can help him."

Samuel focused on Tiago. "You think the Overseer wants to save her friend?"

"I mean, you saw the specs. He handed us a way to disable their ship in less than ten minutes, board it, and rescue Makoto. If things go according to plan, we'd do some real damage. Wouldn't that be nice for a change?"

Samuel had a tightness in the face that spoke of skepticism. "Things never go according to plan, Chancellor.

You're asking me to risk my people on little more than a whim."

Tiago stepped forward. "I'm asking you to trust your gut and do the right thing."

Samuel pointed to Lena. "I want to talk with her. Alone."

Tiago blinked, then turned slowly to Lena, eyebrows raised.

"It's okay," she said. "I don't mind."

Tiago nodded. "I'll wait outside." He turned and walked out of the room.

Samuel ran the wet cloth on the helmet, carefully cleaning every inch of the surface. The helmet had a curious shape. In place of the mouth and nose was a pointed protuberance, and the surface had trimmings resembling metal feathers. The helmet looked like the head of an eagle.

"We've met before," Samuel said. "You remember?"

Lena cleared her throat. "Yes," she said. "At the assembly. You spoke there."

"Before that." He focused his dark eyes on her, and Lena's heart skipped a beat. "At the entrance of Geode. When you were shot. I was there with my team."

She tipped her head as surprise sank in. "You're right. It was you! You pushed me to the side when that dunamis shot. You saved my life."

Samuel clenched his jaw. "You believe in fate?"

She frowned. "Fate?"

"Destiny. You think it's real?"

She swallowed. "No. I don't believe in destiny."

"Why?"

"Because I don't like the idea of an unknown force running my life."

He mused. "No, of course you don't. None with an ounce

of self-respect like the idea. Then, if you believe in free will, why are you here?"

She blinked. "What do you mean?"

"Why are you in Aquamarine?"

She thought of that for a moment. "I guess...I guess I wanted answers."

"I thought you were the Cornucopia." He studied her. "Aren't you here to win a war?"

She shrugged. "I don't know what Wei wanted from me. All I know is that a friend is in danger, and it's my fault. I want to help him. Tiago told me you can make it happen. Please. I'd do anything to save my friend."

"Anything?" He furrowed his brow. "Be careful before offering what you don't know you can give. There might be a price."

"Look, I don't know how much time Makoto has left. Are you going to help us or not?"

The centurion placed the squeeze bottle on the floor, admiring his polished armor. "The chancellor is right. It would be a welcome change to hit the enemy where it hurts." He turned the full regard of his eyes on her. "Well, I guess we'll soon find out if the legend is true."

She blinked. "What...what does that mean?"

"It means yes." Samuel drew up to his full height. "Tell the chancellor that Song's Griffins will rise."

39

STAND

HYPERIST COMPLEX INFINITY, HEXAHEDRAL
ROOM

Gladia

Maria Castellari and Penelope Juno were definitely pissed off. Even the usually stoic leader of the Geocentrics didn't hide her annoyance.

Gladia sat stiffly behind her desk, hands together on the hard wooden surface, her fingertips touching each other to give an impression of confidence. She wasn't confident, but she needed to look the part to keep things under control.

Maria and Penelope exchanged a quick look, then the leader of the Selenians cleared her throat. "Do nothing." Her voice was throaty, each word tight. "That's what you're proposing?"

"No, it's not," Gladia said quickly. "I said I need time to find leverage. That's the *opposite* of doing nothing, Maria."

"Leverage?" Penelope's voice sliced through the air. "You

tried to put Tolomeus on a leash, and look where it's gotten you. He has made his choice. It's time we make ours."

Gladia set her jaw, trying not to blink. "What would you have me do?"

"Publicly condemn his insubordination," Penelope said, counting on her fingers. "Get rid of the councilors who support him and regain control of the Starry Assembly, then cut loose the Ascendents."

Gladia let out a quick, disgusted snort. "Cut loose the… Jesus. Sure. I'm going to do that."

Penelope shrugged. "I wasn't joking."

Gladia smirked. "You're talking about twenty million registered hyperists, for God's sake. It's people who pay membership fees, who work for us. Some of my closest friends are Ascendents."

"Collateral damage," Penelope said dryly. "If they truly are hyperists, they'll choose another party."

"I agree." Maria stepped forward. "Gladia, that man is a cancer. I warned you. To save what's left of HYPER, we must remove him. It's time we separate the wheat from the chaff."

Gladia clicked her fingernails against the table. "Weren't you listening? Tolomeus was fooled into believing the funds were legit. We've got the evidence. I showed it to you."

"I don't care what his fabricated proof says," Maria retorted scornfully. "Tolomeus is a manipulator playing on your good faith."

"You're not thinking—"

Maria held up a hand, palm outward. "Okay, fine. Even if he knew nothing about the funds, which I doubt, the way he acted when this whole thing blew up is enough to fire his ass."

"That's not your decision," Gladia said.

Maria snorted. "Think of what he's done. He made sure

to have the support he needed to challenge you, then stabbed you in the back. Can't you see? He's a coward and an opportunist, and you're still defending him."

"Listen." Gladia pinched the bridge of her nose and squeezed her eyes tight. "Tolomeus felt cornered, he freaked out and overreacted. I know him. He barks but doesn't bite. He won't do anything to harm HYPER."

Penelope stared at Gladia with an intense focus. "You're living in a dream world if you believe that."

"Gladia," Maria interjected, nostrils flaring. "This mess is on *him*. He needs to pay."

Gladia gave Maria a glassy stare. "Look, the Ascendents represent one-fifth of HYPER. There's no way I'm going to handslap all of them for something Tolomeus did out of fear."

"They voted for him," Penelope pointed out. "They're all in this together."

"True that," Maria said, nodding. "And they back everything he does."

"I won't risk open division between the parties, not if it can be fixed."

"How?" Maria almost snarled the word.

"By keeping a cool head," Gladia said, her words sounding strained. "HYPER is one. Without the Ascendents, the movement is reduced to scattered groups."

"I don't share your opinion." Penelope looked Gladia in the eyes. "HYPER is much more than the sum of its parts. It's an idea."

"Exactly." Maria pointed vehemently at Penelope. "Aren't the Apeirons already a *de facto* separated group? Well, we're still here, right? It'll be the same without Tolomeus."

Gladia shook her head. "The Apeirons are part of

HYPER. They recognize the Executive Council and abide by the Starry Assembly's decisions."

"Sure, on paper," Maria said, shaking her head. "Truth is, they do their own thing. They're so secretive we don't even know what they're working on, other than Dodekatheon. They hide inside Serenity and couldn't care less about us."

Gladia crossed her arms and looked at both women. "Look, we can waste time discussing which hyperist group is more at fault here, or we can focus on the *actual* problem."

"Actual problem?" Maria crossed her arms. "Is there anything worse than that snake?"

"Yes, there is." Gladia glared at her. "LAND is on the warpath. Didn't you get the memo? Muchena is using Militarized Space like a presidential election slogan. She's hitting us hard where we're the weakest. We need to deal with her first."

"Then help us clean house," Maria said, her hands clenched into fists. "Open your eyes." She pointed to Penelope and herself. "We're all you've left. The three of us must stand together if we're to survive this storm. Condemn Tolomeus and the Ascendents. It's the only way forward."

Penelope nodded. "I agree with Maria. HYPER is broken. Nothing you do can stop—"

"HYPER is not broken!" Gladia snapped to her feet. "What's wrong with you two? Standing there, talking about a schism to me. *Me*, Gladia Egea, the Last Vertex of the Hexahedron. I exist to ensure HYPER stays united."

Penelope stepped up, eyes unblinking. "Then, perhaps you've exhausted your usefulness."

Gladia's eyebrows drew close together. Penelope's words felt like a knife through her heart.

Maria exchanged a glance with Penelope, then looked

back at Gladia. "Look, all we're saying is that the time to smile at the cameras is over. You did what you could to keep the parties united. It didn't work. Move on. I—"

"Maria—"

"I'm not finished." Maria pointed a finger at Gladia. "I will not stand by and watch you treat Tolomeus like a prodigal son. He's a scorpion. He needs to be stamped on. Soon, I'll make my statement. I'll give you a few days to decide which side you're on."

Before Gladia could reply, the leader of the Selenians broke off communication and her projection disappeared.

"He who chases two rabbits will catch neither," Penelope said, looking at Gladia with her hawk eyes. "You're not seeing clearly. You worry about the top floor of the tower, when you should keep an eye on the base." Penelope severed the connection, and her projection disappeared.

Gladia sagged in her seat, heart drumming against her ribcage. She reached for the cup that sat on the table. As soon as she grabbed it, her hands shook. "Not you again." She slammed her hand against the table, hard. She did it twice more until she registered the pain.

"Not...you...AGAIN!"

She threw the cup against the wall on the other side of the room. It smashed with a resounding crack, splashing coffee onto the floor.

Someone knocked.

"Not now!" Gladia snapped.

The door opened anyway. Arthur stared at the coffee still dripping from the wall. "I take it the chat didn't go well?"

Gladia glared at him. "Your powers of observation are mind-blowing."

The constable picked up the shards from the floor, threw

them in the garbage, then sat in front of Gladia. "What's the word?" He offered a genial smile.

She sighed. "Backup question?"

He raised his eyebrow. "That bad?"

She stared down at her hands. "Let's just say this year I'm not expecting to get Christmas cards from any of the hyperist leaders."

He nodded, held out his hand. Gladia hesitated, then reached out and grabbed it.

"It's going to be alright," Arthur said. "We'll figure this out. I promise."

She smiled and some of the tension eased, like poison seeping out of a wound. "How do you do it?"

He shrugged. "Do what?"

"Keep positive in the face of adversity, when there's nothing but darkness."

"If there's darkness, there must also be a source of light, or you wouldn't know what darkness is."

She blinked. "Poetic."

He grinned. "Feeling better?"

"A bit."

Arthur glanced at the door. "Well, maybe I know something else that can boost your confidence."

Gladia frowned. "What?"

They looked at each other in silence, then Arthur leaned toward her.

Gladia's heartbeat sped up, and a rush of adrenaline coursed through her body. She swallowed as Arthur's face came so close to her his gray-green eyes had flecks within them.

Gladia's interlink trilled, causing her to jump. A quick glance showed Charlotte's comm code.

Arthur cleared his throat and sat back, rubbing his neck.

"What is it, Charlotte?" Gladia asked, putting the call on speaker so that Arthur could hear.

"Ma'am, Muchena is starting her speech," her assistant said.

"Thank you." Gladia interrupted the communication. She turned on the room's projector, careful not to look in Arthur's direction. "Let's see what other thrilling news awaits us."

The reproduction of a crowded square appeared in the center of the room. It was a huge, elliptical space dotted with fountains and ancient-looking marble statues. In the middle of the vast space stood an Egyptian obelisk adorned at the base with four circular basins and as many stone lions, also in the Egyptian style. A projection of the Landist Tetralement hovered a few feet above the obelisk, dominating the entire square.

A stage had been placed at the western end of the square, in front of a sculpture depicting Neptune holding a trident.

Gladia moved a hand, causing the projector to zoom in on the stage. Now the figure of Yvonne Muchena was clearly visible. She was waving at the crowd, like an empress standing in front of her subjects. As the roar of the audience slowly subsided, the landist leader approached the microphone and began her speech.

"One hundred days ago, I took the scepter from Douglas Woodside and led the landist nation." Yvonne breathed in, her gleaming eyes scanning the crowd. "I was afraid. Didn't think I was ready to answer the call of destiny. Woodside asked me to purge the cancer of corruption from LAND and to reform it under a new Tetralement, and so I did. LAND is more united than ever!"

The crowd exploded with shouts of approval. Yvonne waited out the cheers and applause, then she continued.

"We live in difficult times, brothers and sisters. For a quarter century, LAND sought a peaceful solution to the pressing issue of resource distribution. Woodside dedicated his life to this goal. But there are those who denied us that solution, who refused to admit our failure as a civilization, who chose blind progress over sustainability, greed over prosperity, money over people. Never again, brothers and sisters. Never again!"

A multitude of arms shot up in the air, showing their support, calling Muchena's name.

The landist leader raised both hands, commanding silence.

"A sacred crusade is upon us, one we can win only without losing sight of our goal. LAND needs to extend its hand to all groups fighting to preserve Earth and humanity, who care about what happens to this planet and want to defend it, who don't treat it as a credit card without spending limits. That's why, sons and daughters of LAND, I'm proud to announce a powerful ally who'll stand by our side." She turned and gestured with her hand. "Most Reverend Zacharias Hawke, come! Come join us!"

Gladia held her breath and Arthur stared at the projection, eyes wide. They exchanged a dread-filled glance, then returned their gaze to the projection.

A man covered in a white robe entered the stage. He was greeted by deafening shouts. Zacharias embraced Yvonne while several camera drones captured the moment. After exchanging a few words, they walked hand in hand toward the podium, where Zacharias addressed the audience with a fatherly smile.

"The Great Mother Gaea gives her blessings to her

chosen daughter, Yvonne Muchena, and our landist brothers and sisters. This union will provide unprecedented peace and prosperity. We are one now. Nothing can stand in our way."

"Defenders of the landist dream!" Yvonne raised her hand in triumph. "Join the revolution! Become the champions of a newborn civilization! Stand with us as we reclaim our future!"

The crowd went wild, roaring its approval of the union.

"From today," Yvonne shouted over the increasing chorus of voices, "landists and humanists will raise their voices together, fighting for humankind as one entity, one nation. Join us as we gather under the banner of a new symbol, made of the four elements and the strength of Gaea." She pointed toward the LAND symbol over the obelisk, which started changing shape, turning into an open eye, the iris containing the four elements. "I give you the Pentalement!"

"THE PENTALEMENT RULES!" cried out thousands of people.

"LAND! LAND!"

"Gaea dictates the way!"

"United together!"

Gladia turned off the trigoy, the cheers of the crowd still ringing in her ears.

The Hexahedral Room remained quiet. Arthur's face had gone pale, his hands hanging lifeless and loose. That her friend showed so much emotion was a measure of how bad the news was.

"I was ready for the worst," Gladia said, chewing at her lip. "But I wasn't prepared for *this*." She gestured in the general direction of the projection.

"Well." Arthur scraped a hand through his hair. "At least they kept Lucifer out of their party."

She threw him a desperate look. "Can you *not*, please?"

"Sorry." He lowered his head, breaking eye contact. "Not the right time for jokes. Got it."

She barely had the chance to process what had happened when her interlink rang again. She put it on speaker. "Yes?"

This time Charlotte didn't even bother with formalities and just dropped the information. "We just received a new output from the ether."

Gladia swallowed. She met Arthur's gaze. "Go on."

"LAND and Humanitas have begun a public process of merging. Our Data Center estimates that by tomorrow they'll be united into a single mega region of some three hundred ninety million subscriptions and twenty-two ether-aparsecs in size."

Arthur pinched his chin. "That's bigger than Data-Morph." His eyes were glassy, lost in thought.

Gladia braced for what was to come. "What else?"

"The Landist Council and Gaea Temple have released a joint statement. It says... One moment, please." Gladia heard Charlotte typing, then talking to someone else, asking for confirmation about something. "I'm sorry," came back the assistant's voice, sounding strained. "There's a lot of noise on the ether right now. It's hard to handpick legit news. We have confirmed that both landists and humanists have publicly christened the new etheric force with the name 'STAND.' That's all I've got for now."

"All right." Gladia tucked her hair behind an ear, her voice increasingly lower. "Let me...let me know if something else comes up."

"Yes, ma'am."

Gladia closed the call, her vision narrowing as white spots appeared in the corners of her eyes. She had the sensation of being squeezed, like a physical pressure around her throat.

Arthur leaned in while moving closer to her. "Gladia?" He tried to hold her hand.

"Don't." She jerked away, avoiding his eyes. She gasped for breath, a vise tightening around her chest.

"You're not breathing."

"I can't, Arthur." She hugged her knees and rocked back and forth. "I just can't."

"Sure you can." He kept his voice even. "You breathe in through your nose, and exhale through your mouth. Just like this." He demonstrated. "Come on, Last Vertex of the Hexahedron. Show me how it's done."

She glanced at him, swallowed. She breathed from her nose, then blew air out of her mouth.

"That's it," Arthur said with a comforting smile. "Now do it again. Breath in—yes, just like that—and out it goes. Perfect."

Her heartbeat slowed down, and the panic attack slowly subsided. "Thanks," she said in a raspy voice.

He gave her a bright look. "Anytime." He poured water in a glass and handed it to her. "Here. Sip."

She drank.

"How are we doing?" he asked.

She nodded. "Better."

"Good."

Gladia looked at him. "I need you to do something."

"Anything."

She sagged back in her seat, hands falling to her sides. "I can't bring Tolomeus back into the fold, pull Maria and

Penelope by the hair, counter the Planetary's actions, all while Muchena tries to wipe us out."

"I agree," he said calmly. "What do you need?"

She bit her lip. "I need to meet her."

He frowned. "Muchena?"

"Yes. Away from the media, somewhere private."

He blinked. "It's a bold plan."

"I know it's risky, but it's the only sensible thing left. I want to see if I can speak to the woman behind the mask."

Arthur nodded gravely. "All right. I'll use my old contact to see if I can set up the meeting. It worked once. We might get lucky a second time."

40

FAMILY

DÜSSELDORF, HEATHER RAINBOW INSTITUTE

Ramor

"I must warn you," Dr. Airling said, with a note of caution in his voice. "You'll notice significant changes in her behavior."

"Meaning?" Ramor stared at the doctor, doing nothing to keep the edge off his voice. That man had been a pain in the ass since he came back from his trip, fighting every request to speak with Sofia. It took the better part of a week —and lots of pressure—to get the doctor to agree to Ramor's terms.

The doctor avoided Ramor's stare. "Well, the way your sister relates to you will be different, closer to what you were used to when she was healthy, before the...um..." He trailed off, glanced at Ramor before continuing. "Before the violence she suffered. Be aware of that."

"Okay." Ramor crossed his arms. "What do you want me to do?"

"Don't relate events that happened *after* her abduction. We're treading on unfamiliar territory here, and I'm still working out the next move. Be sure to remember that *this* Sofia Deringer is the same person you know, with the same memories, but...well, with no knowledge of today's world. Her mind remains as it was seven years ago, before the GSG9 commando killed the phobaron and rescued her."

Ramor rubbed the back of his neck. "What if she asks me to get her out of here? I mean, that's what I'd ask."

Dr. Airling shook his head. "We probed that need out of her reaction core."

Ramor's eyebrows shot up. "What the hell is that supposed to mean?"

"As I've explained in the document I sent, this is a very advanced method of medical-induced hypnosis. She won't ask questions that'll pull her out of her status of constructed reality. But you have to make sure you keep her grounded in the present. Don't lead her where she's not supposed to go."

"I don't know," Ramor said, grinding his jaw. "It sounds like a deal with the devil."

"It's not," Dr. Airling said, sounding slightly annoyed by Ramor's tone. "It's science."

"Right." Ramor snorted. "When has *that* ever caused any problem?" Before the doctor could reply, Ramor raised a hand to stop him. "Okay, I got it, I got it: Don't be pushy, don't ask dodgy questions, let her lead. I'm good from here, thanks."

"But I haven't explained—"

"We had an agreement." Ramor gestured at the door. "I want my ten minutes alone with my sister. No questions asked."

Dr. Airling hesitated for a second, then nodded. "We'll

be outside if you need us." He walked away and closed the door.

Ramor inhaled sharply as he walked through a passage lined with shelves, at the end of which he found Sofia in her lab coat working with spare parts. She looked happy, like a kid at the park. Ramor couldn't help but smile. It was definitely the Sofia he remembered.

"Ah, there you are, kiddo!" Sofia glanced at him while typing on a tablet. "Be a darling and pass me the Kelferin sequencer; over there." She pointed to a long, narrow object on the other side of the long table, closer to Ramor than it was to her.

"Sure." Ramor picked up the object, then walked around the table and handed it to Sofia, who took it without a word while finishing writing on her tablet.

Ramor stared, fascinated by his sister's small hands repairing a carbon-glass tibia with servo-mechanism joints. After a couple minutes, she put the newly assembled object on the table with a satisfied sigh. "Done." She wiped the sweat from her forehead as she assessed the finished work.

"Looks good," Ramor said.

"Yeah, but it took work." Sofia dropped the object into a box with a post-it note with the word *repaired*. "No idea who the hell produced this garbage." She gestured at the box filled with second-hand autotron parts. "They used gerinonite instead of salvin alloy to connect the joints. Can you believe that? Butchers."

"Yeah," Ramor said absently. "They deserve jail time."

She narrowed her eyes as she studied her brother. "What's wrong, kiddo? You're paler than a ghost."

He straightened his jacket. "I...I wanted to talk to you about something."

"Okay." She shrugged. "What is it?"

He cleared his throat. "I've got a situation." He talked deliberately slow, glancing at his sister as he spoke. "Something I'm not sure how to handle. I thought you might help."

She cleaned her greasy hands with a wet towel, gestured to the chair across the table. "Sit."

He sat. The silence hung awkwardly until Sofia belched. Ramor stared.

"What?" Sofia shrugged. "Had kebab for lunch." She patted her belly. "Went a bit too far with the onions."

He smiled. Yup. That was Sofia Deringer all right.

"So." She gestured at him. "Your problem."

Ramor shifted in his chair. "I know someone who needs help." He crossed his hands on the table and kept them there. "It's a...friend of mine who wants to start an autotronic company." He bit his lip, avoided Sofia's stare. "I... Well, I believe he's getting into trouble. He's a risk taker, you know? How can I convince him he's screwing things up and needs my help?"

She studied him for a moment, then laughed.

He frowned. "What's that for?"

"You're funny," she said with a wide grin. "Erik is giving you a headache but you want to cover him. It's just...well... you're not very good at it."

"What?" Ramor felt his throat go dry. "Sofia, I never said—"

"Oh, come on. You're terrible at lying. Quit using codes. What did Erik do?"

His eyes widened. Sofia saw through his bullshit story right off the bat. Whatever the doctor was doing...well, it was working.

"Hello?" She snapped her fingers. "Anyone there?"

"All right." He unfastened the top button of his shirt. "I

think...I think he's gotten himself into trouble, but he's too stubborn to ask for help."

She nodded. "Go on."

He rubbed his hands down his pant legs. "What would you do to help him without pissing him off? Because I tried. God, I tried. He just doesn't listen!" The last word he almost shouted. He closed his eyes and took a calming breath.

She crossed her arms and looked him straight in the eyes. "Look. You're my brother, and I love you, but you've always been too straightforward when it comes to family. That's a recipe for disaster when you want to coax Erik into doing something."

He sat up straighter, pushing up his sleeves. "I don't understand."

"You treat Erik like hard iron that needs to be hammered to form a shape." Sofia shook her head. "That's not the way you deal with him. He's more like quicksilver. You can't beat him into shape. You must devise a way to guide him, building a path he can flow into effortlessly. Do anything else, and he'll fight you tooth and nail."

Ramor smirked despite his mood. It was oddly appropriate for Sofia to think of her son in terms of metals.

"You got that, kiddo?"

He leaned in, nodded to show his understanding. "So, what would you do?"

She clicked her fingernails on the table, her eyes locked in the distance. "Tell Erik he can't breathe underwater, and he'll drown to prove you wrong. But if you bring an oxygen tank and tell him no one has made it work, Erik'll turn it into a submarine. He loves a challenge."

"Right." He clenched his jaw. "Problem is, how do I get an oxygen tank?"

Sofia studied him for a moment before answering.

"You'll find a way." She squeezed his arm. "You're a Deringer, aren't you? Finding solutions is what we do. Now, it's my turn to ask you a favor."

He jerked his head up, alert. "Shoot."

She bit her lower lip. "Erik is too much like me; proud and stubborn. He can't see past his goals. He needs a guide, and I cannot be that guide. I'm too close to him, too focused on my own objectives. You're a good man and have a big heart. I need someone like you to take care of him, to be the father he never had, to see the things I can't see. That kid has a tough future ahead. He needs someone to share his burden. You understand what I'm saying?"

"Yes." Ramor pulled his shoulders back. "I understand."

"Will you help me take care of him?"

He nodded solemnly. "I promise."

She embraced him and a great burden lifted from his shoulders. They used to be a team, working for the same goal, before the specter of hate robbed him of his sister.

In that embrace, Ramor glanced at Sofia's face, focusing on the white scars on her cheeks, neck, and forehead, leftovers of a dark memory he wished he could erase.

* * *

7 years before

Automaton Industries, Professor Kurosawa's office

RAMOR LOOKS at the man in front of him with a frozen smile. "Eighty percent of the Planetary Court? Jesus." His eyebrows rise to his hairline. "They didn't get to *that* majority even for the Dreyfus Affair."

Kenta Kurosawa rubs his hands on his lab coat before answering, his eyes avoiding Ramor. "Look, I told you it's just rumors, okay? You asked me for an update on the situation. I gave it to you. Personally, I think it's baloney. Official Planetary statements are the only things that matter."

Ramor sets his jaw so hard it snaps. If climate change was refuted by a Planetary statement, this man would deny the existence of the ozone hole. Why can't he admit the rumors are proof the situation is escalating?

Ramor forces a tight smile. No point in arguing. Kenta hates his guts. The snooty bastard thinks Ramor got his position just because of his last name. Fine. The fucker doesn't want to help? He'll help himself.

"Anything to add?" Kenta asks with enough spite to cut steel.

"Nope." Ramor crosses his arms. "Sofia trusted you with damage control, I'll leave you to it." He swallows, feeling dirty just by speaking those words.

Kenta eyes him, his demeanor suggesting he wants Ramor gone. "What else can I do for you?"

"Just need to know where the boss is." Ramor glances around. "Been trying to get a hold on her since I came back, but she went MIA. She's been kidnapped or something?"

Ramor spent the past few weeks in South America, overseeing the opening of a new branch of the Automaton Industries in Buenos Aires.

Kenta avoids Ramor's eyes. "She's busy. Doesn't want to be bothered."

Ramor stops smiling. "She'll make an exception for me."

Kenta frowns. "Why would she?"

"Because she needs my update. In person." Ramor stresses the last word. "The branch in Buenos Aires is key for our expansion in Latin America. She asked for an update when I came back."

Kenta lifts his chin, then tosses his head sharply. He grasps a tablet from the desk and pretends to be busy. "She's in the Research and Development Department, section B-4, Inner Sanctum."

Bingo. Ramor walks out of the room, strides past the hallway until he reaches the first available elevator. He jabs at the call button, tapping his fingers impatiently against the wall while waiting.

When the elevator door opens, Ramor presses the security code and activates the vocal interface.

"Control, reserve this elevator for the next ride. Authorization Deringer, Ramor, Genesis Blue."

"Confirmed, Inspector," the control's voice replies. "What is your destination?"

"Research and Development Department, section B-4, Inner Sanctum."

When he steps out of the elevator, he finds himself in a long corridor. Ramor heads to section B-4 where he finds the thick metal door of the lab closed and the control panel shut down.

He curses under his breath. "Control. Open. Authorization: Deringer, Ramor, Genesis Blue."

"Access denied."

Ramor frowns. "Provide an explanation."

"The president ordered not be disturbed until further notice."

"That right?" Ramor looks around, makes sure there's no one else in the corridor, then he ignores the red light beeping on the access panel, opens the terminal, and tampers with the controls.

"Unauthorized attempt at entering this facility," the

control warns him. "Push attempt rejected. Stand back or you will be...be...bee-e-e-e..."

Ramor grins as he overrides the last set of cascade transconductors. The light turns green.

"Code confirmed," says a more docile control voice. "Access granted."

The doors slide open and Ramor enters a vast room with no windows, lightened by a collection of LEDs encased into the ceiling. The whir of machines working in the background and the familiar smell of lubricant, aseptic, and singed wires tell him his sister is definitely here.

He finds her lying on the floor beneath an Harkan Jet, her back against the metal tiles, face covered by a heat mask as she fiddles with a high-intensity phasic welder. At her side is a fourteen-year-old who looks exactly like her.

"Uncle!" Erik runs and embraces him.

"Hey, champion." Ramor ruffles his nephew's hair. "I swear you're growing an inch every goddamn week. When will you stop?"

Erik grins. "The sky's the limit."

"So." Ramor glances at Sofia, still working. "What are you two up to?"

"Doing some repairs." Erik waves at a bunch of spare parts scattered on the floor. "Mum's upgrading the HarkJet."

"Sounds like fun." Ramor gazes at his sister. "You remember to eat and breathe, now and then?"

Sofia rises from the floor as she removes her heat mask, revealing a smear of sweat and dirt on her cheeks and forehead.

"Pretty." Ramor grins.

Sofia frowns at him. "Weren't you supposed to sign the deal in Buenos Aires tomorrow?" She glances at the entrance, then back at her brother. "What happened?"

"The deal?" Ramor blows through his nose. "That was three days ago, sister."

Sofia blinks. "What day is it?"

"Thursday."

"Really?"

"Really."

"What happened to Wednesday?" She looks around in a daze, hands on her hips. "And Tuesday?"

Ramor chuckles. "Guess they got swept under the rug. Well, glad you two found a nice way to spend the time while I was gone."

Sofia evaluates her brother. "How the hell did you get in? I secured the entrance."

"Please, you're insulting me." Ramor winks at Erik. "A second-class override? Think I was born yesterday?"

Erik chuckles. "You sabotaged the entrance panel?" The boy's eyes glint with amusement.

Ramor shrugs. "I only use my superpowers when I must." He stares at Sofia, this time more seriously. "We need to talk. It's about the PlaCo."

"Boring." Erik rolls his eyes, turns his back to them. "I'm going to get something to drink. Want anything, Uncle?"

"I'm good, champion. Thanks."

"Mom?"

Sofia shakes her head. Erik walks away.

Ramor waits for his nephew to be out of earshot before saying, "Kenta is fucking the whole thing up."

Sofia frowns. "Okay. Spill it all."

"Look, it's a dumpster fire out there. We're sitting on our hands and letting the fire spread. Are you going to do something about that or—"

The lights shut down, and the lab falls into darkness.

Sofia jerks her head up. "What the hell..."

The emergency system turns on automatically, red and orange lights flashing alternatively. Alarms starts to screech, filling the air with their two-tone wail.

Erik rushes to them. "A power loss?"

"Nonsense," Sofia says. "With all the backup generators, it should be impossible. Must be something else." She walks toward the nearest room's control panel and starts typing on the keyboard.

"My phone is out," Erik says, showing his dead cellphone.

Ramor glances at his. "Mine too." He looks at the ceiling. "Control? Control, answer me."

No answer.

"Power control units, internal and external communications, interlink and ether...all down." Sofia's eyes scan the info panel, occasionally typing on the keyboard. "We're cut off from the outside world."

"Cut off?" Ramor tries to ignore the tightness in the chest. "How is that possible?"

"There's more." Sofia presses the *return* key twice. "It doesn't look like a power outage."

Ramor blinks. "Then what is it?"

Sofia's fingers dance on the keyboard, then she pauses. "It's a breach." Her voice is calm, but her eyes betray apprehension.

Erik looks first at Ramor, then at his mother, as if making sure he understood her words. "What?"

Sofia pounds a fist against the wall. "We're under attack."

Ramor jerks his head toward the door, his voice strained. "Under attack? By wh—"

An explosion sends them all sprawling on the floor as boxes and objects tumble all around.

Ramor stares at the door. "What the hell was that?"

"Erik?" Sofia stands up awkwardly. "You okay?"

"I'm good." Erik's eyes are wild with fear. "What—"

Another explosion, this time stronger than before. The ground beneath their feet groans as the emergency lights go out, leaving the room in darkness.

"Get away from the door!" Sofia screams from somewhere on Ramor's right. She barely has enough time to speak when a third blast knocks Ramor off his feet. He curses, heaves himself up, and walks a few awkward steps, but he trips on something hard and falls again.

"Erik?" Sofia's voice is strained, worried. This time, her son doesn't answer. "Erik? Where are you?"

Ramor pushes himself up with effort, smelling burned plastic and charred metal. Someone is trying to blow out the door. With his cellphone's flashlight he finds his nephew, motionless and covered in dust and small debris. There is a deep cut on his forehead, blood oozing out.

"Here!" Ramor calls out. "Erik's here!" He kneels beside him, removes the biggest chunk of metal from his body, and checks his pulse. Ramor fumbles in his pocket, finds his handkerchief, and presses it against the cut.

There is an explosion, followed by a screeching sound. The lab door bursts open from the outside.

Torchlights pour in as people enter.

"Christ," Ramor mutters. He picks Erik up and trudges behind a stack of boxes.

As he carries Erik to safety, the intruders call to each other, giving orders. He catches only clips and phrases. "Capture alive," "reinforcements," "no one gets out." He covers Erik with his body, his heart slamming against his chest. There must be at least a dozen people, and more are pouring in. He needs to find Sofia and get the hell out.

Someone grabs him by the shoulders and he braces for the blow.

"It's me," Sofia hisses.

"You okay?" he says in little more than a whisper.

"I'm fine." She glances at her son. "Erik?"

"He's out." Ramor removes the handkerchief to reveal the cut. "He needs a doctor."

Sofia looks around. "Not through the front. It's guarded."

Ramor peeks over the boxes. "Who are they?"

"Phobarons." Sofia is still whispering. "They're here for me."

Ramor swallows. "How did they get in?"

Sofia shrugs. "We have to do something."

"Okay." Ramor wipes sweat from his brow, trying to think. "What's the plan?"

"See the Harkan?" Sofia gestures toward the general direction of the jet she was working on. "Behind, there's a secondary exit. You'll need a diversion. I'll worry about that."

Ramor stares at her. "You'll worry about... What do you mean?"

"I'll distract them. When they're gone, take Erik out."

Ramor shakes his head. "I can't leave you. You have to come—"

"No time to argue," Sofia cuts him off. "There's no other way."

"Sofia—"

"Shut up and listen." She points at Erik. "Swear you'll take care of him."

Ramor clenches his jaw. "I'm not—"

Sofia grabs him by the shoulders. "Swear."

Around them, the voices get closer.

"I beg you." Sofia swallows, tears welling in her eyes. "Swear you'll take care of him. Swear!"

Ramor swallows. He's never seen his sister beg. Her desperate expression gives him the last nudge.

"I swear," he says.

Sofia smiles. Her face relaxes. "Thank you, kiddo." She sprints in the opposite direction and shouts, attracting the phobarons' attention.

Ramor counts to three, then hoists Erik onto his shoulders and dashes toward the exit.

41

PROMISE FROM A BROKEN PAST
VANCOUVER, KANATA CONVENTION CENTRE

Gladia

The Kanata Convention Centre was completely empty except for two figures standing on the opposite sides of the stage, watching each other like gunslingers ready to draw their pistols. Arthur Strutzenberg was the first to advance, followed in suit by Komla Gbeho, the clacking of their shoes on the hardwood floor reverberating inside the theater.

They stopped half a dozen yards from each other. The surrounding light reflected off the pins on their chests: the Tetralement on Komla's white suit and the Silver Infinity on Arthur's navy blue.

Komla raised a bushy eyebrow as he curled his lips into a wide smile. "So who speaks first? I'm confused." He looked Arthur up and down, his smile turning into a sneer. "I didn't get that part in your message. Should we write this down?

Maybe I can sketch a drawing, so you can look at the pretty pictures and choose. No rush, of course."

Arthur laughed. He outstretched his hand, which Komla shook. "I'm glad to see you too, old viper. Though I must confess, I'm disappointed."

Komla frowned.

Arthur gestured to the Tetralement pinned on the landist's chest. "I was expecting to meet a brand-new member of the 'Standist' family. Haven't they upgraded you yet?"

Komla glanced at his pin, shrugged. "I'm a sentimental man. Make sentimental choices." He grinned. "You shouldn't be worried about me though. What about the Sword of Damocles hanging over your head?"

Arthur studied Komla, then shook his head. "Sword of Damocles?"

The landist poked Arthur's Silver Infinity. "Wearing this thing in broad daylight is asking for trouble. Haven't you read the news? Hyperists are shady. They scheme and lie like there's no tomorrow. They'll even build railguns on orbital ships and start shooting if you let them."

Arthur snorted. "You actually believe that?"

"Well, it's a fantastic story. Makes me want to root for the good guys."

"A fantastic story? It's garbage, and you're too smart to believe the media sludge, so do me a favor and stop pretending you give a damn about Militarized Space. For you, it's just scoring a point. Nothing more."

"Perhaps." Komla scratched his chin. "But when I look at you, my friend, I see a man who's swimming in a shark tank and doesn't even know."

Arthur crossed his arms. "I'm okay with sharks. All they

want is to eat. It's a basic survival instinct, I get that. What I'm truly afraid of are rabid dogs."

Komla blinked. "Can't say that I'm following you."

"Rabid dogs are unpredictable." Arthur gestured toward the other end of the stage. "Take your newly gained boss, for example. She's like a grenade with no safety pin. Woodside was an egocentric bastard, but at least he knew how to steer clear of a psychopath. That's why he kept Hawke at arm's length. I don't get Muchena. Can't she see the man is a disaster waiting to happen?"

Komla shook his head. "She's smarter than you give her credit. We need the priest to get the numbers, but we're the ones holding the leash."

Arthur made a soft growl with the back of his throat. "Oh, come on! You don't believe that crap."

"You don't know me that well, Arthur." Komla glanced over his shoulder. "Well, they must be wondering if we're trying to kill each other with chatter. Are you satisfied? Can we send in for the ladies?"

Arthur gazed at the empty stands, nodded.

"Well, then." Komla tipped an imaginary hat. "Best of luck to you and your boss. You're going to need it." The landist turned around and walked off the stage.

Arthur took one last look around before walking the length of the backstage and passing through a secondary door. Gladia was waiting in the small corridor that connected the dressing room to the stage.

"What took you so long?" Gladia stared at him, hands clasped behind her back. "You two have been out there for ages."

"Just two old hounds sniffing." Arthur gestured at the stage. "She's all yours. Try not to enjoy yourself too much."

∞∞∞

Gladia glanced at her hands to make sure they weren't shaking as Yvonne Muchena emerged from the other end of the stage, walking toward her.

"I'm disappointed," said the landist with a thin smile as she eyed Gladia. "In person, you don't look like much, Last Vertex of the Hexahedron. Are you tired? You look tired."

Gladia returned the smile of the younger woman. "Responsibilities age a person fast," she said, her voice lower than she had intended. "One day you'll look at the mirror and see a stranger staring back at you."

Yvonne gave her a half-shrug, then turned her attention to her surroundings. "So. To what do I owe the pleasure?" She gestured around. "When Komla told me you wanted to meet here, I thought the choice was curious. Why this theater?"

"It's not a theater." Gladia crossed her arms over her chest. "It's an arena."

Yvonne tilted her head to the side. "An arena?"

Gladia nodded. "Fifteen years ago, in this very place, two gladiators entertained millions of spectators while debating over the best ways to spend humanity's resources. I think you know what I'm referring to."

Yvonne's eyes widened. "Of course," she said, looking around as if recognizing the place. "This is where you and Douglas faced each other at Collision."

"A simpler time, that," Gladia said. "When one knew who the enemy was." She walked to the podium at the edge of the stage, then placed both hands on its wooden surface, looking across at the empty seating. "A month after Wei Wang's death, the two gladiators met here." Gladia looked with a vacant stare at the place beside the podium, summoning the phantom of a memory. "Two warriors laying down their weapons, talking frankly with each other to handle a crisis that threatened to end countless lives."

Yvonne looked abruptly back at Gladia, her brown eyes darkly grave. "You and Douglas met in secret?"

Gladia bowed her head. "Woodside called the meeting for the same reason I requested your presence today. After the terrorist attack at Infinity, the deaths of the Hexahedron members, and my attempted murder a week later, the Hyperist Executive was on the warpath." Gladia rubbed her hands together, searching Yvonne's eyes before continuing. "Most of them wanted to mobilize the public opinion against the landists. Everything seemed set to start a chain of violence. In that delicate time, I received Woodside's invitation to meet. On that day, he showed himself to be a man of stature, very different from the showman I knew. He looked me in the eye and assured me that LAND had nothing to do with the attacks, and that he would fire everyone in his council who suggested violence was the only option. Of course, I didn't believe him. I thought it was an attempt to buy time, but when I was on the verge of letting distrust get the better of me, as a proof of his good faith, he gave me this." Gladia handed Yvonne a pair of glasses with thick lenses.

Yvonne arched her eyebrow. "What's this?"

"An object belonging to his sister. Adelaide was her name. Judging by what he said, she was the person he loved the most."

"Why did he give it to you?"

"As a symbol of his good faith," Gladia said. "The next day, Woodside did what he had promised, forcing many pro-violence LAND leaders to resign, publicly siding against violence and giving me leeway. He kept his end of the bargain and I kept mine, discouraging the hyperist demonstrations. On that day, we avoided a catastrophe. That's why you're here, Yvonne. You can be a harbinger of peace or a vessel of destruction." Gladia produced from her pocket a pyramid-shaped object the size of an overripe strawberry.

Yvonne stared at it. "A trigoy?"

"Yes. Here." Gladia handed it to her.

Yvonne turned it over in her hand. "It has a peculiar shape. Doesn't look like any trigoprojector I've ever seen."

"I'm not surprised." Gladia nodded toward the trigoy. "Wei gave it to me. It's the trigoy he used to show me the blueprint of Polaris, years before the word 'hyperist' was invented. He gave it to me just before the rise of Polaris, as a symbol of our friendship. This is the most important object I own, given to me by the person I most respected. Just as Woodside gave me his heart, I now bring you mine. I'm appealing to your common sense, Yvonne. Stop the posturing, the hate, the violence. Please, help me help us before it's too late."

Yvonne blinked. When she looked back at Gladia, her expression looked slightly surprised. "You know, when I was eighteen, an ivory trader told me a story..." She seemed to rifle through several word choices before resuming talking. "There was a small village in the Kinkala district, in the Pool region, close to Brazzaville. The village chief was passionate about astronomy, a rather expensive hobby in a place where people ate once a day if they were lucky, slept in mud houses, and died of diarrhea daily. But the chief was determined to get the most out of his pastime. To fund his expensive passion, he allowed a mercenary gang which passed through that area to select young women from his village. Every month, the brigands would arrive with new, expensive tools for the chief, and he would have women ready to trade.

A new lens was worth a mere child. A new telescope, three grown women."

Gladia's posture straightened, her muscles visibly tightening. "That's terrible."

Yvonne nodded. She weighed the trigoy in her hand, eyes glassy. When she spoke again, her voice grew softer. "After listening to that story, I never looked at the starry sky without thinking of that village chief. Can you imagine? All the lives his hobby destroyed? You're the same, Last Vertex of the Hexahedron. You love basking under the starlight while millions of people die in the dirt." She let the trigoy fall and then stepped on it, breaking it into pieces. "You're a weak leader who's not cut out for what's coming. A war has started, and the first shot has already been fired without you realizing it." Yvonne took a step closer to her, entering her personal space. "It was easy. All it took was to leverage Almagest's greed."

"What?" Gladia flinched back, her lips curling back in disgust. "It was you? You funded the katalamban's project through Juggernaut?"

Yvonne's eyes twinkled with glee. "That's a serious accusation, Last Vertex of the Hexahedron. By all means, spread it through the four winds. See what happens without evidence."

Gladia struggled to keep her emotions in check. She still needed to deal with Yvonne. Nothing had changed. She was there to stop the landist leader and she would do so, no matter the cost. "If you're convinced I'm done, why don't you prove it live?"

Yvonne frowned. "Prove it?"

"A live debate at Collision," Gladia said. "You and I, the Last Vertex of the Hexahedron versus the Elemental Panther. Let the audience decide the winner of this war."

Yvonne's eyes glowed with a predatory light, but it vanished in a second, replaced by an amused expression. "No." The landist leader shook her head. "There's no point. I've already won, Egea. I don't need to get confirmation. I just need to sit back and wait for you hyperists to destroy each other."

Gladia made to reply, but Yvonne turned her back and marched toward the exit.

"Wait!"

Yvonne pivoted.

Gladia clenched her jaw. "Do you understand the cost? Millions will suffer if you continue your campaign of hate."

"I know the cost," Yvonne said. "There's no genuine change without suffering. I learned the hard way. Talking about cost, you know what happened to that village chief? His house was burned down by a black wind that brought long-awaited justice. He died screaming."

Gladia watched Yvonne walk away in the silence of an arena in which she'd lost for the second time.

42

CANTARA'S LEGACY

NASHVILLE, ARK INSTITUTE FOR ADVANCED ETHERIC STUDIES

James

James examined the ninety-six students dressed in the purple uniform displaying the Ark Institute symbol, a black silk ribbon tied around their shoulder to emphasize the solemn moment. He looked to his left; Venus and Ravi returned his gaze. To his right, Angelica stood stiff as a block of granite, her eyes glassy, lost in her own thoughts. Sebastian had found an excuse not to attend the ceremony despite James trying to mend bridges. The etiatros' refusal to take part in the etheric baptism was just the latest snub to James' initiative in favor of the holistic.

James forced himself to focus on the present. All that mattered now were these ninety-six students ready to become his soldiers in the Ether War.

"ADAM," James called out. "I, James Ark, confer the title of 'Domine' to the following candidates." He read the list of fifty-six names displayed on the tablet, then stepped back and looked at Angelica, who nodded and took his place.

"ADAM," Angelica said. "I, Angelica Kam, confer the title of 'Madame' to the following candidates."

When the last name was pronounced, Ravi took Angelica's place. "ADAM, insert in the database that these ninety-six people can now operate in the ether."

"Certification confirmed," the AI responded. "All named individuals are now permitted to operate in the ether as recognized and approved entities. The ether is sovereign."

"The ether is sovereign," Ravi, James, Venus, and Angelica chanted along with the students.

Venus stepped to the center of the stage. "The ether is a timeless stream of consciousness composed of countless parts."

"Let us add our voice, our name, and our time to the stream of consciousness that makes up the world beyond the world," the students repeated in unison.

Venus raised her hands in a gesture of welcome. "Ninety-six new etherions, ninety-six new tools to add substance to the world beyond the world."

"We answer the call and add our flesh, blood, and mind to the timeless stream of consciousness," the students replied. "The ether is sovereign."

"The ether is sovereign," Venus, Ravi, and Angelica stated, completing the ceremony.

"Welcome to the family," James said, clapping his hands, followed by the other teachers.

The students threw the ceremonial sash into the air and poured onto the stage to accept congratulations from their teachers as two servers circulated with plates filled with food and drinks.

The refreshment that followed was pleasant, with

students recalling highlights from the course and enjoying each other's company in a last demonstration of cama-raderie before starting their lives as etherions.

James watched Angelica excusing herself from a group of students and seeking an empty corner of the stage. She sat in a chair, put her untouched glass of champagne on the floor, and stared. He adjusted his jacket, pushed his glasses up, and walked toward her.

"May I?" he asked, pointing at the empty chair beside her.

Angelica blinked, evaluating James for a moment before nodding.

They sat in silence for a solid minute, the students' voices a constant background noise.

"You think they're ready?" She didn't look at him as she asked the question.

He took a slow breath, fingers loosely clasped in his lap. "I think we did what was humanly possible with the time we had."

"Right." Her expression relaxed a little, then she looked at him and smiled.

He frowned. "What's that for?"

"You didn't answer my question."

James gazed at her, enthralled by her straightforward attitude. "No," he admitted. "No, I didn't." He glanced over his shoulder at the students laughing, seemingly uncon-cerned with what awaited them. "Here's what I think. I think Covenant will break most of them." He pushed up his sleeves, avoided Angelica's eyes. "Three-fifths won't survive their first public appearance. Another fifth will decide to give themselves over to the competition when they realize they're fighting an uphill battle. They'll want something less risky, more lucrative. After all, we trained etherions, not missionaries."

Angelica looked at the newly baptized etherions. "What about the remaining fifth?"

He tilted his head to the side. "They would be the hard-core ones, the few who firmly believe in the holistic and have the skill set to spread it. The most adaptable, resourceful, and shrewd, the ones Cantara herself would have chosen. Those will be the people we can count on. But we'll never know until they go through a baptism by fire."

She narrowed her eyes. "You knew this would happen?"

He offered a curt nod. "I needed to separate the weak from the strong."

"You realize they're people, right?"

"I realize what's at stake." He took his sunglasses off. "And you do too. That's why you're here, and not with Sebastian."

She opened her mouth to reply, but nothing came out. She exhaled and said nothing.

"What?" He leaned forward. "Why that face?"

"It's nothing." She shrugged. "I'm just tired."

"No, you're not." He studied her face. "You're worried."

She moved back slightly. "How do you know?"

"You close your eyes when you're tired and pinch the top of your nose." He gestured toward her face. "Your brow furrows and your posture collapses. But when you're worried... Well, when you're worried, your jaw contracts here." He touched Angelica's cheek. "And crow's feet-like lines appear here." He gently brushed the sides of her temple, the contact sending jolts of electricity through his fingers. His hand lingered on Angelica's face longer than he had intended. She looked at him curiously, her eyes unblinking.

James retracted his hand, then cleared his throat. "It's about Sebastian, isn't it?" he said, trying to divert attention from the awkward moment.

"Well." She crossed her arms. "He doesn't help."

He nodded. Angelica and her husband had grown apart since she had been actively involved in the media war against Covenant. James wet his lips. "Why don't we—"

Angelica's interlink ringed. She checked the caller, sighed. "It's Sebastian," she said with a haunted expression. "Mind if I take it?"

"Not at all. Go ahead." He stood and moved away, but slowly, so that he could catch the first part of their conversation.

"Bastian, I don't... What? No, I didn't. You're talking too fast... Slow down..." Angelica shot up from her chair, her mouth hanging open. "Are you serious? No. It doesn't make sense. Hold on. Heading out right now."

She sprinted toward the exit and closed the door behind.

James swept his gaze around and meet Ravi's eyes. He nodded. Ravi made his way through the crowd and out of the room.

∞∞∞∞

Angelica walked the entire length of the hallway, putting distance between her and the graduation room. She looked around, entered the first empty room, and closed the door behind her.

"All right," she said, pacing. "I'm alone. What's happening?"

"This is...fucked...I swear." Sebastian was out of breath, almost wheezing between words. "Not in a million years... would I have...expected it."

"Expected *what*?"

"I'll show you." Sebastian muttered something under his breath. "I'm in room BG33, fourth underground floor. Can you get here soon?"

"Wait, what?" Her hands dropped to her sides. "You're in the Institute? *Now*? When did you get here? I thought you didn't want to—"

"Took advantage...moment of distraction." He paused a second, and Angelica heard typing. "The baptism was my chance to look around...continue my investigation without James or Ravi breathing down my neck. I knew I would find something. I knew it!"

"Investigation?" She touched the base of her neck. "Bastian, what investigation?"

"I had suspicions," he explained. "They led me...follow a trail...rabbit hole. Angy, it's crazy. I...not expect..."

"Bastian?" She tapped at her earpiece. "Bastian, I'm losing you."

"Come...BG33. Don't...anyone. You...alone..." The communication broke off.

Angelica tried to call Sebastian back, but had no luck. "Shit." She exited the room and strode down the corridor to the nearest elevator. She stabbed the button for the fourth underground floor and waited, tapping a foot on the floor until the elevator arrived.

Angelica walked down a corridor with identical doors painted light blue. She scanned the numbers. The door of BG33 was malfunctioning, opening and closing, stopping midway and resuming with jerky movements. The control panel was torn open, a burned hairpin stuck between the access plate and the peripheral transistor.

"Bastian, what did you do?" She stepped inside, sweat gathering on her palms. This floor was used to store unused equipment, but it didn't look like a storage room. Ten high-end consoles lit up the left side of the area. They were active, running on some kind of automated program. At the other end of the room, Sebastian typed frantically on another console.

Angelica sprinted toward him. "What the hell is going on here?"

"It's the holistic." Sebastian was breathing in quick gulps, his hair plastered on his forehead. He looked like he was on some kind of drug. "The holistic causes addiction."

She stared at him. "What?"

"It's in the principal design, hidden within the matrix specifics. The real ones, not the bullshit story James fed us all this time."

"I don't—"

Sebastian grabbed her by the shoulders. "It's been in front of us the whole time. Right here!" He jerked his head toward the consoles lining the other side of the room. "We shouldn't have trusted him. He's a psychopath, Angy. A fucking psychopath. He planned this all along. It's pure devilry. It's—"

"You gotta slow down." Angelica stepped back, and Sebastian released her. "I don't follow."

Sebastian licked his dry lips, inhaled sharply. "Okay... right...sorry." He shook his head to clear it. "Listen. Everything you think you know about the holistic is wrong. It runs on a sub-etheric program designed to affect the subconscious of individuals. It reprograms people to crave more of the connection every time they plug in. Every-single-time. It makes it harder and harder to get out of the loop. It's an addiction, like a drug, but it can't be detected with conventional methods."

"I—"

"It reprograms the way people think, Angy, and it's damn effective. I don't know how...exactly...but the data doesn't lie. Believe me, I know."

She stared at her husband, eyes going wide. "You...tried it on yourself?"

He flinched. "I had to know. *Had* to. Needed the proof, you know? Needed it for you...for the rest of us. Here, see for yourself." He jabbed a finger at his console. Angelica leaned forward to read the data. She recognized the blueprint of the holistic, but there were added parts she had never seen before. For ten minutes she studied the new information. Soon, the implication became crystal clear.

"God." She covered her mouth with a trembling hand. "You're right. This is...this is wrong."

"Yeah," Sebastian said, shaking his head instead of nodding, sweat pooling on his forehead. "We gotta take this information out of the institute. We need to show people. They need to see."

She swallowed. "Why would James do that? I mean...it's the opposite of what he wants."

"I don't know why. I don't care." Sebastian tilted his head back, looking upward. "Needs to be exposed. People need to know. This has the potential to destroy society. This is—"

"Oh, fuck me! You two *had* to stick your noses into the jar, didn't you?"

Angelica and Sebastian turned toward the voice. Ravi was standing at the entrance, his hair sticking messily out of his turban. He was panting, as if he'd been running. He was also holding a Mackenzie Stunner, pointing it at them.

"Ravi?" Angelica stared at the gun. "What are you doing?"

"Nothing, if you shut your month and follow me." Ravi gestured toward the door. "I don't want to drag you, but I'll do it if I have to. One blast, and you'll wish you were never born."

"Think you're going to get away with this?" Sebastian moved away from the console while holding a file folder. "It's over, Ravi. We know what the holistic does. We're going to expose you."

"Hey, genius." Ravi waved the gun at him. "You must have missed the part where I'm holding a stunner on you."

"You can't keep this buried." Sebastian wiped sweat off his face, his eyes dilated, eyelids raised. "And you can't do this without us."

"You mean without *her*," Ravi gestured at Angelica with the gun, taking off his eyes off Sebastian for a second.

Sebastian had been waiting for that distraction. He took advantage and threw the file at Ravi's face. He hit him right in the eye, and Ravi dropped the weapon.

"Sebastian, NO!" Angelica watched, petrified, as her husband threw himself against Ravi.

"Angy! Run!" Sebastian shouted while trying to hold Ravi down. "Call the cops!"

Ravi growled. "You fucker!" He jerked his head back, smashing Sebastian's chin, then pushed him away and punched him in the liver. Sebastian collapsed, gasping.

"Stop!" Angelica cried out. "Stop it!"

Sebastian covered his side, tried to hit Ravi, but the other was quicker, parried the blow with an arm, then grabbed Sebastian's shirt and threw him. Sebastian's head connected with the metal edge of the console, snapping backward.

"BASTIAN!" Angelica threw herself at Ravi without thinking. Ravi was unprepared. He dropped, carried to the floor by Angelica's weight.

"Get off me, bitch!" Ravi used his weight to roll and

knock Angelica off balance. The situation reversed with Ravi on her, pinning her down with both hands. Angelica's hand found the stunner and smashed it against Ravi's temple.

He fell to the side with a curse, but knocked the weapon from Angelica's hand. She stood, gasping, kicked Ravi in the groin while he was down, then scampered toward Sebastian.

"Bastian?" Her husband lay still on the floor, eyes open, blood pooling under his head. Angelica covered her mouth with her palm, stifling a scream.

"What's happening?"

Angelica turned toward the door as James passed through the entrance.

"James!" Angelica breathed heavily, her vision blurry. "Call an ambulance! Sebastian...Sebastian is—"

"Gone." James paced toward her, picking up the stunner on his way. He didn't look at Ravi, his eyes all for Sebastian. "This is unfortunate. You shouldn't have found out this way."

"So it was you." Angelica's voice shook with rage. "You knew about the holistic causing dependency."

He nodded. "I designed it myself."

"Why?"

"The 'why' is complicated, but if you trust me, I'll tell you everything. This is bigger than you, bigger than me, bigger than anything you can imagine. It'll shape humankind forever. Our names will go down in history as saviors."

"God." Angelica shook her head as her posture collapsed. She glanced at her husband. "He was right. You knew."

"Angelica, listen to me." He rested a hand on Angelica's shoulder, gently, reassuringly. "Sebastian...well, he would never have understood. But you...you're different. You're a worthy heir to Cantara. Join me, and together we'll do what she never could. Unite the people of Earth under the same banner."

She pulled away. "You're delusional. You used me for... for what? To subdue people? To make them your slaves? Why?"

Something flashed on James' face as he grabbed her arm, hard. "There's no turning back now. You have to—"

"Get your hands off me!" She pushed him away, but James held her again, this time with more strength.

He yanked her toward him. "You have to listen to me now."

"Let me go!"

"Calm down. You don't know what I...what *we* can do together. Nothing has changed. What we've done these past months...doesn't have to end. It doesn't."

Angelica propelled her elbow backward, slamming James' chin, and he let go. She tried to run, but James grabbed her ankle and she fell face first.

"Please..." came James' voice. "You don't know what's at stake."

"Let me go!"

"I'm begging you. Don't do this."

Angelica kept struggling, trying to free herself from James' hold. She hit him in the face, and the Domine's glasses fell to the floor, breaking.

"No!"

James threw himself at her, pinning her down with his weight. Most of Angelica's blows didn't land. The rest were weak, dictated by fear. James' hands grasped her throat, his fingers pressed against her trachea.

"I didn't want it to end like this." His voice was little

more than a whisper. He sobbed, his eyes wet with tears. "I didn't mean to. I swear I didn't mean to. I'm sorry. So sorry."

"J-Ja-rgh..." Angelica's punches grew weaker and weaker. He didn't seem to notice them as his hands dug deeper into Angelica's throat.

"Ja-a-a-m-sss..." Angelica's leg jerked, the edges of her vision darkened.

"Shh, Angy. Shh," James spoke softly." It'll be over soon...I swear. Shh. Sleep now, Madame of Melody. Sleep. It's time to sleep."

Angelica Kam was vaguely aware of her arms falling to her sides, no longer able to move. Her vision fogged, then the entire world collapsed into darkness and silence.

∞∞∞

James Ark stared at Angelica as the last glint of light disappeared from her eyes. He kept his hands around her throat for what felt like an hour before releasing his grip.

Angelica's head fell to the side, her eyes open, staring into nothing.

"An...Angelica?" James closed his mouth and waited, holding his breath. He swallowed and tried to suppress his sobs.

Angelica's vacant eyes stared at him accusingly.

"I'm sorry," James muttered. "So sorry." He cradled her body, spending the next minute mourning her death, but deep inside he was already working on a way to use this situation to his advantage. He always had a contingency plan. It was what he did best: foreseeing likely outcomes and taking advantage of setbacks. Turning defeat into victory had always been his greatest gift.

Ravi limped toward him, his forehead bleeding. "She's gone?" His tone suggested he knew the answer.

James nodded.

"Fuck." Ravi threw his gun against the nearest console. "We're fucked." He glanced at Sebastian's body. "He's gone too."

James gently laid Angelica's body on the floor, closed her eyes, and then stood up.

"What do we do?" Ravi sounded desperate. "What the fuck do we do? I swear everything went to shit so fast I didn't even... I mean, they just wouldn't listen. I swear they wouldn't listen."

"Get a grip. Our job isn't over."

"Job?" Ravi's mouth fell open, his upper lip curling up. "What're you talking about? There's no way we can hide this." Ravi studied James' demeanor, becoming more upset. "Why do you look so fucking calm?"

James gestured at the two bodies. "Don't you see? We just earned two martyrs."

Ravi stared at him. "M-martyrs?" He stumbled back. "You don't...you don't want to cover this up?"

"No." James gazed at Angelica's lifeless body. "Everyone needs to know."

"I don't understand." Ravi cocked his head while raising his eyebrow. "What's your plan?"

"To turn defeat into victory." James picked up his broken sunglasses.

Ravi shook his head. "James, corpses have a way of pointing out their killers."

"Sure they will. They'll point in the direction we decide." James headed for the exit. "Grab the stunner and leave the bodies. If anybody asks where Angelica is, send them to me."

"I don't—"

"Just do it. Let me handle the rest." James exited the room, doing his best to ignore the sweat dripping down his chin, the nameless feeling of oppression squeezing his chest. They were all things he had learned to live with a long time before.

* * *

9 years before

Nashville, Handal's Institute for Gifted Students

JAMES WIPES the sweat off his forehead while watching the data swirling in front of him. Every single muscle in his body is tense.

Shapes, numbers, and images orbit around him with increasing speed, an organized chaos of information that can help him complete the simulation.

James evaluates the assets he has, eyes scanning for usable bits of data. What's his next move?

"Psi and Tau aligned at the affinity points," he mumbles, like a mantra to sharpen his senses. "Epsilon and Omicron hold up for the moment. But for how much longer? It doesn't matter. If Psi and Tau fall, everything falls with them."

Like a bloodhound spotting prey, James shifts his gaze to the next affinity bond: Xi and Rho. What to do with that? He swallows, his throat so dry it feels like sawdust. *Think, James. Think.* He narrows his eyes, then notices something he missed before. *There.* He knows what do to.

"Xi and Rho are the weak links in the chain." He moves his hands, and the data moves according to his will. Xi and Rho don't have enough mutual affinity points between them. At any moment, the cluster can break the fragile bond they formed, screwing up the whole simulation. He has to fix that. He notices another link out of the corner of his eye. His heart skips a beat. How could he have missed that Xi and Rho are the latest additions on the periphery of the cluster? They're not integrated enough to destabilize the system. They can't do actual damage. James lowers his arms and turns his full attention to the bond between Sigma and Theta. He sees it now. That's the key to completing the puzzle. He needs to work on them. They are the answers. Sigma and Theta...Sigma and Theta...Sigma and Theta...

Adrenaline courses through James' body as ADAM's familiar voice booms within the simulation room.

"James, the synergistic activity between the bank of provinces you have created in *sub quotis* is welding at the desired points of conjuncture." The AI gives James time to absorb the information. "Your attempt at reuniting Sigma with Theta is successfully stabilizing the agglomeration."

James' heartbeat quickens. He's never been this close to reaching his goal. Now it's time to risk it all. He achieved stability in most of the cluster, but it isn't over. The hard part begins now.

"ADAM, I'm channeling my etheric assets to maintain a quantum centric that welds in Omega affinity points with Sigma, rather than Theta. Results?"

"The entropy state of the system is increasing," ADAM replies.

With an effort that takes every ounce of his remaining strength, James calls up additional data in rapid succession. After evaluating the information, he puts all his chips on the table, betting every asset he has left for a desperate final push.

ADAM assesses his action, then comments on it, "James, the Mephisto super agglomerate is gaining subscriptions at a Paretal rate of thirty-two percent per hour. Furthermore, the synergistic activity between the bank of provinces you created in *sub quotis* has successfully completed welding."

James gulps in air. "ADAM, use all my frequency channelers to assimilate the disconnected points left in Mephisto."

"Confirmed," ADAM replies. "Frequency channellers deployed successfully. Your sample system is strengthening in *pro primis*. System entropy is reaching equilibrium."

He's almost there. One last push.

"Shut down all non-vital peripheral assets and use the spare resources for the welding."

"Confirmed," ADAM answers. "All non-essential assets redeployed to assist with the merger. James, the system's entropy has reached equilibrium. The Mephisto agglomeration is now functional and self-sustaining. The simulation has been successfully completed."

James' brow draws in closer, his face tightening. "C-confirm," he stutters, feeling light-headed. "The simulation...is complete?"

"Confirmed," ADAM repeats. "The simulation has been completed successfully."

James drops to his knees, sobbing like a kid. "I did it," he mumbles, shaking. "I...I did it!" He collapses on the floor, panting, half-laughing, half-crying.

"You done mopping the floor?"

James looks toward the room's entrance. Cantara Handal watches him with her arms crossed, an amused smile on her bright red lips.

James tries to stand, but he's so exhausted he barely manages to sit.

"Need help over there, little devil?"

"I...I did it," he mumbles. "Cantara. I did it."

"What was that?" Cantara sits on the ground next to him. She leans toward him. "One more time."

James clears his throat. "I did it, Cantara. It's done." He smiles triumphantly. "The simulation is done!"

Cantara tousles his hair. "Of course, little devil. Of course. Now drink some water. You're dehydrated." She hands him a water bottle.

James pushes the bottle away. "No! You don't understand. I did it. I have created a dominion."

Cantara straightens up a little. She isn't smiling anymore.

"Look. I'll show you." James points at the ceiling. "ADAM. Show the status of the Mephisto agglomeration at the end of the simulation."

The AI obliges.

Cantara stands up and evaluates the data. Her expression turns into a frown.

"I followed your advice," James says, unable to contain his enthusiasm. "I tweaked the program's core and started the simulation again. Same goal, different premise."

Cantara arches her eyebrows. "You did *what*?"

"Remember the story you told me about cheating your way around the impossible? Well, I did exactly that. You were right. With our current type of ether, it's impossible to create a dominion. But if you change the infrastructure of cyberspace altogether, if you build a new scaffold and adapt it to your needs...well, then the sky's the limit." James gestures at the data, proving his success.

Cantara stands to her full height. Her lips press together

in a thin line. James blinks, taken aback by her expression. This isn't the reaction he had expected. Why does she look angry?

"What's wrong?" James asks.

"What's wrong?" Cantara snaps. She points at the data. "This is wrong! ADAM?"

"Yes, Madame."

"Erase all historical data relating to James Ark's simulations. Saved files, models, statistics. I want everything gone."

"Executed," comes ADAM's reply.

It all happens so fast, James has barely enough time to process it. "What...what have you done?"

Cantara ignores him. "ADAM, prevent James Ark's access to this simulation."

James gasps. "Wait—"

"Authorization, Cantara Handal, Sekhmet Gold."

"No!" James tries to stop Cantara, but he's too tired and stumbles to his feet, falling to the ground. He looks up, shaking his head in disbelief. "Cantara, what have you done? What—"

"Confirmed," ADAM talks over James. "The use of this simulation is of now forbidden to Domine Ark."

James stares at Cantara. "Why, Cantara? Why?"

"This flight of fancy is ruining you, James." Cantara turns her back to him. "I won't have my brightest student wasting his time chasing chimeras."

James shakes his head. "It's not a chimera anymore. It happened. You saw it! I created—"

"Nothing!" Cantara cuts him off. "You created *nothing*. You cheated your way into believing you won an impossible scenario. Now listen to me. Your sabbatical is over. It's time you man up and start a real job. I'll set up a meeting with Ermis Donovan. If you like a challenge, that son of a gun will give you one. He'll keep you busy and engaged. Believe that."

Cantara stomps out of the room, leaving James alone in the darkness. He looks up, a chill running down his spine.

"ADAM? ADAM, please, answer me."

The IA remains silent.

James slowly rises, staring at the door, his jaw set so hard it hurts.

Cantara Handal just denied him his right to make a difference.

43

RICANDER

YELLOW SEA, AQUAMARINE

Ariul

❧

Marcius Gaspar hadn't said a word since picking up Lena for her meeting with Cassandra Quinn. The two of them had walked in silence for close to five minutes, entering a section of Aquamarine Lena could only describe as a massive passage partly open at the side to form a colonnade.

Marcius finally came to a stop in front of a frosted-glass door in a metal frame, which gave a glimpse of bright, reddish light inside.

"This is it." He gestured at the entrance. "Now listen carefully. The regent will expect straightforward answers. Make sure you deliver them."

"That's fine by me," Lena said, holding his stare. "Since I expect the same from her."

Marcius' eyes shone like bits of dark ember. "Let's get something straight. You're in a precarious situation. You think you're special, but that couldn't be further from the truth. You trail behind the chancellor's heel like a well-trained dog. Stick to the script, or you'll regret it."

She blinked, taken aback by Marcius' direct manner. "Okay. It sounds like you've got a problem with me. What did I do to piss you off?"

He snorted. "Think I don't know who you are?"

She showed her empty hands. "Um...enlighten me."

Marcius' nostrils flared. "This isn't a game, girl. You can't afford to push the wrong buttons. You're Tiago's creature, but whatever he thinks he's doing, it won't work. If it were up to me, you'd be locked in a cell."

"But it's not up to you, Legatus Gaspar." Lena repeated the title Tiago used to address him. "You know what? You're right. I don't understand a lot about what's happening, but I didn't ask for any of this. Here's something I know, though: I've never been good at taking shit from bullies, and you strike me as one. Only, you're not scary. Where I come from, I've seen people like you chewed up and spit out every Sunday morning."

He glared. He opened his mouth, then shook his head. "You're not worth it." He opened the door and gestured her in.

She lingered for a couple more seconds, then entered.

She wasn't prepared for what awaited: a small green-house with dozens of plants. It smelled earthy and musky; the humidity clung on her skin as she moved forward.

The contrast between the rest of Aquamarine and this verdant oasis was striking. It was almost as if she had stepped into another world.

She knew little about plants, but in one of her summer jobs in Los Angeles she had taken care of a banker's garden in Beverly Hills and had learned to recognize quite a few. As she ventured inside the greenhouse, though, none were familiar.

Lena stopped to look at a group of poppy-like flowers, about thirty inches tall, with an erect stem covered with stiff hairs the color of mud. The flowers inside were black, while the stem was snow white. She moved closer to examine the strange flowers, which rotated in her direction. She jerked back and gasped.

"An Applaudant," came a voice behind her.

Lena swung around and saw Cassandra Quinn sitting on the ground, less than ten feet away. The regent was half-hidden behind a thick group of shrubs that looked almost black in the artificial light. The regent's long, vermilion-red hair was tied back in a braid, and her emerald eyes were fixed on another odd-looking plant she was tending while wearing a pair of thick gloves.

"Extremely beautiful, and dangerously toxic," Cassandra continued, pointing to the flowers Lena had backed away from. "I advise against touching the leaves, but I invite you to admire the beauty of the flowers while it lasts. Won't be long before its seeds burst open and turn the whole thing into feeding matter for insects." Cassandra smiled at her while waving away a couple lance-shaped leaves actively trying to wrap themselves around her wrists. "Welcome to the secret garden of Aquamarine, my small piece of heaven. Would you mind... Damn, these leaves are nosy... Would you mind handing me that spray bottle? It's inside that canister. Over there."

Lena glanced at the ground and noticed a bunch of gardening instruments. She picked up the one described and handed it to Cassandra.

"Thank you." The regent sprayed the plant she was working at and the large leaves stopped moving. "There you go. You can go back to sleep now." She glanced at Lena as she removed her gloves. "Are you okay? You look a little pale."

"Am I okay?" Lena pressed her lips together in a slight grimace. "Well, I'm a bit confused actually."

Cassandra frowned. "About what?"

"Uh... Let's see, by your attitude, for starters." Lena pulled in and then slowly released a deep breath. "Aren't you afraid that I might...I don't know, explode and blow this whole place up?"

Cassandra offered a bemused smile. "What?"

"Well, you made it clear you don't trust me. I'm told the restrainer was your idea, and so was the assembly. You know? The flashy court case you put up a few days ago? Remember that? Sounded like you weren't too happy to have me around. Wasn't that the whole point of the gathering? To make sure I was treated as dangerous?"

"Ah, yes." Cassandra's smile wavered as she shook her head. "To be honest, that was a bit of posturing."

Lena tilted her head to the side. "Excuse me?"

"It's political jargon," Cassandra explained. "It means when someone pretends to have a particular opinion or attitude toward something or—"

"I know what posturing means, thank you." Lena crossed her arms. "What does it have to do with me?"

"Well, the truth is, I think you're a young woman dragged into a complicated situation." Cassandra gave a half-shrug. "You've no clue what's going on. I don't need to be a mind-reader to know that."

Lena squinted. "Then why all the staging? Why the restrainer? Why the trial? Couldn't we just have a simple chat like we're having now?"

Cassandra's eyebrows pulled close and down, creating a

deep crease on her forehead. "It's more complicated than that."

"Why?" Lena spoke through her teeth with forced restraint.

Cassandra lay down the spray bottle. "Have you ever taken care of someone?"

Lena blinked. "I'm sorry?"

"I mean someone completely dependent on you. Have you?"

Lena considered for a second. "Um...well, yes, actually. I worked in a hospice for a season. Some residents couldn't even stand without help. They relied on workers to do pretty much anything, from going to the bathroom to eating."

Cassandra nodded. "Have you ever had to lie, for their own sake?"

The image of an eighty-year-old woman flashed before Lena's eyes. Mrs. Manchester had been an Alzheimer's patient she'd taken care of before she passed away. Lena had to tell the old woman the craziest stories to get her to take a bath or to eat. "Yes," Lena said, slowly. "Sometimes."

"Being in politics is like working in a hospice." Cassandra picked up a pair of scissors and trimmed low-hanging branches. "My job is to reassure the people of the Defensio Project that everything I do, I do for their safety. Using the restrainer was never meant to hurt you. It was a way to reassure my people. And believe me, there are many that would rather have you disposed of with no questions asked."

Lena glanced at the garden's door. "You mean like Marcius?"

Cassandra maintained an even tone. "Marcius is the least dangerous."

Lena gave her a flat gaze. "Meaning?"

"He doesn't know how to use a four-million-dollar combat exo-suit that could level a building."

Lena didn't know what to make of that. Was the regent referring to a dunamis? If Cassandra had shared that information, there must be a reason. Was that a warning or a threat?

The regent continued pruning as she talked. "My title comes with responsibilities. Posturing and questioning is expected. It's a way of venting the frustration of the factions composing the Defensio Project."

"What factions?"

Cassandra jerked free a dry leaf from a plant's stem, then dropped it on the ground. "Any sizeable group splits into smaller groups, each with different ideas. Your coming started something. There have always been different views on how to run the Defensio. Now, these have started taking shape, and people who lurked in the shadows are using you as a pretext to create havoc. My job is keeping that from happening."

Lena bit the inside of her cheek. "You're saying there are others trying to make me look bad."

"I'm also saying that I'm not your enemy."

"Then what are you?"

Cassandra openly stared at Lena with a pained look. "A tightrope walker who's trying to keep a promise."

"A promise?" Lena squinted. "To whom?"

Cassandra's features softened. "We both know the answer. We're all here because of him, after all."

Lena glanced around uneasily. Cassandra meant Wei Wang. What was the regent's connection with the First Hyperist? What was the promise she made to him? Before she could ask, Cassandra walked past her, then bent in front of a small, fragile-looking flower and sniffed at it. "This is a

Ricander." She gestured to the plant. "Extremely beautiful, but even more dangerous than the Applaudant. Its seeds can kill an adult person in less than a minute."

"I've never seen a flower like this," Lena said, then she looked around, as if taking in the entire garden. "Actually, I don't think I've ever seen any of these plants."

"Good." Cassandra nodded. "I'd be surprised otherwise."

"Why?"

Cassandra stood up, looked at the plants. "I created all of them myself. They only exist here, in Aquamarine."

Lena swallowed. "You mean...these are all genetic crossings?"

"Mostly." Cassandra's features softened. "Some are completely new plants, manufactured for specific needs. A few could survive in some pretty harsh environments, like the slopes of an active volcano, the deepest recesses of the ocean, or Mars. Well, kind of. I'm still working on the Martian one actually. Got the cold figured out. Working on radiation, atmosphere, and nutrition now. That's a tough nut to crack. Come see this one." Cassandra motioned to the Ricander with her chin. "This is a genetic cross between a Ricinus and an Oleander, hence the name 'Ricander.' I added a bit of genetic love to make it more interesting. It's one of my favorites."

Lena gazed at the flower, her mind spinning. "You're a genetist?"

"Genetist" was a neologism coined by the media to separate them from the "geneticist," which was a canonic profession, contrary to the genetists, who were seen as rogue scientists with no ethics. She'd heard of the secretive group of people ostracized by the scientific community and mistrusted by NGOs opposed to genetic engineering. The brightest genetists had helped make the Saemangeum Zoo a reality.

Cassandra offered a curt nod, and the sparkle in her eyes spoke of defiance. "I was. A lifetime ago, I worked with Wei. He unlocked my potential, gave me permission to be whatever I wanted to be."

Lena couldn't shake the feeling that Cassandra was mentioning Wei for a reason, but couldn't guess her purpose. "Why am I here?"

Cassandra dusted her pants. "I want us to start over."

Lena raised her eyebrows. "Start over?"

"Yes. We got off on the wrong foot. There's something special about you. I'm willing to admit that."

"So you trust me all of a sudden?"

"The assembly was politics. Now that I've taken care of that, we can figure out a way to understand your position in Wei's plan. What do you say? Want to start over?" Cassandra held out a hand. "Name's Cassandra Quinn. Nice to meet you."

Lena hesitated. Could she be honest about her intentions? Could she trust the regent? Or was Cassandra just playing the part of a friend? Lena had the vivid impression that the Overseer of Ariul was referring to *this* moment when he talked about the chessboard. If this indeed was a game of skill, she'd better learn the rules quickly if she wanted to survive.

Lena swallowed, then squeezed Cassandra's hand.

"You don't need to fear me," the regent said, still holding Lena's hand. "I'm sure Tiago provided a rather colorful image of me, and as a consequence, you walked inside this room carrying lots of prejudice. Truth is, my only goal is to serve the Defensio Project."

"Yes." Lena withdrew her hand. "He told me about you. Said you two had different ways of seeing things."

Cassandra nodded. "The chancellor has an agenda, just like any person. He's not bad, but don't be fooled by his easy-going attitude. He has his own beliefs on how the Defensio should be run, and doesn't like the...shall we call it 'conservative' stance I hold dear."

Lena evaluated the regent. "Tiago doesn't like how you handle the biomechas."

"Among other things. He would have us attack them in force, rather than defend Saemangeum."

"What's wrong with that?" Lena asked.

Cassandra laughed. "They outnumber us ten to one, have more resources and better technology. We've been able to fend them off because we're playing defense, and playing it smart. My five cents? If we followed Tiago's strategy, we would've been wiped out years ago. Call me crazy, but I'm convinced without my approach we wouldn't be having this conversation."

Cassandra had touched on a sensitive subject. Lena decided this was a good time to ask about Makoto. "So you won't attack them because you're scared."

"That's not it." Cassandra tossed the scissors into the bucket. "I won't attack them because that's not the reason we exist. You know what '*defensio*' means? It's Latin for 'defense,' 'protection.' We're here to *protect* Saemangeum, not to start a war."

Lena bit her lip. "Ever heard the adage: 'The best defense is a good offense'?"

Cassandra offered a wide smile that spoke of understanding. "You're asking because of your friend. Makoto, right? You want to rescue him."

Lena's heartbeat quickened. This was it. The whole

conversation came down to this moment. If she could sway Cassandra, convince her that rescuing Makoto was doable, they could do away with the secrecy and the plots. "What if you had a real shot at saving him?" Lena looked straight into the regent's eyes. "What if you had information that made a rescue operation possible?"

Cassandra narrowed her eyes. "Is there something I should know?"

Lena clenched her hands into fists. "Answer the question."

Cassandra shook her head. "No. I wouldn't risk the safety of the Defensio. It's not about your friend. I would do the same with anyone, me included."

"I see." Lena clasped her hands behind her back. It wasn't the answer she wanted, but it was an answer. "I understand what you're saying. I won't interfere with your decision."

"Good." Cassandra opened her arms in a welcoming gesture. "I'm glad we're on the same page. I'll let everyone know you're no longer considered a threat to the Defensio Project. No one will bother you. You're free to go where you please."

"Thank you."

"In return," Cassandra continued, "I'd appreciate if you'd refrain from doing anything that could endanger the peace. Make that promise, and we can work together to find out what Wei had in store for you."

Lena looked the regent in the eyes and lied without hesitation. "I promise."

44

THE HUNTRESS AND THE PATRON

HYPERIST COMPLEX INFINITY, CONSTABLE'S
OFFICE

Gladia

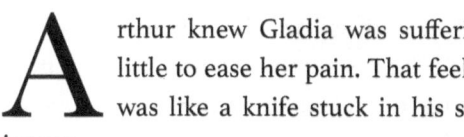

Arthur knew Gladia was suffering, but could do little to ease her pain. That feeling of uselessness was like a knife stuck in his side, impossible to ignore.

His role as Gladia's second-in-command kept him busy, sometimes forcing him to stay away from her for extensive periods of time. He despised those moments. His first responsibility was the safety of the Last Vertex of the Hexahedron, and he felt he was failing her.

For ten years Arthur had worked hard to prevent an attempt on Gladia's life, and for ten years he had been successful. Gladia was alive, the security measures he'd put in place to keep her safe worked, but he always feared he was missing something, that more could be done for her protection.

Arthur stared at the message he was holding, trying hard not to scowl. On it was written a meeting time and geographical coordinates pointing to a location in California. Another commitment he couldn't avoid. He switched on the lighter he was holding and burned the message.

Arthur turned his attention to the broadcasting news service projected by the room's trigoy, which showed a situation deteriorating by the minute. After the speech in Rome, the standists led by the newly formed coalition of Muchena and Hawke had started a fierce campaign against the Hyperist Movement, using the Militarized Space scandal to fuel the fire. All over North America and in many European capitals, the standists organized massive demonstrations to capture the attention of the media.

On the African continent, the Black Wind movement had already destroyed a dozen hyperist installations. In Asia, the governments suppressed the demonstrations for fear of unrest, so the standists used that violence to accuse the governments of militarism and violence. The standists were also pressuring the Planetary Court. The Landist Council and the Temple of Gaea had filed forty-seven requests for sanctions against the hyperists for violations of PlaCo regulations and for endangering worldwide safety. There was a group of a thousand demonstrators shouting slogans around the clock outside the PlaCo headquarters in New York.

The events of the past few weeks would have knocked out anyone, but Gladia continued to wake up at five in the morning and go to bed past midnight to handle those crises. And those few hours of sleep were haunted by nightmares.

Nightmares Arthur felt responsible for.

He switched off the trigoy, and the broadcast disappeared. He rubbed his forehead, then opened the desk drawer, rummaged inside, and emerged with an infinity-shaped pendant. It was a faithful reproduction of Wei Wang's legendary infinity.

Arthur had never looked at it in person, but Gladia had described it multiple times in great detail, along with the phrase engraved on it. He turned it over and read the four words. "Change the whole world."

Arthur closed the drawer and placed the pendant on the desk. He had it made as a gift for Gladia months before, but had never found the right occasion to give it to her. The pendant was still missing a necklace. Since it didn't have one, Arthur could procrastinate, delay the moment he would give it to Gladia. He was afraid she wouldn't like it. Wei was always a sensitive subject around her. What Arthur thought was a gracious gift might not be to Gladia.

"Constable?"

Arthur snapped out of his reverie. Charlotte Encanto had entered his office, her expression flustered.

"I'm sorry, sir," Charlotte said, holding a stack of files. "I knocked, and the door was left ajar, so I thought—"

"Come on in." He motioned for her to come forward.

Charlotte closed the door, then handed the files to him. "This is the data you requested, sir."

Arthur took the files. "The old Herina Sue case from the PlaCo archives?"

"Yes, sir."

He nodded. "Thank you. I'll give it a gander later."

There was an awkward moment of silence, then Charlotte cleared her throat. "Is, ah... Is everything all right, sir?"

Arthur blinked. "Yes. Just busy." He gestured to the trigoy meaningfully.

Charlotte nodded. "I understand, sir." She eyed the pendant in Arthur's hands. "What is that?"

"This?" Arthur shifted in his chair. "Just a gift. Well, I *think* it's a gift."

"For the Executive Director?" ventured Charlotte.

Arthur hesitated for a moment. "Yes," he said at last, surprised by how easily the assistant guessed its purpose.

Charlotte blushed. "Can I...can I see it?"

Arthur looked at the pendant. "Sure." He handed the infinity to her. "What do you think? I've been debating about giving it to her or not. I guess part of me thinks it's lame."

Charlotte's eyes widened as she studied the object. "Sir, is this what I think it is?"

He shook his head. "It's just a copy. A very convincing one, but a copy."

"It's beautiful. I'm sure she'll love it." She returned the infinity.

He opened his mouth to reply, but his interlink beeped. It was the statistics department. He tapped his earpiece to accept the call. "Yes?" There was a brief silence, followed by static. "Damn." He switched off the device with a grimace. "This thing's been acting up for days. I should have gone to the internal communications department on Monday, but with all that's been going on, I've barely had time to breathe."

"Sir, actually, I'm on my way there to upgrade my frequency system." Charlotte leaned forward. "I can mention the problem, if you'd like."

"Thanks." He smiled. "You're a life saver, Charlotte."

"Just doing my job, sir."

"Is there anything you're unable to do?"

She blushed. "Not that I'm aware of."

He gave Charlotte his communication cell and personal interlink frequency.

"And regarding the gift, sir." She hesitated a little, then bit her lip. "I think it's a great idea."

Arthur looked at the infinity. "Yeah," he said, smiling. "I guess all it needs now is a chain. Thank you, Charlotte. I wasn't really sure it was a smart move. You've given me courage."

Charlotte nodded, then walked to the exit, but before crossing it she looked back at him. "Sir, will you be attending the meeting with the Starry Assembly this afternoon?"

"I won't," Arthur said, furrowing his brow. "There's somewhere else I need to be."

∞∞∞

Los Angeles
Venice Beach

The promenade was teeming with people of different ages and nationalities. There were tourists taking pictures, locals walking their dogs, teenagers on rollerblades darting between passersby, and a slew of street vendors and street performers. One of them had set up shop nearby and was entertaining a group of sightseers with circus-like stunts that earned him cheers and a cap full of five-dollar-bills.

Arthur envied those people: they had no threats to handle, no need to watch their back. It was like living in a dream. He would have swapped places with any of them in a heartbeat, if he could bring Gladia with him.

"Good afternoon, Mr. Strutzenberg."

Arthur shifted on the bench as he looked to his right.

The newcomer wore a fedora, a white t-shirt, and a pair of khaki Bermuda shorts.

"Here's some fairy dust for you." His contact set a paper bag beside Arthur. "Make sure you sprinkle the right amount on your lady friend. The recurring nightmares you mentioned in the last reports are making him nervous."

Arthur frowned. "What triggers them?"

The man shrugged. "Could be an indicator that the memory suppressor is weakening, which might point to a side effect of the drug we're not aware of. If the nightmares persist, I'll alert the Patron. God forbid Egea remembers things she shouldn't."

Arthur grabbed the bag and threw a quick glance at the contents: a round pill organizer filled with orange pills. He swallowed, closed the bag, and pushed it to the side. "These meetings are over," he said stiffly. "I no longer need your mindkillers. Don't contact me again." He stood up and made to go.

"How do you plan on keeping her out of trouble?" There was amusement in the man's voice, as if he was genuinely interested in knowing the answer. "Memories aren't easy to ignore, especially when linked to a trauma."

Arthur stopped. "I've had ten years to study the compound. Last month, I replicated it. I don't need you anymore."

The man wearing the fedora crossed his arms and smiled. "Déjà vu. Haven't we had this conversation before? The compound can't be replicated, I thought I made that clear. Even if you replicated it, though, we both know that's not the only reason you keep coming back. If you think these past years have made the Last Vertex of the Hexahedron less appealing to the Huntress, you're sadly mistaken."

Arthur snorted. "Give me one reason I should listen to you."

"I can give you three." The man took his hat off and used it to fan air. "Like the number of her agents watching us right now."

Arthur's hand slid loosely into his pocket. "You're just trying to confuse me. It's cheap, and uncalled for. I don't—"

"The woman with the ponytail who's stretching by that palm tree," the man said, resting his arm on the backrest. "Then there's the lady in green yoga pants who's filming the boardwalk with a projector unit display, and finally the mother in the purple t-shirt with the stroller covered by a yellow veil."

Arthur glanced at the people described, never letting his eyes linger. None of the three women seemed to look in their direction, but the man with the fedora had given rise to doubt, and the feeling of being watched slowly increased.

"There are two reasons they don't interfere," the man continued. "The first, of course, is that we're in a crowded, public place full of people with smartphones, trigoys, and PUDs. It's not the publicity they want. The second reason is the knowledge that I have twice as many men to make sure nothing happens to us."

Arthur stood transfixed, unsure on what to do.

"Why don't you come sit down?" The contact patted the bench. "Let's talk."

Arthur clenched his jaw. "Gladia is exhausted," he said, hating himself for sounding desperate. "She's wearing out. She can't keep up with the pressure."

"She might be exhausted," the contact pointed out, "but she's still alive. I call it a bargain."

Arthur bit his lip.

"Sit down." The man drummed his index finger on the backrest. "I won't ask you again."

Arthur held his breath, then he sat back down.

The man stopped fanning with his fedora, looked at Arthur straight in the eyes. "Understand this: our men are the only thing that keeps the Executive Director safe, and the only thing that compels the Patron to employ them is the assurance that Gladia Egea will keep doing her job."

Arthur drew a breath and released before replying. "We don't need your bodyguards anymore. My starlaukers can easily—"

The contact snorted. "Please, you're being ludicrous. Your precious starlaukers would be squashed like flies by her agents, believe me. I know what they're capable of."

"You're trying to scare me."

"I don't need to. You're already scared to death. But let's say, for curiosity's sake, that I am blowing things out of proportion just to keep you in line. Want to risk being wrong? Are you so confident in your contingency plan to operate without the Patron's help? May I remind you that ten years ago, four of those *things* infiltrated the world's most secure place and killed the world's most protected man? You're not equipped for what's out there, Mr. Strutzenberg. If you think a bunch of men in servo-armor and high-powered blasters make any difference, you're delusional. Gladia Egea would have been killed a thousand times over without our protection."

Arthur glared at him. "What do you want?"

"There are developments you must know. The Huntress went on the offensive. The Patron knows she's fomenting the growing global crisis between hyperists and landists. There's no better way to escalate things than by killing the Executive Director. Keep your eyes open, and trust no one. With the security measures we've built together, the only person who can successfully threaten Egea's life is someone who has direct access to her. Even the Patron can't be everywhere at once. Safeguarding your friend up close is your job, Mr. Strutzenberg."

"I know." Arthur almost growled the last word.

"Splendid." The contact wore the fedora and stood up. "Egea will stay alive as long as she remains useful. I hope I've made myself clear." He started walking away.

Arthur reached out, then hesitated. "Wait," he said with a restless stance.

The man looked over his shoulder. "Yes?"

Arthur's lips were pressed together. He tried to ignore the sinking feeling in his stomach. "Is Hector really your name?"

The man offered an amused smile. "Of course. Did you have any doubt?"

Arthur snorted. "I always have doubts. Isn't that the whole point of these conversations? Convincing me you're in control?"

Hector grinned. "It's good to have doubts, Mr. Strutzen-berg. They might help you keep your friend alive. Regards." He touched the brim of his hat and walked away.

Arthur slumped back on the bench and sighed. Ten years he had known this man, but still didn't know who he really was. It had been this Hector who told him where to find an unconscious Gladia on the beach where she had been attacked ten years before, a Gladia with the memory of what happened the week prior to the attack wiped out. Hector told him she would continue to live as long as her memory remained missing.

For ten years, those pills had removed Gladia's memo-ries of the attack on the Infinity Control Center and the subsequent attack on Cape Canaveral. The medical checks Gladia had undergone had determined that her localized amnesia was due to the trauma, but Arthur knew the truth, and he made sure it remained buried. He knew Gladia too well. If she remembered what really happened, it would lead to her grave.

Arthur would die before letting that happen.

45

THE ETHER IS SOVEREIGN

ATLANTA, DATAMORPH HEADQUARTERS

James

The Museum of the Sovereign Ether was almost empty. The few tourists who showed up didn't look too inclined to spend time inside the building. They mostly browsed around the sections, never lingering in front of one of the info stations. They paced along, like going through the motions of a boring task, then left the museum without looking back.

The whole place seemed under a spell. There was a precarious balance in the air, a feeling of foreboding that made everyone look tense.

One area, more than others, seemed to suffer from that spell. The etherions' hall of fame was completely empty, expect for a figure dressed in black.

James Ark stared at the reproduction of Angelica Kam, his shoulders drawing up, his elbows tucking into his sides.

He took a deep, pained breath and shifted his eyes to the projection next to Angelica. He grimaced. Putting Cantara Handal beside her former student had been a sound strategic choice by DataMorph's marketing team. It worked as nostalgia-baiting, leveraging both women's status and their premature death. Another product packaged to perfection for costumers to enjoy.

In hindsight, Angelica's death had been the worst and the best thing that could happen. He'd lost a powerful ally, but gained a way to checkmate their enemies and win the Ether War. Ironic. Such a gross mistake turned into the resolution to his greatest problem. And all it cost was the life of someone he loved.

"What an absolute bummer."

James pulled his wits into focus. He turned toward the person standing next to him, a plump, middle-aged woman with blonde hair worn in a bob. She was wearing a t-shirt with the phrase *Boss Mom* made of golden glitter. Both Os formed a smiling face.

"Pandora?" James frowned.

"You'd think this place would be teeming with people on a Saturday afternoon, especially with the status of the ether." The woman looked around, pursing her lips. "But then again, maybe not. Maybe folks prefer to see the coming Apocalypse from the comfort of their homes."

James smoothed his jacket. "I was...I was expecting Agate."

"Agate is busy running DataMorph." Pandora looked at him with a motherly smile. "With all the fuss, the poor girl is having a hard time with damage control. Well, you get me instead of her. Happy?"

James rubbed the back of his neck. "Of course."

Pandora laughed. "Oh, James. You're the worst liar. How's Ravi, by the way? Still giving you headaches?"

James' gaze bounced from Pandora to the room's exit. "He is...um...getting used to the new situation."

"Right." She squinted, eyes lit with an inner glow. "So he's complaining about everything, as usual. What about you? You had a busy couple weeks. Lots of balls to juggle, hmm? Your reports have been lacking."

"Well, I..." He cleared his throat. "I didn't mean to—"

"Wasn't an accusation, just a statement." She patted his back in a comforting way. "I take care of my own. The sudden change of plan must have been...ah...taxing." She glanced at the projection of Angelica, then smirked. "In more ways than I can count."

He worked his jaw back and forth, his eyes lingering on Angelica's throat. He remembered how hard it had been to keep his grip around her neck, squeezing harder and harder.

"James?"

The Domine blinked, turned toward her with a glassy stare. "Yes?"

"Haven't gotten lost in the labyrinth, have you?"

"What?" He swallowed. "No, of course. I...I'm not... I'm fine."

"James, James, James." She shook her head. "I've seen guilt a thousand times on as many faces. I know how it looks. Embrace it. You're a survivor. You've clawed your way out of deeper holes to achieve your goal. If that means to kill, you kill. Simple as that. That's why you're part of my team. You're not afraid to do what needs to be done." She tilted his chin with her hands so he looked directly at her. "Tell me who you are."

He inhaled sharply. "I'm James Ark, your Shepherd of Souls."

"Never forget that." She released him. "Angelica Kam and her husband had become a threat to our plan. You took care of that. Move on. No place for doubts in the life of a conqueror."

"Yes." He bowed his head. "You're right."

She narrowed her eyes. "Something else is bothering you."

He hesitated for a second before saying, "What about the Omega Dilemma?"

She shrugged. "What about it?"

He lowered his head and stared at the floor. "I haven't been able to solve the problem, even with ADAM's help. He told me there's no solution."

"Ah!" She took a deep breath, then released it with a satisfied sigh. "You started referring to that thing as a *he*. That's something. Does it mean ADAM is evolving as expected?"

He offered a sharp nod. "By leaps and bounds."

"Outstanding." She smiled. "We're going to need...*him* for what comes next. Oh, about that. How are things going with our shiny white knight? Is Milo giving you any more trouble?"

James shook his head. "The Concentration for Etheric Safeguarding is grappling with many people accusing them of her death." He glanced at the reproduction of Angelica, ignored the sinking feeling in his stomach. "That'll work to our advantage."

"Of course it will." Pandora's face and neck flushed with color. "People loved that woman." She nodded toward Angelica. "Sensationalism will win the cyberspace war for us. Covenant's days are numbered. And then there is

Zacharias' move, of course. He's ready to embrace the holistic. Soon his people will use it as the primary source of accessing the ether. That's tens of millions of good news. The landists will follow, and STAND will be the first portion of the ether to make the holistic mandatory. From that point on, things will fall into place. The Planetary Court will adopt the holistic if they want to avoid worldwide panic. People are dying by the thousands and fear is spreading. As soon as the jurions realize there's an antidote to the Armageddon, courtesy of our lovely doctor here, they won't dare deny it to the masses, or the masses will take it by force. It'll take years, but the holistic will become the bond of humanity." She looked at James. "This is how we remake the world. This is how we reclaim history." She cast a fleeting glance at Angelica and Cantara. "The ether is dead." She turned to look at James with a smile of triumph. "Long live the ether."

Pandora exited, leaving him alone.

James looked at the reproduction of Cantara. Tears streaked his face as he remembered the promise he made to the Black Widow of the Ether. Now all that was left was the ghost of his past that never stopped chasing him.

* * *

9 years before

Nashville, Handal's Institute for Gifted Students

CANTARA HANDAL LIES on the bed, her eyes closed as she breathes deeply.

James caresses her cheek. Her skin is warm and smooth,

like silk left under the midday sun. Cantara murmurs something in her sleep, the side of her eye twitching.

"Cantara?" James leans in. "Wake up."

The Madame flutters her eyes open. A smile blossoms on her face as she recognizes James.

"Good morning." James smiles back.

Cantara blinks. She makes a gargling noise with the back of her throat. Her eyes widen suddenly, her expression shifting from confusion to panic.

"If you're wondering why you can't move or talk," he says, still touching her cheek, "it's because I've injected three milligrams of Paramytosine into your body."

Cantara's eyes bulge. She opens her lips with effort, struggling to talk, but nothing comes out.

"Don't force yourself." James pats her head. "It'll cause you more pain. I don't want you to suffer. I just want you to understand why I did it." He points to the ceiling. "I hung a mirror there, so you can watch."

Cantara's eyes turn upward. Realization dawns on her face when she notices the three dark spots on her naked body. "I thought it'd be poetic justice." He gestures to the three Black Widows crawling over her body. Vaneria is snuggled into her armpit, while Zasha and Anemone are moving across her torso. Three scarlet-red bulges are visible on Cantara's left arm, elbow, and stomach where the spiders have bitten.

Cantara's expression changes. Her lips press together, and there is a tightness in her forehead that speaks of dread. She knows she's going to die. Her eyes search James', the muscles in her neck spasm. She's trying to speak again.

"Fretting will only cause more pain," James warns her. "Won't do you any good."

But Cantara doesn't listen. She keeps fighting, sweat

gathering in beads on her forehead. She raises her chest an inch before collapsing back onto the bed. Her breath is ragged, her face hot and flustered.

"I've always been one for caution." James strokes her neck. "Months ago, I hired some of the best technorists in town to copy ADAM's matrix. It cost me a fortune, but it was worth it." He draws in a deep breath. "It'll take time to recreate what I've done, but I'll get there eventually." His hand brushes her lips, then he kisses her. "You know, I understand why you did it. It was jealousy, wasn't it? Because I could do something you never could. The student surpassed the teacher, and you couldn't take it."

Cantara struggles to open her mouth, but no words emerge. She tries again, this time closing her eyes with the effort of speaking.

"What is it?" He leans forward. "You're trying to say something? I told you it's useless. You can't—"

"Don't...derstand." She swallows, hard. "T-t-h...end... ames. The...en...d."

He flinches back. It must be beyond painful for Cantara to speak. Why is she trying?

"I...didn't...elieve...the...e...nd."

"What?" He frowns.

Cantara tries to work up enough spit to talk, but this time the pain has the better of her. Her mouth opens and closes like a dying fish, then her eyes roll back.

"Here." He holds her head with his hands, and Cantara seems to regain control. "Let me tell you a story. I never told you why I wanted to create a dominion. See, the common person wastes his life fighting small, futile battles because that's what society, family, or friends tell them to do. A battle to win an argument for the sake of it, a battle to get a bigger slice of an inheritance, a battle to follow the latest fad, a battle to keep a job that makes us feel secure, appreciated, feared. They cease to have meaning once the person dies. None of these people ever made a difference. Sadly, we're surrounded by them."

James straightens up, shoulders back. "And then there are the conquerors, the few who realize the lie that clouds our society. The conquerors are people of genius, the leaders, the revolutionaries, who fight, tooth and nail, two or three *real* battles in their life, disregarding everything else. When you showed me ADAM and the simulation, you turned me into a conqueror. Creating a dominion is my battle. That's how I'll make a difference."

Cantara's jaw is set, her eyes bloodshot. She's still trying to talk.

James ignores her struggle. "It wasn't easy to create a replica of ADAM's matrix. I hope the person you sent it to enjoys my copy. No one could distinguish it from the original."

Cantara's eyes widen in surprise.

"Yes," James nods. "Did you really think I was going to let you throw away my treasure after all I've done?"

Cantara opens and closes her mouth, spit escaping.

"Why are you still trying to talk?" James pinches his lips together. "I don't want to see you suffer. I just want to see you die."

Cantara's head snaps back, her eyes wild. "Reason...he had...reason...he...right. He was..."

"Enough of this." He covers her face with a pillow, then presses. "Time to sleep, Black Widow of the Ether." Cantara jerks, legs kicking. James pushes harder. "Time to die."

After less than a minute, Cantara's legs stop twitching.

James swallows. He waits a moment, then another. He

tosses the pillow away, leans forward, feels her pulse. Dead. Cantara Handal is dead.

He stands, swaying slightly as he trudges toward the door. Before stepping out he turns toward his mentor. "I'll continue your legacy, Cantara. I swear it. I, James Ark, will be the one who makes the only difference that matters."

46

EX MACHINA

DÜSSELDORF, MUSEUM OF AUTOTRONICS

Ramor

On-Eni-Fifth entered the museum and walked toward Ramor at a deliberately slow pace.

Until the last moment, Ramor hadn't been sure if organizing the meeting was a sensible idea. He didn't know what to expect. A lot rested on what the autotron would do.

Speaking with Sofia had strengthened his resolve to help Erik. With his sister still in a precarious condition, he was the only family his nephew had left. Erik needed him now more than ever.

On-Eni-Fifth waited for a group of tourists to cross before continuing in Ramor's direction. Contacting the autotron hadn't been difficult. Nayara had traced its interlink frequency using the redundancy path from Erik's own interlink.

Ramor still couldn't wrap his head around the fact that

the eptanidus was actually Sonnie. Over the years, Erik had given it different designations to mask its true identity, and a new chassis to look the part. As an exanidus, it hid behind the designation EN-IN-50, as an eptanidus had used On-Eni-Fifth. The same designation, arranged in different ways to hide its true identity.

The best way to hide something is right under everyone's nose. It was something Sofia used to say, and it must have stuck with her son.

On-Eni-Fifth had escaped the Tronic Purification. Since it had been active since the early 30s, its metakratic core had a decade to develop intrasynaptic pathways of unknown potential. No other model on the face of the planet could boast that level of sophistication.

On-Eni-Fifth stopped a few steps away from Ramor. The autotron looked at him for a long moment, then turned its gaze toward the crowded museum. "Curious you chose this place, Mr. Deringer, although it's not completely unexpected." On-Eni-Fifth looked back at him, tilting its head to the side. "Easier for a piece of metal to go unnoticed in a junkyard, isn't it?"

Beads of sweat formed on Ramor's forehead. "What are you?"

"I am many things." The autotron stood solidly, planting its feet in a wide stance. "The first fully aware sentient being produced in an assembly factory, an experiment in progress, and humanity's fear."

Ramor's heart skipped a beat. The autotron was referring to the Singularity Complex, the vision of the future that artificial intelligence would develop in such a way that humanity would be rendered obsolete.

The engineer in him wondered how the upgrade—or was it better to call it *evolution*?—took place; had it resulted from multiple improvements to the autotron's metakratic core, or was it a structural evolution of the baseline program resulting from being free from the Tronic Purification?

Ramor wiped his hands on his jeans. Nothing could have prepared him for this moment. There was no precedent, no instruction manual to follow. He would have to go with his instincts.

"I'm not afraid of you," Ramor said.

"Nor should you be," the autotron replied. "The Singularity Complex is only as real as humanity allows it to be. It's just a fear, nothing else. If that's your biggest concern, Mr. Deringer, let me reassure you: I'm not here to enslave you."

"My main concern is saving my nephew from whatever hellhole he's dug himself into. You helped me discover your secret and then accepted my invitation. It would seem we both care about Erik's well-being."

"We do."

"Then why didn't you just say you were Sonnie? Why beat around the bush?"

"Because I made a promise."

Ramor frowned. "To Erik?"

"Yes. He asked me not to tell you, and I didn't. You figured it out by yourself."

Ramor snorted. "You told me indirectly."

"Semantics." On-Eni-Fifth raised its shoulders. "I kept my promise. You earned an important piece of information. We both got what we wanted."

Ramor nodded. "I understand Erik is in trouble. What kind?"

The autotron gestured toward the inner part of the museum. "Let's walk."

Ramor followed On-Eni-Fifth toward the section called *The Autotrons in Time*.

They passed through a hallway with smart-glass displays showing information about the history of autotronics, then they entered a less-crowded area.

After walking down a large corridor displaying holos of autotron parts, they stepped into a square room lit by dozens of LEDs. Ramor recognized the long sky-blue line covering the entire southern wall. It was interspersed with dots that signaled years and important events marking the history of autotronics. The first dot was accompanied by the number 2024, the year in which the Triad experiment sanctioned the first working autotron. It was considered by most the official beginning of the autotronics age. Ramor glanced at the following years on the timeline, all the way to the year 2033, where his eyes lingered. That year represented a wound still open in his family's history. The phobaron commandos raided the Automaton Industries headquarters and kidnapped Sofia.

"This way."

The autotron led Ramor outside the timeline room and into a bigger space inside the inner sanctum of the museum. At the center of the area was a gigantic display dubbed *Generations*, which showed the seven autotron models making up the backbone of autotronics: a monidus, a duonidus, a trinidus, a tetranidus, a pentanidus, an exanidus, and an eptanidus.

On-Eni-Fifth pointed to the collection of androids displayed as if they were trophies. "What do you see when you look at them, Mr. Deringer?"

"What do I see?" Ramor blinked. "I see seven autotrons. What do *you* see?"

One by one, On-Eni-Fifth studied the lifeless shells lined up for all eyes to see. "I see a story." It turned to look at Ramor. "Which began with an accident."

Ramor stared at the autotron. "You really are remarkable."

"I'm not." On-Eni-Fifth gazed at him. "You want to see something remarkable? Help us with our project."

Ramor narrowed his eyes. "What project?"

On-Eni-Fifth looked at the seven generations of autotrons. "Human history is a harsh mistress. It teaches us that progress is always threatened by fear. Sofia Deringer knew this. That's why she created us. Our project seeks to continue her mission. You want to help your nephew? Good. I will help you help him."

Ramor squinted. "How?"

"Next week, there will be an unexpected malfunction in the main line assembler of our underground complex."

Ramor blinked. "How do you know?"

"Because I will cause it."

Ramor licked his lips. "You...*what*?"

On-Eni-Fifth nodded, one hard jerk. "This will start a chain of events that will lead Erik to you."

Ramor arched his eyebrow. "What's that supposed to mean?"

"Despite his feelings, Erik will be forced to contact you and ask for your assistance in order to continue our project. I will offer you a chance to help Erik, and I expect you to take it."

Ramor stared at the autotron. "I want to know what the hell you two are doing."

"We are correcting an error in judgment." On-Eni-Fifth looked over its shoulder. "We want to reestablish a historical trend stopped by misinformation. We're going to put humanity's development back where it belongs."

Ramor nodded, but with a tight expression that showed

distrust. "And you're trying to do this in your underground factory, building your top secret autotrons?"

"Autotrons?" On-Eni-Fifth tilted its head, then blinked. "No, Mr. Deringer. We are most definitely not building autotrons."

47

BLACK WATER DOWN
YELLOW SEA, HAMMERER CLASS
BATTLECRUISER UXA MASTODON

Ariul

~

L eft. Right. Up. Down. Cold. Hot. Before. After.
There was no way of telling the difference. Everything was overlapping, wrong, painful; a chaos of memories and feelings that was impossible to untangle.

Makoto Shimao opened his eyes where indistinct shapes danced like shadows. His sight was foggy, and trying to distinguish things had become painful. He felt so tired, so scared. He closed his eyes and hoped to sink into oblivion.

His wish wasn't granted.

A voice. He remembered a female voice, deep and authoritative, and fear seized him. She had asked so many questions and was never satisfied by his answers. What was her name? He couldn't remember. Just thinking about her made his skin crawl.

A presence tromped beside him with heavy steps.

"We should get rid of him." The male voice was a low rumble, grating and filled with spite.

A moment of silence, then a female voice answered. This one was quick and sharper than the first. "We should wait for the Great Mother."

Makoto gasped. *The Great Mother*. He remembered now. *That* was her name.

"He's no longer useful. We should end him."

"We should not jump to conclusions before..."

Makoto lost track of the conversation. He found it increasingly hard to concentrate on words. They bent his mind to the point of pain. He didn't want more pain. He just wanted it to be over.

His consciousness floated into a strange sort of limbo. At the edge there were voices, but he didn't pay attention to them. He was content with floating, waiting out the pain.

Something tugged at him, and he felt jerked toward the voices, toward consciousness.

"He's awake now, Archetype."

Makoto's heartbeat quickened. *Archetype*. They also used that name to call her.

"Ahhhh."

A cold hand stroked his cheek, and he flinched.

"Makoto Shimao is an awful liar."

It was her. She was back, and she was going to hurt him again.

Words were spoken, but Makoto was too scared to care. It was only when she squeezed his arm that he snapped back into the moment.

"That's...that's impossible." It was the male voice, ripe with surprise.

"It's very possible, Goliath. It's the girl, not him. I should have seen it before."

No one spoke for a while, then the man called Goliath said, "What should we do with—"

A piercing, repetitive sound cut his voice off, followed by an explosion. The floor beneath Makoto shook, then the crash of several objects hitting the ground made his head ring.

Something slammed into his shoulder, hard, and he screamed. The voices spoke over each other, and he only caught clips and phrases. "Three groups," "*Mastodon,*" "on the bridge," "directing toward us."

Makoto drifted in and out of consciousness, then something jolted him awake.

"We need to go. Now!" It was a female voice. She sounded urgent.

"I'd rather die than let them control my ship!"

"They don't want to control the ship. They want to *sink* the ship. Want to be here when that happens?"

A noise erupted that sounded like a quick blast. Gunshots. Someone was shooting nearby.

The ground shook again, and the ship groaned under the strain.

The voices were gone.

After what felt like an eternity, footsteps approached.

"Found him!" shouted an unfamiliar voice. "Shit! Kid's hurt. Needs a medic."

Other footsteps, then something poked Makoto's neck. A sharp but brief prick. A rush of warmth coursed through his body, and all his muscles relaxed.

The sound of radio static permeated the room.

"Griffin One? This is Jaguar Three. We found the package. Do you copy?"

"Solid copy, Jaguar Three. What's your whiskey?"

"Starboard side. Section two. Third bridge."

"Solid copy, Jaguar Three. Account for personnel."

"Besides the package, three souls. Lerain, Josh, and Kara."

"Interrogative whiskey for Marauder?"

"We do not know his whiskey. Repeat, we do not know his whiskey. Be advised, six biomecha intruders in proximity of bridge one. Could offer resistance."

"Copy, Jaguar Three. We'll take care of them. Resume rescue operation."

"Roger that."

The static sound ceased.

"Duran, help me get this slab off him. Three...two...one...NOW!"

Someone lifted Makoto and carried him. Every step sent jolts of pain through his body.

Again static noise, followed by a new back and forth.

"Kira, status report? Have you packaged the presents?"

"Affirmative, Griffin One. Charges are plugged and ready to detonate."

"Okay, everybody. Let's get our asses off this death trap."

"Roger that, sir." Other static noise, then the voice said, "Okay, boys. We aren't out of the woods yet. Stay frosty."

A lifetime after, Makoto felt icy wind against his skin, and a spray of salty water hit his face. They were outside.

Someone shouted, "Get him, Rion!"

Makoto felt carried over from arms to arms until he was laid on something warm and soft.

"Kid's strapped, sir. He's ready to go."

"Good. All groups account for personnel."

"Panther and Fox are inside, sir."

"Tiger team? What's your 20?"

"We're all strapped and good to go, sir."

"Okay. Skipper, let's get the hell out of here."

"Roger that, sir. Engines burning. Turning on the heat now."

Makoto started hearing a whirring sound, followed by an increasingly noisier buzz. He knew that sound well. He must be onboard some kind of helicopter. The soundwave pulse created by the rotary motion of the air displaced by the blades was like music to his ears. The vehicle lifted away from the ground below as they became airborne.

Another explosion—stronger than any of the previous ones—followed by a collective cheer.

"Black Water down!"

"Yeah! Burn, baby, burn!"

"Die in hell, motherfuckers!"

"Makoto?" Makoto felt someone gently touching his cheek. "Can you hear me? It's me. Lena."

Makoto swallowed. He opened his eyes, but could only see white. He flinched away, afraid of the light.

"It's all right. Everything will be fine, I promise. I'm with you now."

"Sorry, sweetheart," a hoarse-sounding voice interrupted. "We need to send him to Jolly-Land until Doctor Isaac can give him a proper exam."

Makoto opened his mouth to speak, but tiredness swept over him and then the world fell mercifully into blackness.

48

STARDUST

HYPERIST COMPLEX INFINITY, PANORAMIC TOWER

Gladia

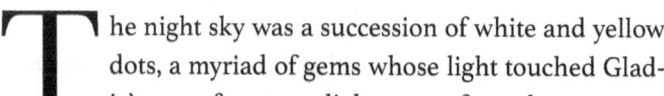

The night sky was a succession of white and yellow dots, a myriad of gems whose light touched Gladia's eyes after many light years of travel.

The Last Vertex of the Hexahedron basked in the work of the universe, made up of more stars than she could count. Each of them was a story forged by time, heat, and gravity.

Thinking about that vastness made her feel small, but also content. It reminded her she was part of an expanse billions of years old, a collective whole that had been there long before she was born and would be there when she was gone. The thought soothed her like nothing else could. It was when the knowledge of being utterly insignificant was combined with an unparalleled sense of fullness.

She closed her eyes and tried to picture what it must be like for people who worked in space. As leader of HYPER, she had visited a few sidereals in low Earth orbit, but she had never gone outside one of the pressurized settlements. She had never taken a spacewalk, never traveled into cislunar or translunar space, never been in the great unknown for more than a day or two.

Many people who worked in space for long periods of time described the feeling of being up there, surrounded by the vastness of the universe, using the name "Communion of Stars." Some said it was like looking through God's eyes.

A space technician told her once that working there was like being born for the second time. There was a moment, he said, when he realized what was truly meant by the phrase: "We are stardust."

Yes. Dust. An infinitesimal part of the universe humans had just started to understand.

"Stardust to stardust," she muttered, turning to the celestial vault. She didn't believe in God, or in the afterlife, but at that moment a part of her wondered if, somehow, Wei was listening.

She breathed in the cool evening air and reluctantly looked away from the sky, down to the world inhabited by humankind.

Sitting atop the Panoramic Tower gave Gladia a view for miles in every direction. The tower was the second tallest structure in the entire mega-complex, and was mostly used by tour guides as the last stop to wow tourists. It gave a magnificent view of the artificial island and of the space elevator Polaris.

Gladia leaned back slightly from the parapet as a gust of wind tousled her hair. She turned her head to the right, where Polaris dominated—like the backbone of the world, going on for eternity. It truly seemed like the "railway to the stars," as Wei had once called it. The carbon nanotube cable was flanked at regular intervals by gravity buoys that followed its path, signaling its presence to the ubiquitous air traffic of ipersedans, shuttles, and drones.

This was where Wei's dream of a space civilization had begun, and where it had ended abruptly with his death. Or so many thought.

Gladia turned sharply when someone opened the terrace's door, causing a swoosh when the metal panel slid into the wall.

Arthur Strutzenberg didn't cross the threshold of the terrace, but his knuckles still touched on the doorframe. He must have knocked several times.

"I'm sorry," he said, clearing his throat. "Thought you heard. Didn't mean to startle you."

"Never mind." She turned back toward Polaris. "Come on in."

Arthur joined her. "Called you via interlink. Didn't get—"

"I turned it off," she said, offering a tired smile. "Needed to be alone for a while."

"I understand." He placed his hands on the railing next to hers. Their elbows touched.

"What's the word?" Gladia asked without looking at him.

"Tolomeus announced the formation of a new Hyperist Executive Council."

She nodded, absorbing the information like a punching bag absorbs blows. "What about Scylla and Charybdis? How did they take it?"

"Not well." He grimaced. "Penelope and Maria have issued a joint statement condemning Tolomeus' actions, and have declared the new executive illegal. They'll hold their own press conference tomorrow morning. Your guess is as good as mine on what they'll say, but I'm pretty sure it won't send our stock skyrocketing."

Gladia rocked in place and rubbed her hands along her crossed arms. She knew what that meant. *Schism*.

Everything she'd tried to avoid since Wei had died had become reality. HYPER was broken. Her worst nightmare had come to pass.

Arthur's hand squeezed hers.

"Nothing you could have done." He smiled, his eyes like anchors that kept her grounded. "We play the hand we're dealt. This isn't the end of HYPER. It's just a steppingstone to make it stronger."

Gladia narrowed her eyes. "How can you say that?"

He shrugged. "I believe in destiny, in second chances, and in never letting bad news spoil your day for too long. What goes around comes around. It's a universal rule. Now things seem desperate, but they won't stay this way. I promise."

She looked at her friend, always by her side when she needed him.

"Arthur, you think—" She stopped short, not knowing how to continue.

He nodded to invite her to go on.

She chose her words carefully. "You think the simulation...you know, what EVA said... You think we'll never become a spacefaring civilization? You think Wei's dream was just that? A dream?"

He stared into her eyes. "That is a dream." He pointed at Polaris, then he placed his hand on her chest. "This," he said, "*this* makes it real. Wei was special because he never let his dreams remain dreams for long. And you, Executive Director, have proven to be a hell of a leader. You've made the word 'hyperist' become a synonym of progress, enterprise, and ingenuity. We'll overcome this crisis, as we've done with all the past crises, and HYPER will be better because of it."

A gust of wind blew between them, stark and chilling. Gladia shuddered. The illusion of security Arthur created was shattered in seconds, and a sense of despair overcame her. The image of Wei with his eyes open and a trickle of blood streaming down his mouth forced itself into her mind, and with it, the emotions that fueled her nightmares.

The side of her vision blurred, and she shook violently.

"Gladia?" Arthur caught her before she could fall. "Are you okay?"

"W-words," she stuttered, finding it harder to breathe. "Yours are just words. I need something concrete. I need results. I have nothing to show for—"

"You aren't breathing." He squeezed her shoulders. "You need to calm down."

"I can't... I just can't stop." She shook her head, hands clasped around her ears. "Everything is failing."

"It's okay. We'll get through this."

"It was my fault. I didn't do enough."

"Look at me."

She bit her lip, then spoke between sobs. "I can't even... to bring everyone together...and he handed me his legacy. To me, Arthur. To me!" Her chest felt heavy, crushed by the burden of responsibility. She couldn't hold back her tears.

Arthur held her tighter. "Gladia, please look at me."

Slowly, reluctantly, she lifted her head, and in that moment Arthur's lips met hers.

Time stopped.

For a second, an hour, or perhaps a lifetime, their lips touched, gently at first, then with growing ardor. Gladia became lost in his embrace. She wanted time to crystalize in that instant; in the arms of the man she loved, under a sky filled with stars.

When Arthur pulled away, it was as if someone had flipped back a switch.

Everything came back in a rush. The cold wind, the artificial lights of the terrace, the unmistakable salty smell of seaweed and iodine brought from the ocean.

The silence between the two lingered for a moment. Gladia, desperate to break it, said the first thing that came to her mind. "You've got some lipstick on your lips."

Arthur smiled. "I'll live." He cupped her chin in his hand. "Care if I get more?"

She smiled.

He kissed her, and this time Gladia snuggled in more closely, enjoining Arthur's embrace, his fresh-cut leather smell she associated with him, rugged and refined.

"You know," he said, holding her closer to him. "This reminds me of something. Might as well give it to you now."

She frowned as she watched him fumble through his pocket. "What are you talking about?"

"Here." He handed her a jewel case.

Her eyes jumped from Arthur to the object he was holding. "What is it?"

"Open it."

She took the jewel case and opened it. It contained a chain with an infinity pendant attached to it.

"A necklace?" She turned the object in her hands. When she found the inscription on the back, she gasped. "Wait. How did you..." She trailed off, unable to complete the sentence.

He shook his head. "Sorry, it's not the real thing. I had it made based on your description."

She studied the object more carefully. She could now

see minor differences with the original infinity, but overall, it was a beautiful reproduction.

"I...I don't know what to say." She looked at him. "Thank you."

"Let me put it on." Arthur moved her hair to the side and secured the necklace. After closing the clasp, he stepped back and admired the result.

"Glorious," he said, grinning. "I've had it for ages. We must celebrate."

"Celebrate?" Gladia burst out laughing. "There's nothing to celebrate."

"Always looking at the glass half-empty, are we? Nah, we deserve a toast. Doctor's orders. Wait here. Be right back."

∞ ∞ ∞

"Arthur? Where're you going?"

Gladia's voice was lost in the distance as Arthur went out the observation deck, walked down a small hallway, and opened the lime-colored door of the storeroom where the guides kept the refreshments. He made his way to a large refrigerator, opened it, and grabbed a bottle. He read the label and pursed his lips. Not exactly what he was looking for, but it would do.

He took a couple glasses from a top shelf, walked out of the room, and closed the door behind him.

"I hope you like Moscato," he said as he re-entered the terrace. "The choice was between plum juice, tomato—" He stopped short. Gladia was on her knees, her hands clawing at her neck and her face purple. She was struggling to breathe.

"Gladia?" Arthur dropped the glasses and the bottle, which shattered with a resounding crunch. "Gladia!" He rushed toward her, his eyes scanning her neck. The necklace was choking her. "Fuck." He tried to open the clasp, but it stuck.

Gladia squeezed his arms. "Ar...th..." She jerked her head from side to side, gasping. Blood seeped into the whites of her eyes. Her fingers dug into Arthur's skin. "Lohv...yo...I..."

Arthur tapped his earpiece. "Strutzenberg to security! I need immediate assistance at..." He broke off, looking at his wrist. "Security? You read me?" Nothing. His interlink was dead. "Shit!" He glanced around, scanning the area, desperate for anything he could use. His eyes found the broken shards of glass. He grabbed one and tried to break the chain. It didn't work. He tried harder, more desperately, his trembling hands causing the shard to cut superficial wounds on Gladia's neck. He tossed the shard aside, his eyes looking for something else.

Gladia produced a gurgling sound, and her eyes rolled back.

"No, no, no." Arthur pulled Gladia from the back, then raised her in a sitting position. "Gladia? Stay with me. Gladia!"

She closed her eyes, her head slumping back like a lifeless doll.

"HELP!" Arthur shouted. "SOMEBODY HELP!" His call was lost in the night. No one heard.

He lay Gladia's body down, placed the heel of his hand on the center of her chest, then put the palm of the other hand on top and pressed down at a steady rate, giving two rescue breaths at the end of each round of thirty compressions. She remained motionless.

"God, no..." He placed his ear on her chest, listening to the void of death. "Not like this."

He tried to resuscitate her time and time again, screaming all the while, begging for help. Nothing changed.

He swallowed, his whole body shaking as he stared at Gladia.

Dead. She was dead. And he'd killed her.

The realization crushed him like a hammer thrown by a vengeful god. He couldn't tear his eyes away from Gladia. After all the protective measures, all the years spent building a fortress around her, they used *him* to get to her. The horror of the paradox broke him.

Him. They used him to kill her.

He gently laid Gladia's body on the ground and then looked up, his eyes fixed on the stars, a thousand judges condemning him.

Arthur walked up the terrace's railing, then turned and looked at the woman he loved. "I'll see you soon."

He jumped.

The fall lasted a lifetime. Memories, feelings, and images flashed before him in a heartbeat as the world pushed down on him with vengeance.

Among these images, Gladia Egea was smiling at him; a shy smile that held surety and sweetness at the same time.

Arthur smiled back. They would soon be together again.

EPILOGUE

When someone knocked at the door, Pandora closed the notebook with the green cover and put it inside the drawer. "Come in."

Charlotte Encanto entered the room and closed the door behind her. "You asked to see me, Great Mother?"

"Ah, Charlotte. Sit down." Pandora gestured to the chair in front of her desk.

Charlotte sat stiffly, a muscle on her check twitching.

"You look uncomfortable, dear." Pandora smiled at her. "Is it too hot in here? The air conditioning has been acting up."

The young woman shook her head. "No, Great Mother. It's fine."

"All right then." Pandora joined her hands. "We better get down to business."

Charlotte swallowed. "Is this about my last report, Great Mother?"

Pandora nodded. "Indeed. I'm surprised. Putting that kevlar thread with the carbon fiber gear into the necklace was risky. A million things could have gone wrong."

Charlotte glanced down at her hands, looking chastised. "Yes, Great Mother."

Pandora studied her. "How did you know Strutzenberg would kill himself?"

Charlotte blinked. "He loved the Executive Director, Great Mother."

"Ah, yes. Love." Pandora gave Charlotte an easy nod. "A very useful weapon. Nothing comes close to its destructive power. You were smart to discover their common infatuation, smarter still at using it against them. Now, with Egea gone, HYPER will implode. Dealing with the scattered remainder won't be a problem. All thanks to you."

"Just doing my job, Great Mother. Sorry I couldn't get it done sooner."

Pandora waved a hand dismissively. "You've done well. You showed initiative, a gift few people possess."

The young woman took in a deep breath, her voice cracking with emotion. "Thank you, Great Mother."

Pandora leaned back and watched Charlotte with an intense gaze. "You know why I chose you, dear?"

Charlotte cocked her head. "No, Great Mother."

Pandora rubbed her hands together, looking the young girl up and down with amusement. "The other candidates were brighter, better prepared, smarter even, but none were more motivated than you."

Charlotte shook her head. "I...I don't think I understand."

Pandora leaned forward, then narrowed her eyes as she studied Charlotte's reaction. "For you, it was personal. There's no better incentive to a job well done than being invested in the enemy's demise."

Charlotte bowed her head. "I'm glad I could be helpful."

Pandora steepled her hands. She had relied on Charlotte's childhood trauma to make sure her commitment wouldn't falter. Her parents had been killed in a clash between hyperists and landists. They were neither member of one group or the other, just people who found themselves in the wrong place at the wrong time. Cultivating the girl's hatred hadn't been difficult. Pandora had known which button to push, and how to plant the seed of vengeance. It had worked even better than she had expected.

The way Charlotte had gotten into the good graces of both Arthur and Gladia had been ingenious, more so if one counted how she planned Gladia's death. Strutzenberg's suicide was a delightful bonus. The man had too much influence over the Hyperist Council. He would have made her job more difficult. With him gone, things would move smoothly.

"So." Pandora tapped her index finger on the desk, her smile spreading. "In light of your outstanding performance, I decided to consider your request to become a dame."

Charlotte's hand covered her heart, eyes glistening. "Thank you, Great Mother. I'm honored."

Pandora nodded. "You've proven your worth. It's just fair."

Charlotte shifted to the edge of the chair, leaning forward with her hands on her knees. "I won't disappoint you. I swear."

"I know you won't." Pandora glanced at the door. "Now, I understand you're going to have a busy month ahead. Don't let me keep you."

"Yes, Great Mother." Charlotte rose from her chair, bowed, and left the room.

Pandora waited for the steps to subside before turning to another door on the other side of the room. "Well?" she said with a snappish tone. "Waiting for an official invitation? The girl's gone."

The door opened and four people came in. Tenoderia Azarova ambled forward, followed by Agate Vultura, who showed a less decisive gait and a stiffer posture. Behind them came James Ark, his shoulders hunched, almost dragging his feet, while Zacharias Hawke strode forward with the easy step of someone who knows he has been chosen by God.

Tenoderia sat in the chair left empty by Charlotte. Agate stood beside her, looking out of place and slightly uncomfortable. James leaned against the wall, his arms crossed, eyes shielded by the sunglasses. Zacharias was the only one to kneel in front of her.

"Let's not stand on ceremonies here, Zacharias." Pandora motioned for him to rise.

The reverend stood, arms spread and voice thick with awe. "As the Archetype commands."

"You really going to turn that girl into a dame?" Tenoderia glanced at the door Charlotte used to leave.

Pandora arched her eyebrow. "You don't approve, friend?"

"She did an adequate job at Infinity." Tenoderia's direct stare lacked warmth. "But elevating her so high, so fast... Well, I think it's premature."

"I haven't decided yet." Pandora showed her empty hands. "I'll consider your opinion."

Tenoderia crossed her arms. "We already have enough dames as it is."

Pandora turned to look at the Domine. "What do you think, James?"

James snapped to attention. "About what?"

Pandora gestured to Tenoderia. "Promoting the girl."

James glanced at Tenoderia, then shrugged. "I think you'll make the right decision, as always."

Pandora narrowed her eyes. Something had changed in his demeanor. Since the Madame of Melody's death, the Domine had grown distracted. She didn't know how bad the damage was, or if it could be fixed, but she couldn't afford a misstep this close to the finish line. She would watch him closely from now on.

"Well." Pandora clapped her hands. "I think we all deserve to celebrate."

Tenoderia blinked. "You want to celebrate?"

"Why not? Everything is going according to plan."

"According to plan?" Tenoderia removed her glasses and wiped them on her shirt. "Were you planning to have the *Mastodon* blown to pieces and to lose Shimao?"

Zacharias stepped forward, his face flustered as he jabbed the Madame twice on the back. "Careful, now. You're crossing a line. Remember who you're talking to."

Pandora raised a hand. "It's okay, Zacharias. I always encourage differing opinions when constructive." She turned to face the Madame, looking squarely in her eyes. "Yes, we lost a battlecruiser and the boy, but we found the Cornucopia."

"Found?" Tenoderia shook her head. "Did I miss something? We don't know where she is, or what she knows. We don't even know what being the Cornucopia means."

"It doesn't matter," Pandora said with an unwavering smile. "We've got time to find out all the answers. The enemy believes it scored a victory. Let them believe. The hardest blow is the one no one expects." She turned toward Agate. "You have what I asked for?"

Agate nodded briskly. "Yes. I found a clear-enough image of the girl searching Gunsan Airport's security system." She handed her a tablet showing an image. "This is Lena Maruishi. The picture was taken last year, on May 12, the day she landed in Saemangeum City. Inside the data file, there's everything I could find."

"Good." Pandora studied the picture. A young woman with long, dark hair looked in her direction, her expression dreamy. "Hello, Lena," Pandora said with a bright smile. "Looking forward to meeting you."

The End

∿

CONTINUE THE OMNILOGOS SINGULARITY SERIES...

Kingdom of Stars, the fourth book in the Omnilogos Singularity series, will soon be available in eBook and paperback format. Preorder your copy now!

GET KINGDOM OF STARS!

ACKNOWLEDGMENTS

Thanks to Alessandro, Alberto, Chiara, Raffaella, Mana, Laura, A'Ryen, and Lena, for reading this story and providing amazing feedback.

You made *War of Pandora* shine.

ABOUT THE AUTHOR

I am an independent author living in Rome, the Eternal City. I grew up writing of falling empires, space battles, mortal betrayals, monumental decisions, and everything in between.

I now spend my days traveling through time and space and, more often than not, writing about impossible but necessary worlds.

When I'm not busy training dragons or mastering the Force, you can find me at MicheleAmitrani.com or hanging out on Facebook at /MicheleAmitraniAuthor.